# SEASIDE
## *Dreams*

Seaside Summers, Book One

Love in Bloom Series

Melissa Foster

ISBN-13: 978-1-941480-02-1
ISBN-10: 1941480020

SEASIDE DREAMS

Cover Design: Natasha Brown

WORLD LITERARY PRESS
PRINTED IN THE UNITED STATES OF AMERICA

## A Note to Readers

When I met the Seaside gang (Leanna Bray's friends) in *Read, Write, Love*, I fell in love with them, and it became apparent that they needed a world of their own in which to come alive. The Seaside Summers series is a fun addition to the Love in Bloom series. Each of our Seaside friends will have their own love story, and I hope you enjoy meeting them as much as I enjoy creating them.

*Seaside Dreams* is the first book in Seaside Summers series and the newest addition to the Love in Bloom series. While it may be read as a stand-alone novel, for even more enjoyment, you may want to read the rest of the Love in Bloom novels (Snow Sisters, The Bradens, and The Remingtons).

*Melissa Foster*

*For the Starfish gang.*
*Here's to Thong Thursdays, chunky-dunking,*
*midnight hamburgers, and Middle Sister wine*

PRAISE FOR MELISSA FOSTER

"Contemporary romance at its hottest. Each Braden sibling left me craving the next. Sensual, sexy, and satisfying, the Braden series is a captivating blend of the dance between lust, love, and life."
—*Bestselling author Keri Nola, LMHC*
*(on The Bradens)*

"[LOVERS AT HEART] Foster's tale of stubborn yet persistent love takes us on a heartbreaking and soul-searing journey."
—*Reader's Favorite*

"Smart, uplifting, and beautifully layered.
I couldn't put it down!"
—*National bestselling author Jane Porter*
*(on SISTERS IN LOVE)*

"Steamy love scenes, emotionally charged drama, and a family-driven story make this the perfect story for any romance reader."
—*Midwest Book Review (on SISTERS IN BLOOM)*

"HAVE NO SHAME is a powerful testimony to love and the progressive, logical evolution of social consciousness, with an outcome that readers will find engrossing, unexpected, and ultimately eye-opening."
—*Midwest Book Review*

# Chapter One

BELLA ABBASCIA STRUGGLED to keep her grip on a ceramic toilet as she crossed the gravel road in Seaside, the community where she spent her summers. It was one o'clock in the morning, and Bella had a prank in store for Theresa Ottoline, a straitlaced Seaside resident and the elected property manager for the community. Bella and two of her besties, Amy Maples and Jenna Ward, had polished off two bottles of Middle Sister wine while they waited for the other cottage owners to turn in for the night. Now, dressed in their nighties and a bit tipsy, they struggled to keep their grip on a toilet that Bella had spent two days painting bright blue, planting flowers in, and adorning with seashells. They were carrying the toilet to Theresa's driveway to break rule number fourteen of the Community Homeowners Association's Guidelines: *No tacky displays allowed in the front of the cottages.*

"You're sure she's asleep?" Bella asked as they came to the grass in front of the cottage of their fourth bestie, Leanna Bray.

"Yes. She turned off her lights at eleven. We

1

should have hidden it someplace other than my backyard. It's so far. Can we stop for a minute? This sucker is heavy." Amy drew her thinly manicured brows together.

"Oh, come on. Really? We only have a little ways to go." Bella nodded toward Theresa's driveway, which was across the road from her cottage, about a hundred feet away.

Amy glanced at Jenna for support. Jenna nodded, and the two lowered their end to the ground, causing Bella to nearly drop hers.

"That's so much better." Jenna tucked her stick-straight brown hair behind her ear and shook her arms out to her sides. "Not all of us lift weights for breakfast."

"Oh, please. The most exercise I get during the summer is lifting a bottle of wine," Bella said. "Carrying around those boobs of yours is more of a workout."

Jenna was just under five feet tall with breasts the size of bowling balls and a tiny waist. She could have been the model for the modern-day Barbie doll, while Bella's figure was more typical for an almost thirty-year-old woman. Although she was tall, strong, and relatively lean, she refused to give up her comfort foods, which left her a little soft in places, with a figure similar to Julia Roberts or Jennifer Lawrence.

"I don't carry them with my arms." Jenna looked down at her chest and cupped a breast in each hand. "But yeah, that would be great exercise."

Amy rolled her eyes. Pin-thin and nearly flat chested, Amy was the most modest of the group, and in her long T-shirt and underwear, she looked like a teenager next to curvy Jenna. "We only need a sec, Bella."

They turned at the sound of a passionate moan

coming from Leanna's cottage.

"She forgot to close the window again," Jenna whispered as she tiptoed around the side of Leanna's cottage. "Typical Leanna. I'm just going to close it."

Leanna had fallen in love with bestselling author Kurt Remington the previous summer, and although they had a house on the bay, they often stayed in the two-bedroom cottage so Leanna could enjoy her summer friends. The Seaside cottages in Wellfleet, Massachusetts, had been in the girls' families for years, and they had spent summers together since they were kids.

"Wait, Jenna. Let's get the toilet to Theresa's first." Bella placed her hands on her hips so they knew she meant business. Jenna stopped before she reached for the window, and Bella realized it would have been a futile effort anyway. Jenna would need a stepstool to pull that window down.

"Oh…Kurt." Leanna's voice split the night air.

Amy covered her mouth to stifle a laugh. "Fine, but let's hurry. Poor Leanna will be mortified to find out she left the window open again."

"I'm the last one who wants to hear her having sex. I'm done with men, or at least with commitments, until my life is back on track." Ever since last summer, when Leanna had met Kurt, started her own jam-making business, and moved to the Cape full-time, Bella had been thinking of making a change of her own. Leanna's success had inspired her to finally go for it. Well, that and the fact that she'd made the mistake of dating a fellow teacher, Jay Cook. It had been months since they broke up, but they'd taught at the same Connecticut high school, and until she left for the summer, she couldn't avoid running in to him on a daily basis. It was just the nudge she needed to take the plunge and finally quit her job and start over. *New job, new life, new location.* She just hadn't told her friends yet. She'd thought she would tell them the minute she arrived at Seaside and they were all together, maybe over a bottle of wine or on the beach. But Leanna had been spending a lot of time with Kurt, and every time it was just the four of them, she hadn't been ready to come clean. She knew they'd worry and ask questions, and she wanted to have some of the transition sorted out before answering them.

"Bella, you can't give up on men. Jay was just a jerk." Amy touched her arm.

She really needed to fill them in on the whole Jay and quitting her job thing. She was beyond over Jay, but they knew Bella to be the stable one of the group, and learning of her sudden change was a conversation that needed to be handled when they weren't wrestling a fifty-pound toilet.

"Fine. You're right. But I'm going to make all of my future decisions separate from any man. So...until my life is in order, no commitments for me."

"Not me. I'd give anything to have what Kurt and Leanna have," Amy said.

Bella lifted her end of the toilet easily as Jenna and Amy struggled to lift theirs. "Got it?"

"Yeah. Go quick. This damn thing is heavy," Jenna said as they shuffled along the grass.

"More..." Leanna pleaded.

Amy stumbled and lost her grip. The toilet dropped to the ground, and Jenna yelped.

"Shh. You're going to wake up the whole complex!" Bella stalked over to them.

"Oh, Kurt!" Jenna rocked her hips. "More, baby, more!"

"Really?" Bella tried to keep a straight face, but when Leanna cried out again, she doubled over with laughter.

Amy, always the voice of reason, whispered, "Come on. We *need* to close her window."

"Yes!" Leanna cried.

They fell against one another in a fit of laughter, stumbling beside Leanna's cottage.

"I could make popcorn," Jenna said, struggling to keep a straight face.

Amy scowled at her. "She got pissed the last time you did that." She grabbed Bella's hand and whispered through gritted teeth, "Take out the screen so you can shut the window, please."

"I told you we should have put a lock on the outside of her window," Jenna reminded them. Last summer, when Leanna and Kurt had first begun dating, they'd often forgotten to close the window. To save Leanna embarrassment, Jenna had offered to be on sex-noise mission control and close the window if Leanna ever forgot to. A few drinks later, she'd mistakenly abandoned the idea for the summer.

"While you close the window, I'll get the sign for the toilet." Amy hurried back toward Bella's deck in her boy-shorts underwear and a T-shirt.

Bella tossed the screen to the side so she could reach inside and close the window. The side of Leanna's cottage was on a slight incline, and although Bella was tall, she needed to stand on her tiptoes to get a good grip on the window. The hem of the nightie caught on her underwear, exposing her ample derriere.

"Cute satin skivvies." Jenna reached out to tug Bella's shirt down and Bella swatted her.

Bella pushed as hard as she could on the top of the window, trying to ignore the sensuous moans and the creaking of bedsprings coming from inside the cottage.

"The darn thing's stuck," she whispered.

Jenna moved beside her and reached for the

window. Her fingertips barely grazed the bottom edge.

Amy ran toward them, waving a long stick with a paper sign taped to the top that read, WELCOME BACK.

Leanna moaned, and Jenna laughed and lost her footing. Bella reached for her, and the window slammed shut, catching Bella's hair. Leanna's dog, Pepper, barked, sending Amy and Jenna into more fits of laughter.

With her hair caught in the window and her head plastered to the sill, Bella put a finger to her lips. "Shh!"

Headlights flashed across Leanna's cottage as a car turned up the gravel road.

"Shit!" Bella went up on her toes, struggled to lift the window and free her hair, which felt like it was being ripped from her skull. The curtains flew open and Leanna peered through the glass. Bella lifted a hand and waved. *Crap.* She heard Leanna's front door open, and Pepper bolted around the corner, barking a blue streak and knocking Jenna to the ground just as a police car rolled up next to them and shined a spotlight on Bella's ass.

CADEN GRANT HAD been with the Wellfleet Police Department for only three months, having moved after his partner of nine years was killed in the line of duty. He'd relocated to the small town with his teenage son, Evan, in hopes of working in a safer location. So far, he'd found the people of Wellfleet to be respectful and thankful for the efforts of the local law enforcement officers, a welcome change after dealing with rebellion on every corner in Boston. Wellfleet had recently experienced a rash of small thefts—cars being broken into, cottages being ransacked, and the police had begun patrolling the private communities along Route 6, communities that in the past had taken care of their own security. Caden rolled up the gravel road in the Seaside community and spotted a dog running circles around a person rolling on the ground.

He flicked on the spotlight as he rolled to a stop. *Holy Christ. What is going on?* He quickly assessed the situation. A blond woman was banging on a window with both hands. Her shirt was bunched at her waist, and a pair of black satin panties barely covered the most magnificent ass he'd seen in a long time.

"Open the effing window!" she hollered.

Caden stepped from the car. "What's going on here?" He walked around the dark-haired woman, who was rolling from side to side on the ground while laughing hysterically, and the fluffy white dog, who was barking as though his life depended on it, and he quickly realized that the blond woman's hair was caught in the window. Behind him another blonde crouched on the ground, laughing so hard she kept snorting. *Why the hell aren't any of you wearing pants?*

"Leanna! I'm stuck!" the blonde by the window yelled.

"Officer, we're sorry." The blonde behind him rose to her feet, tugging her shirt down to cover her underwear; then she covered her mouth with her hand as more laughter escaped. The dog barked and clawed at Caden's shoes.

"Someone want to tell me what's going on here?" Caden didn't even want to try to guess.

"We're…" The brunette laughed again as she rose to her knees and tried to straighten her camisole, which barely contained her enormous breasts. She ran her eyes down Caden's body. "Well, *hello* there, handsome." She fell backward, laughing again.

*Christ.* Just what he needed, three drunk women.

The brunette inside the cottage lifted the window,

7

freeing the blonde's hair, which sent her stumbling backward and crashing into his chest. There was no ignoring the feel of her seductive curves beneath the thin layer of fabric. Her hair was a thick, tangled mess. She looked up at him with eyes the color of rich cocoa and lips sweet enough to taste. The air around them pulsed with heat. Christ, she was beautiful.

"Whoa. You okay?" he asked. He told his arms to let her go, but there was a disconnect, and his hands remained stuck to her waist.

"It's...It's not what it looks like." She dropped her eyes to her hands, clutching his forearms, and she released him fast, as if she'd been burned. She took a step back and helped the brunette to her feet. "We were..."

"They were trying to close our window, Officer." A tall, dark-haired man came around the side of the cottage, wearing a pair of jeans and no shirt. "Kurt Remington." He held a hand out in greeting and shook his head at the women, now holding on to each other, giggling and whispering.

"Officer Caden Grant." He shook Kurt's hand. "We've had some trouble with break-ins lately. Do you know these women?" His eyes swept over the tall blonde. He followed the curve of her thighs to where they disappeared beneath her nightshirt, then drifted up to her full breasts, finally coming to rest on her beautiful dark eyes. It had been a damn long time since he'd been this attracted to a woman.

"Of course he knows us." The hot blonde stepped forward, arms crossed, eyes no longer wide and warm, but narrow and angry.

He hated men who leered at women, but he was powerless to refrain from drinking her in for one last second. The other two women were lovely in their own right, but they didn't compare to the tall blonde with fire in her eyes and a body made for loving.

Kurt nodded. "Yes, Officer. We know them."

"God, you guys. What the heck?" the dark-haired woman asked through the open window.

"You were waking the dead," the tall blonde answered.

"Oh, gosh. I'm sorry, Officer," the brunette said through the window. Her cheeks flushed, and she slipped back inside and closed the window.

"I assure you, everything is okay here." Kurt glared at the hot blonde.

"Okay, well, if you see any suspicious activity, we're only a phone call away." He took a step toward his car.

The tall blonde hurried into his path. "Did someone from Seaside call the police?"

"No. I was just patrolling the area."

She held his gaze. "Just patrolling the area? No one *patrols* Seaside."

"Bella," the other blonde hissed.

*Bella.*

"Seriously. No one patrols our community. They never have." She lifted her chin in a way that he assumed was meant as a challenge, but it had the opposite effect. She looked cuter than hell.

Caden stepped closer and tried to keep a straight face. "Your name is Bella?"

"Maybe."

Feisty, too. He liked that. "Well, Maybe Bella, you're right. We haven't patrolled your community in the past, but things have changed. We'll be patrolling more often to keep you safe until we catch the people who have been burglarizing the area." He leaned in close and whispered, "But you might consider wearing pants for your window-closing evening strolls. Never know who's traipsing around out here."

# Chapter Two

THERE WERE ABOUT a million things Bella loved about spending summers at Seaside, but two of her favorites were spending eight weeks with her best friends and waking to the hoarse cawing of crows. Most people hated the annoying squawks that began the moment the dawn settled around them. It was a sound so unique to her summers at the Cape that Bella reveled in it, and on sunny mornings like today, she welcomed it. She'd spent much of last night thinking about—then trying not to think about—the undeniable shock of heat she'd felt the moment she'd looked into police officer Caden Grant's eyes. She took a sip of her coffee and kicked her feet up on the edge of the table.

"Hey, babe." Jenna joined Bella on the deck. Like Bella, she was still wearing her pajama top and had slipped on a pair of cute cotton shorts over her underwear. That was another thing Bella loved about Seaside. Since the cottages had been in their families for years, they'd spent summers together since they were knee high. Hanging out in their pajamas felt normal.

"Shh. Theresa just opened her front door. She hasn't seen the toilet yet." Bella's cottage faced the laundry building and what they called the big house, which was the original house on the property before it was subdivided and cottages were built. Theresa lived in the big house, and after they were busted by Officer Grant, they'd wrapped up the evening by placing the toilet in Theresa's driveway.

"There she is." Jenna sat beside Bella.

Theresa stepped outside with her arms extended in a wide stretch. Her polo shirt was neatly tucked into her tan shorts, and her short, layered hair was perfectly combed. She waved to Bella and Jenna.

"Morning, ladies."

"Morning," they said in unison as they waved back.

Theresa was in her early fifties, and her life was a bit of a mystery to Bella and her friends. Even though they'd known her for years, they didn't know much about her except that she was an attorney. She was congenial, despite the fact that she'd taken on the position of property manager and queen rule enforcer, but in general, she kept to herself and rarely joined them for community barbeques and gatherings.

"Here it comes," Jenna said under her breath.

Theresa cocked her head to the side, craned her neck forward, and squinted at the toilet. She took a few tentative steps forward. She walked around the toilet and shook her head. She looked up and narrowed her eyes in their direction. Her hands settled on her hips.

"Oh shit," Jenna whispered.

Bella wasn't discriminatory in her pranking. She'd pranked every one of her friends, including the community and pool maintenance guy, who came by every few days to clean out the pool and who was the focus of Jenna's crush. Bella's pranks were relatively harmless, like adding bubbles to the pool or freezing all of Jenna's bras while she was asleep. Her summer pranks were usually met with a laugh and an eye roll, but she'd never gotten a rise out of Theresa.

Theresa spun on her heels and stomped inside.

"Wow, that was quite a reaction," Bella said with a sarcastic tone. She sipped her coffee.

Jenna grabbed her arm. "Oh. My. God."

Theresa stomped out of her house with a book tucked under her arm. She made a show of dropping her pants, then sat her bare ass on the toilet and opened her book. She flashed a wide grin in their direction.

Bella spit her coffee out all over the deck. "Holy crap." She grabbed Jenna's hand and they turned their backs, laughing uproariously.

"Oh my freaking God, did you see that?" Jenna had tears pouring down her cheeks.

Bella clung to Jenna's shoulder. "Oh my God!" she said in a loud whisper. "Is she...Is she still on it?"

"Hold on..." Jenna glanced over her shoulder. "No!" She laughed again. "She's standing next to it and looking over. Oh no!" Jenna tightened her grip on Bella's arm. "Pete's truck just pulled up and she flagged him down."

"Holy crap." Bella covered her mouth to keep from laughing too loudly.

Pete handled general property and pool maintenance for Seaside. He was a quiet man by nature, and he'd give a stranger the shirt off his back. He carried the toilet to the dumpster, shaking his head.

Theresa made a show of wiping her hands, then went back into her house.

"Oh my God. Poor Pete. I feel sorry for him. He's so sweet." Jenna kicked a foot onto Bella's lap and watched Pete climb back into his truck.

He waved out the window. "Thanks for that," he called to them on his way around the cottages to the pool.

"We are going straight to hell," Jenna said. "Did I mention that Pete is wicked sexy?"

"Do you ever not?" Bella shook her head. "Well, chalk one up for Theresa."

"Okay, change of subject before I get all hot and bothered thinking about Pete and have to take a cold shower. Speaking of cold showers...You were pretty wired when you finally went inside. Did you sleep okay, or did you dream about getting handcuffed by Officer Sexy?"

"Handcuffs spell commitment to me, so..."

"Bullshit. You know you dreamed about him. How could you not?" Jenna leaned forward and spoke in a seductive voice. "Six foot something of hard muscle attached to a man who knows how to take control." She leaned back with a sigh. "Sounds almost perfect to me."

"Do you even know who you are talking to? Hello? Major rule breaker here." She pointed to herself with both hands and smiled at Amy when she joined them on the deck. "Me and a cop? No way. Besides, as I said, I need to figure out my life, not find a boyfriend."

"That doesn't preclude you from a quick roll in the sand with Officer Hottie." Amy plopped onto a chair in a pair of flannel pajama pants and a Hello Kitty shirt. The animated kitty had a body like Marilyn Monroe and was sprawled on her side in a seductive pose.

"This coming from Little Miss Proper?" Bella rolled her eyes.

"I am not. I'm just careful about who I sleep with.

14

Besides, it's not like I don't want..." She gazed at Tony's cottage. Tony was the resident hottie. He was a professional surfer and motivational speaker and was too good of a friend to sleep with any of them, much less sweet Amy Maples.

Bella patted her on the arm. "Oh, honey, we know. You've spent years wanting that particular piece of ass. It's time to move on, don't you think?"

Amy sighed. "Let's focus on your love life, not mine."

"How about we focus on my *life* aside from men. It's much more interesting than my nonexistent love life." She spotted Leanna and Pepper crossing the quad and decided it was time to bite the bullet and tell them about the changes she was making in her life. "Besides, I have to tell you guys something."

Pepper bounded onto the deck and went directly to Amy, who lowered her face so the puppy could lavish her with kisses.

"How's my big boy?" Amy crooned.

Leanna stepped onto the deck in cutoffs and a white tank top. Her dark hair cascaded in gentle waves over her shoulders.

"Good morning, girlies. I'm late for the flea market, as always." The previous summer Leanna had begun a jam-making business, Luscious Leanna's Sweet Treats, and now she ran the business out of the renovated guest cottage on Kurt's beachfront property. During the summer she also sold her products at the Wellfleet Flea Market and at other flea markets in the area. "I'm sorry about the window, and I promise to remember next time." Leanna took a sip of Jenna's coffee.

"Sure, you'll remember to close the window," Jenna said. "Now I'm definitely going to install that window lock on the outside."

"I really do try to remember. It's just..." Leanna

held her palm up.

"Things come up and you don't think about it?" Jenna threw her head back and laughed.

"Ha-ha. Who was the hot cop?" Leanna asked.

"Caden Grant. He's Bella's," Amy said.

"He is not mine." The memory of his big hands on her waist, and the heat of their bodies so close, sent a shudder through her.

"Then why did the air sizzle and pop when you were in his arms?" Amy lifted her brows.

"You guys noticed that too, huh?" Bella covered her face with her hands, then met their curious stares with a serious one. "I'm ignoring that particular, incredible connection for now. No men, no commitments, remember? Besides..." She sat up straighter, steeling herself for the gasps and worry that were sure to follow her admission. "I have bigger things to focus on, like the fact that I quit my job."

As if on cue, Jenna and Amy gasped.

"You what?" Leanna asked.

"Because of Jay? You two weren't even serious, and you've worked there for five years," Jenna added.

Bella shook her head. "No, not because of Jay. I mean, that factored into it in a very minor way. It was annoying finishing out the school year and having to see him every day, but my decision about moving is based on more than Jay. My decision about taking a break from men is sort of based on him, though. I don't need to be lied to again, and I'm beginning to think that men and lying go hand in hand."

Leanna reached across the table and held her hand. "Oh, Bella, I'm so sorry. What can we do to help?"

"Nothing. I'm good, actually. Leanna, you're the big reason I decided to throw caution to the wind and quit. You have made such a great life between your

16

jam business and your relationship with Kurt that I thought..." She shrugged. "I'm almost thirty. Why not try to do what I really want to do?"

"I would never base your life on mine, Bella." Leanna's voice became serious. "Do you remember how I used to jump from job to job?"

"Yes, but that was you finding your path. This is *me* finding mine. My new life plan is pretty simple. I've lined up a summer job with the Barnstable County School District to develop a work-study program for high school seniors, and if I'm successful, then I'll get a one-year contract for full-time employment. I know I can make this work, and you know I love the Cape." Bella was still pissed at herself for dating someone she worked with and jeopardizing her reputation at work, but in the end, Jay's lying was the perfect impetus for her to start fresh. She had interviewed for a few other teaching positions since the spring, but she hadn't been interested in any of them, and she hadn't sent out any applications since the summer began. She was excited about her decision, and every day at the Cape solidified her choice. "I can see by your slack jaws that you're worried. I promise, Jay was just the straw that broke the camel's back. I want this change for me."

"What about your house in Connecticut? Your friends? Jesus, Bella. Don't you think this is a little bit of a knee-jerk reaction?" Jenna asked.

"Maybe in the first second it was, but now it feels like the right decision. My boss did say she's holding the job in case I change my mind, but the summer project is really exciting. I brought the concept of putting together a work-study to the school board. It's my baby, my project, and they're as excited about it as I am. Did you know that the unemployment rate among people under thirty on Cape Cod is pretty high in some areas? It's only about seven percent around here, but in P-town it's almost thirty percent. *Thirty.*"

"That's crazy high." Jenna's eyes widened.

"Yeah, tell me about it. I know it's probably skewed somehow because it's a resort town or something, but still. If I can secure a dozen businesses that will commit to hiring twenty-five kids for minimum wage during the school year, with on-the-job training, in positions that can lead to full-time employment after graduation, then the school board will give me a one-year contract. And I know that I can convert that one year into a permanent position once they see how motivated these kids become and how their self-esteem grows, not to mention how their post-graduation opportunities will expand."

"If anyone can do it, you can," Amy said. "But what if it doesn't work?"

Leanna glared at Amy. "If I can make Sweet Treats a successful business, then Bella can create a work-study program. I'm the most disorganized person I know, and Bella is not only organized, but she's smart and incredibly creative." She rose to her feet. "I'm proud of you, Bella. No man is worth feeling uncomfortable every day when you go to work."

"It's really not because of him, although I did use that as my excuse to my boss because she would try to talk me out of the real reason I want to leave. She'd have wanted me to start a new project there, but you guys, I really want to be *here.* You know how much I love it here, and now that I've taken the plunge and put my plan into action, I don't want to turn back. All I have to do now is focus on work, which should be easy if I'm not dating."

"I was just being practical," Amy explained. "I know Bella is capable of doing it, but you know, anything can happen. What if in two months she's stuck without a job? I didn't mean anything bad."

"I know you didn't, Ames," Bella said. "So, now that you know my big news, I have two days of fun before I dive into full-on program development on Monday. Are we still having a bonfire on the beach later?"

"Tony left me a voice mail that he got the permit, so yeah." Amy smiled as she sipped her coffee.

"One day that man will realize you're the best thing since crunchy peanut butter, Ames." Jenna patted her leg. "Bella, on a serious note, are you okay financially? Do you need money?"

Jenna's offer warmed Bella's heart. She wasn't the type of woman to tear up, but if she had been, the compassion in Jenna's voice and her offer to help surely would have made her. Jenna worked as an elementary school art teacher and lived on a shoestring budget. She could no sooner afford to help Bella financially than she could afford to visit Las Vegas.

"It means the world to me that you would offer, but I have a nest egg, so I should be fine for a while. Besides, once my house sells, I can live here, and if the work-study job doesn't lead to a full-time position, I can stay here until I find a job, even if it means traveling all over for interviews."

"You're really doing it." Jenna sighed. "I can't believe it."

"Yes, I'm *really* doing it."

"Well, if it's what you really want to do, then I think it's awesome," Leanna said. "I totally support whatever you want to do."

"I do, too, of course," Amy added. "It's just...Leanna's always been the gypsy in the group. She could pick up at any time and move without missing a beat, and even Jenna and I are more likely to switch apartments, or cars, or even cities, but Bella's always been the one who sticks to things. Gosh, Bell, I thought you'd live in Connecticut forever."

Bella reached for her hand and squeezed. "I know, Ames, but this is a good thing. And who knows? Maybe I'll live here forever. Forever's a long time, and my gut tells me that my forever should start here." Spending summers and school breaks at Seaside had always been Bella's sanity saver. She wondered if she'd enjoy it as much if it were her full-time residence. "How did you like being here during the winter, Leanna? Do you regret your decision to live here full-time?"

Leanna glanced at Kurt setting up his laptop on the deck of her cottage. "I love living at the Cape, and, Bell, I think everything happens for a reason."

"That's because you have a hot, rich boyfriend who spends his days pumping out bestselling novels and his nights adoring every inch of your slinky little body." Jenna raised her coffee in a toast. "To men adoring our bodies."

The others lifted their coffee cups. "Hear! Hear!" Amy said.

"He does those things, but I believe in fate because it's real. You'll see." Leanna came around the table and hugged Bella.

If Bella dared to believe in fate that would mean she had been fated to date Jay, and if that were true, then she was fated to leave a job and the community in Connecticut that she loved. Even though she was excited about the new job prospect, she had to wonder—if she'd been fated to date him, then what other crappy heartache did fate have in store for her?

CADEN STOOD IN the doorframe of Evan's bedroom, watching him sleep. At almost fifteen years old, his toes already hung off the foot of the bed. He looked so much like Caden had at that age, with the same mop of chestnut hair and square jaw. He'd even inherited Caden's cleft chin, which Caden had hated as a kid. He wondered, as he looked at his son, all elbows and knees lying on top of his sheets in his boxers, if he hated it, too. He tried to push away the guilt that pressed in on him for moving Evan away from his friends in Boston, but when his partner of nine years was killed during a robbery, it drove the dangers of his job home.

George Rowe had not only been a damn good cop, but he'd also been Caden's closest friend. Losing George had been ten times more difficult than the day almost fifteen years earlier, when Caden's then girlfriend, Caty Lowenstein, had come to his dorm and placed one-week-old Evan in his twenty-year-old arms. She'd said she was leaving town and that she'd signed custody over to him. He'd been in his second year of college and he'd thought he was in love with her. They'd been dating for five months when she found out she was pregnant. After two weeks of arguing—she wanted to abort the baby and Caden begged her not to—she'd disappeared. He didn't see her again until that fateful day when she set Evan in his arms and took off.

He looked down at his son now, remembering the weight of Evan in his arms and the way he'd turned those serious, trusting, dark eyes up at him. In the blink of an eye, Caden had known he'd never loved Caty, because what he felt for Evan was bigger than anything he'd ever felt in his life. It enveloped him and filled him to his core, leaving no room for anything or anyone else. He'd packed his things and gone home to his parents' house that night. Evan had been his life ever since.

Until last night, when he'd looked into Bella's eyes

and felt a fissure form in the armor he'd worn for all those years. Since the day he became Evan's father, he'd never been affected by a woman that way, which is why now, as he watched the boy who had turned his life upside down and taught him what love was, he allowed himself to think about seeing her again.

"Dad?"

Evan's voice pulled his mind back to the present.

"Hey, buddy. Sorry. Did I wake you?"

"Not really, but it's kinda creepy that you're watching me sleep." He shifted up on his elbow. "Are we still going fishing after your shift?"

Caden had always tried to spend as much time with Evan as he could. Or at least as often as Evan would agree to spend time with him. Teenage angst was clawing its way into their lives, and Caden was doing all he could to keep it from becoming a constant companion.

He ran his eyes over the posters of video and PC game characters on Evan's walls. When they'd lived in Boston, Evan hadn't spent much time playing video and PC games, but Caden had noticed that he was playing them more often lately, and he worried that they were serving as a replacement for friends.

"Yeah." Caden was glad Evan would still go fishing with him, even though he was going through a rough time. "I've got the surf rods ready. About six?"

"Sure. Whatever," Evan said.

*Whatever* had quickly become one of Caden's least favorite words. "What are your plans while I'm at work?"

Evan shrugged.

"Want me to come by at lunch and drop you at the beach?"

"I've got my bike." Evan stretched, and his shaggy hair tumbled over his eyes. When they'd lived in

Boston, Evan had spent the weekends at skateboard parks, hanging out with his friends doing ollies and kick flips. There was a skate park across from Wellfleet Harbor, and Caden had taken Evan there to check it out when they first moved in, but Evan hadn't shown any interest in returning.

"Okay, but remember that the cell phones don't work on the ocean beaches, so call me when you get to the parking lot if you go."

Evan scrubbed his hand down his face. "Got it, Dad. You tell me the same thing every day. It's not like I'll suddenly forget."

"Whatever," Caden said with a hint of amusement, earning him a smile from Evan.

Half an hour later Caden was at the police station, working on reports and thinking about the scene that had unfolded at Seaside. He covered his mouth as a soft laugh accompanied the memory of the half-naked women acting like silly teenagers who had snuck out of a slumber party. The laugh quickly turned to heat, coiling like a snake in his belly with the image of Bella in her silky underwear.

*Holy Christ. What was it about her?*

His chief's voice beckoned him into his office, startling him.

Caden stuck his head through the chief's doorway. "Chief?"

Chief Bassett was a serious man with tufts of strawberry-blond hair and pinkish skin that reminded Caden of a newborn mouse. He motioned for Caden to sit in a chair across from his desk.

"How's it going?" Chief Bassett asked.

Caden shrugged. "Fine."

"Your kid settling in okay?"

The chief had reached out to him several times in a similar friendly manner, checking in in a way that

23

had been rare in the large precinct he'd come from in Boston.

"Yeah. Evan's doing okay. You know how things are at that age. He's having a tough time making friends, but I'm hoping that once school starts that'll sort itself out." He wrung his hands together.

"Moving is tough on teens; that's for sure. You asked about moving to day shifts, and I think we can accommodate that after next week, if you're still interested."

Caden felt himself smile. "Absolutely. That's great. Thank you." He'd been working only a few night shifts each week, but he didn't like leaving Evan alone overnight, even though he checked on him often while he was out on patrol. When he'd first decided to become a cop, he'd known the risks of the job and that night shifts would be difficult. But Caden had always liked rules and structure, and helping people was in his nature. The job appealed to him on so many levels, and the outlook of being indestructible that went hand in hand with youth hadn't allowed him to question the risks. Evan had been just an infant, and leaving him at night, when he was sleeping safely in his crib with his parents in the next room, seemed like a better option to Caden than taking a desk job and leaving him during the day. He didn't want to miss those first few years with Evan. At the time, his mother worked part-time, and between Evan's naps and his mother taking over for a few hours each day, he was able to spend quality time bonding with his new son while paying his dues with the station. By the time Evan went to school, Caden had transitioned to day hours. He hadn't loved the idea of starting over again at a new station, but after George was killed, starting over seemed like a small price to pay for a safer job.

Chief Bassett nodded. "I thought you'd be pleased.

No trouble last night?"

*Not unless you consider running in to a gorgeous blonde trouble.* Caden shook his head. "Nah. Typical night. Any leads on the thefts?"

"No, nothing new, but you know, keep your eyes open."

"Will do." Caden pushed to his feet to return to his desk.

"Hey, Caden, one more thing. Are you doing okay?" The chief's gaze softened.

"Sir?"

"Losing your partner. As I mentioned when you were first hired, I've been through that loss. If you need to talk to someone, I'm around."

It had been almost six months since George died, and Caden felt guilty for having almost gotten used to the idea that he'd never see his best friend again. There was a time when just thinking of George brought a surge of anger and sadness, but over the months, he'd come to grips with it. George and Evan had also been close, and Evan seemed to finally get past that hurt, too. Although there were still times when Caden would forget that George was gone, like when he bought his house in Wellfleet and reached for his phone to call George so he could share his news, or after a long shift when he was alone in his patrol car and he'd catch a glimpse of the empty passenger seat. In those moments, he drew upon the good memories they'd shared, until he felt balanced again.

"Thanks. I appreciate your concern. I think moving was the right thing to do. In Boston I saw him everywhere. Here..." He shrugged. "There's something to be said about starting over."

## Chapter Three

BELLA, AMY, LEANNA, and Jenna were used to the
shock of cold that often trailed sunset like a shadow
on Cape Cod beaches. They hunkered down around
the bonfire on beach chairs with thick sweatshirts and
blankets across their laps. Layers of deep purples and
dark blue surrounded the white globe of the moon,
hovering above the ocean. Soon the sky would darken
and the stars would become visible, but for the next
thirty minutes, Bella had a dusky view of the surf
fishermen lined up on the beach, hoping for one final
bite from a bluefish that had somehow avoided
becoming prey to the seals that had claimed the New
England surf. It struck her how different her life would
be if she lived on the Cape full-time. Would she make
the time to sit on the beach on chilly March evenings
or walk by the edge of the water in a parka,
midwinter?

"Are you bummed that Kurt stayed with Jamie
tonight?" Bella asked Leanna. Jamie Reed was another
Seaside resident. His grandmother, Vera, owned the
cottage next to Leanna's, and Jamie had grown up

spending summers with Bella and the girls.

"Oh, gosh no. But Amy's gonna be mad, because when Tony found out that Kurt was staying, I heard him tell Kurt he'd stay, too." Leanna pulled her blanket up in front of her face. "Don't kill the messenger."

Amy rolled her eyes. "You guys act like something between me and Tony is even a possibility. I told you. I tried to sail that ship and he turned me down. I'm not a glutton for punishment."

"Oh, please. You know damn well that if he asked you out you'd jump at the chance." Jenna bumped Amy with her shoulder.

"Of course. I'm realistic, not stupid," Amy said. "But I won't make the mistake of coming on to him again."

Jenna nudged a rock with her toe, then leaned forward to pick it up.

"Here we go," Amy said. Jenna had been a rock collector for as long as Bella could remember. Each summer she zeroed in on a different type of rock. This summer her fascination was on heart-shaped rocks.

Jenna shot to her feet with her hands on her hips. "Who's coming with me to look for rocks?" She bounced on her toes like an excited kid.

"I thought you had a self-imposed moratorium on rock collecting," Bella reminded her. "Last summer you said your *cottage runneth over*, and that you weren't going to be collecting for a while." Runneth over might be an understatement. Every flat surface in Jen's cottage was adorned with rocks, including various corners of the hardwood floor and the rails of her deck.

Jenna lowered her eyes and twisted from side to side with her hands clasped behind her back. "I know. But I'll only take them if they're absolutely perfect." She tucked her hair behind her ear and her eyes widened with mischief. "And you know how picky I am." She pulled Bella to her feet, then bounced up and down again. "Please, please, please? Just until it's dark?"

Bella rolled her eyes. "Fine. But you owe me big-time."

Jenna threw herself into Bella's arms. "Yay!"

"You're such a fool." Bella laughed and laid her blanket over Amy's lap. "Here you go, princess. Don't drink all the wine without me."

The wet sand was cold beneath Bella's bare feet. She didn't mind walking with Jenna, and she didn't even care that Jenna owned more rocks than any mountain this side of Utah. She couldn't put her finger on why, but she was edgy tonight. She'd told her friends she was giving herself until Monday to start working on the program for the school. She'd also told them that she wasn't interested in sexy-as-hell Caden Grant in that blue uniform that hugged his broad chest and exposed well-muscled forearms and eyes that seemed to look right through her. But the job *and* Caden were all she could think about.

Jenna looped her arm through Bella's. "Thanks for walking with me. I know I won't find any good rocks, but I still like to look."

"I know you do." She loved everything about Jenna, from her obsessive-compulsive need for organization to her flip-flop fetish and her love of rocks. Jenna was always happy. Even when something pissed her off, she had the ability to spin a situation in her mind so her good mood wasn't sucked away.

Jen picked up a rock and washed it off in the surf. She ran her fingers over the rounded edges, then scrunched her nose and tossed it into the ocean.

"Are you nervous about your whole job, house situation?" she asked, bending down to inspect another rock.

"Nervous? You might say that. I'm excited and maybe a little scared, but not really. What's the worst that can happen?"

"You could end up jobless and living in your cottage." Jenna smiled up at her. "Guess that's not really so bad, is it? But it's just not like you to pick up and start over. That's more Leanna's thing. She's always been part gypsy like that, but you're stable Mable." Jenna tossed the unimpressive rock into the water.

"I know." Jenna knew her so well. She'd nailed the reason Bella was feeling edgy before Bella even realized it. "It's totally not like me, but dating Jay wasn't like me, either. I never date guys I work with. I know better than that—or at least I thought I knew better than that. It can only lead to complications with peers and supervisors. Everyone knows that. I've been mulling this over in my mind since spring break, and this is what I came up with. I'm almost thirty, and I worked so hard to get where I was in the school system, and it's been great, but I *am* stable Mable. So even if it weren't great, I'd have stayed for years."

"So, what are you saying?" Jenna stopped walking and gave Bella her full attention.

"Well, as I said, ever since Leanna made her dreams come true, I've been thinking about making mine come true. I think I dated Jay to force myself to make a change."

"Like a subconscious nudge?" The moon rose higher into the sky, glistening off the water behind Jenna.

"More like a conscious and trying-to-ignore it nudge," Bella said. "The whole time I dated Jay, I wasn't connected to him. When I found out he had lied about being divorced and was just separated, I broke it off without thinking twice. And you know what? I knew that second that I was going to quit my job. What does that say about me?"

Jenna leaned her head against Bella's arm and walked farther down the beach. "It says you're normal, like the rest of us. That you followed your heart, which, I might remind you, is exactly what you told Leanna to do when she met Kurt."

"Do you think it's still called following your heart when you make a career and life change, or is that following your mind?" Bella was having a hard time separating the two when it came to the Cape. Everything about the Cape filled her with happiness, from the morning crows to the smell of the salty air, making her heart very much involved with her decision. But this decision was also made with her mind. She wanted a challenge, and the work-study program offered that.

"I think it's both."

"So you don't think I'm nuts? And I'm serious about not dating, too. I think I need to make sure my life is in order before I become some guy-who-can't-be-honest-or-keep-a-commitment's girlfriend."

"I think you're brilliant and fearless, not nuts." Jenna pointed down the beach. "Look, don't you love when the fishermen head back to their cars like little soldiers in a line? It's like the minute the gray sky turns black, they have some secret wave, or nod, or something that alerts them all to fall in line."

Bella squinted at the fishermen with their long surf fishing poles over their shoulders and white buckets hanging from their thick, bare arms.

"Show me a man who's not an asshole and I'll go searching for rocks with you every day of the summer." Bella nodded to two men as they walked past. She turned to check out their butts and walked backward. "God, I love rugged men." *Okay, so maybe I won't swear them off completely. I just won't get involved.* "What's better than a guy in a pair of cargo shorts and a tank top who's not afraid to get his hands dirty and isn't overly concerned with his looks? A man who can take the cold night air against his skin? You know they can keep you warm."

"How about a hot cop without his uniform?" Jenna tugged Bella's arm.

Bella spun around just in time to see Caden Grant's profile as he leaned in close to a teenage boy. Even while he spoke, he had a smile on his lips. It lit up his eyes. He and the boy each carried a fishing pole over one shoulder and Caden also carried a bucket in his other hand. Bella reached for Jenna's hand as she drank in his faded jeans, rolled up at the cuffs. His feet were bare and his gait was as casual as it was confident. And—*holy mother of God*—his white T-shirt hugged his broad shoulders in a way that practically made her drool. He leaned toward the boy, giving him his full attention in a way that felt to Bella like an embrace.

Caden threw his head back with a hearty, deep laugh.

Jenna squeezed her hand. "Close your mouth," she whispered.

Bella followed her advice, or at least she hoped she did. Her brain was busy studying the man who, even without the uniform, had an in-control edge about him that wasn't dangerous or mysterious, but so self-assured and warm that she wanted to be part of his inner circle.

Caden's chin came back to center, and a breath later their eyes connected. The easy, sexy smile that followed did her in.

CADEN STOPPED IN his tracks at the sight of Bella wearing a powder-blue hoodie and a pair of jeans that accentuated her figure. He tried to name the startlingly unfamiliar feeling in his chest. *Full*, was the best he could come up with. He felt full.

He'd been wondering if in his mind he'd exaggerated the instant attraction he'd felt when he'd seen her the night before, but his quickening pulse was all the confirmation he needed to know that what he'd felt was definitely not a fluke.

"Bella. Hi." Caden had been playing a game with himself all afternoon. He told himself that if he ran into her again, he'd ask her out, and if not, then he would stop thinking about her altogether. Then he'd driven by Seaside about six times throughout the day, hoping to spot her so he *could* ask her out.

The breeze blew her blond hair back from her face, revealing thinly arched brows above the warm eyes that had sucked him right in last night. She was even more beautiful than he remembered.

"We didn't really get properly introduced last night. I'm Jenna." The short brunette ran her eyes between Caden and Evan.

"This is my son, Evan. Evan, this is Bella and Jenna. I met them while I was on duty last night." He watched Bella look from him to Evan, then back again. Even at twenty Caden had never felt anything but pride for his son, but now he wondered if Bella felt the same attraction he did, and if so, did his having a son change that?

Evan arched a brow in a look that translated as, *You met a woman?* It seemed too old for his teenage son to be casting his way.

"Hi," Evan said.

Caden stifled the urge to reach over and move his son's hair out of his eyes.

33

"Did you catch anything?" Jenna peered into the bucket.

"Mung," Evan answered. Mung was fisherman's speak for thick seaweed that tangled in their lines.

"Gross. I hate that." Jenna scrunched her nose.

"Yeah, it's pretty gross," Evan said.

"Are you just out for a walk?" Caden gripped the bucket tighter to ease his nerves. It had been so long since he'd been interested in a woman that it took him a minute to get used to his quickening pulse and the tightening in his gut.

"We're having a bonfire." Bella pointed to the fire down the beach. Her friends waved, and Bella waved back.

"Want to join us?" Jenna asked.

Bella shot her a look that Caden couldn't read— she was either pissed or excited—and the two emotions were so far apart that he went with a safe answer, giving her an easy out.

"That's okay. We don't want to impose."

"A bonfire might be fun," Evan said.

"Of course it's fun." Jenna grabbed Evan's arm and pulled him toward the bonfire. "Come on. I'll introduce you to everyone."

The sound of waves breaking filled the silence that stretched between Caden and Bella. Oddly, he didn't feel rushed to break that silence. Just being in her presence felt nice—almost natural. He forced himself to say something, in case she felt uncomfortable, although she didn't appear to, the way she was smiling up at him.

"I guess that means we're staying, but really, if you'd rather we didn't—"

"No. I'd rather you did. Stay." Bella seemed quieter than she'd been the previous evening, and Caden didn't know how to read that, either. A gust of wind swept off the ocean and whipped her hair across her cheek. She shook her head to clear it away. It flew right back again.

Without thinking, he stepped closer and tucked the wayward lock behind her ear.

Bella's eyes narrowed, as if she were uncomfortable. "That means we're married, you know."

She said it with such a serious face that for a second he worried he'd crossed a line in the sand. What the hell was he thinking?

*Oh hell, just go with it.* "Cool. I've never been married before."

Bella slid a confused glance at Evan, who was making himself right at home with the others.

"Evan's mom and I were never married," he explained. Why was he nervous talking about Evan? *That* was new, too.

"Oh," Bella said.

He was sure she was waiting for an explanation, but he'd found that when he shared the story of how he and Evan came to be a family, women got weird, like he was a lost puppy who needed taking care of. He didn't need that shit. He loved his life with Evan, and he'd never regretted his decision to leave school to take care of him.

"So, you sure you don't mind if we hang out for a while?"

"The more the merrier, as long as you don't mind hanging out with a bunch of women. It's pretty chilly. Do you want to go sit by the fire?"

He'd much rather wrap his arms around her. Short of that, sitting by a fire with Bella sounded just fine. "Sure."

At the fire, Jenna threw Caden a blanket. "Here, you and Bella can sit on it."

He almost made a joke about being already married and checked himself before the words left his lips. He didn't need to freak out Evan, although from the looks of things, he was feeling pretty damn comfortable. He had his hand buried in a bag of marshmallows.

Caden glanced at the others. "I hope we're not intruding." He held a hand out to the brunette that had stuck her head out of the cottage window. "I don't think we met last night. I'm Caden Grant. And this is my son, Evan."

"I'm Leanna." She shook his hand. "Evan already introduced himself."

He was glad to hear that.

The skinny blonde waved to him. "I'm Amy. Want a glass of wine? Oh, and, Evan, we have Sprite if you'd like, too."

"No, thanks. I have to drive," Caden answered. The cop in him cataloged that all four of them were drinking.

"That's why we take a cab to the bonfires. They'll pick us up at eleven. Like our personal chauffer," Amy explained.

"Good to know." *Responsible.* He liked that. Caden and Evan hadn't been to a bonfire on the beach, and it wasn't something Caden would have instigated on his own. He was glad for the opportunity not just to see Bella again, but for Evan to be exposed to something new.

Amy handed a plastic cup of wine to Bella, then dug through the cooler and handed a can of Sprite to Evan.

Caden sat beside Bella on the small blanket, hyperaware of their close proximity. Bella's hair swept across her face again.

"Does anyone have a ponytail holder?" she asked.

"No, sorry," Amy said.

The others shook their heads.

"I'm going to the flea market tomorrow and buying three boxes of them. One for my beach bag, one for my car, and one for at home. That way I'm never without," Bella said. "Anyone want to go with me?"

"The Wellfleet Flea Market?" Evan asked.

"Yeah. Do you want to go?" Bella was asking Evan but looking at Caden with a glimmer of hope in her eyes.

"Ev?" *Please say you want to go.* He never thought he'd be hoping his son would want to do something so *he* could spend time with a girl.

"Yeah. I'm looking for a few PC games, and that discount guy is there on Sundays, remember, Dad?" Evan leaned forward with hope in his eyes.

Bella pulled her hair off her face again, and with the next breeze, it blew back in her face.

"Sure, we can go." He tried to contain his excitement.

"Great." Their eyes connected, and for a beat the world stood still. Bella blinked several times, as if she'd felt it too, and then she leaned forward and patted Evan's leg, while Caden tried to catch his breath. "I know that video game guy. We'll negotiate a better deal than the three for twenty." When she turned her attention back to Caden, her eyes were guarded. "Swing by and pick me up at ten?"

"It's a date."

"It's a trip to the flea market," Bella said with a serious stare.

"Whatever it is, be sure to stop by and see me," Leanna added.

Another gust of wind made the fire crackle and sparks fly into the air. Bella's hair whipped around her face again. She reached up with both hands to push it away once more.

"Ugh. I always forget about the wind."

"I can fix that." Caden withdrew his tackle box from the bucket and cut a clean piece of fishing line. He sensed their eyes on him as he gathered Bella's thick, luxurious hair in his hands. He wanted to linger there, with his hands in her hair, so close they'd brush cheeks if he leaned in a few inches. He cleared his throat and pushed the thought away. *Christ.* His son was sitting right there. What was he thinking?

He took Bella's hand in his and wrapped her fingers around the thick rope of hair, holding it in place so he could tie it back. He leaned in close, inhaling her warm, inviting scent, and set to work tying the fishing line around it.

"So, you're a cop and a hairstylist?" Jenna teased.

Bella touched the knotted fishing line and turned to face him. "Thank you. I think you just might be the best husband I've ever had."

Evan's eyes met his—and held.

Caden rolled his eyes to indicate it was a joke, and Evan, the king of eye rolls and *whatevers* answered with a knowing nod.

"Husband?" Leanna reached for a stick and pushed a marshmallow onto it. "Did I miss something?"

"It was a joke. He did something before and I said it meant we were married." Bella finished her wine in one gulp, then reached for a marshmallow.

Jenna shot her a narrow-eyed stare and nodded toward Evan.

"Oh, Evan. I was kidding. Really. We just met last night," Bella clarified.

"It's okay. My dad doesn't even date, so..." He shrugged.

Caden didn't have time to respond before Amy

said, "He doesn't?"

"Nope." Evan stuffed a marshmallow in his mouth.

*When the hell did you become Mr. Social?*

"Why not?" Jenna asked.

"God, you guys. What is this, the Cahoon Hollow Beach Inquisition?" Bella turned to face him. "I'm sorry. You don't have to answer them."

*Shit, yeah, I do.* He wasn't about to let them bat around reasons that would either make him look like a loser or a psycho. "Between work and Evan, there isn't much time for a social life."

"So, like, you never date? Or..." Amy asked.

"Maybe this isn't something we should be discussing right now," Bella suggested.

"I don't care if my dad dates," Evan said.

Caden hadn't dated much over the years, and the few times he had, he hadn't told Evan because he knew they weren't dates that would lead to anything real. Now he read the silent question in his son's eyes. *Why don't you date, Dad?* And he decided that was a conversation best held in private.

"Well, if it makes you feel any better, I recently gave up dating, too," Bella said before loading up her stick with another marshmallow.

"She's kidding," Jenna said quickly.

"Nope. I'm one hundred percent serious. I'm done with commitments." Bella waved her hand in the air.

Her admission hit with the weight of lead, but the harsh looks Bella's friends slid her way were skeptical.

"What's wrong with commitments?" Caden wasn't sure he could keep the fact that he actually cared about the answer out of his voice.

Bella stared at the fire as she answered. "They're only as good as the people who make them."

He saw pain in her eyes, and he wondered how deep that wound went. He needed to change the subject before they got into a discussion that could lead to Evan's mother and make his son uncomfortable.

"So, how long are you guys at the Cape, or do you live here year-round?" A benign topic that would also give him more information about Bella. *Perfect.*

"I live here," Leanna said as she handed out graham crackers and chocolate for s'mores.

"I'm here for the summer." Amy passed a chocolate bar to Bella.

"Same here," Jenna said.

Bella finished cooking her marshmallow in silence.

"Bella? Are you here for the summer, or do you live here?"

She stacked the chocolate on top of a graham cracker, added the warm marshmallow, and then topped it off with another graham cracker. She stared at it for a minute before cocking her head in his direction and answering.

"I'm here until the s'mores run out."

*Then let me run to the store for more marshmallows.*

She took a bite of the gooey treat and licked a streak of chocolate from her lower lip. She had a dab of marshmallow on her cheek, and once again, it felt natural to reach over and wipe it clean with his finger.

Bella narrowed her eyes. *Shit.* There was that invisible boundary again. Maybe she wasn't into him after all.

"I was saving that for later," she said. With her back to Evan, who was preoccupied with his own dessert, she grabbed his hand and brought it to her mouth. His pulse quickened with the expectation of a sensually evocative suck. With wide, amused eyes, she turned his finger sideways and nibbled the sticky

40

marshmallow off like it was corn on the cob.

"I'll teach you not to steal my sugar. Open up." She shoved the s'more toward his mouth.

"No, that's okay." He leaned out of reach to tease her.

"Come on. No one can resist s'mores." She leaned in closer, holding the s'more to his lips. Her knee pressed against his thigh. "You know you want it."

*Hell, yeah, I do.* He took a bite of the sweet, sticky treat. Heat flashed in Bella's eyes as she dragged her finger along the edge of his lower lip and held it up to show him the smear of chocolate before she slowly, evocatively, sucked her finger clean.

*Holy. Hell.*

Beautiful, smart, and sexier than any woman he'd ever met. Bella piqued curiosities and desires that had been slumbering for way too long.

# Chapter Four

SUNDAY ARRIVED WITH the promise of sunshine and a swarm of butterflies in Bella's stomach. She was supposed to be focusing on getting her new life together, not getting all quivery about going to the flea market with a man, and yet there she was, walking into the flea market beside a handsome, charming man and his soft-spoken son. She'd even taken extra care in choosing the brightly colored sundress she wore, and Jenna had insisted that she wear her sexiest bikini beneath, along with matching sandals, because *that man deserves sexy.* She tried not to stare as she ran her eyes over his handsome face. He had a chiseled, square jaw, and today it was peppered with stubble, darker in the cleft of this chin, giving him an edgier—and impossibly sexier—appearance.

The flea market was held in the parking lot of the Wellfleet Drive-In movie theater. They sold everything from designer duds to cheap jewelry and antiques, and even when it rained, the place was packed. They crossed the parking lot toward the sea of vendor tents and booths, set up in long rows for as far as the eye could see, and joined the crowds of tourists and locals looking for great deals they couldn't pass up.

"Can I take off, Dad?" Evan shoved his hands in the pockets of his camo shorts. His hair was damp and uncombed, and in his gaming T-shirt, he blended in with every other teen wandering around the flea market.

Caden withdrew a twenty-dollar bill from the pocket of his shorts and handed it to Evan. "You have your phone?"

Evan held it up, like he'd been asked the same question a million times. He probably had.

"Okay. Text if you need me, and don't leave the grounds."

"I know," Evan said with an exasperated sigh, then disappeared into the crowd.

"He's a sweet kid," Bella said.

"Usually. He's in that stage where testosterone can win out over common sense, so if he appears snappy at times, or disinterested, I apologize ahead of time."

"I'm a high school teacher. I know probably more than I should about teenagers."

"So you're a teacher?" He ran his hand through his thick hair, then placed it on her lower back as they maneuvered through the crowd.

He emitted a confident and tender vibe, and it was such a strange combination that Bella found herself sneaking peeks at him. She tried not to focus on how nice his hand felt on her back, and forced herself to respond.

"I've been teaching in Connecticut for the last five years, but I'm working for the Barnstable County school system this summer. I'm hoping it leads to full-time."

She stopped to look at a display of necklaces, and Caden's hand slipped away. She sensed him behind her, protectively shielding her from the masses as they meandered by. Bella was not a woman who needed protecting, and she'd never had a man treat her like she was. Everything about Caden felt different from the other men she'd dated, and she wondered if it had anything to do with his having a son and being a cop, and protecting others for all those years. It was a strange sensation to have a man she wasn't dating stand so close that she could feel his warmth and smell his earthy, spicy, almost primal scent—and, God, she loved the smell of him.

Bella looked for Leanna, but her vendor space was empty. She wondered what had come up that would cause her to leave the flea market so early, but she knew if it were something bad, Jenna would have tracked her down. *Probably one of Kurt's surprise outings.*

The crowd thickened near a popular L.L. Bean display, and Bella felt his big hand settle on her lower back again as they wove their way through to the next booth. His hand felt nice. Maybe too nice. *I'm not getting involved. It's just a hand.* She rolled her eyes at the thought and reminded herself that she wasn't really going to swear off men, just commitments.

"So you're moving from Connecticut?" He stopped and flipped through a box of CDs.

She was considering how much she wanted to reveal about her current situation when he glanced up with that easy smile that distracted her from her thoughts. She realized she was staring and turned her attention to the CDs.

"You don't share personal details of your life very easily, do you?"

"I just don't want to bore you." Even as she said it, she knew it wasn't the truth. He was so easy to talk to that it took effort not to share everything with him, but she'd made a promise to herself. She knew it would be ten times more difficult to make life decisions based solely on what she wanted if she were involved with a caring, protective man like Caden. He wasn't someone a person just dated. She knew that already. Caden could be a game changer.

"Bore me. Please."

His voice was so full of sincerity that it drew her eyes to his again. Damn if they weren't also honest and interested. *Definitely interested.*

"There's not much to tell. I'm in a transitional period, looking for a new job. You know, figuring things out as I go." *And damn it, why do I want to hold your hand?* She fisted her hands to keep from doing just that.

They continued down the row of vendors, and every time the crowd grew thick, his hand returned to her back. A gesture as possessive as it was protective, it made her warm with desire—and shiver with worry, because being with him felt *that* good *that* fast.

They turned down the next aisle and Caden stopped. He was tall and broad, making it easy for his eyes to dance over the heads of the crowd, finally settling on Evan, talking to a couple of teenagers by the discount game vendor in the next row over.

"I can probably negotiate a deal for him if you want to go over. Everyone here barters."

Eyes still on Caden, he pressed his hand a little firmer to her back. "No, not yet. Maybe he'll meet a friend or two."

"Doesn't he have many friends?"

"We just moved here a few weeks before summer began. He didn't really have time to get to know anyone." His brow furrowed, and his eyes grew serious. He placed his hand on her back again. "Come on. Let's find you those hair things you wanted."

*You remembered.* "It's tough on kids to move, especially teenagers. What brought you to Wellfleet?"

"My partner was killed in the line of duty, and it was a wake-up call. I realized that if something happened to me, Ev wouldn't have anyone. His mom took off a week after he was born, and I haven't seen her since. Other than my parents, I'm the only family Evan has ever known."

He was so open and honest, and his words were thick with love. She felt her resolve soften a little more. She wanted to get to know him better, despite her plan to remain distant.

"I'm so sorry about your partner. That must have been very painful."

When he continued, his voice was thoughtful. "It was. Sometimes it still is, but moving helped." He smiled, but it wasn't the easy smile she'd seen earlier. His eyes remained serious. "I knew moving would be tough on Evan, and it wasn't an easy decision to move away from my parents, but it was more important to me that I work someplace safer. Hopefully, I'll be around for Evan until he's old and gray."

"So you raised him alone?"

"Since the day he was left in my arms." He smiled again, and this time it was full of love, and his eyes filled with pride.

They stopped to look over paintings, but Bella couldn't take her eyes off of this man who had changed his life to protect his son.

"What about you? Has the move been tough for you?" she asked.

His answer came easily. "Nothing is too difficult when I'm doing it for Evan." He shrugged, as if life decisions were that simple.

Bella had made her decision to change her life in a split second as well. Maybe life decisions really were that easy.

"In all honestly, I had to start on the bottom rung here. You know, new department, new city, and all that. It took some getting used to, but hopefully in the long run it will be worth it. What about you, Bella? Have you ever been married?"

She laughed. "Wow. You don't beat around the bush. No commitments, remember?"

"You mentioned that that was a recent decision."

*What is it about you that makes me want to spill my guts?* "It was semi recent. I made the decision not to..." *Date? Get involved in a relationship?* She didn't want to stipulate either so definitively with Caden. "I made the decision in the spring, and no, I've never been married." She was feeling too flustered inside toward him. She needed a little deflection. "And I'm not looking to get married anytime soon, so don't drop to one knee and whip out a ring, either."

He laughed. *Thank goodness.* At least he didn't think she was as crazy as she felt.

"I'm basically starting over, too. I'll be happy to find a job for the fall, sell my house, and settle into a life that doesn't rely on someone else's honesty." *Holy crap. Where did all that come from?* She couldn't stop herself from explaining. "I made a deal with myself that I'd make my life decisions based on me and me alone. Oh God, that sounds terribly selfish given what you've done for Evan."

"You don't have children, so it's different."

"Either you're a great liar, or you're the most understanding man I've ever met. I guess it's different, but what I meant was, I'd make my decisions separate from a relationship. You know, separate heart and mind and all that."

Caden's eyes grew serious. "There's an all that? I thought that when the heart made a decision, the mind had no choice. Huh."

"I'm hoping there's a separation of heart and mind, but if I'm not in a committed relationship, it won't be an issue anyway." *Shut up. Shut up. Shut up. Oh my God, here it goes...* "I have an offer to get my old job back in Connecticut, and I'm trying to build a work-study program here. *That* choice has to come from what I want."

He reached for her hand—even after all she'd said. "Well, I think that makes total sense." He guided her to the next booth, and she was sure her jaw was gaping as she stared at their interlaced fingers. They felt like they belonged together.

"Here's the hair stuff," he said.

She should pull away. She knew she should, but she didn't, despite everything she'd just admitted. She told herself it was curiosity, to see if he would pull away first, but in truth, she liked the feel of him.

She liked *him*.

It was that simple.

And that complicated.

She picked up three boxes of ponytail holders. "I'll take these, please."

Caden withdrew his wallet.

"I think I can afford hair bands." She pulled a ten-dollar bill from her purse and paid for the bands. She wasn't used to men offering to buy anything other than dinner or a movie, and it had never bothered her. In fact, she'd never thought anything of paying for her own things when she was out with a man. Until this very second. She told herself to be careful. Thoughtful, generous, and understanding was a dangerous—and from her experience, uncommon—combination in a man.

They continued down the aisle, and this time he didn't touch her back as they moved through the crowd. She wondered if she'd completely turned him off.

"Thanks for offering to pay, but it's a pride thing." *A pride thing? Oh my God. What the hell is wrong with me? You're trying to be nice and I'm being a bitch.* But it was kind of a pride thing, wasn't it? Bella took pride in being able to take care of herself, financially and in other ways.

"A pride thing? Okay, got it. I didn't mean to imply that you couldn't afford to pay for your own hair bands. It was just a natural reaction to offer, I guess."

"A natural reaction? So you buy things for every woman you go shopping with?" She smiled to let him know she was teasing, but the look he returned was serious.

"I don't usually shop with women, so I guess the answer is yes, because it felt natural with you."

His gaze was so hot, it brought sweat to her brow.

His cell phone vibrated, severing the connection. As he pulled the phone from his pocket, Bella sucked in a deep breath to get her bearings. *Jesus, what is wrong with me?* He was sucking her right into the crazy man world again. The world where decisions were made based on feelings and minds were too filled with lust and anticipation to think straight. Where, for most guys, lies went hand in hand with getting a girl into bed. But he didn't seem at all crazy. She had to be strong. *Fix my life. Then date. Maybe.* A moment later, she felt his body press against her back. *Good Lord, you feel good.* His hands gripped her hips, and he guided her out of the center of the crowded aisle.

He looked down at her with honest, dark eyes, and the last of her steely resolve slipped away. She wanted to kiss that sexy dip in his chin and run her tongue along his lower lip. She wanted to press her hands to his chest and feel the hard muscle beneath the soft cotton. She wanted to be in his arms and feel the passion that fueled him to wrap his life around a child at such a young age—and at the same time, she wanted to turn and run as fast and as far away as she could. Because Bella knew that once she opened the door to her heart, making clear-headed decisions would no longer be easy, and pain was sure to follow.

"That was Evan. Those kids he was talking to want him to hang out with them for the afternoon, so I need to go meet them. Do you have time to hang out? Maybe go to the beach while he's with his friends?"

*No. Definitely not.* The words were on the tip of her tongue, which is why when she heard herself say, "Sure," she knew she was in trouble.

THEY STOPPED AT Caden's house so he could change into his bathing suit. He'd gotten a sweet deal on the three-bedroom rambler, built at the end of a cul-de-sac and just a few blocks from the bay. Since he moved in, he'd had the hardwood floors replaced, renovated the kitchen, and painted the house top to bottom. He had simple taste, and as he watched Bella's eyes moving from the brown sectional to the built-in bookshelves, where they lingered on the titles, then circled back to the glass coffee table, and finally landed on the frames on the mantel, he wondered what she was thinking.

She walked over to the mantel and took down a picture of him and Evan. It was taken at Evan's sixth birthday party, and it was one of Caden's favorite photos. Evan's eyes were wide and his gap-toothed grin was so innocent. The image still tugged at Caden's heartstrings. His hair was long and curly around his sweet little-boy face.

He moved behind Bella and looked over her

shoulder. "Good times."

"I'm glad he met some kids today."

"Yeah. Me too. It's a weird feeling to let him go off by himself with a new crowd, but he's going to be fifteen soon, and if I parent him too much, he'll be an outcast. Too little will open the door to delinquency."

"At least you care," she said. "There are a lot of parents who don't. They leave the kids to video games and the Internet and never even check in on them. It's nice that you spend time together."

"It's nice for me. Sometimes I feel like I'm forcing myself on him."

She smiled, like she completely understood. "That's what being a teenager is all about. They're confused as hell, so it's only natural for their parents to be confused, too. I say, give them rope. Tug them in when they need it, and give 'em more rope when they earn it. If they don't hang themselves, you've done well. If they do, then you probably still did well, but you missed a hint of trouble along the way."

She set the frame back on the mantel and looked at the others. When she continued, her tone was serious but cushioned with compassion.

"What's most important is that if you did miss something, you don't leave him hanging until his eyes pop out and he can't find his way back. You lift him up by the bootstraps and kick him in the ass— figuratively, not literally. Walk with him down a better path. Give him the tools he needs and the understanding to become a better person. Teach yourself to become a better parent; then you both move forward together. A little bruised, a little embarrassed, but whole." She shrugged as if she hadn't just said something that made his world spin.

*You're amazing.* How could a woman who had never been a parent know so much about raising children? "You're wise and beautiful. That's a lethal combination." He felt himself opening up to Bella in so many ways, and after keeping those parts of himself closed off for so long, he wondered if she could feel it, too.

"That's kind of why I'm working on this work-study project for the high school."

He made a mental note about her needing to skirt around compliments and tried again to see if he'd read her discomfort correctly.

"Because you're wise and beautiful?" he teased.

Her cheeks flushed. "Because idle hands lead to trouble, and a lot of parents don't have the income to send their kids to college. So the more kids I can help gain experience in trades, or secure jobs for after graduation, the better chance they'll have at a meaningful future. Whether that's through more schooling that the companies subsidize, or through stronger self-esteem and pride in what they accomplish..." She shrugged. "The path they take doesn't matter, as long as they get there."

"Your passion for helping kids makes you even more beautiful." He couldn't keep the compliment to himself. It was true, and he wanted her to know that. He knew he was pushing, maybe a little too hard, given her wrinkled brow, but he wanted to find out what had caused her to disbelieve compliments, and he wanted to ease the hurt of whatever it was. He moved a little closer, and heat flared in her eyes. She shifted them away and picked up another frame.

She studied the picture of him and George, arm in arm, dressed in their uniforms. It was taken the week before he was killed. George was a stocky man with skin as dark as night and piercing coal-black eyes that could make a criminal wet his pants or a woman melt, depending on the look he slayed them with. He had a laugh that rumbled from deep in his gut, and he was the best goddamn friend a man could have.

"Was this your partner?"

*Was.* Caden's throat thickened. "Mm-hm. George."

Her eyes remained on the photo, but she wrapped one arm around Caden's waist and hugged him close. She stayed there for a beat, with her cheek pressed to his chest and her eyes on the man who had meant so much to him. In that silence, he realized how much he longed to share the pieces of himself that he'd kept bottled up for too long.

The feel of her body against him remained as she moved away and scanned the other photos.

"Are these your parents?" Bella pointed to the picture of his parents, each holding one of four-year-old Evan's hands.

"Yeah. They live in Boston." He made a point of taking Evan back every two or three weeks to visit his parents, and they were due to make another trip soon.

"They must really miss him."

Bella was an interesting mix of brazenness and tenderness, and when she gazed up at him with eyes full of compassion, he felt another emotion that he hadn't felt in a very long time. The urge to climb into a woman's inner circle and allow her into his. He took a step closer and tucked her hair behind her ear.

"They do miss him, and I think he misses them, too." Caden missed this—talking to a woman about things that mattered. Wanting to share them with her and wanting to know more about her and her life. Was she running from someone painful in her past? If so, who was important enough for her to box herself off like she was trying so hard to do? Or was her decision to move as simple as she'd said—a life change she wanted to make? He was no stranger to running from pain. Hell, he'd done it for years. He'd run from the pain of Caty leaving, not so much for him, but for Evan, but he'd had Evan to love and nurture and fill those empty spaces that could have eaten him alive. What did Bella do with all those empty spots she was walling off, and why did he want to be the glue that held her together?

She dropped her eyes, and he felt her shift her weight back on her heels, distancing herself again. Her fingers skimmed his waist, giving him more contradictory signals. One moment she seemed interested in him, and the next, he could practically see her zipping herself into her own private bubble. She ran her tongue along her lower lip and lifted a sensual gaze to his face. He was too damn drawn to her to stop himself from covering her mouth with his.

*Holy Christ.* She tasted sweet and hot and too good for just one quick kiss. His hands slid around her waist to her back, and he pressed her soft curves against him. Lord, he was already hard. Just as he worried that he should pull away, she slipped her hands beneath his shirt and pressed them flat against his back, holding them chest to chest. He deepened the kiss, swollen with desire and aching for more. A sexy, needful moan slipped from her lungs to his, intensifying his desire. He slid his hand beneath her thin dress and cupped the sweet curve of her ass. She rocked her hips into his. Sweet Jesus, they were on the same damn page. He followed her cue and slid his fingers beneath her bikini bottom. He hadn't made out like this in years, and he wasn't thinking, or pushing. He was just going with it. Like everything else with Bella, it felt natural, and he didn't care why. Some things were just meant to be.

His fingertips skimmed her damp center, and he just about lost it. With the next thrust of his tongue, she opened her legs. Good Lord, there was no misinterpreting that she wanted him as much as he wanted her. As she deepened the kiss, he slid his fingers inside her, taunting her—and himself. She moaned again—how he loved that deep, sensual sound—and she spread her legs wider, giving him better access and driving him out of his ever-loving mind. She fisted her hands against his back as he stroked her velvety heat. He couldn't keep himself from tangling his other hand in her hair and tugging her head back, exposing her supple neck for him to taste, suck, ravish. Her skin was sweet and salty, her center warm and wet as he went deeper and took her over the edge. His name sailed off her lips in a hot breath as she clawed at his back. He took her in another greedy kiss and felt her body vibrating against his as they breathed air into each other's lungs, then drew apart in need of more.

He pressed her head to his chest, his fingers still buried deep, until she had the last of her pleasure, and a gratified sigh escaped her lips. Only then did he slide them out. She looked up at him with a sated smile, and he kissed her again, slowly and tenderly, this time. Her hand ran up his thigh, and she stroked him through his shorts. He laced his fingers with hers and brought them to his lips, gazing into her confused eyes.

He shook his head.

"But..."

"Bella, I really like you, but...I can't." The truth came easily. Unfortunately, the pain did, too. "I'm sorry."

She pulled away and looked down at his erection, then met his gaze again with an arched brow. "I could..." She licked her lips.

He leaned down and kissed her softly. "I'm sure you could." *And it would be fucking amazing.* "I don't take intimacy lightly, and you don't believe in commitment." He looked at the photographs on the mantel. He'd never been overly impetuous, but after Caty took off and Evan had been left without a mother, the ramifications of his feelings and his actions were driven home. He'd become even more careful with both. He drew Bella close again and kissed the top of her head.

"I'm sorry. I probably shouldn't have..." *But good Lord did I want to.* He felt his resolve soften at the sight of her flushed cheeks and the desire that lingered in her eyes. He gritted his teeth against the lust that burned within him. "I couldn't help myself. You totally got to me."

She narrowed her eyes. "So, are you like a fetish guy? Make a girl come, then pleasure yourself later?"

The comment was so harsh that he had to shake his head to move past it. Christ, she hadn't even heard the part about commitment. "A fetish...Have you been with guys like that?" The thought turned his stomach.

"No, but..."

"No," he said too harshly. He took a step back. "I'm not a fetish guy. I'm not a make-the-girl-come-and...Jesus, Bella."

"Well, what am I supposed to think?" Her voice hitched, and he realized it wasn't anger that drove her harsh reaction. It was pain, or embarrassment, or maybe both.

She was right. What the hell was she supposed to think? He closed the gap between them, his chest tight with guilt.

"What should you think? I don't know. Maybe that I'm a guy with a teenager who knows that sex has ramifications, or a man who's incredibly attracted to you but doesn't want to be the guy you sleep with and then walk away from." He paced the floor, feeling guilty for touching her and hungry for more of her.

One big confused mix of emotions. "I'm sorry. It's been a very long time since I've felt like this, and I don't really know how to handle it."

She looked away. "Can I use your bathroom?"

*Way to avoid the situation.*

"Of course." He showed her to the bathroom and went to wash up. When he returned, she was looking out the window at the garden in his backyard. He wrapped his arms around her waist and felt her body stiffen. *Damn it.* He loosened his grip and took a step back. She clutched his forearm, holding his arms around her.

She turned to face him and pressed her hands to his chest. "I'm sorry for my bitchy reaction. I was just...I'm in a weird place right now."

"Then we make a great pair." He kissed her forehead.

"Still want to go to the beach?"

She sounded as confused by their connection as he was. "Let me get my suit on, and I promise to try to keep my hands off of you for the rest of the day."

Her voice trailed him into the bedroom. "Way to squash a girl's hopes in one sentence."

*Christ.* Could he get any more confused?

# Chapter Five

"I THINK YOU'RE overreacting." Jenna sat on the floor at the edge of Bella's closet, organizing her sandals and flip-flops while Bella dried her hair. "How would you feel right now if you had slept with him this afternoon? My bet is not great."

Bella turned the hair dryer off and sat on the bed. "I don't know. I only know that when he stopped, I wished he hadn't, and when he said that stuff about me not committing, I wanted to run away."

"Which you did—into the bathroom." Jenna sat beside Bella and rested her head on Bella's shoulder. "Why do you have to classify things? Why can't you just do what you feel and forget commitment or not committing altogether?"

"Why do I classify...? Jenna, you just organized my sandals alphabetically by color. Alabaster, blue, green..." Bella jumped up and planted her hands on her hips. "Because that's what I have to do right now to make sure I stick to my guns until my life is in order. But it's not easy, because being with Caden feels totally different from all the other guys I've dated combined. More *real*. When we're together, things feel right, like we're not just talking about bullshit or putting on our best faces to make a good impression. It's like we skipped all that."

"Because he is real, Bell." Jenna smoothed a wrinkle in the edge of Bella's dress. "You invited him to our barbeque tonight, so yeah, he's a living, breathing guy."

They were having a community barbeque, and despite her desire for no commitments and her confusion over the other day, Bella was excited that Caden and Evan were joining them. She went to the mirror and smoothed her yellow spaghetti-strap sundress, glancing over her shoulder at her butt.

"Don't worry. You look hot," Jenna assured her.

"Lotta good that does me." Bella dragged Jenna into the kitchen, took a bucket of frozen margaritas out of the freezer, and filled two glasses. "Anyway, you're right. It's a good thing we didn't end up doing it. It makes it easier to stick to my plan. No boyfriend will make it easier for me to think more clearly when I'm making my decisions about work." *Liar, liar.*

"You know I see right through that bullshit, right?" Jenna crossed her arms, jutted her hip out, and gave her the don't-even-try-to-avoid-the-truth stare she'd perfected in middle school.

"It sounded good though, didn't it?" Bella arched a brow. "I almost bought it."

Jenna took a drink of her margarita, and ice spilled down her chin and slid between her breasts. "Damn." She watched it disappear into her cleavage. "That feels better."

"You're a freak." Bella threw her a dish towel. "Won't that stain your Good-Times Barbie outfit?"

Jenna had on a short, black sleeveless top and a tan miniskirt. "That's clever, Good-Times Barbie." She wiped her chest with the towel. "What did you want me to do? Fish it out?" She laughed. "Anyway, technically speaking, you could have banged him without a commitment. You'd have stuck to your plan better if you had done the deed and then said goodbye."

Bella took out a head of lettuce and began chopping it on a thick wooden cutting board. "You're doing a great job of making me feel like shit."

"Don't you get it? You invited him and Evan to our barbeque. You *are* seeing him again. If you had slept with him, then, according to your plan, you'd have left it at that. See?" Jenna stole a piece of lettuce and popped it into her mouth.

"Okay, so you have a point. You're not as much of a bitch as I thought you were." Bella tossed the lettuce into a bowl and cut up tomatoes and cucumbers. "I'm not abandoning my plan." *At least I don't think I am.* "We had such a nice day at the flea market and the beach—"

"And his living room. Don't forget his living room."

"Shut up." She tossed a piece of cucumber at Jenna and it stuck to her cleavage.

Jenna snagged it and tossed it in the sink.

"I like him, Jenna. He's sweet with Evan, and he puts Evan's needs ahead of his own, which I think is very admirable."

"Careful," Jenna said in a singsong voice. "That sounds a lot like, *I like him, Jenna, and I hope this leads to a commitment.*"

Bella carried the salad outside. "God, I hate you when you're right."

"Hey, Bell," Jamie, the friend Kurt had stayed home with instead of going to the bonfire, yelled from the quad. "We moved your table and Leanna's. Tony's bringing extra chairs." Jamie's grandmother, Vera, spent summers at Seaside, and Jamie drove in from Boston most weekends to spend time with her.

"You stole my table before you hugged me hello? Get over here, you pest." Bella set the salad bowl on the table and opened her arms.

"Good to see you, gorgeous." Jamie kissed her cheek. The quietest of their group, Jamie, like Tony, was like a brother to Bella. He was soft-spoken and kind, and in all the years they'd known each other, he had never led her astray. She trusted him completely, as did half the world. Jamie had developed a search engine that was second only to Google. "Did I hear that you had a date that lasted all day?"

She shot a look at Jenna.

Jenna held her hands up in surrender. "You know I can't lie."

"It wasn't a date." *Was it?* No. She'd been clear about that at the bonfire, but that was before his living room—and before she invited him to the barbeque, which seemed very dateish to her. *Don't admit it. If you don't say it out loud, it's not a date.* "He's coming tonight. You'll like him. He's a cop, so you can tell him about all the naughty things I do."

"And send him running for the hills? No way. I almost forgot. Leanna and Kurt aren't going to be here tonight. Leanna had a big rush order come in, and she said she needed to work late and get up early."

"Is that why she wasn't at the flea market?"

"Yeah. She got the order early this morning."

"I wish I had known. We could have helped her."

"She knows. I offered, too, but two of her employees are coming in for the evening, and Kurt's on a deadline. She said they'd make it next time." Jamie headed for his cottage. "I'm gonna get the steaks and see how Gram's doing."

An hour later, the smell of sizzling steaks filled the

evening air. Vera and Jamie sat with Amy and Jenna, chatting about their afternoons. There was a fire in the fire pit and citronella candles at the center of each table. Jenna had made a fresh bean salad, and Leanna had left them two loaves of homemade bread with two jars of strawberry-apricot and apricot-lime jelly and a jar of her newest flavor, watermelon jam. Amy had made chocolate chip brownies for dessert, and Bella had already snuck one while no one was looking.

Bella joined Tony by the grill. He had hair the color of sand after a rain, interspersed with streaks of sun-kissed blond, and he wore it long and shaggy on top, shorter in the back. Not only was Tony a world-class surfer, but he was also a popular motivational speaker. Despite his fame, he wasn't full of pomp and circumstance. He was easy to talk to and a good friend to all of them.

Bella inhaled deeply. "That smells amazing."

"What can I say? My meat is sweet." Tony lifted his thick brows and flashed a mischievous smile.

Bella poked him in the ribs. "Pig."

"You left yourself wide open for that one. Where's your date?" He looked at his watch. "Dinner's going to be ready in a few minutes."

"He's not my date, and I'm sure he'll be here soon." Bella wasn't about to admit that she was wondering the same thing.

"Okay, well, I hear not-your-date has a son. That's new for you." He grabbed a plate and loaded it up with steak.

"New? He's not my date, so there's nothing new to consider." *Except maybe that my nerves have been tingling with anticipation for the past two hours.* She caught Amy stealing a glance at Tony and thought what she was feeling must be similar to what Amy felt when she waited for Tony to arrive—even though the man acted completely oblivious to her crush.

"Hey, Ames," Tony yelled. "Can you grab the mayo from my place? I forgot it."

"Sure." Amy looked adorable in her white halter dress and sandals.

Tony's eyes followed her across the lawn.

"Not-your-Amy looks pretty cute tonight, doesn't she?" Bella teased. She was sure that one day Tony would see Amy for the adorably, sweet, smart, fun woman that she was and would be unable to resist her. A little nudge in that direction every now and then wasn't a bad thing.

"She always looks cute." Tony handed her the plate of steak and piled chicken onto another one. He leaned in close and whispered, "Your not-my-date is here."

She turned to greet Caden, and the sight of him in his dark linen pants, white, short-sleeve button-down shirt, and provocative smile weakened her knees.

*Not-my-date is smoking hot.*

CADEN CAUGHT HIMSELF sizing up the man standing beside Bella as he and Evan crossed the lawn. He lowered a hand to her hip and kissed her cheek, silently staking claim to her.

"You look gorgeous."

The heat in her eyes flared between them, and he realized that there was no need to stake claim to Bella. One look at her eyes, and he was sure the world could see how she felt about him as clearly as he could. He held a hand out to the muscular dude in the board shorts.

"Hi. I'm Caden Grant, and this is my son, Evan."

"Nice to meet you. I'm Tony Black, or if it's easier to remember, the guy in the blue cottage." He nodded to the blue cottage behind him. "Here. Let me take that." He reached for the dish of pasta salad that Caden carried in his other hand. "Come on, Evan. I'll introduce you around." Tony and Evan headed toward the others.

"I'm glad you made it," Bella said.

"Sorry we're a little late. Evan got home later than he expected." Evan hadn't called to tell him he was going to be late, and though Caden wrote it off as Evan wanting to seem cool in front of his new friends, he had given Evan a long talk about the importance of checking in. Evan took it well, and by the time they left for the barbeque, he seemed in good spirits again.

"That's okay. Come on. I'll introduce you to everyone."

Caden touched her arm. "Can we just talk for one minute first?"

"Sure. What's up?" She said it so flippantly that he realized she must have been just as nervous as he was.

"I've been thinking about what happened earlier today."

Bella waved her hand dismissively. "Forget it. It's no big deal."

"It might not be a big deal to you, but it was to me. I just want you to know that I totally dig you, and I'm sorry if I hurt you."

"First of all, no hurt on my end. Second, you totally dig me?" Her eyes widened with amusement. "Well, that's good to know. I think you're pretty far out, too."

"*Christ.*" He shook his head. How did she joke so easily when what happened between them had eaten him up all afternoon?

She grabbed his hand and dragged him toward the others. "Come on, hippie boy. I'll introduce you around and we can eat."

Dinner was delicious and conversation came easily. Caden was happy to see Evan enjoying himself.

He had a million questions for Jamie, who was patient and, Caden noticed, didn't speak to Evan as if he were just a kid. Evan was quite computer savvy, and the two were in a heated debate over the future of something technical that Caden couldn't follow. Although he wasn't as technically inclined as his son, he was pretty sure he wasn't following their conversation because he was sidetracked by Bella. She laughed unabashedly, and she kept touching his leg, like they'd been together forever. He wondered if she did that with all of the guys she dated or, if like him, she felt something more between them.

"So, Bell, does Caden know about your rebellious side?" Tony's devilish grin piqued his curiosity.

"Shh." Amy swatted him on the arm. "We don't want to make the man hightail it out of here."

Bella looked up at Caden and nibbled on her lower lip. "I am a little bit of a rule breaker, but not with bad things. Just..."

Jenna got up to refill her wineglass and lined up the condiments while she was at it. "Just things like wanting to climb over the fence and get to the top of the South Wellfleet fire tower, you know, the one that's about a mile from here and off-limits to residents. That kind of not-bad stuff."

"Why the fire tower?" Caden asked.

"Because climbing a water tower is too scary." Bella swirled her glass, then finished her wine.

She was flippant and coy, and Caden had never met anyone quite like her. He listened as they recanted stories of walking down to the tower throughout the years, trying to figure out a way over the barbed wire. He could envision Bella and her friends standing before the fence that surrounded the sixty-eight-foot tower, contemplating the options: *Over? Under? Through?*

She leaned in to him. "Forget the fire tower. Let me tell you about Vera."

"Are you trying to change the subject?"

She narrowed her eyes. "Of course, but really...Vera is a violinist, and she's performed all over the world. I swear, once you hear her play, violin music will never sound the same again."

"Oh, Bella, dear, don't lie to the poor man." Vera patted her short pixie cut. It framed her face in varying shades of silver with flecks of battleship gray at the roots. Her skin held the look of softness that came with age despite the fine lines and deep grooves.

"She's gifted *and* modest," Bella said.

"That's kind of you, dear. But how about you go back to telling Caden about your playful ways while I share my little secret with Evan." Vera turned her attention to Evan. "Evan, dear, did I hear correctly that you have an affinity for computers?"

Evan nodded. "Well, at my old school, I was in the technology club, and we were learning to program. So, yeah, I like them."

Vera patted the chair beside her. "Why don't you come sit here and I'll tell you about Dr. Samuel Masterson, the man who created the first personal computer. I was seventeen, and he was fifty-six. He worked with my father."

Evan moved quicker than Caden had seen him move in the last year, and he hung on to every word she said.

"Looks like you've been outdone by your grandmother, Jamie." Bella patted him on the shoulder.

"I'll happily step aside for her. She enjoys kids so much, and rarely has a chance to interact with them," Jamie said. "Evan's a bright boy, and he really has an interest in technology."

"Thank you. I wish I knew more about computers so I could help him in some way."

"I can teach him a few things when I'm here on the weekends," Jamie offered. "In fact, I'm not leaving until Monday this week, so if you want to bring him by tomorrow evening, I'd be happy to work with him for a few hours."

"That would be great. I'll ask Evan after he's done talking with Vera. Thanks so much."

An hour later, plans for the next evening were solidified and Evan was excited to spend a few hours with Jamie. Caden helped Tony and Jamie bring the tables and chairs back to their rightful owner's decks; then he followed Bella into her cottage with a stack of dishes. He'd expected her cottage to reflect her personality, a little loud with flashes of a softer side. As he stood on the pale and thinly planked hardwood floors in the cozy living room, he was struck by how wrong he was. A cream-colored sofa, layered with pastel, lace-edged pillows, was pushed against the wall to his right. Fresh flowers filled a vase on an end table, and frilly curtains hung around the kitchen window.

The bedroom door was open, and a quick peek revealed a beautifully made bed with a fluffy pink comforter and another vase of fresh flowers on the white dresser. He felt as though he was seeing her most intimate side, and he wondered why she worked so hard to repress her love of femininity.

Bella took the dishes from him and set them on the counter. "I'm really glad you and Evan came tonight, and I know Evan will learn a lot from Jamie. He's a really nice guy."

"Yeah, he seems it. All of your friends seem really nice."

He'd been fighting the urge to reach out and touch her all night. He'd wanted to drape an arm over her shoulder, to feel her pressed against his side, but those were things people did when they were dating—and he didn't know if they were dating or not. She'd been sending conflicting signals all day, but then tonight she'd touched his leg a hundred times even after he'd turned her away earlier in the day.

"Why are you looking at me like that?" she asked.

Unable to stay away, and with a quick glance out the window to confirm that Evan was still engrossed in a conversation with Jamie, he placed his hands on her hips.

Big mistake. It only made him want her more.

"Bella," he said just above a whisper. "I want to go out with you."

She sighed loudly and knitted her brows together, in stark contrast to the desire in her eyes and her quickening breaths. Her reaction worried him, but he wasn't willing to ignore the emotions she sparked in him.

"I can't date," she finally said.

"Maybe what you really mean is that you can't afford to get hurt again."

Her eyes widened so slightly that he would have missed it had he not been looking for an indication that he was striking a chord. She shifted her gaze away, and he drew her chin back so she had no choice but to look at him.

"I know all about being hurt, and although I can't promise that I won't hurt you unintentionally, I can promise you that I will try not to."

Bella pulled from his grasp and walked into the living room, where she flopped onto the couch.

Caden sat on the coffee table across from her and placed his hands on her knees. He felt her stiffen beneath his touch, but again the air around them sizzled, and her eyes betrayed her attempt to avoid the passion brewing between them. He leaned in closer, his hands sliding up her thighs. Her body quivered as his knees moved between her legs.

"Getting hurt sucks." She spoke softly, but her eyes were narrow and angry.

"Agreed."

"I made a plan. No commitments." She crossed her arms and looked away.

"I'm not asking you to break your plan. I didn't realize that I had a plan, but apparently I do. My plan is to not get hurt either, and it's obvious, even after just a few hours with you, that you have the power to hurt me." He had no idea where the words were coming from, but being with Bella pulled the truth from him.

That brought her eyes back to his.

"So what are you saying? I'm totally confused. You made it clear today that you don't want to sleep with me because I can't commit."

"That's funny. I thought I made it clear that I *wanted* to sleep with you, but I wouldn't because you won't commit." He slid his hands to her outer thighs, and she closed her eyes for a beat. When she opened them, desire was still there.

"Well, I still can't commit," she answered.

"*Won't*, but that's okay. I'm not asking you to commit. You don't know me from Adam, and you're right. I don't know you very well, either. Both are reasons why we shouldn't sleep together."

Confusion filled her eyes again. He squeezed her outer thighs, and she placed her hands on top of his and slid them to her inner thighs, so close to her center that he could feel the heat radiating from her.

"Then what do you want?" she asked in a breathy voice.

"To spend time with you tomorrow night while

Evan is with Jamie. Call it whatever you want."

"Not a date," she said adamantly; then she moved his hands higher. His fingertips grazed her panties.

"Not a date." Jesus, he wanted to carry her into the bedroom and make love to her, commitment or not. But he wasn't about to allow his heart to get torn to shreds, and Bella had the power to do it. She opened her legs and leaned forward, and his willpower fell away. He covered her mouth with his, taking her in a deep, sensuous kiss.

"Touch me," she whispered against his lips.

He slid his fingers into her wetness, and holy hell, he knew better. This wasn't going to make it any easier for him if she walked away. He shot a look out the window. Evan was still deep in conversation with Jamie. *Thank God*. Bella arched against his hand. He swept her into his arms and carried her into the bedroom, locking the door behind them. He backed her up against the door as she fumbled with the button on his pants.

"Caden," she said in one hot breath.

He clutched her wrist and held it against the door. "No." He laved her neck with his tongue, loving the way she breathed harder with every stroke. Her eyes fluttered closed as he ground his hips into hers and filled his free hand with her breast.

"You're so beautiful, Bella."

He took her in a rough kiss, trying desperately to thwart the urge to drop to his knees and taste her most private area. She reached for his pants again and he drew back again and stared into her dark, wanting eyes. She licked her lips, and he kissed her again, slowly, sensually, memorizing the feel of her mouth against his. Holding her to the door with his hips, he lifted her dress and had to close his eyes for a beat to try to restrain the need that gripped him. He just had to taste her belly, the soft skin that lined the sexiest pink panties he'd ever seen. He kissed his way across her belly, feeling her body tremble with need. The scent of her arousal drew him lower. One stroke of his tongue against the damp fabric of her panties drew a groan from his lungs and a wanton moan from hers. She clutched his shoulders, urging him to continue. Like kissing Bella, one taste of her was not enough, but he knew nothing short of being inside her would be enough, and with his son so close, he forced himself to stifle the urge to throw her on the bed and make love to her.

He broke from her grip and rose to his feet, taking her in another rough kiss, capturing her pleas in his mouth. He had no business kissing her like she was his world, or intimately exploring her body, when she might never be willing to give him what he needed, but he was powerless to walk away from Bella. He'd already committed, even if she hadn't.

He forced himself to tear his lips away from hers.

Eyes still closed, she said, "It's not a date."

His lips curved into a smile, and he whispered, "Not yet, it's not."

## Chapter Six

BELLA STRUGGLED TO remain focused Monday morning and to not let her mind wander to Caden. She wasn't the type of person who usually moved that fast with men, but with him, she couldn't stop herself. No matter how hard she tried to convince herself that it was shameful and that she was sending the wrong message to him—*no commitment, but ravish me, please*—she couldn't. What they did didn't feel shameful. It felt incredible, passionate. Right.

She forced her attention back to Dr. Wilma Ritter, the superintendent of Nauset Regional High School. Wilma was tall and willowy, with salt-and-pepper hair that she wore in a messy bun. She had a limp handshake, and based on the fact that they'd been walking around the school since Bella had arrived, the inability to sit still.

"We've been pushing for this type of program for years, but there was never enough budget, or the right person to head it up, or..." Wilma waved her skinny hand in the air. "I'm just glad you're giving it a shot."

They walked down a long corridor lined with

lockers. Wilma rattled on about how much red tape was involved in doing anything with the school system.

"It's the same everywhere," Bella agreed. "In Connecticut we had the same trouble. It's amazing to me that professional sports teams have more money than they could ever spend, and our educational system barely scrapes by."

Wilma pushed open the heavy door and waved Bella through. They were behind the school, facing a grassy field that led to a thickly wooded area. Bella followed Wilma down a sidewalk, along the side of the brick building.

"I have a list of businesses that I've been putting together since they hired you. Companies that might have an interest in supporting the program, both nonprofit and for profit." She stopped walking and nodded toward the edge of the woods. "This is what I wanted you to see. Every year we have a few kids who tend to get into trouble. For whatever reason, that spot has become a gathering place for them."

"What do you mean a gathering place? Do you mean that any kids who hang out there are high-risk kids?" Bella didn't see any kids hanging around the area.

Wilma nodded, then took Bella by the arm and guided her back toward the double doors. "Well, it would be irresponsible of me to lump them together definitively, but for the most part, yes. Why they come here during the summer, instead of *anywhere* else, is beyond me, but they come by every few days. It would be great to get those kids involved in something to occupy their time. During the school year, the good kids avoid that area like the plague."

They went back inside the school and walked back toward Wilma's office.

"What kind of trouble, exactly? And if you're sure they're getting into trouble, can't you speak with their parents?" She wasn't quite sure why Wilma thought it was imperative to show her that area instead of just mentioning it.

"Oh yes. We've taken all of the appropriate steps. People like to think that parents can control their teens, but we know better." She nodded knowingly at Bella. "There's only so much parents or teachers can do, which is why I hope your program might help get those kids and others like them involved in something more productive."

"That's the driving force behind it, and the hope."

"You asked about the type of trouble they get into, and that's a little hard to define. They're the kids who bring tension into the classrooms. You know the type. They interrupt class with jokes; they're generally disinterested and sneer at the kids who are trying to actually learn. They jaywalk, too."

"Jaywalk?" Bella stifled a laugh.

"Don't scoff. That's where it all begins. It doesn't take much to move from breaking small rules to landing in jail."

Bella followed Wilma into her office and refrained from telling her that it was that type of thinking that also led kids to trouble. If they were assumed to make bad choices, they often felt a need to live up to the assumption or to walk farther down Bad Decision Alley.

Wilma leafed through a file cabinet and withdrew a manila folder. She handed it to Bella.

"This is the list I mentioned. There are also companies noted that you might want to stay away from." She whispered, "Unsavory business owners."

As Bella headed to her car, she didn't know what was worse, knowing the high school was run by a busybody like Wilma, who appeared to be looking for trouble and willing to spread gossip based solely on her opinion, or the fact that she couldn't wait to go home and share her own gossip with her friends. She hadn't known what Wilma was like before she accepted the summer position, but it wouldn't have curbed her enthusiasm any more than it did now. She was in this for the kids and the intellectual challenge.

Back at her cottage, she changed into her bathing suit, gathered her laptop, phone, a notebook, and the manila folder, and headed down to the pool. She'd rather go to the beach, but without Internet, she'd have no hope of getting any research done.

She found Tony and Jenna lying in the sun. Tony's hands were clasped behind his head; his sculpted body was already evenly tanned. Jenna wore a string bikini that was in danger of splitting at the very thin seams.

"You two shouldn't be allowed out in public with bodies like that," Bella teased.

Tony squinted against the harsh sun. "You're not so bad yourself. How was your first day of school?"

"More importantly," Jenna interrupted. "I didn't get to talk to you last night after the barbeque. Wanna spill on the mysterious twenty minutes when you and Officer Sexy disappeared into your cottage?"

Bella glanced at Tony and said, "The school was a fact-finding mission, and it was interesting." She sighed at Jenna. "Twenty minutes in heaven." Bella set up her laptop on a glass table and shifted the umbrella so she could see her computer screen.

Jenna held her hand out to Tony. "Five bucks."

Tony reached for his wallet. "Jesus, you guys get more action than I do."

"We didn't do *that*, so don't pay her." Bella stretched out on a chair beside Jenna in the sun.

"I thought you had to work," Jenna said.

"I do, but I want five minutes of sun before I hunker down and do real-world work." She closed her eyes and sighed.

"You still have to pay me," Jenna said to Tony. "The bet was if they hooked up, not if they had sex, and twenty minutes in heaven says way too much to be innocent."

Bella remembered the look in Caden's eyes when she guided his hands to the promised land, and the feel of being in his arms. Oh, how she'd wanted to stay in his arms. Forget the ecstasy of kissing him. Just being that close to his warmth and feeling his heart beating against her as he carried her to the bedroom was heaven. He felt safe and sure, and his words held promise for so much more than lust.

"And that smile says even more." Jenna touched her arm. "Care to share?"

Bella sighed. "He's confusing."

"Like women aren't?" Tony quipped.

"I never said that. I know I confuse the hell out of him." She'd been thinking about what he'd said all night. *I thought I made it clear that I wanted to sleep with you, but I wouldn't because you won't commit.* She'd also been thinking about what Jenna said about not classifying their relationship. The truth was, Bella was a classifier. She had never been the type of woman to date more than one guy at a time, and she didn't have any interest in that now, either. She also knew it probably seemed silly to tell Caden or her friends that she didn't want to date or commit when she was clearly interested in Caden, but it didn't feel silly. It felt like she was trying to stand firm to her convictions—even if she and Caden were already doing intimate things that she didn't normally do outside of a committed relationship.

Maybe life choices weren't as easy as she'd hoped.

And if she were honest with herself, it wasn't Caden who was confusing at all. It was her.

"What kind of guy won't...you know...with a woman who's offering no strings attached?" Bella asked.

"The gay kind," Jenna answered.

"I'm going to put on my therapist hat for a minute." Tony sat up and leaned his elbows on his knees.

"You're not a therapist. You're a motivational speaker and a surfer, neither of which qualifies you to wear a therapist hat." The truth was, Bella had gotten lucky in the male friend department. Tony's advice was usually spot-on.

"Fair enough," Tony said. "Then I'm putting on my man hat, and I know I am qualified to wear that. First of all, since when are you looking for a scrump and dump?"

Bella rolled her eyes. "I'm not looking for a scrump and dump. I just don't want to have a scrump-and-be-lied-to or a scrump-and-make-bad-life-decisions experience."

"Because you dated some asshole who told you he was divorced and he was really working things out with his wife? What power did that guy have over you to make you change who you are? You're Bella Abbascia, the epitome of strength and confidence. You're beautiful and smart, and you built an amazing career for yourself. What did that guy do to you for you to leave that all behind?" Tony rose to his feet and paced beside Bella's chair. "And if he did something so bad, then why the hell didn't you call me so I could beat the shit out of him?"

"Excellent point," Jenna said as she rolled onto her side and put on her sunglasses.

Bella rose from her lounge chair and sat at the table with a sigh.

Tony came to her side and placed his hand on her shoulder. "You're not alone in this, Bella. No matter what it is."

"I know." She leaned back and kicked out a chair. "Sit down."

Tony lowered himself to the chair, and Jenna joined them on Bella's other side.

Bella pressed her palms flat on the table and drew in a deep breath. She'd held the truth in for months, and it would be a relief to get it off her chest. It would also be a slap in the face, and she knew how much that slap would sting. And she knew that she could spill her guts to Jenna, Tony, or any of the other friends here at Seaside, and they'd soothe that sting with more love than she could ever hope for.

"Okay. The truth is, it wasn't him. It was me. It *is* me. This was my decision any way you cut it. Jay was nothing. He lied to me. Yeah, that stung, but I broke up with him the moment I found out. But changing my life—taking *control* of my life?" She shook her head. "That's all me, baby. I took a good look at my love life and my professional life. And trust me, it wasn't easy to take off the rose-colored glasses and open my eyes, but I did. You're right, Tony. I'm strong, and you know what? I'm not sure that's a great thing when it comes to relationships. I'm loud. I say things that can be harsh or misconstrued. I joke about things that other people might not, but I like who I am."

Jenna lifted her brows. "We love who you are."

"Thank you, Jen. I love you guys, too." She sighed. "I just realized that maybe the reason relationships don't work for me is that I'm not supposed to be in one. It seems like we women are always looking for Mr. Right, and I realized that I don't *need* Mr. Right. I just need to be happy with myself, and I am. So, I decided to take charge of my life and make a change. Sink or swim. And part of taking charge of my career and my life is setting aside the pathetic need to be in a relationship."

"Bella—" Tony began.

"No, let me finish. You guys know me. I'm a no-bullshit person. What you see is what you get with me, right?"

Jenna nodded.

"Pretty much, but you hide a lot, Bell, even if you don't want to admit it," Tony said.

"I hide?"

"Yeah. You tuck away parts of yourself. I can't explain it, but I've known you long enough to recognize it. It's not a bad thing. It's like when I'm surfing. The people I meet around my competitions want to know me because of what I stand for, not who I am. So around those people, I don't show my real self. You kind of do the same thing. Maybe it's not the loud part of you that makes relationships difficult, but it's keeping that other part of you walled off that, I don't know, creates a gap. Guys feel that, you know. When you women think we don't know you're hiding something, we totally see it."

She chewed on that thought for a minute. There was probably some truth to it, but she wanted to finish her thoughts, and she was too distracted to define those pieces of truth just then. She pushed the thought away to deal with later.

"Okay, maybe you're right in some ways. And you're also right, Tony, about me not fucking around for the sake of fucking around."

"Wait. Hold up." Jenna held her palm up toward Bella. "Timmy Brown? Taylor Marks? Do either of those ring a bell?"

"Okay, so maybe there were a few times. God, Jenna, what were we? Twenty-two? But it's not a habit, and you know that. I might talk big, but I want love like everyone else does. I want the stupid white picket fence and the, *Hi, honey; I'm home,* and all the other bullshit that goes along with it."

Tony shrugged. "Okay, but why can't you have that and a career?"

"Don't worry. I'm not some desperate woman who thinks she's not worth being loved." She rolled her eyes. "God, I'm so *not* that person."

"We know that." Tony reached out and touched her hand. "I was just worried that you gave up everything because of a guy."

"Nope. He was just a nudge to get off my ass and do what I really want to do. I'm a realist. I can handle this, and it's a good thing. I might actually get to live in my favorite place on earth and fill my creative soul with a challenge." She inhaled deeply, feeling her smile fill her with happiness. "So my very long-winded answer about why he had the power to hurt me is that he didn't. He lied about his wife and about his commitment to me, and yes, that stung, and maybe it even made me worry about guys knowing how to *not* lie. I am only human. But I didn't make my decision to change my life and my dating habits *because* of Jay. I did it because of me. I happened to realize what I wanted at the same time that I broke up with him." She shrugged again.

Tony sat back and crossed his arms. He slid a concerned look to Jenna.

Jenna shrugged. "The woman does know how to take control."

He shifted his eyes back to Bella. "I can't argue with that. You're right. It's actually a ballsy move."

"Thank you."

"What about not-your-date?" Tony asked. "What's your plan with him? He brought his kid over. Chances are he's not a scrump and dumper."

"Not-my-date and I have a not-a-date tonight. Speaking of which, now that I've spilled my pathetic guts, I need to get some work done so I can be ready by six."

CADEN STOPPED AT the hardware store on his way home from the station to pick up extra window and door locks for the house, and while he was there, he picked up locks for Bella's cottage, too. There had been another break-in last night, and he was not taking any chances. He put his bags on the kitchen table and unbuttoned his shirt.

"Ev?" he called down the hall.

Evan didn't answer.

"Evan?" He knocked on Evan's bedroom door, and a minute later, Evan opened it. His hair was uncombed, his shirt was wrinkled, as if he'd pulled it from the hamper.

"Hey, Dad. Sorry. I didn't hear you." He went to his computer and studied the screen. "We're going to Jamie's at six, right?"

"Yeah. I need to shower and change, and you should, too." He moved behind Evan and scanned the monitor. "What's Python?"

"A program."

"For?" He felt out of touch with Evan lately, and he didn't like it. His interest in computers was just one aspect of the distance that had crept between them. He'd decided last night that he was going to do whatever he could to spend time with Bella and explore his feelings for her, and now he made another commitment. He was going to study up on technology so he could at least understand the basics of the things

Evan was interested in.

"There was another break-in last night."

"I know." Evan's eyes remained trained on the computer screen.

"How do you know?"

Evan pointed to the computer. "That stuff's public information. Wellfleet has a daily crime report that they publish."

"And you read it?" Caden thought he knew his son pretty damn well, but he never would have guessed that he'd have an interest in a crime report. He wondered what else Evan was reading that he didn't know about. He had parental controls on the computer to keep him off of porn sites, but he of all people knew there were other dangers lurking out there.

"Dad, you're a cop. Haven't you drilled safety into my head since I was, like, two?" Evan shook his head. "You always say that it's the people who don't pay attention to their surroundings that get themselves into trouble."

"That can get hurt, actually," he corrected him.

"Whatever. You know what I mean. Besides, what's the big deal? Someone broke into a few cars and a cottage. They took a laptop and a couple bucks they had lying around." Evan shrugged.

"What's the big deal? Seriously, Ev?"

Evan sighed. "You know what I mean. It's not like they killed someone, or they robbed them of everything they owned."

Caden lowered himself to Evan's bed and rubbed his temples with his finger and thumb. "Ev, you know how wrong that attitude is, don't you?"

Evan shrugged.

"How is it that you can remember what I said about knowing your surroundings but not about respecting other people's property?" Caden watched

83

his son turn and face him. He might be running on hormones, but his face still held the soft qualities of a boy, and it was that softness that eased Caden's worry.

"I remember. It's not like I'm the one doing it, Dad. I'm going to study computers tonight. Remember?"

Caden smiled. "Yeah. I remember."

Evan turned back to his computer. "I like Bella."

"Yeah. She's nice."

"And hot."

Caden raised his brows. *Hot?* His son was looking at women as hot?

"Yeah, she is pretty hot," he admitted.

"Are you going out with her tonight?"

Evan asked it so casually that it took Caden by surprise.

"Why *don't* you date, Dad? Is it really because of work and me?"

"You? Buddy, I don't date because dating takes time, and in case you haven't noticed, I don't have much free time."

"So make it." Evan spun around in his chair again. "She's obviously into you. She looked at you all night, and she did the whole hand-on-your-leg thing."

"What do you know about the hand-on-the-leg thing?"

Evan laughed. "I'm almost fifteen, not in second grade. There are YouTube videos about picking up girls and taking hints."

"There are?" *And you're watching them?*

"Yeah. You should watch them. There's this one guy, MasterDater—"

"MasterDater?"

"I know. It's a stupid name, but he's really smart. He goes over everything." Evan waved his hand in the air. "How girls like eye contact, and they hate when you talk about yourself. And how if you aren't

84

interested in what they have to say, you shouldn't even consider dating them, because girls love to talk. He says you have to smell good, too, or girls won't like you."

"Really? There are videos on that stuff?" Caden made another mental note to look up this MasterDater dude.

"Heck yeah. There are videos on anything and everything on YouTube."

"Wait. Does he go over sex stuff, too?" Caden had had *the talk* with Evan when Evan was twelve. He'd come home from school one day talking about a boy who made out with a girl in the bathroom, and that spurred weeks of detailed conversations about sex and love and the importance of respecting women. Caden had expected to feel funny talking to Evan about those things, but Evan was a very practical kid, and he didn't blush or act embarrassed. He wanted to understand it all, and it made for easy, open lines of communication.

"Nothing that you haven't already told me about. He talks more about not pushing girls into stuff than the actual activity, if you know what I mean."

*Activity? That's a great word.* He was impressed with Evan's attitude and pleased to hear that he was researching the more respectful parts of dating than the sexual side. He also wasn't naive, and he knew that Evan could be cushioning the truth.

"Anyway, are you going out with her tonight?" Evan asked.

He'd hoped he'd avoided the question altogether. "Yeah, but it's not a date."

"Why not?"

Caden pushed to his feet and headed for the door. "I need to shower, and you need to get cleaned up, too. Remember to put on a clean shirt."

"Yeah, yeah. I know. But you can't avoid the question. Why isn't it a date?"

He couldn't explain something he didn't understand himself.

"It's complicated," he said before heading to his room.

# Chapter Seven

BELLA HEARD CADEN'S truck roll onto the crushed-shell driveway in front of her cottage. Her stomach did a little flip.

"Oh my God. He's early." Bella turned away from Jenna and Amy and took a quick look in the mirror. She didn't usually wear pink in public, and when she bought the pale-pink, strapless, crushed-cotton minidress on a whim one summer, she'd thought she'd wear it around the quad when she and the girls were hanging out. She had yet to wear it, even around the quad, but when they were searching for just the right outfit, this one spoke to her.

"Better that he comes early now than later," Amy said with a devilish grin.

Jenna laughed. "Did our Ames really just say that?"

"There won't be any coming later," Bella said with a serious voice, though she wasn't as confident as she sounded. He'd made her feel damn good—*twice*—and the idea of bringing him pleasure in return made her icy nerves turn white-hot.

"Yeah, right." Jenna patted Bella's butt.

Amy peered out of the bedroom window. "He's gonna knock on the door," she whispered. "Hi, Caden!" Amy waved out the window.

"Oh, hey, Amy." Caden's deep, sexy voice settled in Bella's ears like a tease.

"Come on in." Amy turned around with a wide smile. "Not-date time." She pretended to clap her hands.

"You guys are sure I look okay?"

"Hold on." Jenna disappeared into the bathroom and came out with Shalimar perfume. She spritzed it on Bella's neck, then bent and shot it up her skirt.

"Really, Jen?"

"Hey, just in case." Jenna dragged her out of the bedroom.

Caden met them in the living room, looking devastatingly handsome in a pair of jeans, a gray button-down shirt, and a pair of leather sandals. He held a brown bag in one hand and a bouquet of pink roses in the other.

He dragged his eyes down Bella's body. "Wow. You get more beautiful every time I see you."

"Thanks. I just threw this old thing on," Jenna said, twisting from side to side.

Bella held his stare, ignoring Jenna's joke. It was hard not to ignore everything else when his eyes said, *I want to kiss you* and her mind replied, *Oh God, yes*.

"You're not looking so bad yourself." Bella felt as though they were moving in slow motion as they each stepped forward.

"Hi," he said softly. "These are for you."

"They're my favorite. Thank you." He smelled like strength and a warm embrace. Bella lifted up on her toes, and he met her halfway for a sweet kiss. She felt the bouquet slip from her fingers and heard Amy padding into the kitchen. The running faucet told her

Amy had snagged the bouquet and was putting it in a vase. When their lips parted, Bella remained on her toes. She felt his fingers touch hers, and only then did she come back down to earth.

"I also brought you something else." He lifted the bag between them. "There was another break-in, and I noticed that you had pretty simple locks on your doors and windows."

"You bought me locks?" Bella peered into the bag. She glanced at Jenna and Amy and knew they could hear her silent remark. *He bought me locks!* Locks were a whole different level than flowers. Locks showed that he cared about what happened to her. That thought conjured up all sorts of futures.

"I know it's not a very romantic gesture, but this isn't a date, so…"

"But you brought me flowers. That's pretty dateish." *And I love it.*

"Okay, maybe you got me there. But when I saw them, they screamed your name. I really had no choice but to bring them to you."

Bella didn't think before she reached up and stroked his clean-shaven cheek. His skin was baby soft. She ran her finger along the sharp line of his jaw, then went up on tiptoes again and kissed the dimple in his chin.

"That wasn't a date kiss, either. Your dimple was screaming *my* name."

He tightened his grip on her hand, and the room became ten degrees hotter.

"Okay, kids. On that juicy note, we're outta here." Jenna grabbed Amy's hand. "Let's go, sugar pop. I've got a bottle of Middle Sister with our name on it."

Amy pointed to Caden. "Have her back before midnight or she'll turn into a pumpkin."

"I'll have her back by ten. I have to pick up Evan

from Jamie's." He set the bag of locks down on the coffee table.

"Oh, don't worry about that. We'll tell Jamie that if you're late to bring Evan to us. Don't worry. We won't corrupt him or anything. We'll just make him watch chick flicks, maybe pull a few tears from the boy." Amy waved as she headed out the door.

"You really do have the most incredible friends." Caden placed his hands on Bella's hips and drew her close again.

"I'm pretty lucky that way. Apparently, I also have the most incredible not-a-date."

Their lips met again, this time in a deep, delicious, tongue-plunging, hip-rocking, moan-inducing kiss that stole Bella's breath and turned her legs to mush.

When they drew apart, he pressed his cheek to hers. "What is it about you? I feel like I've been waiting for you my whole life."

*OhGodohGodohGod. I feel it, too.* Bella's heart was open despite how much she was trying to keep it under lock and key. She had no hope of escaping the emotions that swelled between them. A string of worry threaded its way into her mind. She slipped into self-protection mode and thwarted the truth.

"Maybe we're both gluttons for punishment."

He took her hand as they went outside to his truck. Bella left the door to her cottage unlocked and Caden turned back.

"Don't you want to lock it?"

"We always leave them open. Everyone's here, so it's not like someone's going to break in while we're gone."

Caden rubbed the back of his neck. "Do you realize how dangerous that is? What if everyone leaves, or if someone cases the area and realizes that the doors are left unlocked?"

Bella stepped closer and grabbed his collar, then pulled him down so they were eye to eye. "Your cop is showing."

He kissed her nose. "So is your cuteness. Lock it. Please? For me?"

"*Ugh.* Fine." She stalked back and locked the door, secretly enjoying that he cared enough to push the issue. "Satisfied?"

He arched a brow. "Very. I know your belongings are safe *and* I got a great look at your ass."

"You're impossible," she said with a laugh.

He opened the truck door and helped her in. "You know you love it." His truck smelled masculine and safe, like him.

"So what do you have planned for our not-a-date?" she asked as he started the vehicle.

He drove out of the development with that panty-dropping smile Bella loved so much and reached across the seat. "Hold my hand and maybe I'll tell you."

This was dangerously enjoyable. *He* was dangerously enjoyable. Bella put her hand in his, relishing the feel of it.

"Never mind," she said with a comfortable sigh. "Don't tell me. I want to be surprised."

It was a nice warm evening with a gentle breeze. They drove through Eastham and headed into Orleans with the windows open, holding hands and listening to music. With most men, Bella felt pressure to fill gaps in conversation, but with Caden the silence was comfortable, maybe even comforting. He already felt familiar, and holding hands drove that feeling deeper.

A few minutes later, he parked in front of the Orleans Book Stop. The Book Stop was located in a small white saltbox-style house that had been renovated into a bookstore. Caden held the door open for Bella and bowed dramatically, sweeping his arm before her.

"After you, madam. I hope you don't mind bookstores."

"Interesting choice for a first not-a-date, but a good one. I love bookstores, probably a little too much. You haven't seen the stacks of books on the far side of my bed."

He reached for her hand, and she followed him around a wide display of books.

"We only made it to the bedroom door, remember?" He squeezed her hand, and she flushed with the memory.

She moved in close and whispered, "Yes, I remember. You're a naughty boy." The heat in his eyes made her want to kiss him again.

"It's you," he said easily.

"*Tsk*. I'm the naughty one?" She glanced at the teenage girl behind the counter, who appeared to be too busy texting to eavesdrop on their conversation.

"No. You make me want to be naughty," he teased.

"Oh." She hooked her finger in his jeans, trying to remember how to breathe.

"You're torturous," he said. He took her finger from his waistband and turned back to the books. "Books. Focus." He slid his eyes toward her, and she licked her lips. "Christ, Bella."

That was too fun of a reaction not to do it again.

He snagged her hand and hurried down to the lower level. Her pulse quickened as they wound their way through two aisles of books and he cornered her against the bathroom door. She loved this game of cat and mouse, and when he pressed his hips to hers and she felt his desire, she couldn't help but hook her finger in his waistband again. He glanced up at the security camera in the corner of the room, and when their eyes connected again, a streak of lust spiraled through to her core. He tangled his hands in her hair and kissed her like he was a soldier who'd just come home from the war.

"I...This..." He scrubbed his face with his hand and turned away. It was all she could do to watch him close his eyes for a breath, then turn back, looking as hot and flustered as she felt. Through gritted teeth and a harsh whisper, he said, "I don't want just hot sex with you, Bella."

She felt playful, and seeing him so flustered sent a thrill through her. "So you *are* a fetish guy."

His eyes darkened and narrowed, pinning her to the door. "No. I want hand holding and talking and whatever the heck else people do to get to know each other. I want to cook you dinner and watch stupid movies that make you cry."

Her heart melted a little. She wanted all those things, too, but she knew if she opened her mouth, she'd deflect his words with something stupid like, *I don't cry*. She didn't want to deflect Caden.

He ran his fingers along her cheek, then through her hair as he brushed it away from her face. His hand came to rest on the back of her neck.

"I want the other stuff—the hot sex—too," he admitted with a tender gaze.

That made them both laugh.

She forced herself to push past the deflection that came so easily. "Me too."

He pressed a kiss to her forehead, sealing their sentiments.

They left the bookstore forty minutes later with two books about computers, so he could get a feel for Evan's hobby, and a novel she'd wanted to read. When they got in the truck, he handed her a pink bookmark with a lacy ribbon on the end.

"I thought you might need this for your book."

"Thank you." She ran the ribbon over her fingers. He'd given her two pink things in less than two hours. No one, not even her friends from Seaside, bought her pink things, and they knew she loved pink, but they also knew that the Bella she presented to everyone else in the world wasn't a girlie girl. She'd left *that* Bella behind ages ago—at least publicly. She looked down at her dress. *Until now.* She wondered what it was about Caden that made her feel safe enough to bring out a part of herself that she'd hidden for so long.

She studied him as he drove around the corner to the harbor and parked by the pier. He seemed very aware. Aware of her, aware of everything around them, the other cars on the road, people walking down the sidewalk. She assumed that came with being a police officer—and a father—and it made her feel a different type of safe than the safety she felt with regard to being herself.

Caden turned off the truck and leaned across the seat. "Has anyone ever told you that you're beautiful when you're contemplating?"

"Has anyone ever told you that you're handsome when you're...being?"

He shook his head. "For a woman who doesn't date and doesn't want a commitment, you sure say things that seem girlfriendy."

*Oh boy.*

"Huh." *Girlfriendy.* She made a mental note to calm her comments as she watched him come around and open her door. *Girlfriendy.* He reached for her hand, and she shifted in the seat and pulled him in close so they were nose to nose.

"*Girlfriendy* should not be in our vocabulary. It's like *dating.* Got it?"

"Is that the toughest voice you've got?" He pressed

his lips to hers. "Because I'm not buying it."

She wasn't buying it either. She liked being with him too much, and she was about as good at hiding it as a leopard was at hiding its spots. Behind Caden, the sun was setting, casting reflections of the boats on the still-as-glass water in the harbor. Peaceful would describe the scene for most people, but the way Bella was swooning, romance-inducing seemed more fitting.

She stepped from the truck, and Caden draped his arm over her shoulder. She snuggled right in before she realized that it was *too easy* for them both.

"Excuse me." Bella looked up at him with a tease in her eyes. "That is very *boyfriendy*."

"I'm calling your bluff. So smile and put your damn arm around me."

"That whole take-charge thing is pretty sexy." She slid her arm around his back and hooked her thumb into the waistband of his jeans.

"Babe, I'm pulling out all the stops. Full-on picnic tables for dinner and plastic wineglasses. You'll fall so hard for me you'll be wishing you met me ten years ago."

*I already do.*

## Chapter Eight

BELLA COULDN'T REMEMBER ever being out with a man when everything they did, everything they talked about, every glance, every touch, felt so right. True to his word, they'd eaten dinner on a cloth-covered picnic table using plastic utensils and plastic wineglasses—and Bella felt as though she were the richest, and the luckiest, woman in the world. What Caden hadn't told Bella ahead of time was where he was taking her after dinner. They climbed the metal stairs to the top of the South Wellfleet fire tower. The higher they climbed, the chillier it became. Bella's heart was beating so fast, she clutched the railings to keep herself grounded. She couldn't believe he'd gotten permission for them to climb the tower she'd been practically drooling over for so many years. This was her ultimate rule-breaking moment, and she loved that they were doing it together, even though he had permission to take her up to the top, so she wasn't technically breaking a rule. It was still thrilling after so many years of anticipation.

She stood in the room at the top with her back

against Caden's warm body, his arms circling her waist, and gazed out over Wellfleet, wishing they could stay there all night.

"Do you know how many years I've dreamed of coming up here?" Bella leaned back against his chest. The view was more spectacular than she'd ever dreamed. The tips of tall pines gave way to the moonlit bay. Just down the road, the grassy mounds snaked through the ink-black water of the marsh, looking ominous and hazy. Though she couldn't see the ocean, she knew it was in the opposite direction, just beyond the darkness.

"How many years?" Caden kissed her cheek.

"It feels like my whole life. How did you make this happen?"

He pressed his cheek to hers. "Pulled a favor from a friend."

He kissed the spot below her ear and guided her down to the floor. She sat between his legs with her back against his chest, gazing up at the stars. The breeze sent goose bumps up Bella's limbs, but Caden's warmth enveloped her.

"Do you mind if I take a picture of us?" He pulled out his cell phone and held it at arm's length.

"Not as long as you text me a copy." She smiled and he clicked the picture.

"I've had a really good time tonight." Bella traced a muscle on his forearm with her index finger.

"Me too. I think it's the best not-a-date I've ever had." He tightened his arms around her.

*Not-a-date*. This was definitely *not* not-a-date, but admitting that would send her right down a road that opened her up to either getting hurt or not being able to make clear decisions. The realization worried her just enough to tuck it away. She wanted to—*had to*—stick to her guns about figuring her life out before getting involved in a real relationship.

*This feels real.*

*Very real.*

She suppressed the urge to admit just that and forced herself to use that energy toward getting to know him better. If she had hopes of one day allowing the feelings blooming between them to flower—after her life was figured out and she was settled—she needed to understand who he was, the bad and the good.

"Can I ask you a personal question without ruining the romantic vibe we have going on?" Bella asked.

"I'll tell you what. How about you ask and we'll see how it goes? I can't imagine what you could ask that could change how amazing it feels to be with you."

She turned sideways, curling her legs up against his thigh. She ran her finger down his chest. "I love how open you are with me, but if you'd rather not talk about this, I would understand."

He kissed her lips. "I have nothing to hide."

"Okay." She lowered her voice with the sensitive question. "What was it like raising Evan when you were so young?"

"That's the scary question? I've been asked that question a lot over the years, and I usually give an answer that won't lead to more questions, like, *Amazing*, or *Totally worth it*."

Bella felt his heart beating calm and even. He gazed up at the stars, and when his eyes met hers again, she sensed his honesty before the words even left his lips.

"When I showed up at my parents' house that first night, I was so full of love and hurt that I'm not sure I was able to even think clearly. Or maybe I was thinking clearly for the first time in my life. If you want to know if I ever questioned my decision to raise him, the answer is no. Not even at the most difficult times."

"How did your parents handle it?"

"My parents..." He paused, and a smile warmed his eyes. "They were looking at their twenty-year-old son and their grandchild. How do you think they reacted? They were scared shitless about me leaving college and thrilled about this little baby boy that was a part of me. A part of our family."

Bella shifted in his arms, and finally his eyes met hers—warm, loving, and without regret. Like him.

"They tried to convince me to go back to school. They even offered to raise Evan, but there was no part of me that wanted to go back to that life. It was as if the minute Evan was mine, all that drinking and partying was from another lifetime altogether."

"They say that the love you have for a child is unlike love you have for any other."

"Without a doubt. That was true in my case. My father has always been a strong influence in my life. He's the kind of man who always—*always*—does the right thing." A soft laugh slipped from his lips. "He taught me to hunt and fish, and he taught me to value friendships over nonsense. Everything he did, it seemed, held a lesson about responsibility, and the way he was—is—with my mother was like a silent lesson in love." He shrugged. "Anyway, I had their support, and it made everything a little easier."

They talked for a while longer about his parents and raising Evan. Bella had hoped the conversation might naturally lead to Evan's mother, and when it didn't, it made her even more curious. She pressed her hands to his chest, and when he leaned forward and kissed her, she almost let the subject go.

"What?" he asked softly.

She knitted her brows together, trying to figure out how she had already become transparent to him, just as when he ran his finger down her cheek and asked her again, she knew there was nothing she couldn't ask him.

"You said you were full of love *and* full of hurt."

His mouth twitched, and he lowered his forehead to hers and closed his eyes.

"I was," he admitted.

"I'm sorry," she whispered, and kissed his forehead as he'd kissed hers.

"It was a tough time." He inhaled deeply, and when he spoke again, his eyes never wavered from hers. He clearly had nothing to hide.

"I thought I loved Caty, Evan's mom, but the moment I held Evan in my arms, the love I felt for him was overwhelming. I knew that second that I didn't love Caty. And even though I knew that, it still hurt when she left. The hurt for myself was little more than momentary. But the pain I felt for what Evan would experience, having been abandoned by his mother, once he was old enough to understand, was anything but momentary. I worried day and night about how it might affect him. The truth is, I still worry about that."

"Do you think it's worth trying to get in touch with her to see if they can build a relationship now?"

His lips curved into a smile, and he pressed another kiss to her lips. "You're a thoughtful person, Bella, and I love that about you. I think most women would find the mother of my child a threat."

"This isn't about me. This is about Evan and what's best for him."

"I know it is, which is why you're so remarkable." He paused long enough for those words to sink in. "I haven't seen Caty since she left Evan with me. He's gone through stages of wanting to know about his mother, and I tracked her down and opened the door for her to get to know him, but it's like she's wiped that slate clean."

"I can't imagine a woman leaving a child behind like that, but I guess we never know what's going on in a person's head. She probably had reasons that were valid in her mind."

"There you go again." He ran his finger along her bare shoulder. "It would be easy to jump into a diatribe about how awful of a person she is, but you didn't go there. I don't go there either, even though, when Evan was younger, the pain over not having a mother would sometimes bring him to tears." He paused, and in his eyes, Bella saw him struggling with what she assumed were memories. "It's a little selfish to say this, but in a way she did Evan a favor. I think it would have been worse for him to be raised by someone who didn't truly love him, or resented him, than to be given a chance to be loved completely without that kind of stress in the house. It probably sounds weird, but I think it took a lot of courage to do what she did."

Bella pressed her cheek to his chest, her palm flat over his heart. *Now who's the remarkable one?*

Caden wrapped her in his arms again. "There's something else you should know, Bella, since we're being so honest on our not-a-date. Even though she didn't love me, and even though she has been absent for so many years, if she ever wanted to see Evan, or if Evan wanted to track her down himself, I would never stand in their way. I love him too much to do that."

He lifted her chin and gazed lovingly into her eyes. "But no matter how she might have changed, or what she had to say, I could never love her. I've learned over the years what love feels like, and it's either there or it's not. It was never there with her. She was an infatuation. It was love at first sight with Evan, and that love was so powerful that I knew if I ever fell in love with a woman, I'd know it the minute I met her."

He lowered his mouth to hers, quieting the voices in her head and answering her unspoken questions.

"Caden," she whispered against his lips.

"Hmm?"

*Thank you for being honest. Thank you for coming into my life. This is the best date ever. I'm falling for you hook, line, and sinker.*

"Thanks for pulling out all the stops."

CADEN PARKED AT Bella's cottage and they walked across the quad hand in hand. They'd turned a corner tonight, and he'd been seconds away from admitting that he'd known he loved her the first moment their eyes connected. He'd had to kiss her to keep the words from tumbling out for fear of scaring her off. She didn't have to tell him that she had the same intense feelings for him as he did for her. Like with his parents, it was as present as the air they breathed. He had a sense that he had to be careful with Bella. That as strong as she liked everyone to believe she was, her heart was fragile.

Bella stopped short of Jamie's cottage. "I almost forgot to tell you that when I was at Nauset High today, walking outside with the principal, she told me that troublesome kids hung around the back field of the school, by the woods."

"Troublesome?"

"She seems like a gossipmonger, so I wouldn't get overly concerned. She said they jaywalked. I mean, that's hardly troublesome, but I wanted you to know. You know, you're a cop, so maybe you guys need to know that stuff? I don't know."

"You're too cute."

"Hardly. Maybe it's worth mentioning that area by the woods to Evan for when he goes back to school."

Caden glanced at Jamie's cottage, thinking about Evan and what he'd said about reading the crime report and loving that Bella was thinking about him, too. "I'll mention it to him."

Bella leaned in close and whispered, "I jaywalk all the time." He heard a cottage door open, and Bella placed her index finger over her lips. "Shh."

Pepper, Leanna's fluffy white Labradoodle, bounded toward them from around the corner of her cottage. Bella knelt to love him up. Pepper barked and licked so excitedly that he tumbled onto his back.

"What are we shushing?" Leanna peered over the railing of her deck.

"Leanna! You're back." Bella smiled up at her. "I was telling Caden not to tell anyone that I jaywalk."

"Now you're corrupting an officer of the law?" Kurt appeared behind Leanna. "How's it going, Caden? I heard the two of you were out on a date."

At Kurt's voice, Pepper ran back onto the deck. Kurt looked down at the pup. "Hey, buddy. Hold on a sec."

"Nice to see you again, Kurt, but uh...we're not exactly dating." God, it sucked to say that.

Kurt and Leanna exchange a confused look. "Oh, sorry. I thought Tony said you were out on a date."

Bella hooked her finger in his pocket. "Some things don't need labels."

He couldn't have said it better himself.

"Hey, we're thinking about chartering a boat and going deep-sea fishing next Tuesday. Do you guys want to go?" Kurt asked. "I think most of the community is going."

"That sounds great." Bella turned hopeful eyes to Caden. "Can you and Evan make it?"

"I start working days soon, so I'll have to check the schedule. If I'm clear, yeah, we'd love to go. Evan loves fishing." The way she instantly included him and Evan with her friends made him feel good all over.

"Great. Well, if you have to work, Evan can still come with us. I'll make sure he doesn't become shark bait."

"Sounds great. Speaking of Evan, I need to go relieve Jamie of him." He kissed Bella on the cheek and went to retrieve his son.

Evan talked about how great it was to work with Jamie from the second they left Jamie's cottage until they reached Bella's.

"And Vera played her violin while Jamie walked me through some programming steps. She's really good, Dad. You should hear her play."

Caden smiled when he saw Bella sitting on the deck.

"I take it you had a great time?" Bella asked Evan.

"Jamie showed me some really cool stuff. I can't wait to go home and try to do it on my own." Evan headed for the truck.

Caden joined Bella on the deck. She looked adorably inviting with her feet propped up on the chair in front of her and her long legs bare to the tops of her thighs, where her sundress had gathered and draped over the sides. Caden placed one hand on each side of her chair and leaned in close.

"I'd really like to see you again."

"Me too." She snuck her hand between his arms and his torso and gripped his shoulders. Using him for leverage, she pulled herself up so their lips met.

"Should I call you?" he asked.

"I almost never carry my cell with me, so if I don't answer, just show up. I'm pretty easy," she said as she lowered herself back onto the chair.

"You're anything but easy." He held her gaze.

"Good. Then I'm doing something right."

He glanced at her cottage, fully aware of his son waiting for him and not wanting to tear himself away from Bella even for a second, much less for hours on end.

"Can I come by and install those locks for you after work tomorrow?"

She rolled her eyes. "If you must, but wear something sexy." She raised her brows in quick succession. "I like my handymen in leather tool belts and work boots."

"You're impossible."

"Yeah, we've pretty much determined that already."

He shook his head. "Okay, I'll be here in full workman garb, but..." He rose to his full height, pointed a finger at her, and tried his best to put on a serious face—though he felt a smile pressing at his cheeks. "It's not a date."

She rolled her eyes again. "Obviously. Now get out of here before I drag you inside and do dirty things to you."

"If that's what you promise to your not-a-date, then I can't wait to be your real date."

# Chapter Nine

STILL AMPED UP from his evening with Bella, Caden awoke early the next morning and went for a run on the beach. Running usually cleared his head, and he wanted to try to get a handle on the emotions that had his pulse quickening at the very thought of her.

Sweat beaded Caden's brow as he ran across the wet sand at a fast pace. A cool breeze swept over his heated skin. He reveled in the momentary chill. He passed a man with his young son building a sand castle, and it sparked a memory of taking Evan, then a curious toddler, to the beach with his parents. As a child, Evan had been an early riser, and Caden had made a habit of rising before the sun so he could be showered and dressed before Evan woke up. That summer, Evan's internal alarm clock had gone off even earlier, and by six o'clock each morning, Caden had breakfast packed, blankets, and towels stowed in the stroller, and a very happy Evan anxiously awaiting their walk to the beach. In their sweatshirts and shorts, they built sand castles and walked along the shoreline in search of rocks and shells until it was a reasonable hour for Evan's incessant toddler chattering to wake up his parents.

He cherished those memories.

He picked up his pace when he came to a couple walking hand in hand. When Evan was younger, Caden would fall into bed at night too exhausted to think about being with a woman. But there were times when he'd pass a loving couple whispering to each other, or nuzzling on a park bench, and part of him ached for a lasting, intimate relationship. But they were only flashes of longing for what he'd never allow himself to have, and after a few minutes, the urge would pass and his life would be whole again. Spending time with Bella brought those lonely times to the forefront. He was no longer a kid raising a baby and building a career. He was a man with a teenage son.

*A teenage son.*

He couldn't imagine how the time had passed so quickly, and he didn't want to think about a few years from now, when Evan would be off to college, and shortly thereafter, be the age Caden was when Evan was born. His mind drifted back to Bella, to the look in her eyes when they were talking up in the fire tower and the love he felt radiating from her when they'd kissed. He'd sent her a text when he arrived home last night with the picture of them he'd taken, even though he knew she probably wouldn't check it until the next time she needed to make a call. He couldn't help himself. It was a simple text, but he hoped it brought a smile to her beautiful lips.

He ran back down the beach the way he'd come, and when he reached the access road, he ran toward home. He reached up and touched his cell phone in the armband he wore when he ran and wondered what it would be like not to be tethered to it every minute of the day. He'd noticed that Bella and her friends didn't carry their phones everywhere like most people did. He'd never had the pleasure of feeling so free. He wouldn't want to. He liked being only a phone call away from Evan—and now from Bella, as well.

The house was quiet when he arrived home. He did a few sets of push-ups and sit-ups in the living room. Still warm from his workout, he filled a glass with ice water and went outside on the deck to cool off. His cell phone vibrated, and Bella's name appeared on the screen, spurring another quickening of his pulse.

A picture popped up on the screen, and he laughed out loud. Bella was standing in a colorful beach cover-up with her hair pulled up in a high ponytail. Her hand formed the shape of a heart in front of her chest—thumb to thumb, her knuckles bent and pressed together. To her right, Amy held a sign with a red arrow across the top that pointed at Bella. The sign read SHE MIGHT. Beside her Jenna held a sign that read WANT TO, on Jenna's other side, Leanna held a sign that read DATE YOU.

When he'd her sent the photo of them this morning, he'd given it the caption, FUTURE DATERS. He thought it might make her laugh, but this...*this* made his heart so full he thought he might burst.

He texted back, *I like my girlfriends in leather and lace, no boots required,* and hoped she'd get the reference to her handyman comment the evening before. He paced the deck as he waited for her response. When it didn't come right away, he worried that he'd sent the absolute wrong message.

After fifteen minutes, he went inside to take a cold shower and mentally orchestrated an apology. He could drive over and explain face-to-face that it was a joke. The last thing he needed was for her to bring up the whole fetish thing again. He knew she'd been kidding about the fetish stuff, but he also knew he had been out of the real dating realm long enough that he was probably behind the times with what was appropriate and what wasn't when texting a woman. He probably would have been better off sending a damn naked selfie. The thought made him cringe— he'd never understand the fascination with sending pictures that anyone could hack into.

He showered and changed, and when he came out of the bedroom, Evan was standing in the kitchen wearing nothing but a pair of cargo shorts and a troublesome grin—and staring at Caden's phone.

"Uh, Dad? I thought you and Bella weren't dating."

"We kind of are now. I think." Caden reached for the phone.

"I'd say you are for sure." Evan laughed as he poured himself a bowl of cereal.

Caden glanced at the phone. *Holy hell.* He wasn't sure which was worse, the fact that he was getting turned on by Bella's selfie, or knowing his son had just seen his girlfriend wearing nothing but a pink lacy nighty and a pair of knee-high leather boots.

WHEN BELLA HAD taken on the summer project, she'd thought local businesses would jump at the chance to hire high school students. They were cheap labor, they needed to get good grades to graduate, so they were likely to be responsible, and the business owners would be helping the kids to be better prepared for their future. It was with those hopes that she set out that morning to meet with three separate business owners. Her first stop was with Wellfleet Automotive, a company that had not only been on Bella's list of possibilities because she'd read an interview with the owner in an archive of the *Cape Codder* newspaper, but also one that was on Wilma's list. From the article, he seemed down-to-earth, and since he'd gotten his start in the business as a teenager shadowing his father, who had owned two auto shops at the time, Bella hoped he'd be open to the idea of joining the work-study program.

Wellfleet Automotive was located off of Route 6, making it easy for kids to get to whether they were driving, biking, or taking public transportation. The one-story building was built at the bottom of a long, sloped driveway. Bella stepped from her car and smoothed her dress as she assessed the property. A bank of tall trees shaded the parking lot. The temperature was cooler in the shade, which was a welcome relief to the warm morning. The lot was lined two cars deep. *That has to be a good sign. They aren't hurting for business.* The building had three bays, two of which were open. Two men were moving about in the center bay, and in the far bay, she saw a pair of jeans-clad legs sticking out from beneath a truck.

Bella walked into the center bay and was surprised when neither the tall, dark-haired man in blue coveralls manipulating a wrench, nor the short stocky man peering beneath the hood of a car, greeted her. When she'd called to make the appointment with the owner, Mr. Healy, he was a little gruff, and since he'd put her on hold three times during their brief conversation, she'd written it off to the call interrupting his busy schedule. Now she wondered if the entire staff was less than friendly.

"Hello?" Bella called to them.

Both men looked up at her, then went back to work.

*Nice.*

The bay smelled like oil and gasoline and felt ten degrees colder than just outside the door, but that might have been from the creepy vibe of *Jay* and *Silent*

*Bob.*

"Excuse me. I'm here to see Mr. Healy." She walked toward the man with the wrench.

He had a thick middle and jowls that jiggled when he turned. He nodded toward a door to the right.

"Thank you." Bella was beginning to wonder if she'd made a big mistake.

Inside the waiting area a young couple sitting in vinyl chairs against the far wall glanced up from the magazines they were reading, gave her a quick once-over, then turned their attention back to the magazines. Bella stepped up to the counter and rang the silver bell. Heavy footsteps sounded before she saw the giant man who owned them come through the door, hulking toward her. He had to be six seven or taller, with linebacker shoulders and a square head that reminded her of Lurch from *The Addams Family*.

He splayed the largest hands Bella had ever seen on the counter. "Help you?"

The combination of Mr. Healy and this being her first time giving her spiel made her stomach knot up. She glanced at the couple, who were still engrossed in catching up on the latest gossip, giving her a second to gather her courage.

"I'm Bella Abbascia, here to see Mr. Healy."

A smile softened his weathered cheeks and gray eyes. "I'm Healy. Come around the desk and follow me."

She followed him through a door at the back of the cramped reception area and into a surprisingly neat office with a window facing the woods.

"Have a seat," he said with his back to her as he went to the other side of the desk and lowered himself into a leather chair that conformed to his large body.

Bella sat in the chair across from him, noting the dust-free bookshelves, the neat stack of papers on the desk, and the lack of mechanic's stench that the bays and the front office seemed to be drenched in.

"Bella Abbascia." He had a smoker's voice and followed his words with a loud sigh. "Is your father Milton Abbascia?"

Bella tried to hide her surprise. "Yes."

He smiled. "Concord station wagon, Buick LeSabre."

She furrowed her brows as he rattled off the cars from her youth.

"Some people remember faces; for me it's names and cars. I worked with my pop before I took over. Your name isn't common, so I looked through the old records, and yup. The guy I remembered—tall, rail thin, serious minded. I assumed he was your father."

Relief swept through her. Her father was all those things, plus a careful and meticulous man. If he trusted the Healys, then she knew she could as well.

"He's driving a Taurus now." She crossed her legs and drew her shoulders back, concentrating on, and pushing past, the nervous energy that had her fidgeting with her purse.

"Mr. Healy, I know you're busy, so I'll try to be succinct. As I explained on the phone, I'm working with the school system to put together a work-study program. Have you hired a teenager as an apprentice or mentored any of the local kids?"

His eyes grew serious again. "We hired a kid a few years back. Rat stole two hundred dollars."

*Great.* "That's unfortunate, but not all kids are like that. The program I'm putting together is geared toward helping those who can't afford to go to college, or perhaps don't have an interest. I'm asking local businesses to help these kids learn trades and responsibility. We're talking only about fifteen hours a week at minimum wage."

He leaned forward and rested his massive forearms on the desk. "Bella. Is it okay if I call you Bella?"

"Yes, of course." By his serious tone, she knew she was about to be turned down, and she fought to keep the irritation from her face.

"Bella, what you're doing is commendable, but winters around the Cape are very different from summers. It's pretty desolate, and kids aren't as inclined to ride their bikes to a job they'd rather not be doing in ten-degree weather."

"You're on public transportation."

"True, but they have to pay for that transportation." He lifted his thick, graying brows. "I could give you ten practical reasons why a kid would do a shitty job or not show up for work, but you're a smart woman, so I won't play that game. I'll give you one honest answer.

"I'm not willing to spend time training kids that I don't know and trust. I've had the same employees for the past eleven years. We run an efficient business, and as much as I want to help the kids around here, I've been burned once, and that was enough."

"Mr. Healy, you got your start working with your father. Many of these kids don't have that option, so I'll ask you this. What options would you have had if your father hadn't owned this shop?" Bella held his gaze, hoping he'd soften to her plight.

He narrowed his eyes and leaned back in the chair. "Great question, and one I've thought about a million times in the last twenty years. I'm not sure what my options would have been. But I've spent a lot of years building a business people can trust. The residents here rely upon me to do business fairly and to provide quality work." He shrugged as if he'd provided an answer.

"How does hiring a student who can learn and grow from your efforts hinder that business?"

"If I could be assured they were here only to learn, that would be one thing." He pushed to his feet. "Come with me." He led her out the office door, through the reception area to the parking lot, where he pointed to a car. "See that red Corolla?"

"Yes."

"It was broken into two nights ago. The radio was stolen, along with some CDs. The checkbook the customer had in the glove box was left behind. That tells me kids were involved, because a practiced thief would have taken the checkbook and known what to do with it a few towns away. Letting teenagers in is giving them an open door to scoping out inside jobs." He crossed his arms over his chest. "Like I said, I've been burned once. It's been a long time since I was a kid, and I know every generation says the next is worse than theirs was." He shrugged. "I can't do it, but I appreciate what you're trying to do, and I'll tell you what. Let's see how the first year of the program goes. If the businesses don't end up with more trouble than they asked for, I'll consider it for the following year. Maybe some of the larger companies can hook you up this year."

Bella drove straight to the Chocolate Sparrow and bought a hunk of fudge. She needed a dose of sugar to chase away the ills of reality. She sat outside the little white shop with a thick chunk of peanut butter fudge, silently giving herself a pep talk. Of course she'd run in to this type of thing. Why would she think otherwise? Teenagers were teenagers. They weren't wired to be well behaved all the time, but if they didn't have the opportunity to focus on more productive ideas and challenge themselves in ways that were conducive to a responsible future, then what did people expect? Idle hands...

She closed her eyes for a second and tilted her head up toward the sun, thinking about Caden. In a few hours, he'd be at her cottage installing extra locks to ensure her safety. She still thought the locks were unnecessary, even with the recent break-ins. There had never been any trouble at Seaside. Someone was always home, and they were tucked away from the main road. She felt safe there. But she loved that he cared enough to do it, and she was excited to see him again.

After his comment about calling her, she made a point of bringing her cell phone with her today. She pulled it out now, and her cheeks flushed with the thought of the selfie she'd sent him. The first racy picture she'd ever sent a man. Boy, he sure was tugging her toward the edge of Love Mountain. She looked at their picture, which she'd set as the wallpaper on her phone.

Bella was nothing if not practical, and as she stared into his dreamy eyes and ran her finger over the image of his windblown hair, she knew the feelings that were making her feel warm all over were coming too fast. They went against her plan to figure out her life, but, boy, did she like Caden Grant. He was about as committed as they came, having raised his son alone for all those years, but that didn't necessarily mean he'd be as committed to her. Or even if he started out as such, that he'd remain that way. Hell, she knew men didn't come with guarantees, the same way she didn't come with one.

Her mind drifted to Evan. He was a sharp, respectful kid, and she could tell by the way he interacted with Caden that they had a good relationship. Mr. Healy's adamant rejection and Wilma's speculation about wayward teens fueled her desire to get the program off the ground for kids like Evan, who wanted to do and learn more than what was readily available to them. She finished her fudge, which took the edge off her frustration, and headed to her next appointment with rejuvenated hope.

Almost three hours—and three rejections—later, Bella drove down the back road that ran parallel to the ocean on her way to Seaside. Four kids on bikes came flying out of Payton's Campground directly into her path. She slammed on the brakes, and with her pulse racing, she recognized Evan's mop of chestnut hair and long, skinny legs as he pedaled away. After the initial shock of almost running them over subsided, a flood of childhood memories came rushing back. *She and the Seaside girls pedaling their own bikes to the beach, flaunting their bikini bodies, waving to cute boys, then spending all day in the sun. Evenings spent gathered around the pool, rehashing their long afternoons in the sun, and sneaking out to sit in the darkness and whisper about things they hoped to do when they were older.* Not much had changed. They were still the same close-knit friends they'd always been, and she hoped, as she drove into Seaside and parked in front of her cottage, that Evan was building the same type of cherished memories.

"Hey, girlfriend." Leanna waved from her deck as Bella stepped from her car. She held up a muffin. "Come over and try my newest creation."

"Thank you," she said as she took the warm muffin from Leanna. "Somehow the peanut butter fudge I bought from the Chocolate Sparrow didn't hold me over. I'm starved." She took a bite and her eyes widened with the delicious burst of banana and cranberry melting in her mouth. "Leanna, this is…" She swallowed the last of it. "Scrumptious."

"Hmm." Leanna crinkled her nose. She wore a pair

of cutoffs and a tank top streaked with red jam and muffin batter. "Jenna said it was orgasmic, so I'm thinking that scrumptious is a level below that."

"Was Pete here when she said it?" Bella asked.

Leanna's eyes widened. "Oh, right. She was talking about Pete. I swear, you guys are always much quicker on the uptake with things like that than I am."

"Nah, it's just that it's Tuesday, and every Tuesday morning, Jenna's thinking about Pete and orgasms she hopes he'll one day induce."

Kurt came out of their cottage. "I'm not sure I'll ever get used to hearing you guys talk about men like we're here only to pleasure you." He wrapped his arms around Leanna from behind and kissed her neck.

"Mm." Leanna reached up and stroked his cheek. "Why? Because you hate doing it so much?"

"No. Because it makes me wonder what you guys said about me." Kurt kissed her again and sat down at his laptop.

"We didn't have to say a thing. You guys said it all by leaving your windows open." Bella blew Kurt a kiss.

He shook his head and began typing.

"How's the project? Did you get any companies to sign on yet?" Leanna walked with Bella over to her cottage.

"No. I met with four today, and two turned me down flat. The other two were receptive, but noncommittal. I just don't get it. It's like everyone's afraid to hire teenagers." Bella hadn't asked Leanna to take part in the program with her jam business because she knew Leanna would say yes just to help her out, and she didn't want to put her in that situation in case she really didn't want to be part of the program.

Leanna followed her inside. "I'm sorry it didn't go well, but I can't imagine that all of the businesses will

118

be that way. If anyone can sell this, you can."

The fact that Leanna didn't offer to join the program confirmed to Bella that not asking her had been the right thing to do. "I hope so."

"I know so. Want to get your mind off of it and go down to the pool with me? Kurt is writing for another few hours, so I thought I'd hang out there. Jenna and Vera are already down there."

"Sure." Bella went into the bedroom and changed into her bathing suit, and then they headed down to the pool.

Jenna and Vera sat beneath an umbrella, engrossed in a game of gin rummy. Jenna had a glass bottle of Perrier on the table.

"Jenna, if Theresa sees you with glass by the pool, you are dead meat. Rule number seventeen: no glass on the pool premises."

"Theresa's not here, but I'll keep an eye out for her car. Thanks for killing the joy, babe."

"Nice to see you, ladies." Vera wore a floppy white sun hat and the same white cover-up she'd worn for the last three summers. Dark spidery veins mapped her pale legs. She smiled up at them and pointed to the empty chairs. "Sit, please. Jenna is letting me win again."

Jenna blew out a breath. "Oh, please. I think Vera was a card counter in a previous life. Either that or she's using marked cards." Jenna ran an assessing gaze over Bella. "Uh-oh. Hard day at the office?"

"You could say that. I didn't think this was going to be easy, but I didn't think I'd be shot down every time." Bella sprayed sunscreen on her arms and legs, then handed the bottle to Leanna. "Maybe my pitch is off or something."

"Gin." Vera laid down her cards.

Jenna rolled her eyes and put her cards on the

table. "Okay, I'm out for a bit. Congrats, Vera. I owe you about a million dollars."

"You owe me nothing. It's kind of you to play with an old lady like me." Vera patted Jenna's hand, then turned her attention to Bella. "You know, Bella, Evan was quite a gentleman when he was at our house. I enjoyed spending time with him."

"I'm glad to hear that." She thought of him speeding out of the campground on his bike. "They moved here a few weeks before summer, and Caden said he hadn't made any friends yet, but Evan met a few boys at the flea market the other day."

"Yes, that's what he told Jamie. It sounded as if they were getting on just fine," Vera said.

"They might be. I saw them riding bikes on my way here. I know Caden is nervous about him going off with a new crowd, so I hope they're good kids."

"I hope so, too. He seems like such a sweet boy." A smile spread Vera's thin lips. "You're very fond of this man, aren't you, dear?"

"That's one way to put it," Jenna said as she dragged her chair into the sun.

Bella shook her head at Jenna. "Yes, Vera. I am, but I'm trying really hard not to commit to a relationship while I'm putting the pieces of my life together."

"Why is that?" Vera asked.

"Well, as you know, I'm trying to get the work-study program off the ground so I can get a full-time job, and then I need to sell my house in Connecticut. My life isn't exactly stable at the moment, and I think adding a relationship into the mix just makes it more confusing."

Vera patted her hand. "Bella, dear. Your life is stable. You've always been stable. You're just in a transitional state of your stable life. Sometimes having a relationship makes everything else easier to deal with. Sometimes all it takes is that one piece of the puzzle to pull the rest of them together and have them all make sense."

*A transitional state of my stable life.* Bella looked away and let those words settle in. *Could Caden be the missing piece in my life? No. I don't need a man.* But Vera wasn't saying she did. "As much as I'm trying to deny what you're saying so I can stick to my no-commitment rule, I know what you're saying makes sense, Vera."

"You mentioned to me that the man you were dating in Connecticut had lied to you about getting back together with his wife, and I know you well enough to realize that you probably have had enough of men lying to you." Vera leaned closer to Bella and lowered her voice. "Sweetie, if you live your life afraid to be hurt, you're not really living your life, are you?"

Bella sighed. "Tell me this, Vera. Does wisdom really come with age, or did you have all this figured out when you were our age?"

"No, honey. At your age I was fumbling through my emotions just like the rest of you. Once you have more wrinkles than orgasms, that's when wisdom sets in." Vera smiled, as if she knew she'd just blown them all away.

Bella laughed. "Hopefully, I have a long time before that happens. I really do like Caden, and I like Evan. Maybe I should just bite the bullet and stop fighting my feelings for him." Vera had just given Bella the validation that she hadn't realized she was waiting—maybe even hoping—for. "Yes, you know what? You're right, Vera. I think it's time for stable Mable to throw caution to the wind and give this thing between us a name. I'm going to *date* him."

"Good for you, Bella. I know it's hard for you to feel like you're breaking your promise to yourself, but think of it as renegotiating the plan. That's how it was with me and Kurt," Leanna said. "You guys remember how scattered I was, trying to make things work, and Kurt sort of brought all of my chaos into focus."

"Trust me, Leanna. We all hear him bringing your chaos home a little too often." Jenna wiggled her eyebrows.

Leanna blushed.

"Now, now, girls. You're not kids anymore. Making love is part of coming together as a couple. It's a beautiful part, and...Oh, now, there's a thought. Bella, does it bother you that Caden has a son?" Vera's voice was serious.

"Bother me? No. It's not like it's an option for him to *not* have a child."

Vera smiled warmly. "That's a very smart way to look at things. I think some women might feel jealous."

"Of his son? I guess some women might, but Evan was there before me, and he's Caden's world. Besides, I don't think a person has room only to love a child or another adult. If they did, marriages with children would never work." She thought about Caden and how he'd changed his whole life for Evan, and she wondered if he would have turned out to be the man he was if Evan hadn't been in his life.

"I think you can tell a lot about a man by his children, and Evan is a lovely boy." Vera had known Bella and the others since they were toddlers and their families first bought the cottages. She'd always been careful about injecting her opinions on Bella and the others. The fact that she was offering her opinion now meant a great deal.

"Evan is lovely, but I've been working with teenagers for a long time, and if there's one thing I know for sure, it's that even good parents can have delinquent kids." Bella stretched her legs in the sun.

"And the opposite is true, too. Delinquent parents can have really well-behaved kids. I don't think there's a formula."

"Maybe that's the answer for your project," Vera suggested.

"What do you mean?"

"When we spoke the other day, you mentioned that the project was for kids who might otherwise have too much time on their hands and get into trouble, but what about kids who are looking to break the cycle? Those children who *want* to learn a trade, or want to do more with their lives but they aren't necessarily being forced into it. I'm not saying to use those words, but instead of presenting the program as a saving grace for kids who might be destined for delinquency, how about selling it as a program for kids who are trying to better themselves because they want to? Like Evan learning from Jamie. No one forced him to come over, or to make another date with Jamie next weekend."

Bella drew in a hopeful breath. "Vera, you're brilliant. Maybe I've been looking at this all wrong. Maybe it should be a little bit of an exclusive program." Bella stood and paced. "Maybe the application should be expanded to include more than the fields the kids are interested in and why, but what their goals are after high school. And, taking it even further, we can add an essay requirement about why a company should hire them. Nothing big, just a few paragraphs." She wrapped her arms around Vera.

"Thank you! This sounds so much more appealing. I mean, no kid is going to write an essay unless they want a job, right? And it would make them really think about the fields they are interested in." Bella sat back down. "And the kids who need the program but aren't as inclined to fill out the paperwork can be recommended by the guidance counselors, so they have an in. They'd have to complete the same forms, of course, but maybe then we add…Wait, that sounds like we're playing favorites. That won't work."

"Bella, you're not saving the world. You're developing a program for those who want to better themselves," Leanna said. "I think the idea of an essay is a good qualifier. Think about it. Do you really want to sell companies on a kid who is in it only for the time out of school, or do you want to really help the kids who want to be helped?"

"Don't forget, guidance counselors can recommend to the kids that they take part," Jenna added. "And the ones who follow through are more likely to do a good job anyway."

"True. And the application already requires teacher and personal recommendations. You know what?" She gathered her towel and hugged Vera again. "I'm going to text Caden and tell him that we're officially dating and then I want to work on this. I have a new boyfriend and a pitch to develop!"

## Chapter Ten

EARLY AFTERNOON FOUND Caden taking a report for another break-in at Duck's Pond. The pond was located off a back road, at the bottom of a hilly, wooded path. Like many ponds on the Cape, the parking lot was a good distance from the water, and unfortunately, it made for an easy target for vehicle break-ins. He took the report and then drove down the main drag to the center of Wellfleet to grab a soda from the Wellfleet Market.

He parked behind the church and was crossing Main Street when he noticed Evan and his friends sitting on their bikes in the gravel area beside the market. He recognized two of the boys from the flea market, Mike and Bobby. Unlike Evan, both boys wore their dark hair cut short, while the others had longer hair, like Evan.

"Ev," he called as he approached.

Evan's shoulders dropped as he reluctantly stepped from his bike. "Be right back," he said to the others.

"Hey, buddy. How's it going?" Caden eyed the boys

on the bikes, and when Mike shifted his eyes away, Caden had a funny feeling in his gut. He wrote off the discomfort to a combination of the distance he'd felt between him and Evan and to not knowing Evan's new friends. *This too shall pass*, he hoped.

Evan stared at the sidewalk and kicked at a stone. "Fine."

"Where are you guys heading?"

Evan shrugged.

Evan's friends rode to the edge of the gravel area, where they were waiting for him, obviously trying to signal Evan that they were ready to leave. Caden slid them a narrow-eyed stare. He wasn't about to be rushed, but he was also walking a fine line of not wanting to embarrass Evan with his new friends.

"Dad, can I go, or did you want something else?" Evan asked.

He didn't like the way Evan wasn't looking at him or answering his questions. "You know I don't like you loitering. What's your plan?"

Evan shrugged again.

"Damn it, Evan. Are you going to just ride circles around Wellfleet? Head over to someone's house and play a game? What's the deal? And look at me when I'm talking to you."

Evan lifted his eyes. "Beach, I guess."

Caden didn't like his reticence one bit, but he'd cut him some slack this time. "Fine. Stay out of trouble, and remember to be home in time to go to Jamie's tonight."

"Whatever." Evan walked away.

Caden opened his mouth to call him back, then thought better of it and shook off his irritation. He knew that being a cop's kid had all sorts of things that came along with it, including new friends looking shady with nervousness even if they weren't bad kids.

A uniform could make the calmest of kids jumpy. He'd let this go with Evan, but he'd have the station secretary run a background check on the two boys Evan had met at the flea market—just to be sure Mike's shifting eyes were only a sign of a typical nervous teen around a cop.

AT THE END of his shift, Caden was poring over the crime reports from the night before when he received a text from Bella. Her smiling face filled the screen with the caption, *Guess who this is?*

He texted back, *The hottie who likes leather boots?*

What was she up to now, and why the hell did she still make his body fill with anticipation like he was sixteen years old? His phone vibrated a minute later.

*Your new girlfriend. Yup, it's official. Alert the media. We're dating. That is...if you still want to. If not, well, check out the racy boot pic, and you'll change your mind. Xox.*

Caden was laughing when Kristie Palken, the executive assistant for the station, stopped by his desk with the report he'd asked her to run on the two new friends Evan talked about most often, Bobby Falls and Mike Elkton. He shoved his phone in his pocket and cleared his throat, but there wasn't a chance in hell he'd be able to stifle his grin.

Kristie chewed bubble gum like an addict. She was never without a pink wad, and she blew bubbles midconversation in the most annoying fashion, but she was efficient as hell, and after working with cops for the last ten years, she was savvy enough to actually get blood from a stone.

"Okay, spill it. What's got you looking like the Cheshire cat?"

"Nothing. What've you got?"

"Uh-huh. I've raised a teenager. I know what a

juicy secret looks like, and you, my friend, are totally in that secret zone." She smiled and blew a bubble. "It's okay. It's a small town. I'll find out eventually if it's worth knowing. Anyway, I've got your info." She wiggled her plump bottom into the chair across from Caden.

"And?" He tried to read her expression, but she was looking past Caden at two officers joking around behind him.

She blew a bubble and shrugged. "I've got nothing on them. They go to Nauset High, parents are respectable, no history of delinquency on either."

Caden breathed a sigh of relief.

She shifted her eyes back to him and blew a big bubble, then sucked it back into her crimson lips. "Is this a case of little boy growing up and his daddy being overprotective, or did you have a reason to worry?" Kristie was a single mom with a twenty-year-old daughter, and the way she tossed her red hair over her shoulder and then narrowed her eyes and set her stare on Caden told him that she'd been there and done that.

"They acted a little nervous around me earlier today, but it must have been the uniform. And the superintendent of the high school said there were some troublemakers around, so I was just checking." He shook his head. "I'm glad they're not troublemakers."

"Wilma Ritter?" She waved her hand in the air. "Willa thinks any kid who's not a robot is trouble. What does your gut tell you?"

"I only met them briefly a couple of times, but they seemed like normal kids."

"Cops usually have good instincts." She leaned across the desk and stopped chewing long enough to lower her voice. "Spend time with them. Let them know you're a cop and you're watching them." She pointed her index finger and her second finger at her eyes, then pointed them at Caden. "You'd be surprised how a little fear can instill good behavior in kids." She walked away with a curt nod.

Caden knew damn well what fear could do. It could backfire as easily as it could instill good behavior. He'd have to find a middle ground and hope those kids weren't trouble in the first place, because he also knew that if a kid was set on getting into trouble, sometimes there was no deterring him.

He read over the reports one last time before heading home for the evening. There were three vehicles broken into, each within a few miles of Bella's cottage, and in the late afternoon another cottage had been hit. Luckily, no one was home at the time. His muscles tensed with the thought of anything happening to Bella.

Caden drove home thinking about how important Bella had become to him. He wanted to protect her as much as he wanted to protect Evan, and even though she wasn't quite as forthright with her emotions, he knew in his heart that her feelings were just as strong for him.

His cell phone rang on the way into his house. *Evan.* "Hey, buddy."

"Hi, Dad. Do you mind if I hang with Bobby and Mike tonight? We're gonna play video games at Bobby's house." Evan sounded excited.

Two thoughts fought for Caden's attention—his son's safety and a few hours alone with Bella. He had an instant reaction of jumping at that time with Bella, but the father in him made him slow down and ask the right questions.

"Are his parents going to be home?"

Evan sighed. "Yes."

"You're not going out anywhere? You'll be there all night?" In Boston Caden had known most of Evan's friends' parents. Not knowing the adults who would be in charge of the boys was new to him, and refraining from being overprotective was a struggle.

"Yes, Dad." Evan's annoyance came through loud and clear.

Caden's gut told him to stop by and meet the parents, but he trusted Evan, and he didn't want to make his son appear to be a daddy's boy. Kristie had already given him both of the boys' parents' names, addresses, and phone numbers. He decided to give Evan a little rope and hope he didn't hang himself.

"Okay, but be home by ten. Do you want me to pick you up?" He felt like he was sending him off to preschool for the first time. At least with preschool he could sit in his car and watch Evan playing safely under the guidance of the teachers. This was much scarier.

"Nah. I've got my bike, but can we say eleven instead?"

"Evan."

"What? I had a curfew of eleven back in Boston. And it's summer, Dad."

The frustration in Evan's voice shot straight to the center of Caden's chest. He was right. It wasn't an unreasonable request, and it would give Caden an extra hour with Bella.

"Okay, but not a minute later."

Caden showered and changed, excited to spend a few hours alone with Bella. On his way out the door, he grabbed his leather tool belt. He loved this little ruse they were playing, and he intended to make the most of it.

He pulled over to the side of the road before driving into the Seaside complex. He removed his shirt and wrapped the leather tool belt around his waist, feeling the thrum of anticipation. He caught a glimpse of himself in the rearview mirror and shook his head. He had no chance of quashing the smile from his lips. He tilted the mirror so he could see his abs. He worked out often and he was in great shape. As he confirmed that fact, he felt incredibly silly. He hadn't done anything even remotely similar to this since his college days, when he and a group of his buddies went to an Anything But Clothes party wearing nothing but plastic beach inner tubes and their private parts.

He pushed the mirror back into place and leaned his head back. *What am I doing?*

He pulled out his cell and brought up the picture of Bella in her lingerie and leather boots. The mischievous glint in her beautiful eyes gave him confidence.

Hell yeah, he was *so* going to do this. He threw the truck into drive. After he parked at Bella's cottage, a quick scan of the immediate area told him that no one was outside, which was good, because while he loved the idea of surprising Bella in his shirtless, boot-clad getup, he knew damn well that there would be no hiding the thought behind the outfit.

With a deep breath, and his stomach doing all sorts of funny things, he climbed from the car.

"She's at Leanna's." Tony came around the side of the cottage and assessed Caden's outfit with a knowing smirk.

"Christ." Caden closed his eyes for a beat and shook his head.

"Dude, let me get her. Trust me. You don't want those girls seeing you like that. Bella yes, but Jenna? Man, she'll eat you alive."

Caden couldn't even thank him, he was so embarrassed. He banged his forehead against the door, then reached for the buckle on the tool belt to take the damn thing off.

He heard their giggles before he could get the tool belt off. *Fuck.*

"Oh, come to mama," Jenna teased.

"Damn. You are one hot handyman," Bella said as she came up behind him and patted his butt.

"Wowza," Amy said. "I told you that lingerie, leather boots outfit would put a spark in your relationship."

"Holy Christ." *We needed a spark?* What else could he do but roll with it? Caden turned, threw his hands up in the air, and spun around slowly. "There you go, ladies. Get an eyeful, because it's the only one you're gonna get."

"Dude, you're upping the ante here big-time. How are we supposed to keep up?" Kurt and Leanna followed Jenna onto the deck.

"Well, you know. You've already got Leanna, so you probably don't need to do this stuff anymore. I'm still wooing Bella." Bella trailed her fingers lightly along his abs, with such a lustful look that he was thankful the tool belt was hanging in front of his junk.

Kurt shook his head. "If you think it ends after you're together, boy, you've been out of the dating scene for too long. I know I was." He pulled Leanna close, and she wrapped her arms around his waist.

Bella hooked her finger into the belt and smiled up at him. "I love that you came over ready to work." She lifted her brows and nibbled on her lower lip.

*Holy hell.* He shot a look at the others.

Tony held his hands up in the air. "I tried, dude."

"Thanks, man."

"If you thought we'd miss this, you were sorely mistaken." Jenna and Amy made no effort to hide their gawking.

132

"If you're going to drool over me, you'd better have a few dollar bills ready."

Bella put her hand flat on Caden's chest. It was warm and soft, and even with all the people around them, he couldn't help taking her in his arms and kissing her.

"Hi, sexy," she said. "Kurt and Leanna were helping me write up some of the stuff I need for the project I'm working on. We can finish tomorrow."

"No need. It'll take me some time to get these locks on. Why don't you guys finish and then we'll spend time together."

She ran her finger down the center of his chest. "Will you stay dressed like this?" She fluttered her lashes and nibbled on her lower lip.

Did she have any idea how crazy that drove him?

He glanced at the others, talking among themselves but still close enough to hear them. Being with Bella had calmed his nerves, and he no longer felt embarrassed. It struck him that Bella's friends had already become *that* comfortably familiar to him.

He shrugged. "Why not."

Bella went up on tiptoes and kissed him. "Hot damn! And in case you didn't get the memo, we're dating, so you can totally do boyfriendy things."

He lowered his cheek to hers. "I got the memo and the racy selfie. Do you really think I'd have dressed like this if I didn't think we were dating?"

Her smile didn't falter.

"Does this mean you're committing to seeing only me, or do you plan on dating anyone willing to don a tool belt?"

She drew back and searched his eyes. "I am totally breaking my plan for you, you know."

"I do know." *But I'm hoping your new plan will include me and Evan.*

133

BELLA HAD A hard time focusing on the marketing pitch and designing the outline for the work-study program with Caden walking around half naked. They'd been trading heated glances that made her feel like a high school girl crushing all over again. Only Caden was not a high school boy. He was one hundred percent man. She wondered what he was like in high school. Was he strong and silent, a little mysterious, the way he was as a man? Or did that come with being a father or simply growing up? Had he been a jock or a studious nerd?

She imagined he was a sexy combination of both.

Bella brought her attention back to Kurt, staring at his laptop and tweaking the marketing plan for the work-study program. Leanna claimed to think better when her hands were busy. She'd made a catastrophe of Bella's kitchen, while baking bread and calling out ideas for them to jot down. Now Leanna was poking around in Bella's refrigerator.

"I think you've got a solid plan." Kurt turned the laptop toward Bella. "I just changed a few words here and there."

"Really? It doesn't suck?"

Kurt laughed. "Of course not. What you had before didn't suck, but this is even better. I like the new spin on it."

Leanna pulled a fresh loaf of bread out of the oven, filling the small cottage with the delicious scent of warmth and comfort. "You know I'd sign up for the program if you really wanted me to."

"I know you would, but there's no need. I'm going to make this work. I just have to be creative."

Leanna closed the refrigerator door. "Where'd you hide the jam?"

Bella opened the refrigerator and pulled a jar of

Luscious Leanna's Sweet Treat apricot-lime jam from the door and waved it at Kurt and Leanna. "Want some?"

"Don't sweat it. I can never find anything in my fridge either," Bella assured her.

Caden came out of the bedroom, where he'd been installing the last of the new locks on the window. "It smells like heaven in here."

"Leanna made bread." Bella glanced at Leanna's dirty T-shirt. "As you can see by the flour, sugar, and"—she leaned in close to look at an oily streak on Leanna's jeans—"butter that she's wearing."

"That's my girl." Kurt kissed a streak of batter from Leanna's cheek.

"Hey, cleanliness and creativity do not go hand in hand." Leanna began gathering the bowls and utensils she'd used. "That's a banana, cranberry, almond loaf, and this mess is a small price to pay."

"Agreed," Bella said. "Leave it. I'll take care of it. Thanks for your help, you guys. I couldn't have done it without you."

"Of course you could have, but if we didn't keep you busy, Caden wouldn't have gotten any work done." Kurt reached for Leanna's hand. "Come on, babe. Let's go check on Vera and give them some privacy."

"Thanks for helping Bella and for giving me time to get the locks installed," Caden said. "Now at least I know she's got ample security."

Leanna opened the door to leave. "Like she'll lock her doors? See ya guys."

"Tell Vera we said hello," Bella called after them.

Caden placed his hands on her hips. His fingers slid beneath her billowy tank top and skimmed her waist as he touched his forehead to hers.

"Do you feel good about what you've accomplished?" His breath was hot, his voice rich and seductive.

Bella's body hummed with anticipation. She wrapped her arms around his bare back, feeling the muscles she'd just spent more than an hour watching flex and bunch beneath his taut, tanned skin. God, he felt good.

"Yeah," was all she could manage. "How about you?"

He lifted her chin and kissed her softly. It was the kiss of a man who had no place else that he'd rather be, tender and full of promise.

"That depends. Will you use these new locks?"

*I'll do anything you ask.* "Mm-hm."

"Then yes. I feel better knowing that you're a little safer."

"I never thought I needed protecting, but I have to admit, there's something about *you* protecting me that feels good."

"Yeah?" He lowered his mouth to her neck and trailed kisses to her ear. "Everyone needs protecting." He licked the shell of her ear, then whispered, "Even tough women who make plans."

Bella closed her eyes, relishing the sound and feel of him.

"Are you sure you can commit to me?" he whispered.

*Oh God, yes.* A shiver of worry skittered up her spine. With her eyes still closed, she whispered, "I know I can commit, but you might find I'm not all you were hoping for."

He pressed his lips to her cheek. "You're exactly the woman I've hoped for."

Her throat tightened.

Caden drew back and cupped her cheeks in his big, strong hands. "Look at me, Bella."

She forced herself to open her eyes, and the

136

compassionate, loving look in his told her everything she needed to know, and his words drove that feeling home.

"I'm not afraid to commit, and I'm not afraid to love." He searched her eyes, pausing, Bella assumed, long enough for his words to sink in.

"But we're adults, and Evan's still just a kid. I'm not a free agent, Bella. My life includes Evan, and always will. My decisions affect him, so if there's any chance you're going to run scared, then let's take things slow."

She tightened her grip on him. "Slow? It doesn't matter what we call it, Caden. Our hearts and bodies don't know *slow*. At least not when we're together. You've weaseled your way into my heart so fast. I have no desire to go slow with you. I just want to...Oh, Caden, I don't want to make a life decision about my job, or my house, and then get hurt. I need to make those decisions without the rest, but that seems unrealistic."

He brushed her hair from her forehead and tucked it behind her ear. "Then how about if we just make damn sure we don't hurt each other? Because I need that same level of commitment from you. I can't afford to be hurt. Evan doesn't need a lovesick father making his life more complicated."

"I don't cheat or lie. I never have," Bella said adamantly.

"Neither do I."

He sealed his mouth to hers in a tender, drawn-out kiss that made her long for more.

"Tell me what I need to know before I take you into your bedroom and make sweet love to you until neither of us can remember how to talk."

She could barely breathe, much less think straight.

"I...I break rules," she managed.

The left side of his mouth quirked up. "In the bedroom or in general?"

She placed her hands on his bare chest and felt his heart beating as fast as hers. Every breath, every second, pulsed with heat. She forced herself to answer.

"Both." She didn't really break rules in the bedroom, but now, with him, the idea was tantalizing.

"Holy...I'm not a cop in the bedroom." He lowered the strap of her top and kissed the curve of her shoulder, sending her mind reeling. "Tell me about the rules you break outside the bedroom."

He ran his tongue along her collarbone. Bella closed her eyes, relishing the feel of his body against hers, his tongue on the skin above her breasts, the feel of his arousal against her belly.

"Fireworks," she said in one long breath.

"You see them now?" he whispered. "Or you use them?" He slid his hands up her ribs, making her feel small and feminine—and crave the feel of them on her breasts.

"Both." Another breathy word. She couldn't help but bring her lips to his chest. He smelled like passion and strength. Earthy, musky, and sweet all at once. She kissed the arc of his pecs, nipping at the muscle.

"I can't break the law," he whispered.

She heard restraint in his voice. "I would never ask you to."

His eyes darkened as he grazed the underside of her breasts with his thumbs. *Oh God, yes.* She couldn't have pushed words from her lips if her life depended on it. She was too focused on his thumb brushing over her tight nipple. She felt ripe and ready, hot all over.

He kissed her again, then whispered, "Tell me all the bad stuff now so we go into this with our eyes open."

He slid his thumb from her nipple, and before she

could stop herself, a little wanting sound escaped her lips. He captured her mouth with his and took her in an impatient, tongue-thrusting kiss. When he drew back, she was dizzy, drunk with desire.

"Eyes open, baby. No secrets, no lies, no hidden agendas."

She opened her eyes, and his hungry gaze brought the truth to her lips.

"Skinny-dipping." Oh God, he was going to run out the door if she kept spewing her rule-breaking ways.

His mouth quirked up again. "You *are* a naughty girl." His thumbs brushed the sides of her breasts.

"Tell me." She kissed his chest again and forced herself to continue. "Your bad stuff."

He sealed his mouth over the curve of her neck, pulling a moan from her lungs. His lips grazed hers as he answered.

"I've been a single dad for a very long time."

He cupped her breasts, and she sucked in a breath at the gratifying touch.

"And I'm a cop," he whispered. "No bad stuff."

He lowered her other shirt strap and kissed his way across her shoulder. A light breeze blew through the kitchen, and Bella realized the only thing between them and the outside world was the screen door. He took her in another knee-quaking kiss and slid one hand to her ass.

"Only fantasies," he whispered against her lips.

The thought made her damp.

He slid his eyes from hers to the door. "Of all the things I haven't had a chance to do." He kissed each corner of her mouth, then pressed a soft kiss to her lips. "Like make love to a woman outside."

Bella's knees weakened. *Outside.* "Like, on the beach?" She was beginning to realize that her rule-breaking ways were pretty tame. She'd never had full-on intercourse outside, and the idea of making love to Caden outside revved her up even more.

"Too open." He kissed her again. "Indecent exposure."

"The woods?" she offered.

He touched his forehead to hers again. "Bella."

"The pool?" she asked softly.

He met her gaze. "You are going to get me in trouble."

She laved his nipple, feeling it tighten with every stroke of her tongue.

"Holy Christ." He tangled his hands in her hair and took her in another deep kiss.

She wanted to be closer, to feel the weight of him on top of her. To feel him buried deep inside her.

He drew back, his eyes jumping over hers. "Bella, if there's more, tell me quick."

"I. Can't. Think."

She pulled him down for another kiss, and they stumbled into the bedroom. Caden kicked the door shut and kissed her so deeply that she felt as if she were floating on a cloud. He tasted deliciously sweet, and hot, fervently plunging his tongue into her mouth, tearing his lips from hers only long enough for her shirt to slip off; then they were mouth to mouth again. She fumbled with the buckle on his tool belt and heard Tony's laugh filter through the open window.

Bella froze.

"Window," she whispered.

He moved quickly toward the window. Bella dashed out the bedroom door with her arms crossed over her chest. She closed the window over the kitchen sink and pushed the cottage door shut. Bella took a second to get ahold of herself before she lost all control and climbed Caden like a tree. She pressed her hands flat on the door and leaned her forehead against it, breathing deeply.

She sensed Caden behind her before she felt him unhook her bra. His hands circled her from behind. Heat radiated from his bare chest. He rocked against her, brushed her hair from her shoulder, and lowered his mouth to the back of her neck. She shed her bra and reached behind her, clutching his hips as he gyrated against her. His hands slid up her ribs, stopping short of her breasts again. She couldn't take it. She needed him to touch her again, to take her breasts in his hands and—*Oh Lord. Oh yes.* He slipped one hand down the front of her shorts, cupping her sex and teasing her with his fingers. Her body heated with desire as he sucked and kissed, nipped and licked her neck, taking her right up to the edge. She rose onto her toes, urging him deeper.

"You like that," he whispered against her neck.

She moaned, arching against his probing fingers. In the next breath, his hands gripped her shorts and pulled them off. He turned her roughly in his arms and pressed his body to hers, her back against the wooden door. He pressed barely there kisses to her cheeks, her chin, her neck, everywhere except her lips, making his way slowly down her neck, then back up to her face again. Every feathery tease heightened her anticipation.

"Caden, please." She was ready to crawl out of her skin and into his.

He placed one hand on each side of her head and pressed his thighs to hers. She leaned forward to kiss his luscious lips and he pulled away.

"No rushing."

He traced the edge of her lips with his tongue. Each time she moved forward, wanting to taste him, to feel his mouth consume her, he drew away. He trapped her lower lip between his teeth, then sucked it into his mouth and soothed it with his tongue, taking Bella up on her toes again. She caressed him through his shorts as he drove her out of her mind. He kissed along the edge of her jaw, and she closed her eyes, giving in to the torturously slow progression he was lavishing on her, feeling as though she might come apart from sheer anticipation.

"You taste so sweet," he whispered against her cheek.

He ran his hands up her outer thighs, lingering at her hips, then caressed her inner thighs. She rocked her hips, silently pleading for more as he finally, blissfully, lowered his mouth to hers and took her in a long, soulful kiss. She fumbled with the button on his shorts. He made quick work of shedding his boots and shorts. He reached for his wallet, pulled out a condom, and tore it open with his teeth.

"I'm on the pill." She saw hesitation in his eyes. "I'm clean, Caden. I got tested in the spring. I've been on an *all about me* path, and the first step was making sure I was clean."

He leaned his forehead to hers. "It's not that. Caty was on the pill, too."

Hearing her name stung in this intimate moment. But he'd asked for honesty, and she wanted to give— and receive—nothing less. She caressed his cheek, and when she went to kiss his lips, this time he didn't pull back.

"Okay," she whispered, and she helped him roll on the latex sheath.

THE LOOK OF understanding in Bella's eyes nearly overwhelmed him. He couldn't wait a second longer to be inside her. He lowered himself to a chair and guided her hips as she straddled him. They both sucked in a breath as she took in every inch of his thick desire until he was buried deep. She was so beautiful, loving him in sync with his own efforts. He tangled his hand in her hair and brought her lips to his for another passionate kiss. Caden loved kissing Bella. Her mouth was soft and eager, and every stroke of her tongue was sensuous and filled with more than just the carnal lust that drove them together, which is why he took his time, savoring every second of each magnificent kiss.

Bella gripped the back of the chair as he thrust faster and harder. He moved her hands to his shoulders.

"I want to feel you." Caden's eyes were dark and serious. "All of you. Your strength, your need, your body trembling against me."

Heat flared in her eyes. He took her breast in his mouth, sucking her nipple and then grazing it with his teeth while stroking between her legs with his other hand as she took him in deeper. Her grip tightened on his shoulders. Her fingernails cut into his skin as her eyes closed and her lips parted.

"Come for me, baby," he urged.

He'd been in a hurry to get inside her when he sank to the chair, and now he had to have more of her. He grabbed her hips, thrusting harder, faster, and taking her up, up, up. Her inner muscles pulsed around him, tightening over and over again in quick succession.

"Caden," she cried out.

Her hips bucked, and he cupped the back of her head and locked lips with her again, devouring her mouth as she came apart. His body ached for more of her; even buried to the hilt wasn't enough. He wanted to fuck her, make love to her, cherish her, and take care of her all at once—and he recognized the significance of those feelings. *Every fiber of my being loves you.*

He rose to his feet, their bodies still joined as one, and carried her into the bedroom. She rested her cheek on his shoulder with a contented sigh, and when he lowered her to the bed, she reached for him again. He took her in another ceaseless, impassioned kiss that he hoped told her how much she meant to him. He stroked the roof of her mouth, the ridges of her teeth, the parts of her that were usually overlooked. He wanted Bella to feel safe enough with him to expose, and to embrace, all the parts of herself that she tucked away from the rest of the world.

Her lips curved up, and her eyes were so full of desire that there was no room for misinterpretation. They were totally together in this. He pushed into her again, and she felt too damn good to take it slow. He gripped her hips and drove into her over and over again. She wrapped her legs around his waist, lifting her hips to meet each thrust, and when she sealed her mouth over his neck and sucked, she sent a bolt of heat so deep inside him that he couldn't hold back any longer. She clung to him, thrusting her hips and clawing at his back as she followed him over the edge in her own exquisite release.

They lay together for a long while afterward before Caden was willing to drag himself away from Bella long enough to take care of the condom. When he returned, Bella was lying on her side, facing the opposite direction. He climbed onto the bed and wrapped his body around her.

"It seems unfair that we have to spend tonight apart," he admitted.

"I was just thinking the same thing."

"I haven't spent the night with a woman since college."

She turned toward him and caressed his cheek.

"Do you miss it?"

"Honestly? I haven't really thought about it until now. It's different when you have a child depending on you. I wanted to be home with Evan. There wasn't a woman in the world who could make me want to spend a night apart from him." He kissed her softly. "Until you."

"Caden." She snuggled against him.

"I promised honesty, and the truth is, I don't want to be away from Evan, especially since he's been giving me more flack lately, and he seems withdrawn."

"That's not good. Do you think he's just going through a hard time, or are you worried that there's something else going on?"

"I don't know. I feel like he's challenging me."

"I call it the I-don't-need-parents stage. You remember what it was like to feel old enough to not need to be checked on, don't you? When your parents graduated from being the people who knew everything to the dumbest people on earth? It comes a few years before the oh-yeah-you-weren't-so-dumb-after-all stage, which usually hits around twenty or so."

"I hope you're right." He kissed her lips. "All I know is, I also don't want to be away from you."

"I thought you were just being sweet, but you're serious."

"Dead serious." He held her gaze.

She kissed the dimple in his chin. "Spending the night together isn't an option. We both know that."

He pulled her on top of him. "Okay, Little Miss Rational. Isn't the woman supposed to be the one craving cuddle time?"

"Oh, I do crave cuddle time with you." She ran her finger down the center of his chest, and it made him want her all over again. "But I'd never try to come between you and Evan, or try to coerce you into spending time away from him. I love and respect the type of father you are."

She nibbled on her lower lip and her eyes filled with mischief again. "So...You want to make love to a woman outside?"

He rolled over with her in his arms so she was beneath him again.

"No. I want to make love to *you* outside, but I won't."

She raised her brows. "Oh, yes you will."

He laughed. "I'm a cop. I think that would be the totally wrong thing for me to do."

"Then we'll be careful and find a place no one can possibly catch us."

"You, Bella Abbascia, are a very bad influence." He kissed her again. "By the way, I didn't see any rule breaking in the bedroom. All talk no action?"

"A girl can't pull out all the stops in one night."

"That's what I was counting on."

# Chapter Eleven

ALL BELLA HAD ever needed at the Cape was a few sundresses, flip-flops, towels, and bathing suits. Food and drinks were bought on the fly, and days began when her body decided it was time to wake up and ended when she and her friends were too tired to stay awake any longer. She'd spent so many summers turning off the part of her brain that required watches and calendars that it was a huge adjustment for her to get used to paying attention to the day of the week, or the exact time. In her mind, the Cape meant seven or eight weeks of immersing herself in her friends, stockpiling memories to carry her through until spring, when they would return for a long weekend of catching up.

She knew today was Friday because of her appointments, but also, and weighing on her mind more heavily at the moment, it was Caden's last night shift, and he was excited to switch to day shifts so he could spend more time with her and Evan in the evenings. She sent him a quick text. *Yay! It's your last night shift! Walking into the clinic. Wish me luck! Xox.*

The cell phone was a welcome addition to her summer accessories. She and Caden had traded flirty texts over the last two days when he was working nights and she had been tied up in meetings with businesses and school administrators to discuss the new angle of the program. He'd called her each evening, and their conversations flowed naturally, like they'd been dating for years. He was interested in her project, and she loved hearing about Caden's and Evan's days. Evan had been more attitudinal lately, and she'd reassured Caden that was to be expected at his age and with all the changes he'd been through recently, but she knew from teaching teens that parents took the worst of teens' attitudes and she felt for him.

With her new pitch in mind, she assessed her crinkled cotton minidress in her car window, then entered the clinic with her head held high.

*I can do this.*

*I will do this.*

Wellfleet was a tourist town that tripled in population over the summer. Winters in the small town were desolate in comparison, and because of that, doctors tended to practice in larger cities, like Hyannis, which was forty-five minutes away. It was only nine o'clock in the morning, and every chair in the waiting room was filled with coughing, sneezing, and puffy-eyed patients as well as two people with wrapped appendages. The clinic was a godsend for the tourists, handling everything from strep throat to broken bones.

Bella waited in line behind three women, the first of whom was speaking to a stern-faced, middle-aged receptionist who held a clipboard in one hand while writing on a notepad, while also speaking to another employee, a skinny woman with tattoos snaking around her neck and shoulders. The skinny woman's pitch-black hair was sculpted into spiky points that darted out from her head at various angles, complemented by eyebrow and nose piercings.

The door opened, and a man carrying a screaming baby entered the lobby, followed by a heavy woman with a toddler attached to her hip.

The tattooed woman shot a glance at the door, then called over her shoulder, "Bones. Front and center."

A tall, rangy guy wearing jeans and P-TOWN ROCKS T-shirt, who couldn't have been more than twenty, looked up from behind a metal desk.

"Got it." Bones hustled to the counter and took the clipboard from the stern-faced woman. His thin lips curled into a smile that softened his bony features and further confirmed his youthful appearance.

"Please fill out your name, insurance information, and—"

"I don't have insurance," the patient whispered.

Bones leaned closer, softening his gaze. "No worries. You can still receive medical care. We have a benefits specialist who will work with you. Just fill this out, and we'll call you when it's your turn."

"God bless you," the woman said.

When she turned toward the waiting area, Bella noticed a red rash covering the right side of her face. Bella had been lucky enough not to need medical attention while at the Cape, but she was pleased to hear that the clinic didn't turn patients away.

Bones handled the next two people in line with the same effortless patience. A woman in scrubs peered into the office behind him.

"Perry, Mary needs you," the woman in scrubs said.

The tattooed woman said something to the stern-faced woman that made her smile. She touched her shoulder as she passed on her way to tend to whoever Mary was.

"Ma'am?" Bones thrust a clipboard toward her.

"Oh, sorry." *Way to space out, Bella.* "I'm not here as a patient. I'm Bella Abbascia, here to see Ms. Blankenship."

"Sorry about that. If you can find standing room in the waiting area, I'll track her down."

"Perfect. Thank you." Bella was impressed by the swift efficiency of the operation. While she waited, a woman in scrubs had come out three times to call patients into the back, and each time the woman's eyes were compassionate. Though they were obviously overwhelmed with patients waiting to be seen, she didn't appear to rush them through the door.

The tattooed woman came through the door. "Bella Abbascia?"

"Hi, I'm Bella."

"I'm Perry Blankenship. Sorry to keep you waiting. Come on back."

Bella followed her down a wide hallway lined with patient rooms. She'd first guessed Perry to be in her midtwenties, but as she took a closer look, she noticed fine lines around her eyes and mouth and eyes full of wisdom that came only from experience and probably put her closer to her mid to late thirties.

"We'll be in here." She led Bella into an office barely big enough for the metal desk, file cabinet, and chairs inside. "Fridays are pretty crazy around here."

Bella sat in one of the chairs in front of the desk, and instead of sitting behind the desk, Perry sat in the chair beside Bella. She let out a breath before turning a warm smile to Bella.

"Welcome to our busy little clinic," Perry said.

"It's run very efficiently. Thank you for taking the

time to see me. I'll make this quick so you can get back to work. I've been hired by the school board to put together a work-study program for high school seniors."

Perry smacked her thigh, and her eyes widened with excitement. "Great idea."

"Yes, that's what we thought, too. The goal of the program is to provide hands-on training for kids who are looking to better themselves, to encourage self-confidence and independence and help them learn skills they can use toward a productive future."

Perry waved her hand to silence Bella. "Responsibility, self-worth, it's all wrapped up in helping others. Like I said, great idea. What do you need from me?"

Bella swallowed the urge to say, *Really?* "I'd like you to consider making the clinic part of the program and committing to hiring two seniors through the work-study program. They're limited to no more than fifteen hours each week and paid minimum wage."

"We drug test."

"Fine. We don't want kids using drugs any more than you do." Hope swelled in Bella's chest.

"They'd have no access to medications, obviously, and until we can gauge their abilities and trustworthiness, they would be confined to working in the admin area." Perry leaned forward with excitement in her voice. "But if we find a stellar student who shows promise, I'm not opposed to keeping them on after graduation to learn the ropes of becoming a certified medical assistant or a lab tech."

"Thank you. That's all we can hope for." Bella's feet lifted up onto their toes in a silent happy moment. "We're finalizing the documents, and I'll be happy to—"

Perry's office door opened and Bones poked his

head in. "Perry, Doc Winston is on line four. He said it's urgent."

"Oh good. Tell him I need one minute. Oh, Bones, this is Bella Abbascia. She's coordinating a work-study program for the high school."

He thrust a hand toward Bella. "Barry Goodman, but everyone calls me Bones. Nice to meet you."

"Bella, would you mind wrapping up the details with Bones? I need to take this call."

"Not at all." Bella rose to her feet.

"I wish there was a work-study program when I was in high school. Having something to do with my time might have saved me from a pregnancy at eighteen. Not that I begrudge my daughter. She's *amazing*." Perry's voice filled with pride. "Thankfully, she graduated last year *without* a baby in her belly. Let's hope this catches on."

When Bella left the clinic half an hour later, for the second time that week, she felt like she was walking on air. This one definitely came in second to making love with Caden, but it was a damn good feeling. She climbed into her car and headed toward Orleans for her next appointment.

CADEN PULLED INTO the parking lot of Nauset Beach to take another report on a vehicle break-in. Evan was at Nauset with his friends today, and Caden had texted him when he left the station to let him know he'd be there shortly and would like to touch base. He knew Evan would only get the text if he was by the snack area or parking lot, but at some point he'd see it. He'd texted Bella hours ago, and he assumed either her meetings were going well or she'd forgotten to take her phone into the cottage, because she still hadn't responded. When his cell vibrated, he hoped it might be her. He was surprised to receive a return text from

Evan so quickly, since cell phones didn't work on the beaches. He read the text.

*Still here. Leaving soon to go to Bobby's.*

Caden texted him back. *I'm here. Meet by snack bar in twenty mins?*

He stepped from the patrol car and scanned his surroundings. A woman wearing shorts and a blue bathing suit stretched tight over her muffin top waved at him as he crossed the parking lot.

"Officer, they took my wallet and cell phone," the woman said frantically. Her wet, dark hair stuck to her flailing arms. "I can't believe it. All my contacts, my calendar, my *life* is on that phone."

"Ma'am, slow down. I'm Officer Grant, and I'll be happy to take the report."

"Thank you. I just can't believe my stuff is gone. I mean, really? I'm at the beach, for God's sake. Who steals from people at the beach?"

Caden peered into the car. "Was the car locked at the time?"

She rolled her eyes. "No. I didn't want to lose my keys on the beach."

*Of course you didn't.* Caden had long ago stopped being surprised by the naïveté of people. "Tourist towns are prime targets for thefts. I'd suggest that you keep your vehicle locked from now on."

He jotted down the license plate number and the make of the vehicle.

"I've been coming to the Cape forever, and there has never been any crime."

Caden scanned the parking lot as she blew off steam, ranting about how little respect people had for others. He spotted Evan and a group of kids unlocking their bikes from the bike rack by the snack bar. He took the report as quickly as he could and wondered how many more would roll in before the end of the evening. Then he went to talk to Evan.

Evan and a handful of friends sat on their bikes, front tires angled toward one another in a circle. Two of the boys carried towels around their necks, and three wore backpacks strapped to their backs. They were all laughing as he approached.

"Evan." The laughter silenced, and Caden sized up the group. They looked to be between fourteen and sixteen—hard to tell at that age. Mike and another boy shifted their eyes away again.

"Hey," Evan said.

*Hey?* Not, *Hey, Dad?* That rubbed Caden the wrong way, but he cut Evan slack again and chalked it up to the whole cool image thing boys went through at his age.

"What's your plan?" Caden asked with a tone that was more serious than he'd have used if Evan were by himself.

Evan shrugged. "We're going to hang out at Bobby's."

Bobby looked over at the sound of his name and nodded. "Hey, Mr. Grant."

"How's it going, Bobby?"

"It's cool," he answered with another nod.

Caden sensed the boys watching him. Thinking of what Kristie had said, he slid the other boys a serious stare followed by a smile.

"I'm Caden's father," he said to two boys he hadn't met.

"I'm Brett," the blond boy said.

"David," the darker-haired boy said.

He picked up on their bouncing legs and glanced at Evan again. Caden was used to kids being nervous around him when he was in uniform, but it had been a very long time since he'd had to evaluate kids he didn't know as friends for his son, and he found himself scrutinizing every twitch.

"Hey, Ev, come talk to me for a minute." He lifted his chin and indicated for Evan to walk with him.

Evan climbed off his bike with a tortured sigh.

Caden waited until they were far enough away from the others to talk to him. He set a narrow-eyed stare on his son to let him know he was serious, but spoke with his normal fatherly tenderness.

"How's it going?"

Evan shrugged. "Fine."

"Did you have fun at the beach?"

"Yeah." Evan watched a girl walk by.

"Ev, I'm in a weird position here. I don't know these guys, but I'm getting a funny vibe. Should I be worried?"

Evan's eyes tracked another bikini-clad girl. "No."

Caden touched his shoulder to draw his eyes to his. "Look me in the eye."

Evan met his gaze; the muscle in his jaw clenched.

"If you tell me these guys are good kids, I'll trust your word, but if they're trouble, you know our deal."

Evan rolled his eyes.

"I want to hear it." He'd drilled a very simple—and in his eyes, freeing—rule into Evan's head since he was a little boy. Through the years, Evan had always lived up to his side of the deal, and Caden had lived up to his side, too.

"Come on, Dad." Evan shifted from one foot to the other.

"Don't *come on, Dad* me. You're going through a big transition with a new town, new school, new friends."

"Exactly. That's why I don't need this shi—stuff."

Caden's gut clenched. He shot a look over his shoulder and didn't like the way the other boys were watching them like hawks. He hated to do it, but he drew upon the deep, fatherly voice he rarely needed to rely on with Evan.

"That's exactly *why* you need this shit. You tell me the deal and that you still respect it, or you can get on that bike and head home. And before you say anything, know that your word is about the only thing that matters. I'm on your side, Ev."

"Yeah, right." Evan kicked at the ground.

He crossed his arms and set an icy stare on his all-too-adolescent son. "Yeah, right? I've never been anything *but* on your side." Caden knew things had been brewing between them for a while, but this was not the time or the place he wanted them to come to a head.

Evan flashed his own icy stare. "If you were on my side, we would have stayed in Boston."

Caden held his stare. He hated this push-pull, and he'd fooled himself into thinking that maybe they'd avoided it altogether. That maybe if he was a good enough dad, they'd make it through Evan's teenage years unscathed. George had warned him enough times that he was living in a dream world with that notion, and he'd brushed off George's comments because George wasn't Caden, and Caden believed that his dedication to Evan would make their relationship different from any other parent-teenager relationship.

Boy, had he been wrong.

"Fine," Evan relented. "The deal is, if I tell you the truth, no matter what it is, you won't punish me, but if I lie or hide the truth, I'll get nailed. Satisfied?"

He hated having to tighten the reins, but the challenge in Evan's eyes told him it was time.

"New rule. Home by ten."

"But—"

"Evan, this isn't a negotiation. Home by ten o'clock. Off the streets and inside someone's home by nine. I want to know where you are at nine, and I want to receive a phone call at ten telling me you're at home, not a text. Got it?"

Evan turned away with his teeth clenched tight. "Yeah, you really trust me."

He took a step away, and Caden grabbed him by the arm. "I do trust you, but I don't know them, and this *new* you, the one who challenges his father? The judgment is still out on him." He took him by the shoulders and leaned down so they were eye to eye. He knew the intimate hold would be a little embarrassing for Evan, but he did it as much to drive home the fact that he loved him no matter what happened between them as he did to let the other boys know that Evan had a father who cared about him. His gut ached at the way Evan's entire body went stiff, and the fire in his son's eyes drove that pain deeper.

"This uncomfortable part of our relationship is new to us both, and I know there are parts of it that you can't control, and there will be parts that I can't control either." He'd sworn he'd never make Evan feel bad about pushing the envelope, and he was finding it a difficult tightrope to walk. "Ev, you don't need to like me, but you do need to know that I love you." He felt the tension in Evan's shoulders ease just a hair and continued with the hope that Evan was really listening. "And I'll be damned if I'm going to ignore what my gut's telling me about these kids. My job is to protect you, so no matter how hard it is for either of us, we'd both better get used to it."

Evan shrugged out of his grasp. "They're my friends, Dad."

"I know. I get it. Let's just make sure they're the right friends."

He watched Evan walk away and felt as though he

was losing him a little more with each step. He questioned again if he'd done the right thing by moving. He'd made it for almost thirteen years on the force without getting killed. Should he have pushed his luck by staying and hoped for the best? It was a question he'd asked himself a million times, and he knew he'd ask it of himself a million more times before Evan came out on the other side of his transition into manhood.

Inside the patrol car, he checked his cell, but still there was nothing from Bella. He called her, and the call went to voice mail. He needed a Bella fix. Forty-eight hours was too damn long to go without seeing her.

He played the conversation with Evan over and over in his mind on the way to Seaside. He was certain he'd done the right thing by flexing a little parental muscle, but it still made the muscles in the back of his neck pinch tight. A thread of guilt tightened inside him. In Boston, time off had meant Caden would have more time to spend with Evan, watching him show off at the skate park or hanging out at the house while he and his friends bopped in and out during the day as they went from one of their houses to the next, doing whatever kids did. Lately, Evan preferred to spend time with his friends instead of his father, and Caden allowed Evan extra time with them because *he* craved time alone with Bella. That guilt had been nagging at him over the last forty-eight hours while he'd been working nights and wishing he could be with her.

He drove up the sloped gravel road into Seaside and parked beside Bella's car in her driveway. He waved to Amy as she came out of the laundry room.

"Aw, no tool belt today?" Amy held a laundry basket against her hip and pulled the laundry room door closed with her free hand.

"I think my chief might have a heart attack if I wore that to work."

She crossed the gravel road. "You obviously have a male boss."

"Very male." Caden looked at her basket. "Do you need help?"

"You're such a gentleman. No, thanks. I've got it. Bella's still at the beach with Jenna. Want me to tell her you came by?" Amy tucked her hair behind her ear.

"Sure. I'll try to come by later while I'm on patrol, but it may not be for a few hours, if I'm able to at all." He noticed that Amy had her bathing suit on beneath her dress. "Why aren't you at the beach?"

"Hey, Caden. How's it going?" Tony waved from the deck of his cottage. His hair was tousled, which seemed a perpetual state for Tony, and it gave him the look of always having just come from the beach, which, by his board shorts and lack of a shirt, Caden imagined he had.

*Just had a run-in with my son, can't find my girlfriend, and I'm sure I'll have three more thefts to deal with tonight. Life is grand.*

"Great. Just stopped by to see if I could catch Bella." Damn, he missed her.

"I was with them at Cahoon, but the sun's really warm today, so I came back to get some things done." Amy shifted the laundry basket to her other hip. "She'll be bummed she missed you, but she had a great day and I know she'll be excited to tell you about it."

"Yeah. I've been texting her, but if she's at Cahoon, she won't get them until she leaves." He ran his hand through his hair and debated driving over to the beach, but the chance of catching her in the parking lot was nearly zero. "Can you just ask her to check her phone?"

"Sure." Amy shifted her eyes to Tony and her cheeks flushed.

The dispatcher's voice came across the radio in his patrol car. "Thanks, Amy. I've got to take this. She can text me, and if I get a break, I'll swing by again." He waved to Tony, took the call, and headed back to Nauset to handle another vehicle break-in report. He had a feeling it was going to be a very long night.

BELLA AND JENNA stayed on the beach long after the sun went down. Her hair whipped across her cheeks, reminding her of the night Caden tied her hair back with fishing line. He was always doing thoughtful things like that—taking care of her in ways that no man had done before. He was different in so many ways from the other men she'd dated, and she realized that she was different when she was around him, too, and even though she wasn't her snarky self, she liked the softer woman she became when she was with him.

Jenna pulled her chair closer to Bella and draped a blanket over their legs. "You look like you're deep in thought."

"Thinking about Caden." She inhaled the cool, salty air, and her mind drifted to Caden's fantasy. Bella had always been adventurous, and she'd never been especially modest. Having sex in places other than the bedroom wasn't new to her—tents, cars...been there done that. Outside, though? That had always carried a trace of danger, but the thought of doing that with Caden didn't feel dangerous at all. Caden wouldn't let them do anything dangerous. Maybe they could find an adventurous, private spot to satisfy his fantasy...

"Aren't you always thinking about Caden?" Jenna wore a sarong draped around her shoulders and it blew behind her like a colorful mane.

"Am I a total loser for tossing away my convictions

so quickly and agreeing to date, aka commit to, Caden?" She had tried to get herself to believe that she might be making a mistake or setting herself up to get hurt, but being with Caden didn't feel anything but right.

Jenna reached for Bella's hand and cupped it between her own. "Bella, Bella, Bella. Haven't you learned anything from me? Convictions are meant to be broken." She reached into her bathing suit top and pulled out three small rocks.

"Jenna." Bella laughed. Ever since they were little girls, Jenna had found creative ways to carry rocks home from the beach. She would put the tiniest of rocks between her gums and her cheek and then forget they were there. Her cleavage was another favorite hiding place, and Jenna's cleavage could hide a boulder.

"I can't help it. I love them." She ran her index finger over a gray-white rock. "They're not perfectly heart shaped, and they're not perfectly gray or white, but look at them." She petted the rocks in her palm. "Can't you just see them on my coffee table beside the big one that looks like an ostrich egg?" Her eyes widened, and she flashed that killer smile of hers and blinked her eyes in rapid succession, the same way she had when she was fifteen and had scored a date with the hottest surfer at the beach.

"Yes. I can totally see it there." Bella leaned her head on Jenna's shoulder. "I needed this time with you. I wish Amy had stayed longer. I've missed spending our days at the beach this summer."

"Me too. But this is all for a good reason, and next summer we'll be back on track with the beach all day and hanging out at night." Jenna gasped. "Oh no."

"What?" Bella scanned the water, thinking that Jenna saw someone in trouble.

"You can't date Caden."

"What?" Bella turned to face her. Jenna's thin brows were drawn together. Her eyes were full of concern. "Why not?"

"Leanna has Kurt, and we see her maybe half as much as we used to. If you and Caden stay together, then next summer we'll only see you half as much." She shook her head. "No, this isn't good. We can't lose you, too."

"You'd never lose me, and we see Leanna a lot. She and Kurt stay at Seaside all the time. I mean, it's different with him around, but you love Kurt. We all do."

"I totally love him, and from what I know of Caden and Evan, I really like them, too, but it's different." Jenna tucked her rocks back into her bathing suit top.

"Yeah. But it's kind of better, too. I'm happy for Leanna. She's never been happier, and you know how much Kurt adores her. He moved from New York to be with her. That's love." Caden had moved from Boston to the Cape for Evan. *That's love, too.*

"I know, but what if you end up with Caden? Amy's cute as a button. She'll get swooped up next. Jamie'll show up here one summer with a computer geek girlfriend, and Tony...Hell, he'll have a harem. Then it's just going to be me, lusting after Pete." She covered her face with her hands. "Oh, God, Bella. I can't be a forty-year-old-woman lusting after Pete."

Bella laughed. "Wow, a little dramatic, aren't we?" She patted Jenna's arm. "You aren't going to be a forty-year-old woman lusting after Pete. He'll be long married by then." She leaned away and Jenna swatted her arm.

"God, I hate you." Jenna feigned a scowl, but her teasing eyes gave her away. "You watch. That man will be mine before I'm thirty-five."

"I should hope so. That gives you five and a half years. If you can't snag your man in that long, then maybe it's time to move on." Jenna had been nursing a crush on Pete for years, but while she was a total extrovert around everyone else, she turned into a mousy introvert around him.

"Bite your tongue."

"Can we get back to me for a minute?" She used her foot to bury Jenna's foot beneath the sand.

"Always." Jenna wiggled her toes free from the mound of sand, and Bella went to work covering her foot again.

"Here's the thing. I'm not worried about dating Caden, and I wonder if that means I'm already not paying enough attention to red flags or something. We're already serious. Super serious. I mean, Jenna, serious like I've-never-been-this-serious-in-my-life type of serious. And what if my house doesn't sell? Then what will I do? What if the job doesn't come through here? What if it does but my house doesn't sell? Then what will I do?"

"The answer to the first question is that I'm not seeing any red flags. I think Tony was right. The guy's been a single dad for fourteen years. He's a committer for sure. As far as the rest goes, you're asking a lot of questions to a woman who isn't holding a margarita."

"You're right. Sorry. That was the big question that I was stressing over." She folded her chair and gathered her belongings. "But if you think I'm seeing clearly, and you know I trust you to not let me fall into some dark man-abyss, then let's go home and we'll fill you up with the good stuff."

"First of all, put that shit down and look at me." Jenna stood with her hands on her hips.

Bella dropped her beach tote and looked at her.

"Here." Jenna pointed to her eyes.

Bella stared into her eyes, and Jenna leaned in so close Bella thought they might bump noses.

"Nope. Those eyes are wide open and wiser than mine will ever be."

"You're such a fool." Bella picked up her tote.

Jenna swung her tote over her shoulder, and they carried their chairs up toward the parking lot. "I say trust your gut with Caden Too-Good-To-Be-True-Grant." Jenna stopped at the bottom of the dune.

"Why'd you stop? Let's go. I want to stop at the package store."

Jenna pointed to the top of the hill, where Caden stood beside his police car.

"Oh my God!" Bella ran up the dune with Jenna laughing as she hurried behind. Bella was out of breath by the time she reached the parking lot. She dropped her tote and ran into his open arms.

"I'm sorry to just show up." He kissed her quickly and shifted his eyes to the people watching them.

"Sorry," she whispered. She cleared her throat. "I forgot you're *at work*, and I'm glad you just showed up." She raked her eyes down his body. She hadn't seen him in uniform since the night they'd met, and damn he looked hot. But Bella wasn't looking at the same things the other women were ogling in the gray evening light. She saw past the six-pack abs and the sculpted body that she knew lay beneath his handsome uniform. She pushed aside the clean-shaven cheeks that she loved to touch and the sense of pure hunky male that he radiated. As she drank him in, she saw the person he was on the inside. The way he loved Evan and would do anything to keep him safe. The way his eyes dampened as he talked about losing his best friend and partner and the way those same expressive eyes never wavered from hers when she spoke. When she added those qualities to his

164

intelligence and the way he touched her, as if bringing her pleasure was what he lived for, well, who on earth could be sexier than Caden Grant?

"Bella." Jenna elbowed her.

Bella startled out of her thoughts. "Oh gosh. Sorry. What are you doing here?"

"I've been trying to reach you all day. Amy said you were here a few hours ago, and when I still couldn't reach you, I got a little worried."

"He worried," Jenna whispered.

"Yeah, I know." Bella glared at her.

"I'm going to put these things in the car. Nice to see you, Caden."

"You too, Jenna," he said, then drew his eyes back to Bella.

"I missed you," she whispered.

"Me too." His eyes darkened.

"It was so nice to spend the day with Jenna that we decided to stay late. Did you get my text?" Bella had to fight the urge to reach out and touch him again. To hold his hand or hook her finger into the waistband of his pants. That hug and peck would have to hold her over until he was off duty.

"Only the one you sent before you went to the clinic. That's why I was worried." He stepped closer and placed his hand on her hip.

*God, I love that.*

Heat spread from beneath his hand across her hips, coiling down low in her belly. Bella forced the lascivious thoughts away for now.

"Sometimes I hate cell phones," she said. "I sent you a text after my meetings. I signed up four more companies today." She went up on her toes to kiss him, then remembered he was at work and bit her lower lip as she sank back down to her heels.

He smiled and tightened his grip on her hip. The

combination told her he wanted to kiss her just as badly. "That's awesome. We should celebrate."

"Well, it's only a third of what I need, but it definitely gives me hope."

He ran his finger down her cheek, then tucked her hair behind her ear. He'd done that a dozen or more times and it still sent a shiver through her.

"I'm so happy for you, Bella. Evan made plans to spend a few hours with Jamie tomorrow. Want to spend the day together? Then go back to my place and have dinner with me and Evan?"

"I would love to." She thought of the last time she'd been at his place. Her cheeks heated with the memory.

"Good. We'll celebrate your success."

She could think of a hundred ways she'd like to celebrate with him when they finally got time alone again, and none of them included food. Unless she counted whipped cream as food. She shook her head to clear her mind.

"How was your day?"

"It was fine." He drew his brows together, and a shadow of worry washed over his face. He was definitely not *fine*.

"I'm sorry if I worried you."

"Oh, babe, it's not you. I just..." He rubbed the back of his neck. "I don't want to bum you out. It's nothing."

She stepped closer. If they'd been alone, she'd have wrapped her arms around him and held him until the tension left him. "Bum me."

"I just had to take a hard line with Evan. It's nothing, really. He got a little too big for his britches. It just sucks that I had to do it." He shrugged, but she read frustration in his eyes.

"I'm sorry. That must be difficult."

"It's not that it's a hard thing to do. It's knowing

166

what can happen if I don't. I see kids getting into trouble all the time, and it was bound to happen at some point, with the move and his age…"

"Teenage angst is like a rite of passage." She reached up to touch his cheek but caught herself and lowered her arm.

He reached for her hand and smiled. "It's a funny thing, isn't it? I want to reach out and touch you, too." His radio sounded from his car. "I'm sorry. I have to run, but I'm glad you're okay."

"Don't worry about me. I'm always okay." She realized that her gut response was one that didn't allow herself to be taken care of, and she also realized that Caden had seen that, too, and he still tried to find a way around it.

"Yeah, well. I'm a cop *and* your boyfriend. It's my job to worry, and I care for you, so worrying about you comes naturally." The radio sounded again, and he pressed a quick peck to her lips. "I have to go. I'm off work tomorrow. Want to spend the day together?"

"More than anything in the world." She didn't even care what they did.

"Great. If I get a break, I'll stop by later. Otherwise, I'll call for sure and we'll make plans."

Jenna drove up just as Caden pulled away. "Ready, lover girl? Or do you want to stand there and swoon a little longer?"

She put her chair and tote in the trunk of Jenna's car and climbed into the passenger seat. "I have a feeling I'll be swooning over that man for a very long time."

"What happened to the girl who was worried about sticking to her convictions?"

Bella leaned her head back and closed her eyes. "A very wise friend told her that convictions were meant to be broken."

## Chapter Twelve

THE NEXT MORNING, Bella was in the shower when she heard Jenna calling for her from the bedroom.

"Bells? Belly? Bella!" Jenna stormed into the bathroom where Bella was showering.

Bella peered out from behind the shower curtain. Jenna wore a red bikini and a pair of cutoffs. She thrust a plate of something that resembled mangled bread toward her. "Good Lord, Jenna. What is so urgent?"

"After seeing you and Caden together at the beach last night, I decided it was time to take action with Pete. He arrives in ten minutes, and I wasn't sure what time you and Caden were leaving. Sorry to barge in."

"No, you're not."

"You're right. I'm not. You don't mind, do you?" She didn't give Bella a chance to answer. "I need you to try this." She shoved the plate closer to Bella.

"I'm all wet." She didn't mind Jenna barging into her bathroom. In fact, the day Jenna stopped treating Bella's house as her own would be a very sad day for her. One that Bella hoped never happened—even when they were old, gray, and saggy. With Leanna and Kurt coming together, and now her and Caden, maybe they needed to think up a sign that they were getting busy inside and not to come in. *Like the proverbial sock on the doorknob.* The thought made her smile.

Jenna scooped up a hunk of whatever it was and shoved it into Bella's mouth. "Pete loves pumpkin, so I made orange pumpkin bread, but I didn't have enough butter or flour, so..." She furrowed her brow. "How is it?"

"Jen..."

Jenna plopped down on the toilet lid. "God. I knew it! I have been baking the damn thing for an hour."

Bella drew the curtain closed and finished showering. "Why don't you just get something from Leanna? She always has good stuff."

"She's at the flea market already, and besides, I really wanted to try to get his attention, you know?" Jenna went to the mirror and brushed her hair, then used Bella's eyelash curler.

"Hand me a towel."

Jenna tossed her one.

"That red bikini will get his attention, Jen." She stepped from the shower and looked at Jenna in the mirror. "Look at you. You're gorgeous, you're smart, you're compassionate, and you're funny. Jenna, you don't need extras. Just be you."

Jenna's shoulders dropped. "I've been being me around Pete for years, and either he's gay or he's just not into me."

Bella ran a comb through her hair. "He's just shy, and when you're around him, you're shy, too. Why don't we have a barbeque and you can invite him? We'll liquor you up, and you'll be yourself again instead of lost in your Petey crush."

"Maybe I should invite him to go with us on the

fishing trip."

Bella shrugged. "Sounds good to me." She went into the bedroom and put on a yellow bikini and a short, sheer, cover-up.

Jenna went into Bella's closet and brought out two pairs of flip-flops—one pale yellow, one light blue—then held them up next to Bella. "Did you and Caden decide where you're going?" She put the yellow flip-flops on the floor, and Bella slid her feet into them.

"The beach." Bella lowered her voice. "He's never done the deed outdoors."

"Bella!" Jenna's eyes widened. "He's a cop. You can't delinquentize him!"

Bella arched a brow. "Says the girl who pretty much eggs me on with every slightly bad thing I ever do."

"That's you, not a cop."

Bella rolled her eyes. "Do you really think I'd suggest that we do anything that could get him in trouble?"

Jenna arched a brow.

"Have some faith. I'll try to behave." *Maybe.*

At the sound of tires on gravel, Jenna looked out the window and gasped.

"He's here."

"Caden?" Bella asked.

"Pete!"

Bella pushed her toward the door. "Go."

Jenna circled back to the bathroom and grabbed the plate. Bella took it from her hands. "Leave that here and go. Try to put together a coherent sentence."

Jenna straightened her bikini top and smiled. "Do I look okay?"

"Crystalline-blue eyes, boobs like Salma Hayek, and an aura of sweet and sexy that could melt ice. I think it's safe to say you're a walking, talking, instant hard-on in a four-eleven package." She hugged her quickly and pushed her out the door. "Talk to him. Practice saying, *Hey, sexy,* on the way down."

Jenna waved a hand behind her as she headed toward Pete's truck, which was parked by the pool. Bella went around her cottage and peeked around the corner, watching Jenna. Jenna was slightly pigeon-toed, with a natural swing to her hips that would have looked like a mockery on anyone else, but it looked sexy and natural on Jenna. She slowed by Tony's driveway and smoothed her hair. *Come on, Jenna. You can do this.* Jenna's shoulder lifted, then fell, as if she'd taken a deep breath.

"Who are we spying on?" Caden's arms wrapped around Bella's waist from behind and he kissed her cheek.

"Jenna's going to invite Pete on the fishing trip." Bella inhaled his minty, citrus, warm scent, and every sexual nerve in her body awoke. "You smell amazing. What is that?"

"Tommy Hilfiger. I figured you might want something different."

She looked over her shoulder and inhaled again. "I always love the way you smell." His skin glistened in the warm sun, and when he bent to kiss her, he closed his eyes. She loved his eyes. They were warm and expressive. She could see what he was feeling in his dark eyes, and when he opened them, they told her that he was exactly where he wanted to be.

"There she goes." Caden nodded toward Jenna.

Pete was in his midthirties, with a body that could stop traffic and a mop of thick brown hair. He had a welcoming smile that could ease a scowl from the devil. He set down his tools and leaned casually against his truck, giving Jenna his full attention. Who wouldn't in that hot red bikini?

"She must be talking, right? He looks like he's listening." Bella's pulse quickened, as much with anticipation of Jenna's potential date as for Caden's close proximity.

"Sure. What's the big deal?" Caden asked.

"You only know the Jenna we all know. She's a pistol, but around Pete, she's a wallflower."

Pete nodded and Jenna's arms went behind her back. She linked her hands together, lifted her shoulders, and kicked at the gravel with one foot.

"He said yes! Oh, I'm so happy for her."

"How do you know?" Caden asked.

"Her body language. That shoulder scrunch was like her happy dance." She turned to face Caden, and without thinking, she hooked her finger into the waist of his bathing suit. He sealed his lips over hers, and for a minute she debated skipping the lake altogether and taking him inside for a day of frolicking in the sheets instead of the sand. She forced herself to push those thoughts away, realizing she'd had to do that an awful lot lately.

"How's Evan?"

"He wasn't thrilled about last night's earlier curfew, but he was fine again this morning."

"One thing you can count on with teenagers is that they're completely inconsistent." Bella headed inside, and they gathered her beach tote, towels, and the lunch she'd packed for them. "I remember what it was like to be that age. I would hear myself say something bitchy to my mom, and it was like I couldn't stop myself if I'd wanted to."

"Yeah? Then the next few years should be fun. You might want to run while you still can." Caden carried the cooler outside, and they packed the truck for an afternoon at the lake.

"If I can teach a classroom of teenagers, I think I

can handle one." They climbed into the truck, and she leaned across the seat and kissed him. "You can't get rid of me that easy."

"Then I'm a lucky man."

BELLA AND CADEN went to Fisherman's Landing, a large lake shaped like a figure eight that wound beneath a bridge and disappeared behind a bank of trees on the other side. A wooded trail led from the parking lot to the beach. There were a handful of rowboats, pedal boats, and kayaks tied to a small dock. The rental kiosk was down the beach to the left. They walked down the narrow stretch of beach in the opposite direction of the boat rentals, past families with small children darting in and out at the water's edge, past the roped-off swimming area, and found a quiet spot at the far side of the beach.

Bella lay on her back in a yellow bikini, which tied at the hips. Her hair spread out like threads of gold around her beautiful face. Caden couldn't stop himself from stealing glances at her. Her eyes were closed, her lips slightly parted, and it was all he could do not to climb on top of her and kiss her until she begged for more.

"I can feel you looking at me." Eyes still closed, Bella smiled.

"Caught me." He leaned up on one elbow and ran his fingers over her stomach. Her skin was soft and warm from the sun.

"That feels nice."

"You're telling me?" Caden glanced behind him to make sure no one had moved closer to them. When he was sure no one could see them, he leaned over and kissed the crest of her breast, just beyond the yellow triangle of stretchy fabric.

"Mm. That felt good, too." She shifted onto her

side, stretched her arm along the blanket, and rested her head on it.

Caden leaned on one elbow and ran his hand along the curve of her hip as it dipped to her waist, then up her ribs. He moved closer, so their bodies were almost touching. The closer he got to Bella, the hotter, and harder, he became.

"You're dangerously sexy, babe," he admitted.

She draped her arm over his waist and pressed her hips to his. "Have you looked in the mirror lately?"

He exhaled a breathy laugh and sealed his mouth to hers. She met his desire with a needful, eager kiss and eased onto her back. Caden slid his leg over her thighs and the skin-to-skin contact spurred him to deepen the kiss.

"Bella," he whispered against her lips, then kissed her again. "I feel like such a letcher around you."

She looked up at him through a sexy haze of desire so thick he had to kiss her again.

"If you're a letcher, then what does that make me?" She ran her fingers up his back and brought her mouth to his shoulder.

Holy hell. The warm, sensual strokes of her tongue on his heated skin nearly did him in. When she drew back, her eyes darkened seductively. A quick sweep of their surroundings confirmed that they were far enough away from anyone else that as long as he kept his back to the other side of the beach, he could tease her right back without being seen.

He slipped a finger beneath the tie on her hip and slid it along the seam of her bikini bottom. The crease of her thigh was warm and inviting, and when she opened her legs for him and narrowed her eyes with a challenging look, his pulse quickened. He leaned down and grazed her lips with his. He'd never done anything like this before—right out in the open—and it amped up the thrill a zillion times. He couldn't resist brushing the damp skin between her legs with his finger.

"You are a naughty, naughty girl, Bella Abbascia." He trapped her lower lip between his teeth and sucked. Heat flared in her eyes.

She wrapped her slender fingers around his wrist and opened her legs further, pressing his fingers against her wetness. He glanced over each shoulder in a way that he hoped was casual, trying to mask the urgency racing through him, and he wondered if the risk they were taking was making this as exciting for her as it was for him. When he met her gaze again, Bella dragged her tongue across her lower lip, leaving it glistening wet, and pulling a groan from his lungs.

"Touch me," she whispered.

"How about you let me lead?" He kissed the corners of her mouth and licked the glistening streak on her lower lip while stroking her into a sea of desire.

"So wet," he whispered against her cheek.

She arched against his hand, pleading for more. He brought his mouth to her neck and kissed a path to her ear.

"You can arch and plead all you want. You're not getting what you want until I'm good and ready," he whispered.

"You're so unfair."

"Am I?" He sucked her earlobe, and her hips bucked against his hand.

"Caden," she said in one long breath.

"I love hearing my name come off your lips like a plea." He dragged his tongue across the crest of her breast, feeling her shudder beneath him. Her breathing hitched, and he knew she was getting close to coming apart. She gripped his wrist, harder this time, and tried to push his fingers inside her.

"Don't worry, babe. I'm not gonna leave you

hanging." He kissed her lips and she opened her mouth, greedily sweeping his mouth with her tongue. He pulled back, now in full tease mode, and pressed featherlight kisses around her lips.

"Un-fair." Her eyes fluttered closed, and her arm drifted to the sand beside her.

Her lips parted as he traced them with his tongue. He stilled his hand between her legs, pressing his fingers against her slippery folds, and used his thumb on her swollen, most sensitive area. She gripped the edge of the blanket and arched her neck back. He covered her mouth with his and took her in a deep, soulful kiss, swallowing the sexy little sounds that she tried so hard to repress as she came apart beneath the heat of the sun. When their lips finally parted, her eyes fluttered open. He withdrew his fingers, grazing her overly sensitive nub and causing her to suck in another breath. She wrapped her arms around his neck and pulled him into another mind-numbing kiss.

"Holy cow, Caden. I've never...you know, without penetration." She closed her eyes for a beat and he touched his forehead to hers.

"Wow," she whispered. "Wow."

*I'm so in love with you.* He silenced the words that ached to be heard with another soft kiss.

BELLA DIDN'T KNOW how long she lay on her back with her eyes closed, trying to quell the desire that snaked through her veins and stole her ability to think clearly, but when she finally opened her eyes, Caden was about fifty pages into a novel. He was perched on his elbows beside her. He squinted against the sun.

"Hey there, beautiful."

"Sorry for zoning out." She rolled onto her side and ran her hand along the muscles that flanked his broad back.

"Don't be. I'll take it as a compliment." He leaned over and kissed her.

"You blew my mind. Literally." She smiled and gazed into his eyes. She could lie right there beside him all day long and be perfectly content. *Happy*, she corrected herself. *Perfectly happy.*

"Can't ask for more than that." He set down his book. "Do you want to rent a boat?"

"Sure."

They walked down the beach hand in hand, and for the first time in a very long time, Bella felt like she was part of a real couple. She'd never felt very connected to Jay, so he'd always felt a little like a friend with benefits. Even with the other guys she'd dated throughout the years, she'd never felt the same deep connection she felt with Caden. Holding his hand wasn't high school exciting. It wasn't a precursor to sex. It was so much more than those things. Holding Caden's hand felt like their lives were joining together and becoming one. She could see herself years from now sitting on the beach reading beside him; she could picture him graying around the temples with crow's feet around his beautiful dark eyes. None of those thoughts were part of her summertime plan, and yet they were there, as real and as present as the man who instilled them.

Caden rowed them out to the middle of the lake. Children's voices drifted farther into the distance, birds flapped as they landed on the water, and Bella soaked in the peaceful moment.

"I kind of like this whole setup." She leaned back and stretched her legs out in front of her, wiggling her toes between Caden's bare feet. "You can row me around anytime you want. You know, if you get bored one day and just feel like being a sexy, shirtless water taxi."

He shook his head, but his smile reached his eyes. "Can I?"

"Uh-huh. I mean, I wouldn't fight it or anything."

Bella spread her towel out on the metal seat and lay horizontally, dangling her toes in the water. Her arms fell limply to her sides, and she closed her eyes. It had been a perfect morning, and now, as the boat moved swiftly through the water, the comfortable silence that had become familiar no longer surprised her.

From behind closed lids, a shadow darkened the sky and the air cooled as, Bella assumed, they passed beneath the bridge. When her closed lids were struck by the blazing sun again, she knew they'd passed through to the other side. The lake was large, and in all the years Bella had been going there, she could count on one hand the number of times she'd seen people go beyond the bridge. She kept her eyes closed and listened for sounds of others. She liked drifting along without knowing exactly where she was, letting Caden make the decisions of where they were headed. She trusted him, and that thought nestled into her heart like a bear bedding down for a long, cold winter.

She heard the sweeping of the oars in the water cease and felt the boat drifting slower. She heard Caden sigh. He sounded as relaxed as she felt, and she wondered what he was doing, but the moment was so blissfully peaceful that she didn't dare open her eyes. The boat rocked, and she sensed Caden's closeness before she felt his mouth on hers. She opened her lips and welcomed his warm, loving kiss. Every stroke of his tongue was deep and sensuous. She kept her eyes closed, relishing the anticipation of not knowing what might come next. She willed her hips to remain still, and when his big hand slid beneath her bikini top, a quiver spiraled in her belly. Her nipples hardened between his index finger and thumb. He kissed her like he was making love to her mouth, and her mind drifted far, far away. When he lowered his mouth to her breast, she gasped and opened her eyes, quickly looking around the empty lake, before he reached up and brushed her lids closed again.

"No one's around. I promise."

She closed her eyes, trusting him completely. The risk heightened the excitement, and she hoped he was feeling the same thrill as she was. He grazed her sensitive nipple with his teeth, and she sucked in another breath. She reached for him, eyes still closed, and felt his hip, then followed the line of it to his firm ass. He moaned, then dragged his tongue between her breasts and whispered against her lips.

"I swear I love more about you than your body. I really do." He kissed her softly, and she opened her mouth and tried to deepen the kiss, but he drew back, teasing her once again. Every sensation magnified with each hot breath as he whispered against her ear, "But I want to be inside you."

She fisted her hand in the fabric of his shorts and licked her lips.

"You know that drives me crazy." He kissed her again, and she opened her mouth wider, trying to take more of him.

His big hands gripped her hips and held on tight as he brought his mouth down to her belly, leaving her panting in his wake. He licked along the edge of her bikini bottom.

"I love how you tremble when I touch you."

*Tremble. Touch. More.*

His hands left a hot trail as they slid up her body and he filled them with her breasts. *Oh God, yes.* She felt his tongue drag along the center of her chest and swirl in the dip of her collarbone. He nibbled the edge of her jaw, bringing her nerves to the surface of her skin. Jesus, he could make her come again without ever entering her. She sensed his face over hers, and she forced her eyes open and met his gaze.

His eyes slid to the water, and the edge of his lips curved up. "Up for a swim?"

*Hell yes.* Her mouth still wasn't working. He sank to his knees beside her and drew her close.

"I don't have a condom," he whispered.

Her heart was beating so hard she was sure he could feel it. She forced herself to speak. "I really am on the pill. I'm not a college girl just looking for sex, or someone who forgets to take the pill religiously and willing to risk a pregnancy."

He touched his forehead to hers. "I know, Bella."

She quieted, letting him make the decision. She wanted to be close to him, to be with him in every sense, and as he contemplated the situation, she was hit with a thought so powerful that it drew her back. She could see herself having a child with him.

"I haven't risked this since Caty." He pressed his hands to her cheeks and gazed into her eyes with the most serious look she'd ever seen on him. Her pulse quickened from the unsureness of what it meant. His jaw clenched, and his eyebrows drew together. His eyes swept over the empty lake. They were alone, so very alone. It felt like they were the only people on earth.

"We don't have to..." she offered.

"I want to, Bella. I want you. I want you in every way possible." He kissed her then, and she couldn't hold back any longer.

She grasped at his shoulder, his back, his hair, whatever she could reach. He was kneeling beside her. She pushed him back on his palms, then pulled the top of his suit down and took him in her mouth.

"Oh, sweet Jesus," he said through gritted teeth.

She swallowed him deep, stroking him with her tongue. He was sweet and salty and hot—*oh so hot.*

"Good Lord, Bella."

His voice was thick with need. Heat seared through her as she placed a hand on either side of him and kissed her way up his body. His chest heaved with every jagged breath.

"Water." A command. Another desirous thrill.

He stepped over the side and reached for her.

"Come to me, baby."

She leaned toward him, and in one swift move, he had her in his arms, the cool water warmed in seconds. He sealed his mouth to hers and kissed her like he needed her in order to breathe. His powerful legs kept them afloat as he pulled the string on one side of her bikini bottom and the fabric fell away, connected only by the thin thread on the other hip. Without missing a beat, still lip to lip, tongues urgently colliding, he pushed down his swim shorts and thrust into her. Bella's head fell back with the force of him. He filled her completely, and as he drove into her, she felt every stimulating inch stroking her into a frenzy of tingling nerves and pulsing need. He grasped the side of the boat for leverage, holding on to her with his other powerful arm.

He tore his lips from hers, breathing hard and holding her tight against him.

"Caden." She paused to catch her breath. *I love you.* "I...I've never done this before. You're my first outside lover."

"I hope to be your last." His eyes darkened, piercing through to her soul, as he thrust in deep and loved them both over the edge.

## Chapter Thirteen

AFTER SPENDING THE afternoon lying on the boat, then dozing beneath the warm sun, Caden thought the urge to tell Bella he loved her might have subsided, or at least lessened to a nag rather than a continuous, all-consuming need he could barely contain. Boy, had he been wrong. He fought the urge to share his feelings with every breath he took. After they arrived back at her cottage, Caden wanted to savor their last moments alone. He still felt a tether of guilt over those thoughts because of Evan, but all it took was one look at the love in Bella's eyes for him to push that guilt aside and bring her hand to his lips.

"Sorry I introduced you into a world of debauchery?" Bella's cheeks pinked up against the tawny glow of her fresh tan.

"Hardly a world of debauchery, and that was my idea, remember?" He leaned across the center console and touched her cheek. "Wait right there." He stepped from the truck and opened her door. Bella shifted in her seat, placing her legs on either side of him. Caden folded her into his arms and breathed in the coconut scent of her suntan lotion.

"Mm," she murmured. "Quite possibly the best Saturday ever."

He drew back and gazed into her eyes. He knew committing to seeing him was a big step for Bella, and hell, it was a big step for him, too. He thought about her as much as he thought of Evan, and he couldn't deny that he cared about her as much, too. But would he scare her off if he admitted it to her? All afternoon he'd tried to gauge her feelings for him, and he thought they were definitely on the same page, but what did he know? He hadn't allowed anyone into his heart for years.

"If you keep looking at me like that, you're going to make me worry," Bella said. "You look like you're debating breaking up with me."

He smiled and touched her cheek. "Just the opposite."

She drew her brows together.

"I think I'm falling in love with you." His feelings didn't tumble or jump from his lips. They came easily, softly spoken and smooth as silk. They were true, so damn true.

In the space of a breath, Bella's eyes widened and her lips curved into a smile. Then her eyes narrowed and she hooked her finger into the waist of his bathing suit. Her lips parted—every second felt like a lifetime as he waited for a response that he could understand.

"Caden," she whispered. Her eyes searched his and her mouth opened, as if she were going to say more; then she trapped her lower lip between her teeth.

He brushed her hair from her shoulder. "I can't help it, babe." His voice refused to speak louder than a whisper, and in this intimate unveiling of his heart, a whisper was all that was needed. She rested her forehead against his chest and wrapped her arms around him. Caden stroked her hair, wishing she'd say more—and wondering if he'd made a mistake by saying as much as he had.

Bella lifted her head at the sound of Vera's violin. He repressed the heartache brewing inside of him in an effort to give Bella whatever space she needed to digest his words. When she finally looked up at him again, he still couldn't read her thoughts.

It took every iota of his strength to step back and give her physical space as well as emotional room to think.

"I guess I'd better get Evan."

"Caden." She reached for his hand and drew him close again. "I feel it, too, but I'm scared. What if I don't get a job here? What if my house doesn't sell? My real estate agent left a message and I haven't checked it yet. What if I have to move back to Connecticut because it doesn't sell?"

He knew her well enough to sense that what she was really worried about wasn't any of those things. He also knew her well enough to know that she might not want to admit the truth, but he had to try to get her to open up to him. At least to the idea of them.

"What if I lie to you?" he whispered. "What if I hurt you? Isn't that what you really mean?"

She shifted her eyes away.

"Bella, I understand. Take all the time you need. Take years if you need it. One day you'll see who I am and understand that I don't take commitments lightly."

"I know that." She tightened her grip on his hand. "I feel the same way you do. When I'm with you, everything feels right." She pressed her lips together and her eyes grew serious. "Know what scares me the most? When I'm with you, I let myself be vulnerable, and if you know me, you know I'm anything but vulnerable."

"Bella..."

"Let me finish, because this is hard to admit out loud. If any other man had said they wanted to put locks on my doors and windows, I'd have sent them away. If they showed up at the beach when I was there with my friends just to make sure I was okay, I'd have thought they were too possessive and found excuses to distance myself from them. If they—"

Caden ran his hand through his hair and blew out a loud breath. "So, basically you're saying that I've done everything wrong."

"No," she said quietly. "You've done everything right, Caden, and for the first time in my life, I've allowed myself to let someone do those things."

"Okay, now you're confusing me. So that's a bad thing?"

"Yes, that's a bad thing." She held her hands up as if she were making total sense, and for the life of him, Caden had no clue why. Nothing she was saying made any sense to him. "Don't you see?" she pleaded.

"Treat me like a student and walk me through it, because honestly, no. I'm completely at a loss. Isn't it good that you feel comfortable enough with me to allow me to do those things?"

"Yes. It's a good thing, but it's like standing on a street corner naked and waiting for the guy you're dating to drive by—and every time he does, you wonder if he's going to throw tomatoes or whistle."

She nodded again, as if she were making sense. She probably was, but not in man-speak.

"Come again?"

"*Ugh!* Okay. Listen carefully. This morning I noticed that there was a loose board on my deck, and my first thought was, *Oh, Caden can fix that for me.*"

"Sure. I'm happy to." He never considered himself a complete novice in the world of women, but now he was having his doubts.

"That's just it. I know you will, and before you, I'd have thought, *Let me get my hammer.*" She held her palms up again. "See the issue? With you I let myself be a...a..."

"Girlfriend?"

"A *girl.*"

He couldn't stifle a laugh. "Sorry, but uh, if you weren't a girl, then you and I would definitely never happen."

"*Tsk.*" She playfully pushed his chest and smiled. "A weak girly girl. I left that girl behind in high school, and I worked really hard to become a woman who could be completely self-sufficient. But I'm so darn comfortable with you that I let you do things I can— *and should*—do myself."

He did the only thing he could do. He wrapped her in his arms.

"Bella, Bella, Bella. It's okay to be a girly girl. In fact, I love your strong, efficient side as much as your girly girl side. What's the worst that happens? You let me do a few things you can do on your own, and in return I let you lead me down a path of allowing myself to have a life separate from my son?"

"Yes." She smiled up at him. "That's exactly it. Then if you hurt me, I have to get used to doing all those things again."

"And if you break up with me? I'd have had a taste of life with you, and after being with you, there's no going back. So we're in the same boat." He kissed her lips and felt her smile. "This would have been a lot easier if you'd just said that you feel the same way but you're afraid of becoming too reliant on me."

She jumped from the truck. "That's what I did

say."

Caden shook his head to try to clear his confusion.

"Just to be sure I understand. You *are* falling for me? And it's okay if I do things for you and treat you like a girly girl sometimes? Or should I not fix the deck and bring you flowers?"

She grabbed her tote from the back of the truck and swung it over her shoulder. "Falling for you, *check*. Bring me flowers, *check*. Fix my deck?" She went up on tiptoes and kissed the dimple in his chin. "You're the first guy who picked up on my love of pink. You can fix my damn deck as long as you know I'm completely capable of doing it myself."

"Has anyone ever told you that you're a challenge?" He took the tote from her arm and carried it to the deck.

"No," she said as she unlocked the door. "They usually call me a pain in the ass."

"Well, there is that, but a welcome pain with a fine ass."

## Chapter Fourteen

BELLA MADE PASTA salad and brownies to bring to Caden's for dinner, and when violin music weaved its way into her window, she decided to bring a few brownies to Jamie and Vera for being so nice to Evan. She found them on their deck. Jamie had a cocktail in one hand, and his other hand tapped a beat on the glass table. Vera smiled and continued playing.

"I thought I smelled something delicious. I figured Leanna was baking," Jamie said. He pulled out a chair for Bella.

"I only have a sec. I'm on my way to Caden's for dinner, but I wanted to bring these by and say thank you for letting Evan hang out with you." She set the plate on the table.

Jamie looked relaxed in a pair of shorts and a loose cotton shirt. He didn't shave on the weekends because, *It makes me feel like I'm really on vacation.*

"He's an interesting kid. He's smart as a whip, but I get the feeling he's struggling a little," Jamie said.

Bella heard what he said through teacher's ears and lowered herself into the chair. She knew that it was often outsiders—teachers, coaches, neighbors— who picked up on issues with teenagers before their parents did.

"Caden said he's going through a teenage phase. I hope he wasn't rude to you or Vera."

Vera stopped playing and laid the violin in her lap.

"That was beautiful, Vera," Bella said.

"Thank you, dear." Vera turned her attention to Jamie. "I wonder, Jamie, what did you see with Evan? He seems like a very pleasant young man, and he's shown quite an interest in what you are teaching him. He seems to enjoy listening to me play as well."

"He is a really nice kid. He just seemed distracted today. He was texting a lot more than he did last time, and I could see that he was struggling to give me his full attention." Jamie sipped his drink. "Can I get you a drink?"

"No. I'm okay, thanks. I think most teenagers feel like they need to be plugged in twenty-four seven or they'll miss something. And he's just made new friends, so that might be part of it. I'll have Caden talk to him. I don't want him to be rude to you." She made a mental note to speak to Caden about Evan's phone etiquette.

"No, you don't need to do that. I actually really enjoy teaching him. Last winter a buddy and I taught a workshop to a dozen or so teenagers. Even when Evan's not fully tuned in, he's more engaged than most kids when they're paying full attention, and he's respectful, which I appreciate. Especially with Gram."

Vera patted his hand.

"Are you coming into town to go fishing with us, or do you have to work?" Bella asked.

"We're both going," Jamie answered. "I took off work to go. I can't miss out on all the fun."

"This will be like old times," Bella said. "With the

addition of Kurt, Caden, and Evan. I guess we'll need a bigger boat."

"Don't forget Pete. Jenna said he's coming, too." Jamie nodded with a grin that said, *She might just reel him in after all.*

"Should be a great time."

"I feel so blessed to see each of you grow up," Vera said. She patted Jamie's hand again. "If only we could find a nice woman for Jamie to settle down with."

"Gram, please. I think I can find my own woman." He smiled at Vera.

"Bella, I'd like to attend your wedding before my old heart decides to retire," Vera said.

"You'll live for another fifteen years, which gives me plenty of time," Jamie assured her.

"Don't worry, Vera." Bella rose to her feet and placed her hands on Jamie's shoulders. "Look at how cute this guy is. He's smart, sweet, and he likes kids. If worse comes to worst, you and I will set up an online dating profile and you can handpick his woman."

Jamie covered Bella's hands with his and looked up at her. "Paybacks are hell. Just keep that in mind."

Bella ruffled his hair. "I'll remember that. Have you guys seen Amy? I wanted to tell her something. Her car's here, but I can't find her anywhere."

"She and Tony went into town to get stuff for a barbecue." Jamie wrinkled his brow. "Want me to tell her whatever it is?"

"Nah. I'll catch her when I get back tonight. Thanks."

An hour later, Bella was sitting with Caden and Evan eating dinner on their back deck. The yard was lined with pitch pine trees, and the deck ran the length of the house. It was quiet, save for the music filtering through the screened doors that led to the living room. A cool breeze swept across Bella's toes. She'd worn jeans and a hoodie in anticipation of the cool evening, but she fought the idea of wearing close-toed shoes in the summer.

"This was delicious, Caden. Thank you for cooking." He'd made a shrimp and rice dish that, like him, was just the right amount of spicy and sweet.

"Dad's a pretty good cook." Evan didn't look up from the text message he was typing on his phone.

Caden draped an arm across the back of Bella's chair. "Can't live on chicken nuggets and fries forever." He patted his stomach.

"I could, but you won't let me." Evan glanced up at Caden from beneath his thick bangs.

"Old fight, different town." Caden shifted his eyes to Bella. "Evan had a few friends in Boston who ate fast food for lunch and dinner most days. Being the odd man out was tough sometimes, but I didn't want him eating that garbage all the time."

"I think that's nice," she said. "You're lucky, Evan. Think about what it would be like if your dad was an awful cook."

Evan shoved his phone in his pocket and shrugged. Bella noticed he wasn't nearly as engaged as he'd been at the barbeque, and as Evan withdrew his phone from his pocket again and Caden sighed, she knew she didn't have to mention Jamie's concerns.

"Ev, how about you give the texting a rest for a while?"

Evan continued texting.

The muscle in Caden's jaw jumped. "Ev," he said in a stern voice.

Evan sighed, finished texting, and shoved the phone back in his pocket.

"Thank you." Caden smiled, but Bella could see that it was forced, and she tried to ease the thickening tension.

"I saw you riding your bike out of Payton's Campground the other day. Do you have friends staying there?"

"Payton's?" Evan squinted and shook his head, as if he had no idea what she was talking about.

"Yeah. The campground behind our development? I took the back road home the other day, and you and your friends flew out of there on your bikes, or at least I thought it was you." She smiled at Caden, but it was wasted. His eyes were locked on Evan. "It brought back memories of riding our bikes to the beach when we were younger. It's one of the most fun things I remember about summers here. There were times me, Jenna, Amy, and Leanna would leave Seaside in the mornings and not come back until dinnertime."

Evan shook his head and fiddled with the arm of his chair. "I wasn't at a campground. It must have been someone else."

"Payton's had a break-in the other day." Caden pulled his arm from Bella's chair and turned his attention to Evan.

Bella felt the heat of his scrutiny and she wasn't even the focus of it.

Evan shrugged again, and when he met his father's gaze, his eyes were cold, his voice serious. "Like I said, I don't even know the place. Can I be excused? My friends are all online, and I want to play a game with them."

"Don't you want to stay and visit a few minutes?" Caden asked.

Evan rolled his eyes, and Bella set her hand on Caden's tense thigh.

"It's okay. He'll have more fun playing with his friends than entertaining me."

Evan lifted hopeful eyes to Caden.

"Fine. You're right. Go ahead, buddy, but take your

193

dishes inside."

Evan gathered his dishes, and before he walked inside, he turned back to Bella and Caden. "Thanks for dinner, Dad. Bella, I'm glad you're here, and thanks for introducing me to Jamie. He's cool."

After Evan went inside, Bella leaned closer to Caden and said, "Breathe, Dad."

Caden shook his head. "Jeez. It's like he changed overnight, isn't it?"

"He's making friends, settling in."

"I hope that's all it is. What made you think it was him coming out of Payton's?" His voice was serious again.

She shrugged. "It looked like him, but kids all look alike these days. Shaggy hair, shorts, T-shirts. He said it wasn't him, so obviously I was wrong." *I hope I was wrong, given his reaction.*

Caden nodded, but she could tell he was chewing on the information.

"You're worried?"

He shifted her chair so her knees were between his legs. "Not really. I trust Evan."

"I know I draw on what my mom said a lot, but she used to say that when you have children, you teach them right from wrong, giving them the tools they need to make good decisions, but you can't force them down the right path." She leaned forward, and he met her halfway, so they were eye to eye. "Then all you can do is hope they do the right thing."

He kissed her and smiled. "She's right, but the fatal flaw in that thinking is that you only know if they've made the wrong decision after they've already made it. That's the part that's hard to swallow. I spent my life taking care of Evan. Now my job is the same, to keep him safe, but it's hindered by a teenage attitude."

"Oh yes, that fine line between boy and man."

"It would be easier if we hadn't moved. I knew his friends, and they were good kids. Here the kids are a mystery to me. I saw them in town, and then again at the beach the other day, and the kids were, I don't know, rougher, maybe. Hardened in a way that his old friends weren't."

Bella leaned back in her chair. "Well, this *is* a tourist town, so I'd imagine that the kids who live here year-round probably spend summers the way I did. I was always with a pack of friends, riding bikes from one place to the next. It wasn't the ocean breeze that blew through my hair at that age. It was newfound freedom. I had a bike, a new teenage body, and friends who wanted to have fun. Life was good. And what makes it even better for kids who live here year-round is that a new crop of hot girls or guys arrive weekly."

Caden rose and began clearing the table. "Let's not go there. I'm still getting used to him wanting to text someone more than he wants to hang with me."

"Maybe it's me he doesn't want to hang with. It's an adjustment for him to have to share you."

"It's not you. He told me he likes you, and that you're..." Caden arched a brow. "*Hot.*"

Bella smiled as she carried the dishes inside. "At least you know the boy has good taste."

"Christ." Caden followed her inside. "He saw that picture you sent in your sexy little nightie and boots."

Bella gasped. "Oh my God. He did not."

"Sure did. But he decided you were hot before that."

She fisted her hands in his shirt and buried her face in his chest. "I'm so sorry. I'll be more careful."

"It didn't seem to faze him. He just asked if we were dating." Caden lifted her chin and kissed her. "I'm so glad we are."

"Mm. Me too. I'm sorry about being so wishy-washy today. I'm definitely falling for you and Evan."

Caden narrowed his eyes. "Me *and* Evan?"

"You're a package deal. How could I fall for you and not him?"

"He's not easy to fall for at the moment," Caden said with a serious tone. "But you couldn't have made me happier than you did by including him."

"He's just being a teenager, and besides, I've seen flashes from the non-testosterone zone, and I like them. He's not going to be a teenager forever. I would like to spend time with him, though. I can't just monopolize you."

"I think at the moment he's happy to let you monopolize me." He kissed her again. "When we first moved here, we went surf fishing a lot. We'd get up at five o'clock in the morning, some days before school, and last night when I asked him if he wanted to go this morning, he said, *Get up at five? No way.*"

"That doesn't mean he doesn't want to spend time with you. It means he's realizing that he can be separate from you. He can sleep later and go out and have as much fun with his friends as he would with you. He's cutting the umbilical cord."

Caden leaned against the sink and folded her into his arms. "Like I said, I get it. It's just not easy. He'll always be my number one responsibility, and I'm not giving that up because he wants some freedom."

"You shouldn't give it up. Just don't take it personally."

"What are you up for? Want to go for a walk? Watch a movie? Sit outside and count the stars?"

Evan burst from his bedroom mumbling under his breath. He stormed out the back doors and paced the yard.

Caden stepped toward the door, and Bella grabbed his arm. "Don't you want to let him blow off steam first?"

His concerned eyes locked on Evan, then shifted to her, then back to Evan. "He never storms off."

"If you follow him, won't he just snap at you?" Bella felt Caden's muscles tense.

Caden shrugged from her grasp. "Let him snap."

Her heart went out to Caden as he stalked out the door. She knew all he wanted to do was fix whatever had sent Evan into a tizzy. If Evan was anything like the teenagers she knew, when Caden asked Evan what was wrong, Evan would snap, *Nothing*, in a spiteful way that would cut Caden to his core, when really, whatever had sent Evan storming outside felt bigger than life in his teenage mind.

She went into the living room and sat down on the couch, debating whether she should leave and give them time alone. She didn't hear any yelling, which she took as a good sign. After twenty minutes, Bella began to wonder again if she should leave. She went in search of Caden so she could bow out of the evening politely. She found them sitting on the steps of the deck with their backs to her, both leaning their elbows on their legs. Evan's narrow shoulders and waist looked even smaller beside Caden's broad body. Bella hesitated by the screen door, unsure if she should interrupt them. She didn't want to leave without saying anything, and simply by being there she knew she was putting added pressure on Caden to return to her.

She opened the screen door, and they both glanced over their shoulders. Evan's eyes were hidden beneath his hair. Caden's were dark and serious.

"Hey." She hoped she sounded casual. "I think I'll take off."

"Bella, stay." Caden came to her side.

"You don't have to leave," Evan said from the

steps.

She had no idea if she should leave or stay. They both sounded sincere, but she didn't want to take Caden's attention away from Evan when he needed him most.

"I'm sorry," Caden said.

He might have wanted her to stay, but she knew that a bigger part of him needed time alone with Evan.

"It's okay. Evan needs you more than I do right now. Thanks for dinner. It was amazing."

He touched his forehead to hers. "I'm sorry, babe," he whispered.

"Don't be. I'm a big girl. Besides, I had you all to myself today." She kissed him and felt his disappointment tangle with hers on the way out the door.

## Chapter Fifteen

BELLA PULLED INTO Seaside still nursing her disappointment. She was happy to see everyone hanging around the fire pit in the quad. She could use a few laughs.

"Bella! Tony made Talking Monkeys." Jenna hurried over to Bella with Pepper on her heels. She looked like a teenager in her purple hooded sweatshirt, jeans rolled up at the ankles, and purple flip-flops. "Where's your man?" She looped her arm into Bella's and pulled her across the grass.

Pepper clawed at Bella's legs, and she knelt to pet him. He rolled onto his back and Bella scratched his belly.

"Evan needed a little daddy time."

"Well, good." Jenna touched Bella's back with her knee. "I needed a little Bella time."

"That's why I love you." Bella kissed Pepper's fluffy head and rose to her feet.

"C'mon, Pep." Kurt's stern voice had Pepper bounding back to him.

"Remember when he used to sneer at Pepper?"

Jenna whispered.

"Love changes everything." *Everything is an understatement.*

"How'd it go today?" Jenna's eyebrows jumped. "Did you break him of his goody-two-shoes ways?"

Bella laughed. "Actually, I think it was the other way around."

Jenna's eyes widened. "Yeah? Mr. Straitlaced Sexy Uniform has a bad-boy side?"

Amy jumped up, sending her chair to the ground. "Bells!" She was wearing a pair of flannel pajama pants and a long sleeved T-shirt and ran with her arms open wide, nearly toppling Bella over when she fell against her.

Amy stumbled back a few steps, and Tony caught her in one strong arm. She swayed on her feet and ran her finger along Tony's chin. "Well, helloooo there, sexy."

"Okay. I think I'd better take our little girl home." Tony wrapped an arm around Amy's shoulder, and she melted against his side.

"Holy crap, Jen. You let her get two sheets to the wind?" Bella glared at Jenna.

"Hey, it's Tony and his Talking Monkeys." Jenna poked Tony's side. "We were just hanging around eating dinner, and he came out with a couple pitchers and, well, you know Amy and drinks that taste like candy."

"I'm taking care of her, aren't I?" Tony scooped Amy into his arms. She wrapped her arms around his neck, closed her eyes, and sighed.

"She's going to hate us if we let you carry her home." Bella put her hands on her hips and shook her head. "Jenna? What's the vote? Let him bring her home and we tuck her in?"

Amy patted Tony's chest. "Sexy man can tuck me

in."

Tony shrugged, and the right side of his mouth quirked up.

Bella poked his chest as she spoke. "Tony Black, if you take advantage of this situation, I swear I will cut your balls off in your sleep."

Tony looked down at her finger and shook his head. "I didn't take advantage when she *wanted* me to. Do you really think I'd take advantage of her now?" He disappeared into the darkness between Vera and Leanna's cottages with Amy safely in his arms.

"Do you think that means he's never going to be interested in Amy in that way?" Jenna asked.

Bella sighed. "I'm not sure, but she's going to be furious with herself, and with us. And I really wanted to go chunky-dunking tonight." Chunky-dunking is what Bella and her friends called skinny-dipping.

"We can still chunky-dunk. We'll get Leanna, and the three of us will enjoy a little moonlight nakedness." Jenna dragged her over to the fire, where Leanna and Kurt were cuddling on a bench, kissing between whispers.

Just watching them kiss made her long to be cuddled up in Caden's arms, kissing his lips, smelling his masculine scent. God, how could she miss him so much already?

"Good evening, smoocheroos," she said to Leanna and Kurt.

Leanna rested her head on Kurt's shoulder, turning the knot of longing in Bella's stomach a little tighter.

"You're back early," Leanna said.

Bella shrugged. She wasn't in the mood to talk about her date being cut short.

Jamie sat in a beach chair on the other side of the fire, wearing a pair of faded Levi's and a sweatshirt. He used his bare feet to push a chair toward Bella. The fire reflected in his dark eyes as he handed her his plastic wineglass full of Talking Monkey.

"How's it going, blondie?" Jamie asked.

She didn't know why she thought she'd keep the night's happenings to herself. She wasn't very good at it, and if she didn't answer, then her friends would think something awful was going on. She guzzled Jamie's drink.

"Damn, that is good. Let's see...Poor Ev had a teenage moment tonight, so I'm here instead of kissing my hunky boyfriend. Amy's being tucked into bed by her dreamboat, but she's too shnockered to realize it, and I can't go chunky-dunking tonight because Amy will be *really* upset if she misses out on both Tony *and* our midnight sneak into the pool."

"Speaking of which, anyone seen Theresa?" Bella asked. She shifted her eyes away from Leanna and Kurt as they nuzzled against each other's cheeks.

"Yeah. She's in bed." Jamie nodded toward her house. "She reminded us to put out the fire, yadda, yadda, and turned in."

She took another sip of Jamie's drink and handed it back to him. "One day we'll have to drag her butt out here to join us. I think she has a side that we haven't seen yet."

"We'll liquor her up," Jenna suggested.

"We'd have to sneak it into her. She never drinks, and I would worry about slipping anything to anyone, so we'll have to find another way to loosen her up. We'll think of something. Did you guys have fun tonight?"

"Always," Jamie said. "Kurt read us the first chapter of his new manuscript, *Deadly Thoughts*."

"Ugh. I can't believe I missed that."

Kurt pulled his lips from Leanna's long enough to

respond. "Don't sweat it. I'll let you and Caden read it anytime you want."

She loved how her friends included Caden as one of their group.

"Thanks, Kurt. Did Leanna tell you about how well the new pitch worked? I have three new signups, and I'm meeting with the school board this week. I think I might just be able to pull this off after all. Now, if only my house would sell." She'd checked her message from the Realtor, and she was hopeful about the three showings she had scheduled this week.

"Fantastic." Kurt reached down and petted Pepper. "I guess if you and Caden decide you're really serious, then you'll definitely want to be here. If that's not motivation, I don't know what is."

"I think we're pretty serious." She grabbed Jamie's drink and finished it, hoping it would quell the ache of missing Caden. Jenna dragged her chair next to Bella's, and Bella took her drink and finished it, too.

"Where's the pitcher?" Bella asked.

"Why? Do you want Tony to carry you to bed, too?" Jenna asked.

"I like him, Bella. I'm glad for you. He seems like a good guy," Kurt said.

"Thanks. I think so, too, Kurt."

Jenna spun around and looked in the direction of Amy's cottage. "Why isn't Tony back yet?"

"As a matter of fact..." Bella grabbed Jenna's hand and dragged her to her feet. "You're coming with me. You should have been watching out for her."

Jenna hurried along beside her. "What are you doing? If she is with him, you can't barge in there."

"He's not going to be with her in *that* way. It's Tony, for heaven's sake. But what if she's puking? She would be mortified if he saw her like that." Bella slid open Amy's glass door. The cottage was silent. Bella and Jenna tiptoed into the bedroom clutching each other's hand.

"Oh my God," Jenna whispered.

"Shh." Tony held a finger to his lips. He was sitting on Amy's bed with his back propped against the headboard and Amy snuggled beneath his arm. Her hair was in a ponytail, and she looked a little green.

"What happened?" Jenna lifted her knees up high as she tiptoed overdramatically around the bed.

"She got a little sick, so I pulled her hair up. Every time she lay down, she felt sick again." Tony shrugged.

Bella's heart melted. He was so compassionate, but come morning, if Amy remembered that he'd taken care of her, she'd want to run away as far and as fast as she could.

"We'll take it from here. Thanks, Tony. It was so nice of you to stay with her." Bella climbed onto the bed. "And if by the grace of God she doesn't remember you taking care of her when she wakes up in the morning, you have to promise to take this to your grave."

"I hear you cut off people's balls. I'll never tell a soul." He kissed Amy's forehead and held her up while Jenna climbed into his spot. With Bella on her other side, they wedged Amy between them. "I'll get you guys her barf bowl just in case."

Tony went into the other room, and over Amy's head, Jenna mouthed, *Barf bowl?* Bella shrugged.

Tony came back with a big plastic bowl that Amy kept on top of her refrigerator and set it on the bed next to Bella. Bella turned it over in her hands. She'd never known Amy to throw up in this particular bowl, but Tony having tied back Amy's hair and designating the bowl as a barf bowl were such compassionate gestures that she went along with it.

"Thanks, Tony."

"If you need me, you know where I live. Take good care of her." He looked thoughtfully at Amy before leaving through the sliding glass door.

"What was *that* all about?" Jenna whispered.

Bella shrugged and brushed Amy's hair from her forehead. "Look at her. How can he not fall for her? It kind of pisses me off, actually. She's everything a man could want. Why can't he see that?"

"Because he's all a woman could want. Why would he ever tie himself down to *one* woman?" Jenna leaned back and kicked off her flip-flops. "Besides," she whispered. "She can't get hooked up with a man before me. I'll be all alone, and I hate that."

Bella sighed and reached for Jenna's hand. "We'll always have each other." The comfort she took in knowing her friends would always be there was exactly the comfort she knew Evan drew from his father. She closed her eyes, and the disappointment she'd felt earlier in the night subsided.

"Jenna?"

"Yeah?"

"I feel a little guilty because when Evan needed Caden, I was bummed to lose out on spending time with him."

Jenna squeezed her hand. "That's okay, sweetie. That's because you care. If you weren't bummed, it would be a bad sign."

"But it was a selfish thought. Of all people, I know how much teenagers need their parents, and I'd never want to come between them."

"Bella, honey, you weren't competing for Caden's attention or trying to take him away from Evan. You have to honor your feelings of missing the man you're involved with and separate that from the rest. There's no guilt involved with missing someone. I would bet that Caden's feeling the same way."

She smiled to herself. "Yeah, you're probably right. I wasn't mad or anything, just a little sad to leave."

"It's okay, Bell. Close your eyes. Barfy here will be up every hour."

Bella curled onto her side and draped an arm over Amy. "I hope she doesn't remember how she got here."

Jenna curled around Amy's other side. "I hope you guys still make time for me when you're both in serious relationships and I'm alone."

They heard the sliding glass door open and then close. Leanna peeked into the bedroom. "Do you have room for one more?" she whispered. "I miss you guys." She climbed onto the bed behind Bella.

"What about your man?" Jenna asked.

"My man knows how important you guys are to me. He loves me no matter where I sleep." She draped her arm over Bella.

"We do, too," Bella said. "You guys?"

"Hm," they mumbled in unison.

"I think I love Caden."

"We know," they said at the same time.

"We do, too," Jenna said. "He makes you too happy for us not to, even if I'm green with jealousy."

Bella drifted off to sleep, feeling safe and happy and on the right track.

# Chapter Sixteen

CADEN RAN AT a fast pace along the beach. It was only six o'clock Sunday morning, far too early to call Bella, but he'd been up half the night worrying about Evan—and his relationship with Bella—and he needed to blow off some energy. Evan hadn't given him any insight into what was bugging him beyond having played a PC game *with a group of assholes.* He'd tried to get Evan to open up more, but Evan had clammed up, and Caden didn't press the issue. He was glad Evan had told him as much as he did. They'd watched *The Replacements,* and by the time Evan went to bed, he seemed more like himself again. It had been a while since they'd spent any quality time together, and he realized that as Evan spread his wings of freedom, the opportunities to spend time together would become few and far between.

Caden felt horrible about Bella leaving early, and he'd called her before he'd turned in for the night, but he still hadn't heard back from her, which made him worry that she was upset about their evening being cut short.

Bella's comment about Evan not wanting to share him had also nagged at Caden. He'd asked Evan last night if he had an issue with him dating Bella, and Evan had been adamant about being fine with it. He'd gone so far as to say he was glad Caden was finally *getting a life* and that Bella was *cool*. But Caden couldn't help worrying that adding his relationship with Bella to Evan's list of stresses—moving from Boston, having to make new friends, going to a new school—might be too much. That reality cut like a knife, and rather than contemplate what it would mean and what the remedy might be if it *were* too much, he pushed the awful feeling away.

As he headed home, feeling no less confused than he had at the beginning of his run, the sun burned through the gray morning and smiled down on the beach with a promise of a glorious day. Caden could think of a hundred things he wanted to do with Bella today, and the truth was, even if they did nothing at all, it would be more than enough.

BELLA AWOKE TO the smell of eggs and coffee Sunday morning. Amy was sprawled across the center of the bed with her arms and legs splayed as if she'd fallen face-first and hadn't moved since. Jenna was curled up along the headboard hugging a pillow, and Bella was so close to the edge of the bed that if she rolled over she'd tumble to the floor. How many mornings had they awoken in a similar fashion since they were little girls? Bella smiled at the familiar scene.

She padded softly out of the bedroom and was not surprised to find Amy's counters covered with flour, sugar, eggshells, and other accoutrements of Leanna's morning meal. Bella was greeted by the homey scent of warm baked goods. She put her arm around Leanna, who was busy cooking omelets.

"I think I love you."

Leanna smiled. Her hair was still damp from a shower, and she smelled of soap and floral shampoo. "Because I'm messing up Amy's kitchen instead of yours?"

"No. Maybe," Bella teased.

Leanna pulled a tray of muffins from the oven.

"You are a goddess. I hope you know that." Bella reached for a muffin, and Leanna slapped her hand. "I take it back. Meanie."

Leanna laughed. "Can you get the jams from the fridge?" She put the muffins on a decorative plate. "Kurt's down at the bay running, but he should be back soon. I thought we could eat out on the deck."

Bella tried to sneak a crumb from the pan, and Leanna pointed a finger at her.

"Okay, June Cleaver," Bella teased.

Jenna came out of the bedroom with her hair askew, blinking the sleep from her eyes. "Something smells delicious."

Bella pointed to the muffins, and Jenna reached for one. She got slapped, too.

"Aw, come on, Mom. Just a taste?" Jenna stuck out her lower lip.

"You guys always eat the tops and leave the rest. Can't you wait just until Kurt comes back? Then you can tear them apart." Leanna carried the muffins outside.

As soon as she was outside, Jenna turned to Bella. "She slapped my hand."

"Mine, too. She just wants to do something nice for Kurt." Bella grabbed coffee cups and plates, wishing she had woken up in Caden's arms and made him coffee and muffins. She wondered what he was doing and how things had gone with Evan.

Jenna snagged jam and butter from the

refrigerator, then gathered utensils and napkins. They brought everything to the table on the deck in front of the cottage, and Jenna went back in to check on Amy. She came back out with the coffeepot and creamer.

"Sleeping Beauty is totally zonked." Jenna poured coffee for each of them. "Where's Pepper?"

"Kurt took him with him on his run. I'll get sugar." Leanna went inside and returned a few minutes later. "I slept like a baby last night. Did Amy get up at all?"

"Not that I remember," Bella said as she fixed her coffee.

"She kept grabbing my boob in her sleep and mumbling." Jenna pulled off her sweatshirt from the night before. She tugged at the tank top she had on beneath.

"There wasn't much room. It's not like she could avoid them," Bella teased.

Jenna put her hands under her boobs and pushed them up. "Jealousy will get you nowhere."

*Speaking of jealousy...*Seeing Leanna and Kurt last night had twisted all sorts of jealous twines in Bella's stomach. She knew she'd done the right thing by leaving Caden and Evan alone, but that didn't stop her from *wanting* to be with them.

Jenna leaned across the table and squeezed Bella's hand. "Your face is all pinched, so either you need to get laid or you need to get something off your chest, and given that you and Officer Hottie nipped that first one in the bud, what's going on?"

Bella sighed and shook her head. "It's nothing."

"I wasn't going to say anything, but I noticed it, too." Leanna kicked her feet up on the chair beside her. "And you'd better spill soon. I have to be at the flea market early today."

"By early you can only mean nine thirty instead of ten, right?" Jenna snuck a piece of a muffin. "Like *late* early?" Leanna would be late to her own wedding for sure. She arrived everywhere late, no matter how much she tried to be on time.

Leanna pointed to the muffins and glared at Jenna, but her smile told of her softening resolve. "Ha-ha. I want to get there by eight. Remember Carey?" Carey sold records at the flea market, and the previous summer he'd had the booth next to Leanna. Booth placement changed often at the flea market, and Leanna was glad when he'd texted and said he was going to be beside her again for the next few weeks.

"He's that hot young guy, right?" Jenna asked.

"He's not that young. He's twenty-five," Leanna said. "He has the booth next to mine this week, and we were going to try to catch up this morning before the crowds come in."

"How does Kurt feel about you and Carey?" Bella picked at the muffin she'd snuck when Leanna was inside.

Leanna rolled her eyes. "You're kidding, right? Remember last year when Carey kissed me? I told Kurt, remember? He trusts me. Besides, Kurt's coming, too."

"That's another thing I don't get." Jenna kicked her feet up on a chair and leaned back. "How come you get a guy who changes his whole life to be with you, and Bella gets a cop who finally, after a million years, takes her up in the fire tower—which, by the way, I'm totally jealous of—and I can't get Pete to look at me like a woman?"

"I thought he was coming fishing with us next weekend," Bella said.

"He is. But you know what he said?" She lowered her voice. "Fishing? That sounds great. It's been a while since I hooked a big one."

Leanna and Bella exchanged an eye roll.

"You're the queen of innuendos, Jen. How can you be so blind to Pete's?" Bella shrugged.

Jenna drew her brows together. "You think..." Her eyes widened. "No." Her face grew serious again. "Maybe you're right. *Oh my God*. You see? Now not only can I not speak around the man, but my brain goes all wonky, too. Maybe I should just forget him altogether."

That incited another eye roll from Leanna and Bella. Jenna would never forget Pete.

Bella turned at the sound of Caden's voice. He and Kurt were jogging up the road from the entrance. His bare chest glistened with sweat, and when their eyes met, his easy smile sent her to her feet.

"Caden." She hurried off the deck.

"I found him on the access road to the beach and we got to talking," Kurt explained. Kurt joined the others on the deck, leaving Bella and Caden alone.

Caden went to Bella, and when she opened her arms, he held his hands up.

"Sweaty," he warned.

"Don't care." She hugged him close, and when he leaned down and kissed her, her world righted once again. He was dripping with perspiration, but he still smelled like Caden, and that was a smell that she couldn't get enough of.

"How's Evan?"

He wiped his forehead with his arm. "He's good. He didn't tell me much, just that he played a game with a group of assholes and it pissed him off. I'm sorry about last night, babe. I didn't want you to leave, but he needed me."

"I know. It's okay."

Caden lowered his voice. "Were you upset?"

"No." It was a gut reaction, and she realized, not a completely honest one at that. "I wasn't upset, but a little disappointed. I know that's stupid and childish of me. I don't begrudge Evan for needing you, or you for being with him, but I did miss you."

He touched her arm, and his eyes warmed. "Me too. I missed you like crazy, and when you didn't return my call, I thought..."

"Oh God. I'm sorry." She shot a look at her car, where her phone, and her purse, were probably still on the passenger seat. "I'm still not used to carrying my phone. I got home and everyone was by the fire. Amy was hammered, and the girls and I slept here last night."

"Here?" He glanced up at the others on the deck.

"Yeah. Like a litter of puppies on Amy's bed." She stepped closer and touched the waistband of his running shorts. "I'm so happy you're here."

He moved her hand from the fabric. "So am I, but if you do that, everyone will see just how happy." He kissed her again and checked his watch.

"Do you have to get back home?" she asked.

"I promised Evan we'd go boogie boarding at the ocean today. I would really love it if you'd go with us. I know it's not a very romantic date with a teenager around, but at least we'd be together." He reached for her hand.

"Do you think I'd miss a chance at going to the beach with you? I'd love to, but if Evan would rather have time alone with you, that's totally fine." She suddenly realized that despite how she was feeling last night, she really was okay with being excluded. She'd miss him, but how could she feel anything but good about the man who was doing right by his son?

"I'm sure he won't mind, but if it'll make you feel better, I'll check with him when I get home. But you'll need to find your phone if you want to know the answer."

"I've got muffins," Leanna called from Amy's deck.

Caden waved. "Thanks, but I've got a long run back."

"I can drive you home," Bella offered.

"That's okay. Enjoy your friends, and I'll text you when Ev gets up."

He kissed her goodbye, and before she joined the others at Amy's, she retrieved her phone and listened to Caden's message from last night.

*Hey, babe. Sorry about tonight. I miss you, and I wish you were climbing into bed beside me and falling asleep in my arms. Call me when you get a chance.*

She texted a response. *I would have given anything to fall asleep in your arms, but we did the right thing for Ev, and that's what matters most. One day it'll be our turn. Xox.* She read the message again, then deleted *One day it'll be our turn* before sending it. She didn't want to seem too eager, even if her heart was already hoping for a future.

## Chapter Seventeen

*ONE DAY YOU'LL do just that. BTW, Evan said it's cool. Meet us here around ten? Xox.*

Bella read Caden's text message for the tenth time in as many minutes. He was hoping for a future as much as she was. She sent him a text saying ten was fine. Then she showered and packed her beach tote, excited to spend the day with them.

An hour later, Evan answered the door wearing a blue bathing suit that hung to his knees. "Hey. Come on in." Evan smiled as he stepped aside.

"Hi."

"Dad'll be out in a second. He's on the phone." He waved to the couch. "You can sit down if you want."

"I'm okay, thanks. Are you sure you don't mind if I come along?"

He flashed the same easy smile as Caden's. "Nah. It'll be fun. I'm gonna grab a shirt." He disappeared down the hall.

"Damn it." Caden's voice came down the hallway. He stepped into the living room clutching his cell phone.

"Hi." Bella crossed the living room, and the irritation in Caden's eyes stopped her cold. "What's wrong?"

Evan appeared behind him, arms over his head as he slithered into his T-shirt.

"Ready, Dad?"

Caden looked from Bella to Evan. "One of the guys called out sick today. I've got to cover his shift."

"Man, that sucks," Evan said. "I was looking forward to going."

"I can still take Evan. I mean, if you want to go while your dad's at work."

"You don't have to do that." Caden's tone softened.

"Do you mind, Dad?" Evan asked, surprising them both.

"Do I...? No. I think it's great if you both want to go. I'm just pissed that I won't be there." He reached for Bella's hand. "Are you sure you don't mind?"

"A day at the beach with Evan is hardly a hardship." She glanced over his shoulder at Evan. "Evan? You sure?"

"Yeah, I'm in." He grabbed a beach towel from the kitchen table and slung it over his shoulder. "Do you have our boogie boards?"

"I've got them in the truck. Why don't you go grab them and we'll be right out." He tossed the keys to Evan.

Caden placed his hands on her hips and drew her close. "I'm so sorry."

"It's okay. Duty calls. I'm glad he wants to go. It'll be fun, but I'm sorry you have to work."

"Low man on the totem pole for a while." He kissed her forehead.

"Like everything in this world, you've got to pay your dues before you can rise to the top. Luckily, there are no dues to be paid in boyfriend world. You're

216

already on top."

He pressed his cheek to hers. "Speaking of on top..." He nuzzled against her neck and sent a thrill through her body.

"Careful making promises you can't keep."

"Oh, I intend to keep it." He covered her mouth with his, and his kiss filled her with all sorts of delicious promises.

The door swung open, and they both took a startled step back.

Evan crossed his arms and shook his head. "It's not like I don't know you two kiss."

Bella felt her cheeks flush.

Caden cleared his throat. "Cells don't work on the beaches, so call me when you guys leave? The shift is from eleven to seven, and if he gets too mouthy, just bring him home."

"Dad," Evan snapped.

"I'm kidding," Caden said. "Sort of. Behave, okay?"

Evan rolled his eyes. "Whatever."

Bella loved that Caden cared enough to say it, but she was pretty sure it was unnecessary. Evan seemed like he was in a fine mood, and she probably handled teens better than she handled adults.

"We'll be fine. Anything I need to know? Rules for the ocean?" Even though Bella wished Caden was going with them to the beach, she knew they'd have fun and she was glad for the chance to spend time with Evan. Maybe she could find out what types of things were going on in his teenage brain and help ease the rough spots.

"Evan's a good swimmer, but you know, just keep an eye on the undertow and look out for sharks, of course."

"Oh my God. Can we go? Please?" Evan tossed Caden his keys before heading out the door.

Caden caught the keys in one hand, then pressed a soft kiss to Bella's lips.

"Have I told you lately how great you are?"

"No, but between that and the promise of you being on top, the day's looking better and better."

"GRANT. COME IN here, will ya?" Chief Bassett waved him into his office.

"What's up, Chief?"

"Have a seat. We've got a lead on the thefts." Chief Bassett pushed a stack of papers across the desk. "An eyewitness put two teens hanging around the Dunes the day of the theft." The Dunes was a cottage community in South Wellfleet. The property was heavily treed, making visibility from the road into the community nearly impossible.

Caden scanned the report.

"Can they identify them?" Caden asked.

"No. But this confirms what we've thought all along. Kids looking for trouble." Chief Basset locked his hands behind his head. "Now we just have to catch them."

"Chief, the description is pretty vague, don't you think? Two teenage boys with darkish hair." Caden met his serious gaze. "That describes half the population. Hell, that describes Evan." The thought made his gut ache. "Thankfully, he was home with me last night, so that's one Wellfleet teenager off the list."

"I know. It's not much to go on, but when you're out on patrol today, spend your free time trolling the rental communities and the beach parking lots. See if anything stands out. They're hitting cars and cottages during the day, with a few rare exceptions, like over at Healy's."

"I'll keep my eyes open." Caden rose to leave.

"Grant, sorry to pull you in on your day off. Your

218

dedication is duly noted." He nodded a dismissal.

"Thanks, Chief." Even though he knew Evan wasn't involved, he was glad he was spending the day with Bella. The less time he had to get roped into something like this, the better.

BELLA SAT ON a beach chair at the edge of the surf and, with Evan's safety in her hands, she finally understood why her parents were so overprotective of her when she was growing up. Every time Evan disappeared under the waves, the pit of Bella's stomach sank and she held her breath until he reappeared on the other side. Riding waves and smiling when he broke through the surface, Evan looked so different from the brooding teenager she knew him to be at times. It was funny how a dark hoodie and a cell phone could change the image of a person.

He came out of the surf shivering; his hair fell long and streaky across his face. He crossed his skinny arms over his chest and squinted against the sun.

"Wanna boogie board with me?" he asked.

"I haven't been boogie boarding for a while, but heck yeah." She wrapped the Velcro strap of her board around her wrist and stepped into the icy water.

"My dad loves to boogie board." Evan carried his board over his head while Bella clung to hers for warmth.

Her teeth were already chattering.

"Come on!" Evan waved her out deeper. He eased his rangy body onto the board and paddled over the next wave.

Bella turned to the side, clutching her board as the wave crashed against her. Evan paddled toward her and reached for her hand, then pulled her through the next wave.

"Climb up on your board," he directed. "We'll ride the bigger waves in."

She did as he instructed. Somehow boogie boarding seemed easier when she was eighteen. They paddled out side by side with the sun warming her back.

"You've done this before, right?" he asked.

"Of course. It's just been a few years."

"Such a girl," Evan teased.

Bella spied a big wave rolling toward them. "I'll show you what a girl can do." She spun her board around and rode the wave all the way up to shore. The icy spray of water on her face and the rough sand on her thighs as she climbed the bank brought memories of her childhood rushing back. Her heart thundered in her chest as she paddled out to do it again.

"Awesome!" Evan hollered.

She rode the next few waves and wondered why she'd ever stopped boogie boarding. *Oh yeah. Boys.* She'd given up boogie boarding for lying in the sun in a bikini and flirting with lifeguards and hot boys in surf suits. She had turned into a *girl*, and now that she was back on a boogie board, she decided that maybe she'd given it up too soon. She smiled at the thought. In one sense she'd become a girl, and in another she'd cast away being too girly in lieu of taking care of herself— and with Caden, she realized, she had the best of both worlds.

"Come on, daydreamer." Evan splashed her as he waded back out into the deeper water.

Bella was definitely not too girly to give it right back to him. She paddled out and splashed him, then dunked him under the water. They splashed and laughed so hard, neither noticed the next wave mounting until it crashed over the top of them. Bella tumbled against the hard, scratchy sand, and when she broke the surface her first thought was for Evan's safety. She spun around and scanned the water.

"Evan?" she hollered. She pushed through the waves, frantically looking in both directions.

"Hey!" Evan was about twenty feet down the beach from where she was. He waved his arms over his head and—*thank God*—he was smiling.

She ran through the surf. "Oh my God. I thought I lost you."

"Whatever." He splashed her again. "Guys don't get lost."

"Oh, I am *so* going to get you." She dunked him under again, then jumped on her board and paddled out into the deep water. They boogie boarded until Bella's body was numb from the cold; then they made their way up the beach, shivering and covered in goose bumps. Bella lay on the blanket, soaking in the warmth of the sun.

"Hey, Bella, thanks for bringing me here." Evan sat in the beach chair, piling sand up beside his feet, his eyes tracking an attractive young brunette walking along the shore.

"Anytime. I love the beach, and I've had a lot of fun. I forgot how much I loved boogie boarding." She shaded her eyes with her hand and caught his gaze. "I should thank you."

"Hardly." He rested his head back and closed his eyes.

"Let me know when you're hungry and we'll head up to the snack bar." Bella closed her eyes and listened to the sound of the surf and the din of the people on the beach. Evan was as easy to be with as Caden was. Without his phone, he seemed to breathe easier, and Bella realized, she thought that held true for most people.

A few minutes later Bella felt a shadow steal her

warm sun; then the blanket shifted. She opened her eyes and found Evan sitting beside her. His arms rested casually on his knees as he gazed out over the ocean.

"I'm sorry about last night. I didn't mean for you to leave early."

Bella opened her eyes, and he kept his trained on the water.

"Don't worry about it. I don't ever want to come between you and your dad." She closed her eyes again, proud of him for apologizing. It was a difficult thing to do at that age, and she appreciated the confidence it took for him to do it. The silence that followed was surprisingly comfortable.

"When you were growing up, what did you do here during the summers?"

Bella sat up beside him, leaning back on her palms. "Oh, I guess the same stuff kids do now. We had the cottage, so I was always with Amy, Jenna, Leanna, and pretty much the same friends for most of the summer. We rode our bikes to the beach when we were your age, or to the flea market, and just hung out together. And at night we gathered around the fire pit roasting marshmallows, or if we wanted to escape the parents, we'd hole up in one of our cottages and just, I don't know, talk or play games at night. Not much has changed, actually."

His solemn expression remained. "You were lucky that the other kids in the development were like you and not assholes." He glanced at her. "Sorry. I mean—"

"I know what you mean, and it's okay. I say it too sometimes." She smiled to ease his discomfort, but his eyes remained dark and serious. "I guess if they were annoying, I wouldn't have enjoyed it as much, and I probably wouldn't spend any time with them now." She'd counted her lucky stars for her Seaside friends more often than there were stars in the sky.

"You must really miss your friends from Boston."

He shrugged.

"What kinds of things do you do with your friends here?"

He shrugged again and pushed sand around with his feet. "Video games and stuff. The beach sometimes. I don't know." He was quiet again, and a few minutes later he said, "It's different than it was in Boston."

"Night and day, I'd imagine." Feeling the serious turn of the conversation, Bella sat up straighter. "I'd imagine it's a different type of change for you than your dad sees in his life."

"Dad's life sucked before you came along." A hint of a smile lifted his lips.

*Wow.* That was interesting. "I doubt it sucked. I mean, he obviously misses your grandparents and his friends, but he seems to be happy here."

"Yeah, I guess. But he didn't have a life. He had work and me, and then we moved, and now I'm the one without a life."

*Ouch.* So the move was far more of an issue than either Caden or Evan were letting on—or maybe than Caden even realized.

"So you don't like the kids you've met here?"

He shrugged again. "They're okay. They're just different from my old friends." He threaded his fingers together and cracked his knuckles.

"I'm sorry you had to move."

Evan was quiet for a long time. He moved sand around with his feet, watching a group of children running from the surf and a group of teenage girls gathering their towels and umbrella and walking down the beach.

"I guess I'm glad we moved, after what happened to George." He shook his head. "I always knew my dad's job was dangerous. I'm not stupid, or anything, but when you grow up seeing someone all the time and then they're gone forever, it's kind of unreal." He swallowed hard and turned his face away from Bella.

If she weren't afraid of embarrassing him, she'd pull him into her arms and hold him. She'd brush his hair from his face and tell him it was okay to feel sad and angry about George, and moving, and his friends. She'd let him yell and cry and kick sand if it made him feel better; then she'd hold him again until he got all that bottled-up frustration out of his system.

"I'm sorry." She wasn't sure what else to say. Talking too much would make him more emotional, which would probably lead to him clamming up out of embarrassment. Talking too little would say she didn't care, and she did care. Desperately.

He rose to his feet and pulled his shirt over his head. "Wanna eat? I'm getting hungry."

*Deflection.* She knew it well from her students. "Yeah, sure." There were so many things she wanted to ask, like if he'd talked to his father about how he felt. She thought he must have, but teenagers were experts at camouflaging their emotions—even from themselves—with anger and attitude.

Bella pulled on her cover-up and grabbed her wallet from her tote.

"Shit." Evan turned his back to the dunes.

"What's wrong?" She shaded her eyes and looked up toward the path that led down the dunes from the parking lot. She didn't see anything out of the ordinary.

"Can we go?" Evan grabbed his towel and boogie board.

"Yeah. I was just getting my money."

"No. I mean, like, leave." He grabbed the second boogie board and picked up her tote. A deep V formed between his brows, and his narrow chest rose and fell with each heavy, agitated breath.

"Sure. Why are you in such a hurry?" She scanned the beach again. There were people lying out on the beach, kids filling sand with buckets, and lifeguards sitting high up in their chair. She wondered what had caused his reaction.

"Just hot."

Bella grabbed the beach chair and blanket, and they crossed the hot sand. Evan walked at a quick pace with his eyes glued to the path that led up the steep dune. When he shifted the boogie boards in his arm to block his face from the right, Bella was sure something was up, and she quickly surveyed that part of the beach.

She was pretty sure that the two boys Evan had met at the flea market were walking along the base of the dunes, fully dressed in shorts and tank tops. For Evan to leave the beach in order to avoid them could only mean there was some sort of trouble brewing. Bella was so tempted to ask why he didn't want them to see him that she had to bite the insides of her cheeks to keep the words from slipping out.

They packed their stuff in the car and drove away in silence. Evan clenched his jaw repeatedly as he stared out the window.

"Mac's okay for lunch?" she asked, hoping to ease the tension.

"Sure. Whatever."

Bella drove through the center of Wellfleet, along the main road that was home to art galleries and cozy restaurants.

"Have you and your dad been to the gallery walk?" The gallery walk was a popular tourist attraction on Saturday evenings, when the galleries offered free wine and cheese to patrons and local artists came out to meet the customers.

"No." His voice was flat as he stared out the passenger window.

"It sounds boring, but it's really pretty fun. We usually go to the juice bar or the pizza place and eat, and afterward we fill up on ice cream at the pier."

He slid her a blasé look that either meant she sounded like a stupid adult who was trying too hard to make a kid feel better, or that she was speaking a foreign language. She was pretty sure she was guilty of the first. She pressed her lips together and silently chided herself for doing just that. *Ugh.* She was turning into an adult in ways that she swore she never would.

They parked at the Wellfleet Pier, and as they walked across the parking lot in a bubble of uncomfortable silence, Evan kept his eyes trained on the ground. Bella wished she understood what was going on, but she knew better than to push. She tried to ease the conversation into a safe subject as they neared Mac's Seafood.

"What are you hungry for?" she asked.

Mac's was built at the edge of the parking lot on the beach. Lines at least twenty people deep led to several walk-up windows. On the far side of the cedar-shingled building, where a covered deck met the beach, there was a handful of picnic tables packed end to end with customers.

"Whatever." He eyed the menu, and Bella noticed that he was breathing a little easier than he'd been at the ocean. "Burger, I guess."

Bella was in the strange position of feeling like she was young enough to relate to anything Evan might be willing to share with her, when in reality, she knew that the way she saw herself was very different from a teenager's perspective. As a high school teacher, she was well aware of the dichotomy, but as Caden's girlfriend, everything she knew about dealing with teenagers felt different with Evan.

She was beginning to see even more clearly how remarkable what Caden had done the other night really was. He'd done what he believed to be the right thing for Evan, regardless of how uncomfortable it was for him. And he hadn't seemed the least bit hesitant. *Let him snap.*

What was even more remarkable was that it had worked. It had brought them closer together.

They made their way through the line, and as they waited for their food, Evan kicked the sand with the toe of his flip-flop. "Sorry I made you leave the beach."

"It's okay. I was getting hot anyway." She was struck not only by the sincerity in his voice, but by the fact that he was apologizing again. That was pretty unusual for a teenager, and she knew that was a testament to how Caden had raised him.

She hoped Evan might reveal his reasons for leaving, and again it was torture having to refrain from asking. She was so used to saying what she felt that it took extra effort to navigate this touch-and-go conversation. She wasn't Evan's friend or his teacher. She was his father's girlfriend, and her heart was tied to both Caden and Evan. She didn't want to make a mistake that might alienate her from Evan, or make him uncomfortable, but her gut told her not to completely ignore what she'd noticed, either.

They picked up their food and decided to sit on the knee-high wall at the edge of the parking lot by the marina, with their trays balanced on their knees.

"Are you excited to start school in the fall?"

"Sort of, I guess." He took a bite of his burger. "I'm looking forward to the technology club more than school. School kinda bites." He smiled. "Crap, you're a teacher. Sorry."

"It's okay. Hopefully, I'll be teaching again."

"What do you mean hopefully? I thought you were teaching?"

"I was a teacher in Connecticut, but the program I'm putting together has to be accepted before I can get a full-time job here."

"In Connecticut? I thought you lived here." Evan set his burger on the tray. "You *don't* live here?"

"It's a little complicated. If the work-study program is accepted, I'll probably move here full-time."

Evan's voice grew serious. "So, if the program isn't accepted, will you go back to Connecticut?"

Bella shrugged. "I haven't decided yet. I do have a job offer there, but there's a lot to consider." *Like where your dad and I are heading.*

"But..." He turned away. The wind whipped his hair away from his face. He looked at Bella, and she couldn't miss the concern in his eyes. "Does Dad know you might move back to Connecticut?"

"Sure. He knows it's a possibility." They hadn't discussed it in very much detail, but they'd touched on it as a possibility. Against her plan, and against what she'd promised herself, she couldn't deny that the idea of leaving Caden made her stomach hurt.

Evan shook his head. "So you might move away?"

"Well, I hope not, but it's a possibility, I guess."

He got up and carried his tray back to the restaurant. She followed, and after they returned their trays, she tried to get his mind onto something else.

"Do you want to walk the pier?" she asked.

"Nah. Can you take me home?" He shoved his hands in his swimsuit pockets.

"Sure, but, Evan, I don't want you to think that I'm moving. At least that's not my plan." *My plan.* Meeting Caden hadn't been part of her plan either, and it was the best thing that had ever happened to her.

"If there's one thing I learned this year, it's that life doesn't always go by what we have planned." He stalked into the parking lot.

Bella couldn't have agreed more.

WHEN CADEN'S SHIFT ended, he checked in with Evan and then stopped by Bella's. She and Amy were sitting by the pool even though it was dusk. Bella's laughter filled the air. He loved her laugh, whether she was laughing raucously at a joke or flirtatiously against his neck when they were intimate. Both made him warm all over. The gate to the pool creaked as he pulled it open, drawing Bella's attention. Her smile lit up her eyes, and when she jumped up to greet him, he knew he looked just as happy. He waved to Amy, and after waving back, she crossed her arms on the table and rested her head on them.

Bella fell into his arms and lifted her eyes to his. Jesus, he'd missed her.

"Hey," she said in a soft voice.

"Hey yourself." He pressed his lips to hers. "Is Amy okay?"

"Yeah. Just nursing a hangover from hell. Luckily, she has no memory of Tony being there when she threw up, so at least she's not embarrassed on top of it."

"A hangover? Ouch. I'm sorry." He glanced at Amy and wondered how different it must be for Bella when she was in Connecticut. Did she have friends she was close to there, too? "Thanks for taking Evan out today. He said he had a great time."

"Yeah, we did. Did he say anything about practically running off the beach to avoid seeing his friends?"

"No." Caden thought about Evan's recent snappy

and sullen behavior. "He probably didn't want them to see him with you. You know, the whole teenage independence thing. I have tomorrow off, and I asked him if he wanted to go to that go-cart and batting cage place in South Yarmouth. When we first moved here, he loved it. But he had no interest in that either."

"I hope you're right, but maybe you can find a way to talk about it without telling him that I mentioned it? He seemed a little stressed."

"Okay, I will." She felt so good in his arms, and she smelled like the ocean. He wanted to spend the evening with her. They could go for a walk, then watch a movie, rub each other's feet, or read on the couch. He didn't care what they did. He only knew that nothing felt right without her by his side.

"I was hoping we could go for a walk or something, but it looks like Amy needs you, so can I call you later?"

Bella glanced over her shoulder at Amy. "I'm sorry. Thank you for understanding. It isn't often that she needs me, but she's feeling a little down today. She never drinks—well, none of us do, really, except when we're here on vacation, but Amy is a super lightweight. She's, like, pixie light, and she drank like she was a heavyweight."

"Don't be sorry." When they kissed again, it was painful to break away. "I hate not being with you every night. It feels like you should always be right there with me."

"I feel that way, too." She glanced at Amy. "You could stay if you want."

"That's okay. Enjoy your time with Amy. You don't get much of it when you're apart for nine months out of the year. Besides, I had Evan time the other night; you should have girl time."

"Thank you for understanding."

He touched his forehead to hers. "Babe, I'd do anything for you. I'm off work tomorrow. Do you want to do something?" He could spend every minute with Bella and it wouldn't be enough.

Her lips curved down in an adorable frown, but the ache it caused wasn't cute at all.

"I have meetings scheduled with a few companies, but afterward, definitely."

"Definitely." He pulled her close again. "Call me when you're done and we'll figure it out." He looked back at his truck, knowing he should leave, but every part of him wanted to stay. He forced himself to take a step back, but he kept hold of her hand. Even the short distance between them felt too far apart.

She smiled up at him and pressed her other hand to his abs. "Why does it get harder and harder to say goodbye?"

"I think it's what happens when you fall for someone." *Forget falling. I think I've base jumped.* "I'll call you before I go to sleep later, but, babe, good-night phone calls aren't enough."

"I know."

"But for Evan's sake, it has to be for now."

"I know that, too."

# Chapter Eighteen

BELLA WAS STILL thinking about last night's good-night phone call with Caden when she parked in front of the office of The Geeky Guys (TGG) Monday morning. She loved that he called to say good night each night before he went to sleep. She slept better having his voice as the last she heard before her head hit the pillow, but last night she'd wanted to crawl through her cell phone and climb into his arms. Although neither had crossed the invisible line of saying *I love you,* their feelings hung in every word. She'd never forget the longing in his voice when he'd said, *I can't wait to fall asleep after making love to you and wake up with you in my arms.* She wondered if that was what Vera had alluded to when she'd asked if Bella minded that Caden had a son. There *were* challenges when dating a man with a child, like not spending the night together and worrying about someone other than themselves at all times. She missed Caden at night, and she woke up in a bed that never used to feel empty, longing for him to be there with her, but she didn't begrudge Caden for having

Evan. She was falling for Evan as quickly as she was falling for Caden.

She liked Evan, whether or not he was going through a tough time. There wasn't a teenager on earth who didn't go through trying times. She could tell by the way Evan handled himself around other adults that he would come out on the other side as a good man. He'd been raised by Caden, after all. Bella also knew that when he acted out around Caden, he did so because he felt safe doing it with his dad. Evan knew that Caden loved him unconditionally. No one could behave all the time, and if a child couldn't act out occasionally in front of those who loved them unconditionally, then where could they?

Bella took a deep breath and tried to push away thoughts about her personal life and mentally prepare herself for gaining TGG for the work-study program. Getting her professional life in order had to be her primary focus. *Especially if I hope to stay here with Caden. Stop it. I'm making my career decisions separate from him!*

*Yeah, right.*

Okay, she was trying to.

TGG was the only computer shop within twenty miles of Wellfleet. They handled computer repair, designed websites, and handled a multitude of other computer-related services. Jamie had suggested that she try them, and as she walked into the one-room office, she wondered if they'd be able to afford to hire anyone at all.

Five sets of eyes turned toward Bella when she stepped inside. Six desks were paired off, facing one another in the center of the room. The walls were lined with deep metal shelves, littered with CPUs, monitors, electronic gadgets, and other digital paraphernalia.

A twentysomething guy with black framed glasses and jet-black hair cropped short on the sides and spiky up on top rolled his chair a few feet back from his desk.

"Hi. Can I help you?"

"Hi, I'm Bella Abbascia. I've got an appointment with Frank Kohler."

The guy peered around his computer monitor at the man sitting behind the desk across from him. "Frank, you're up."

Frank had one hand on his forehead as he peered at his monitor with his thick blond brows drawn together. He held up one finger. "One sec, Bell."

*Bell?* While she waited, she quickly assessed the office. Four men, one woman, and one unoccupied desk. The employees appeared to be in their midtwenties and early thirties, dressed casually in shorts or jeans, and as far as Bella could tell, not at all bothered by the fact that she was standing there.

"Holy shit." Frank smacked the desk.

"Frank." The skinny blond girl who was sitting closest to Bella chided him. She smiled and Bella realized that she was probably closer to twenty than midtwenties. "He's been crunching that program for hours."

"That's okay." She made a mental note to address foul language if by some miracle they were able to hire any of the students.

Frank rose to his feet, his fingers flying across the keyboard. "Just one sec, Bell. I'll be right there."

She wondered if he'd misunderstood her name. A few minutes later he waved her over and pulled a chair from the unoccupied desk.

"I'm Frank." His handshake was firm, but his hand was soft. Based on that and his pale skin, Bella doubted he spent much time away from his computer.

He was just a few inches taller than her, with short blond hair and blue eyes that held the excitement of whatever issue he'd just solved. "Sit down. Talk to me."

"Congrats on whatever you've just accomplished," she said to break the ice.

"Thanks. I've been trying to crack that algorithm for days, not hours." He shot a look at the blond girl, who rolled her eyes. "Stace doesn't work on the weekends like I do. Anyway, tell me about your work-study program."

*Stace.* She assumed that was short for Stacy, and that Frank was one of those guys who didn't need friendship or an invitation to shorten someone's name. Bella explained the goals of the program and what type of commitment was required from each company that signed on.

Frank leaned back in his chair and called to the guy sitting behind the desk to his right, "Sam? Whaddaya think?"

Sam, a dark-haired, clean-cut guy, was poring over a manual of some sort. "Sounds good if they're not morons."

Frank shrugged. "Not exactly a politically correct answer, but he's pretty much right. Anyone we hired would need to be familiar with computers on some level. I'm all for on-the-job training, but they've gotta have the basics. You know, understand what batch files are, have some HTML knowledge. Any kid who has a real interest in computers will know those things, and experience with Python, Java, or Ruby is a big plus."

"Python? My friend's son is learning that now."

"Is that the kid Jamie Reed is teaching? He said something about helping a kid learn Python when he told me about the program. We'd love to help someone that motivated."

She was surprised Jamie had mentioned Evan. "He's not a senior, so he's not eligible for this program, but if you're interested, I'm sure Evan would love to shadow you. He was in the technology club in Boston and he's just recently moved to Wellfleet."

"Sure. Why don't you give Evan my number and we'll see where it goes with him."

"I'll do that." She could barely contain her excitement for Evan.

"How about an application that asks about the basic computer stuff? Any kid can go to Codeacademy online, and if they're really driven, they can learn the things we need on their own." Stace walked around the desks and put a hand on Frank's shoulder. "My big brother's a hell of a mentor."

"You're siblings?" She ran her eyes between them.

"Yeah." The girl held out her hand. "Stacia Kohler. I go to UMass. I'm only here for the summer, but I'd be happy to work with you to outline the basic requirements if Frank says it's a go."

"It's a go," Sam said over his shoulder.

"Well, I need to know who has signing authority for TGG, because we'll require legally binding signatures for the contract."

Both Sam and Stacia pointed to Frank.

"Sure. If you can work with Stace to develop a general list of requirements, we can try this out. I assume it's a set number of hours each week at minimum wage." Frank glanced around the desk at the guy with black hair. "Mark, can you put together some type of—" He turned his attention back to Bella. "Is this by school year or by semester?"

"School year."

He turned back to Mark. "A nine-month guideline of expectations, things we can teach them, that sort of thing?"

"Sure." Mark looked up at Stacia. "Stacia can help me this weekend." He smiled in a way that made Stacia blush.

Stacia put her hand on her hip and narrowed her eyes. "Okay, but I'm still not going out with you." She turned her attention back to Bella. "Stop by my desk when you're done with Frank and we'll pencil in a date to go over things."

Bella went over the documentation with Frank and set up a time to discuss modifications to the application with Stacia. By the time she left the office, she had also received recommendations from Stacia for a bakery and a CPA office that might be interested in becoming part of the program.

When she got in her car, Bella picked up her cell phone to call Caden and saw that she'd missed two calls from Kelsey Trailer, her old boss. She hadn't spoken to Kelsey since she left for the summer. Kelsey had extended an offer for Bella to return to her old job. She refused to believe that Bella really wanted a change. Who wouldn't? Bella was as stable as the day was long. She arrived early for work every day, missing only two days out of the last two years, and she stayed until her work was complete each afternoon. Bella had been good at hiding her secret hankering for something more fulfilling—in fact, she wasn't sure she really believed she'd ever make the change. Until last spring, when it all clicked.

Bella knew Kelsey wanted an answer that Bella wasn't ready to give. She called her back before calling Caden.

"Bella, how's summer in Wellfleet?" Kelsey asked.

She pictured Kelsey behind her desk, her blond corkscrew curls framing her face, wire-rimmed glasses firmly balanced on the bridge of her nose, and a warm, hopeful smile on her thin lips.

"It's beautiful, as always." There was no doubt in Bella's mind. She wanted to be at the Cape, and she realized, she was proud to have made that decision *before* meeting Caden. Since she had no offer for permanent work here yet, she needed to keep the door to her old job open, even as a last resort.

"I'm just going to cut to the chase here, Bella. Jay quit, so there's no reason for you to quit. There was no reason before, but I understand why you wanted to get away from seeing him every day. So, what do you say?"

Bella digested the new information. "He quit?" For a split second she wondered why he'd quit, but she quickly realized that she didn't really care. She still wasn't keen on the idea of going back to work in Connecticut or to a school where she'd dated a coworker, even if he was no longer there. She was excited about the prospect of the work-study program—and then there were Caden and Evan. The truth was, she couldn't imagine not being with them. She closed her eyes for a beat to get ahold of her emotions. *Separate mind and heart. Separate mind and heart.*

Nope. Didn't work. They were tied together in a knot only an experienced boatman would be able to disassemble.

"Yes. He gave his notice last week, and I waited to call in case it was a momentary lapse in judgment. But he's serious. So does the offer look any better to you now?"

"I...Kelsey, I need to think about it." Five years she'd worked there, and in those five years she'd made close friends, and she'd bonded with families and students. She had a life there that was comfortable and safe.

*I have a boyfriend here who holds my heart in his comfortable, safe, reliable, strong, sexy, loving hands. Yeah, great separation there, Bella.*

"That's fine, but I need to know before August fifteenth. We have another teacher on the line, and she needs a decision so she can move forward one way or another." Kelsey sighed, and when she continued, her voice held the emotion of a friend rather than a boss. "Bella, we all love you. You know that. Don't let one bad relationship throw you off course. You have a career *and* a family here."

Bella promised to give her a decision by the fifteenth, which was only two weeks away. She had a meeting with the Barnstable County school board on Wednesday, and now she felt like there was a fire under her ass. She drove down the road to the Chocolate Sparrow and called Caden on the way.

"Hey, babe." The smile in his warm voice eased the tension in her chest.

"Hi. I've got good news for Evan. You know that company in Eastham, The Geeky Guys? They want to talk to him about shadowing them to learn more about programming."

"Really? That's awesome, but what about Jamie?"

"Jamie's only here during the summer, so it works out perfectly. If Evan's interested, of course." She told him about the people in the office and the technical things Frank had mentioned as prerequisites.

"I've been reading about HTML and other technical things that I'll never have a use for, in those books we got at the bookstore."

She loved that. "You have?"

"I have to do something to keep my mind off of you at night." He spoke seductively quiet. "Not to mention, this way I won't become the loser dad who is totally oblivious to Evan's interests."

"You're such a good dad. Did you talk with him about the beach?"

"Not yet. I don't want it to be obvious that you mentioned it. Besides, he's in a very teenage mood right now. This opportunity should turn that around, though. I think you just got ten degrees hotter."

Bella laughed. "You're so cute."

"Cute? Totally not what I was going for. Do I have to come over dressed as another Village People, YMCA guy?"

"You're already a cop. Wasn't there a cop in that group?" She narrowed her eyes and grinned, even though he couldn't see her. "Maybe tonight we'll play cops and robbers."

"I'll bring my handcuffs," he said in a teasing voice.

"Don't bother. I have my own." She said it just to hear his reaction. She did have a pair of pink fuzzy handcuffs that she'd bought in Provincetown as a gag one night with the girls, but she'd never used them with a man. Come to think of it, she thought they were in her house in Connecticut and no longer at the Cape.

She was met with silence.

"Um...Caden?" Shit. She wondered if she'd crossed a line.

He cleared his throat. "Hold on. I'm trying to get an image out of my mind."

She breathed a sigh of relief, and after they made a plan to get together later in the evening, she drove toward her next appointment revved up in more ways than one.

CADEN WAS GETTING ready to go see Bella when Evan threw the front door open and slammed it shut. *Goddamn it.* He was already tired of this teenage attitude.

"Hey." Caden shot him a look.

Evan stalked into his room and slammed that door, too. Caden had had just about enough of this behavior, regardless of if it was typical or not. He knocked on Evan's door, and when Evan didn't answer, he walked into the room. Evan stood at the window with his back to Caden.

"What's going on, Evan?"

Evan slid his hands in his pockets and rounded his shoulders forward.

"Ev?" When Evan didn't acknowledge him, he took a step closer and forced himself to tether his anger. "Evan, look at me when I'm speaking to you." Caden didn't like having to pull the parental look-at-me card, but he liked being ignored even less.

Evan turned with his neck bowed, eyes trained on the floor.

"What's going on that's got you slamming doors?" Life was so much easier when Evan's biggest issue was fighting over a toy car in a sandbox or wanting a new cell phone. This world of him having a life that felt separate—and far too secretive—from Caden was bullshit.

*It's normal teenage bullshit*, he reminded himself.

*I fucking hate this.*

Evan shrugged.

"Look at me." Evan lifted his eyes, and Caden hated the feeling of what he did next—looked for bloodshot eyes and heavy lids. He was relieved that Evan's eyes were clear, even if brooding and angry.

"I know you're going through a lot right now, but I won't have you slamming doors and ignoring me. If you want to talk, I'm here. If you want to keep it to yourself, that's fine, too, but I won't be ignored when I ask you a question. Got it?"

"Whatever." Evan sat in front of his computer.

Caden blew out a frustrated breath and paced the

small bedroom. "No. Not *whatever*, Evan. That's not even an option as an answer."

"Fine. I've got it." He clicked something on his monitor, and a PC game emblem filled his screen.

"Ev." *Do you want to talk?* He knew him well enough to know he didn't, but leaving the room without talking felt wrong. *Too wrong.*

Evan looked up at him and opened his mouth as if he were going to say something; then he turned back to his computer.

*Aw hell.*

"I'm right here if you want to talk."

Evan pushed back from the computer and fidgeted with the edge of the chair.

Caden sat down on Evan's bed and waited.

"Can we take a trip back to Boston soon?" Evan asked.

"Absolutely. Want to see your friends?" *Stupid question.* Of course he did, just as Caden wanted to see his parents.

Evan nodded.

"We'll plan a trip, but, buddy, is something going on with your friends here? You never used to come home angry after hanging out with friends."

Evan shifted his eyes away. "The kids here aren't my friends, Dad. They're just kids to hang with, shoot the shit. You know. But they're not my friends. They don't even like the same things I do. It doesn't matter. I'm not hanging out with them anymore. They suck."

Caden felt a little guilty for being relieved, and that guilt merged with the realization that this was his fault for moving them out of Boston.

"That stinks. I'm sorry, Ev. Hopefully, when you start school, you'll meet kids who are interested in the same things you are."

"Whatever." He turned back to his computer.

Caden rose to his feet. "It's not whatever to me. It's important to me that you're happy, and I'm sorry we moved, but I still think it was the right thing to do."

"Because of Bella or because of the job?"

The question hit him like a punch to the solar plexus, but it was the innuendo behind it that pissed him off.

"I'd never jeopardize your well-being or your happiness for anyone, Evan. Not even Bella." He strode out of the room, then hesitated, as the words hit a little too close to home. He drew in a deep breath to calm his anger and turned back to his son.

"Listen, buddy, I can stay in tonight if you want to hang out."

"No thanks." He didn't miss a beat in his game.

Caden stood in the doorway, mired in guilt and struggling with indecision. He knew that staying home wouldn't help. Evan would be chained to his computer for the next few hours regardless of where Caden was. He wrestled with the message he'd be sending by leaving. Would Evan think he was less important than Bella? Or was Evan using Bella as a manipulation to derail Caden from whatever was behind his bad mood?

Caden studied him, fully engrossed in a PC game, and decided this was probably a case of the latter. "I'll see you later, buddy. Call if you need me."

He pulled up to Bella's ten minutes later, and when she answered the door with smiling eyes and open arms, he breathed her in. The guilt and anger that felt like a companion only moments ago dissipated with Bella's warm embrace.

"God, I missed you," he whispered.

"I missed you, too."

He lowered his mouth to hers, and when their lips met, the lingering guilt was swept away. How could he feel guilty about being with someone who meant so much to him?

"I bought a bottle of sangria. Would you like a glass?"

"I don't want to move from holding you in my arms." He kissed her again, deep and slow. He wanted nothing more than to disappear into her, but he also wanted to talk to her about Evan. He forced himself to draw his lips away. "Sangria. Sure."

He followed her inside. She reached up to retrieve wineglasses from the top shelf of the cabinet, and the sundress she had on lifted, flashing the sweet curve of her ass. He couldn't keep himself from circling her waist from behind and nibbling on her neck.

"You look delicious in that outfit."

She leaned against him, tilting her head to the side, giving him better access to her neck. He kissed his way up to her earlobe, then laved it with his tongue.

"Caden," she whispered, then turned around.

He sealed his lips over hers. His arms slid to her lower back, and he pressed his hips to hers.

She smiled against his lips. "Is it bad that I want to make love to you every time we're together?"

He touched his forehead to hers. "Good Lord, no. I was thinking the same thing." He inhaled deeply.

"We should talk, right?" She bit her lower lip and wrinkled her brow.

"Probably. We should go outside and cool down before that look you're giving me gets you in trouble and I carry you into the bedroom." He wanted to bury himself inside her and lose himself in her love, and afterward, when the guilt and pain were pushed too far away to recall, they could talk, but he knew that was backward. Talking with Bella would make him feel better, and then he could make love to her with a clear head.

They moved in silence, carrying the wine and glasses outside. Bella's cheeks were flushed, her eyes seductive and dark. They sat beside each other on the deck chairs, restraint tightening his nerves and written all over Bella's face as they tried to calm their desires. He drew her legs onto his lap and moved his chair closer; then he poured them each a glass of sangria.

"You guys are still going fishing with us tomorrow, right?"

"We wouldn't miss it for the world."

She smiled. "Good. I picked up four new businesses for the work-study program, and TGG referred me to two other companies and I'm meeting with them on Thursday." She wrapped her arms around his waist and pressed her cheek to his chest.

"That's fantastic."

He clinked his glass to hers. "To a full-time job at the Cape."

"I can't imagine that this isn't going to come through as a full-time job." She sipped her wine and traced the condensation with her finger. "I also got a call from my old boss. She wanted to let me know that Jay quit."

Caden's stomach clenched. He knew how much she loved working there, and with Jay out of the picture, he wondered if her excitement over the work-study program and their relationship was enough to keep her at the Cape. He settled a hand on her thigh.

"She said she needed a decision by the fifteenth, so I have another two weeks."

He was unable to read her steady gaze. "And how do you feel about it?"

She ran her finger along the edge of her dress. "Conflicted."

"About?" was all he could manage. Did she want to be with him, or did she want to move back to Connecticut?

She sighed. "There's a lot to consider. On the one hand, if this job comes through, it's because I created something valuable that could really make a difference in a lot of kids' lives, and that's exciting. On the other hand, I have a life in Connecticut and friends and a job that's secure." She ran her finger along his forearm. "And then there's us to consider, too." She leaned forward and kissed him.

"I'm glad to hear you say that. I know you want to make your decision free and clear of our relationship, but, Bella..." He stopped himself from saying more. This was her decision.

"I know."

He took her hand in his. "I adore you. I know your life is up in the air right now. I also know that what we have is worth considering."

"I know. I've never felt this way before. I couldn't *not* consider us, Caden."

He kissed her again, silently thanking her for caring enough to keep him in her mind while she decided their fate.

She took another sip of wine. "My realtor also called. She has a verbal offer on my house and expects to have it in writing tomorrow."

"That's good, right?" He took a drink, then ran his hand along her thigh. He loved her legs. Hell, he loved her, and he would have told her tonight, but with the job and house offer on the table, he worried she might think he was saying it just to keep her there.

"Yeah. I think so. I mean, I came here with the intent of starting fresh. New job, new digs, new life. Now at least the option is stronger, but I still don't have the offer from the school board here." She smiled, fisted her hand in his shirt, and pulled him down so they were eye to eye. "Even though I didn't come here looking for a new boyfriend, I'm really glad I found you."

He kissed her again. "I think I found you, remember?" He slid his hand up the outside of her thigh, beneath her dress. "I sure do. Your hair was caught in Leanna's window, and your black silk panties were begging to come off."

She tightened her grip on his shirt. "Only for you."

How was he supposed to concentrate on anything other than how good she felt when all he wanted to do was love her until all the other complications disappeared? She released his shirt and settled back into her chair.

"You know you're killing me, right?"

"That's my evil plan." She finished her wine and went into a slow, off-key rendition of Carly Simon's "Anticipation."

"I was thinking more along the lines of 'You Shook Me All Night Long' by AC/DC."

She laughed. "Okay, okay. We should be serious. How's Ev? Did you talk with him about the job?"

"Serious, huh?" He rolled his eyes, but it was a farce. He loved that she cared about Evan. "Not yet. He came home pissed off, so I thought I'd wait until he was in a better frame of mind. You were right, though. He doesn't like those other kids. He said he's not going to hang out with them anymore." He debated telling her what Evan had asked him about moving and Bella, but with everything else that was going on, he refrained.

"Wow. I wonder what went down." Bella's brows drew together.

"He didn't tell me much, just that they weren't like his old friends. I'm going to take him back to Boston this weekend for a visit."

"That's great."

He scooted his chair closer to Bella's. "Would you consider coming with us for the day?" The idea had come to him as they were talking. He hated the idea of spending any time away from her, and he was looking forward to showing her where they'd lived and introducing her to his parents.

"Are you sure?"

He pulled her onto his lap and ran his fingers through her hair, then drew her lips to his. She pressed her hands to his cheeks and deepened the kiss.

"I love when you do that," he admitted.

"Kiss you?"

He shrugged. "Kiss me, touch my cheeks like they're yours." He wanted to fill his senses with her like she filled his heart. He wanted to taste her arousal, hear her voice gasping his name, and feel every inch of her luscious, naked body beneath his.

He stood with her in his arms, carried her inside, and laid her on the bed. This time he remembered to close the bedroom window; then he closed her bedroom door, leaving no room for interruptions. He stripped down to his skivvies and lowered himself to the bed, taking her in a deep, passionate kiss. When he drew his lips away, her eyes fluttered open.

"Come back." She wrapped her hand around the back of his neck and pulled him to her again.

He didn't need the help, but, boy, did it turn him on. He would kiss her until her body was on fire and her thoughts melted together. She felt so right beneath him, soft and feminine. He felt her love for him in every stroke of her tongue. He grazed her lips with his, and when she arched to meet him, he drew back. A seductive moan slipped from her lips. He loved feeling her writhe with need as she rocked against him. He grabbed the hem of her dress and lifted his body as he drew the thin fabric up and over her head and tossed it to the floor, exposing lacy, yellow lingerie.

"Jesus, Bella. You're so feminine and sexy you make me lose my mind."

She scrunched her nose. "I'm hardly feminine."

He glanced down at the pink comforter, then ran his tongue along the ridge of her lacy bra. "Why do you hide it? What happened that you feel like you have to be so strong?"

She turned her face away but not before he saw the pain in her eyes. He touched his forehead to hers.

"Tell me, baby."

"It's stupid. No one but Jenna, Amy, and Leanna know about it."

He kissed her mouth, her cheek, her forehead again. "You don't have to tell me. But one day I want to share all our secrets."

That drew her eyes to his. "Tell me a secret and I'll tell you."

He smiled at the tit for tat presented with mischief in her beautiful eyes.

"Okay." He propped himself up on his elbows beside her. "The truth is, moving was hard. I was scared as hell to move away from Boston. It was the hardest decision I've ever made. I was scared about starting a new job, afraid that Evan would hate me, afraid that my parents would need me and I'd be two hours away."

"Oh, Caden." She leaned up and kissed him softly.

"And now I'm scared that I've messed up Evan for good."

He rolled onto his back beside her, surprised at the truth streaming from his subconscious. He'd never admitted his fear to anyone before, or just how deep it ran.

She stroked his cheek. "I'm sure you didn't mess him up for good. He's just settling in. This time next year he'll have forgotten how hard it was; he'll have new technology club friends. You'll see."

"I hope so. It would kill me if I realized that although I moved here with the sole intent of protecting Evan, I had somehow made the worst decision of his life, while it was the best decision of mine." He closed his eyes for a beat, and when he opened them, he noticed Bella's eyes were damp.

"You're such a good dad, Caden." She pressed her lips to his, and her voice turned serious. "Are you considering moving back to Boston?"

He shook his head. "I moved here for a reason, and that reason hasn't changed. I just have to believe that it was for the best. That it was fated to be."

"You believe in fate?"

"Well, I think you and I were destined to be together. And I also think you're skipping out on sharing your secret." He kissed her again, then ran his finger down her cheek. "Why do you pretend that you don't have a love of all things girly?"

"I don't pretend. It's just not part of my personality." She ran her finger along his arm.

"But it is, babe. You're very feminine."

"I'm brash, and loud, and take charge." She furrowed her brow, and it made him smile.

"You are self-confident, independent, and secure. But you're also feminine. You wear dresses every day. You walk with graceful steps, and your hips swing in an extremely feminine fashion. You flirt like a seductress, and sometimes you get this look in your eyes when we're talking." He breathed her in, giving himself a second to catch his breath. "It's tender and sweet. Your essence is girly, babe, no matter how much you try to deny it."

Her cheeks heated. "I don't try to. I just don't share it with many people. I like knowing that I can bang nails into my own deck and move furniture, or..." She rolled her eyes. "Whatever else I need to do. And as a woman, when you can't do those things, I think it makes you vulnerable. It lessens your strength and independence."

"Does Amy do all those things?"

She laughed. "Oh my gosh, no. Neither does Jenna."

He arched a brow. "So, I don't get it. Do you have any less respect for them?"

"Of course not." She lay flat on her back and covered her face with her arm. "It's just my thing. I can't even believe I'm telling you this. Really, when did you enter the zone that has always been reserved for just my Seaside girlfriends?"

"Since we fell in love," he whispered.

She reached for his hand, needing the safety of him while she exposed her secret. "I was really girly when I was a teenager, but it seemed like every time I asked a guy for help with anything—my car, carrying something heavy—they always wanted something sexual in return. I learned pretty quickly that guys tended to take advantage of girly girls, so I decided not to be that person anymore, at least not publicly. Is that a big deal? That I keep my girly side private and only share it with those I really care about?"

He shifted so she was beneath him. "It is a big deal to me, to be included in those you care about." He kissed her chin, then moved down her body to her belly and slipped her pretty lacy panties off with ease. "I adore your girly side." He took off his briefs and positioned himself on top of her again. She pressed her fingertips into his hips as he kissed her again.

"Are you in a hurry?"

"I miss you." She licked her lips. "Would you rather I got my handcuffs and took you every which way on my terms?"

He took her in a greedy kiss, aroused by the thought of being restrained by her.

"One day I'd love to see you take control." He kissed her again. "I want you to drive me to the edge and then make me wait." He lowered his mouth to her breast and dragged his tongue across her nipple, earning a gasp of pleasure from Bella. He slithered back up her body, the tip of his arousal eager against her wet center.

"But not tonight, lover girl." He kissed her softly. "Tonight I just want to be close. No games, no props, no diversions. I just want to love you."

She arched to greet him as he buried himself deep inside her. Their bodies joined as one—and the rest of the world faded away.

# Chapter Nineteen

THE NEXT MORNING Bella stood on the deck of the fishing boat docked at the marina, anxiously watching for Caden and Evan to arrive. The sun beat down on her shoulders and a gentle breeze brushed across her back. Everyone from Seaside except Jamie and Vera had arrived early. They were too excited to wait at the cottages. Amy, Tony, and Leanna were at the helm talking with Joe Bloom, the owner of the boat, while Kurt prepared a comfortable place for Vera to settle into inside in case she wanted to get out of the sun. His thoughtfulness was endless.

Jenna paced the deck in her red bikini top and a pair of cutoff shorts. "What if Pete doesn't show up?"

Bella shaded her eyes from the sun and peered in the direction of the parking lot. "Then we'll go out and catch some fish and have a kick-ass time without him."

"I know that." Jenna put her hands on her hips. "But what would it *mean*?"

"That he's an idiot and it's time for you to move on." Bella draped her arm over Jenna's shoulder, but Jenna shrugged out of her reach.

"You're a total buzzkill." Jenna tugged at her bikini top.

"Oh, stop. He'll show up. The real question is where are Caden, Evan, Jamie, and Vera?" She leaned against the wooden railing.

"Well, don't worry. If they don't show up, you can always move on." Jenna smirked.

"*Ugh*. Jenna, I was kidding. I just wish Pete would jump at the chance to be with you." Bella turned back toward the parking lot. "There they are." She pointed to Caden and Evan. Pete was nowhere in sight.

"Pete isn't with them." Jenna rolled her eyes. "See? He's totally not interested."

"Don't jump to conclusions." Bella went to greet them.

"Sorry we're late." Caden looked sporty and handsome in a pair of khaki shorts and a white tank top. He carried a small duffel bag and raked his eyes down Bella's body. He settled a hand on her hip, leaned in close, and said quietly, "Love that bathing suit, babe."

She had worn an emerald-green bikini that accentuated her bust, along with a white cotton miniskirt. She loved getting a rise out of Caden, and the suit earned her another lascivious look.

Caden pressed a kiss to her lips. "I'll go put our stuff inside and be right back."

"Sounds good." She turned her attention to Evan, who was scrolling through texts on his phone. "Hey, Ev. How's it going?" Bella said.

"Good. Thanks for hooking me up with TGG. I called on the way over, and Dad's taking me to meet them Friday." Evan wore a black tank top, revealing his gangly arms. He quickly scanned the boat. "Where's Jamie and Vera?"

"There not here yet, but hopefully they'll get here

soon." She watched Evan cross the deck and join Amy, Tony, and Caden.

Her heart went out to Jenna, standing at the edge of the boat, peering over the parking lot. "He'll be here, Jenna."

"I'm not so sure." Jenna nodded toward Jamie coming up the dock. "Where's Vera?"

"No idea." Bella wondered that, too.

Jamie waved as he approached. His thick, dark hair stood on end against the breeze.

"Hey, sorry I'm late." Jamie stepped onto the boat. "Gram wasn't up to coming, but she sent chocolate chip cookies for Evan."

"Lucky kid. Is Vera okay?" Bella asked.

"She said she was really tired. I think she had second thoughts about spending the day on the water. You know how she is about ruining other people's fun. If she got tired or hot, she wouldn't mention it. She'd rather suffer in silence than make a boat turn back." He rubbed his stubbly chin and turned compassionate eyes to Jenna.

"Jenna, don't kill the messenger, but Pete stopped by and said he had a pool emergency."

Jenna rolled her eyes. "What kind of excuse is that? A pool emergency?"

"Jenna, he does pool maintenance," Bella reminded her. "I'm sure it's not an excuse."

"Whatever. You know what? Men suck." Jenna touched Jamie's arm. "Not you, of course." Jenna stomped off toward the far end of the boat.

"Sorry." Jamie shrugged. "For what it's worth, he seemed pretty bummed about missing the fishing trip."

"You know Jenna. She'll shake it off in five minutes and be back to her bubbly self. Please do me a favor, though. Can you clue her in that Pete was bummed?

You know it feels like a rejection even if it was a valid excuse."

"Sure." He followed Jenna across the deck.

Bella watched as he gave her the news. Jenna hugged him, and Jamie said something that made her laugh; then he slung his arm over her shoulder and offered her a cookie. She was glad to see Jenna smiling again.

The boat moved swiftly through the water as they left the marina and headed out into the open water. Bella and Caden leaned against the railing at the bow of the boat. The crisp air stung against her skin, but beneath Caden's protective arm, Bella was toasty warm.

"Evan's really excited about TGG. I don't think I properly thanked you." He kissed her cheek. "It means the world to me that you include Evan in your thoughts."

She turned toward him, and her hair whipped across her cheek. Caden reached over and gathered her hair in his big hand and held it away from her face. "That's how you first stole my heart, remember?"

"I remember." He glanced at Evan, feverishly texting on his cell phone.

She loved the way he was conscious of acting appropriately in front of Evan. It made their stolen kisses even more special. Heck, she loved everything about him, stolen kisses or heated, exposed kisses, and it still surprised the heck out of her, because she'd been dead set on sticking to her plan.

"I missed you last night." He moved so close she could see his long eyelashes tangling at the corners of his eyes.

She felt her cheeks heat up as the others joined them.

Caden took a step back, but the heat of him

remained.

"None of that kissy-face stuff, please. It's depressing me." Jenna pushed her way in between them. "I'm instigating a five-foot rule." She pointed to Leanna and Kurt, standing arm in arm. "You too. Five feet between you at all times. Give a girl some slack, will ya?"

"You're such a nut. Jamie said Pete was bummed about not coming with us."

"I know. But Jamie's so sweet he probably made that up." Jenna smiled at Jamie.

"I'm not that nice," Jamie said as he joined them by the railing.

The captain cut the engine and the boat slowed.

Amy ran to the railing. "Oh good. Now we get to fish. I'm so excited."

"Fish barbeque in the quad tonight?" Tony whipped off his shirt. Caden, Kurt, and Jamie followed his lead, and the bare-chested men began readying the fishing lines.

"Who needs Pete with this much eye candy around?" Jenna slapped Jamie's butt.

Bella caught Caden's eye and blew him a kiss. "You're telling me?"

Tony was helping Amy with a fishing rod. "Hey, Ames," Jenna called. "Hands off Tony's rod."

Amy blushed.

Bella laughed, glad Jenna was back to her old self.

Bella couldn't tear her eyes from Caden. She could still feel his hips against hers, his muscular thighs, heavy and tense as they joined together last night.

"Hey, girlie. If you keep looking at him like that, his son is going to learn a lot more than fishing on this trip." Leanna bumped her shoulder against Bella's.

"Sorry." Bella turned away from Caden. "Now I know how you felt with Kurt. I've never felt like this before."

"Neither had I. Remember how it freaked me out?" Leanna shifted her eyes to Kurt and sighed. "He's everything to me, Bell."

"I know, and I get it. I feel the same way about Caden, and of course Evan." She glanced at Evan, who was still texting. "As a matter of fact, I think I'll go talk with him a little and see if I can get him away from his cell phone for a few minutes."

"Hi, Ev." Bella sat beside him.

He pressed the lock button on his phone. "Hey."

"Don't you want to fish?"

"In a minute." Evan shifted his eyes away, and when he brought his attention back to Bella, a chill ran up her spine at the frightened look in his eyes.

"You okay?"

He looked away again and fidgeted with his phone. "How long are we going to be out here?"

"A couple hours, I guess. Is something wrong?"

He looked at Caden, then dropped his eyes to his phone again. "I can't get any service. I had it back at the dock, but I've lost it."

"That happens a lot out here. Is something going on that you need service right now?" She didn't like the way his demeanor had changed since he arrived.

He shrugged again.

"Ev, if something's wrong, I'm sure Joe can get in touch with someone for you."

"I'm cool."

"Ev, come take this line." Caden waved him over to the railing.

Evan shoved his phone in his pocket and joined Caden. Caden handed him a fishing rod, but Evan's expression didn't change.

"Remember when you caught that big one two summers ago?" Caden asked Evan.

Evan handed him the pole. "I don't want to fish." He stalked to the other end of the boat, leaving Caden to stare after him.

Bella reached for the pole. "I'll take it. You should go to him. I think something's wrong."

"He's just moody." Caden draped an arm over her shoulder, holding the rod in the other hand, and nuzzled against her neck.

"I don't think so." She watched Evan standing farther down the deck with his shoulders hunched forward as he scrolled through his phone. He fisted his hand around it and punched the air.

"Babe, he's just going through something right now. You even said he'd get through this hard time just fine." Caden turned back toward the water.

An uneasy feeling drew Bella's eyes back to Evan.

Amy squealed. "I've got one!"

Distracted by Amy, Bella glanced back at her, despite her mind still being on Evan.

Tony came up behind her, dwarfing her small frame with his large body, as he reached around her and helped her bring in the line.

"Hang on tight," he guided her. "Good. Now reel it in slowly. That's it."

"Okay. Okay." Amy smiled brightly. "I got a fish!"

"Way to go, Amy," Jenna cheered from the other side of the rail, where her own line hung in the water. "I knew you'd snag one before me." She threw her head back and laughed. "Get it?" She elbowed Leanna.

"You're so silly." Leanna bumped her with her hip.

In the excitement, Bella slipped away and went to Evan. He turned away as she neared, a move that screamed trouble in Bella's experienced mind.

"Evan, you sure you don't want to fish?"

He nodded.

"Well, you're missing out on a good time." She

leaned on the railing and looked out over the water. It was a warm, sunny day, and she only wished Evan could enjoy it.

His eyes were hidden by his hair, but she had a clear view of his clenching jaw. He was throwing off the same troublesome vibe she'd felt when they left the beach.

"Evan, if there's something—"

"Nothing's going on, okay?" He breathed heavily through flaring nostrils.

*Holy crap, what are you dealing with?*

"Okay. Okay. Sorry." She took a step away.

"Wait." The tremor in his voice stopped her cold. He crossed and uncrossed his arms. "I don't know if something's wrong. Everything's messed up."

"Evan, *what's* messed up?"

He clammed up again, and she wanted to shake him into talking.

"Hey, guys." Caden's voice cut through the silence. He ran his eyes between the two of them. His smile faded, replaced with a piercing, worried stare. "What's going on?"

Evan shot a look at Bella. She tilted her head and softened her gaze, as if to say, *This is all you, buddy.*

Evan shifted his eyes to his father again. He crossed his arms over his chest, but he couldn't hide the fearful vibe that radiated from him.

"It's Vera."

Two words that hit like a bullet to Bella's chest.

Caden closed in on him. "*What's* Vera?"

"I don't know." Evan drew in a jagged breath. His voice was shaky and angry, and his eyes welled with tears. "I don't know, okay? Those guys sent me a text, and I think it might mean that they're doing something to her cottage. I don't know, Dad, and I swear I have nothing to do with it."

Without a word, Caden stalked inside and grabbed his duffel bag. He pulled out some sort of radio and called in a report to the station for someone to get over to Vera's cottage.

"Evan?" Bella placed her hands on his shaking shoulders and stared into his damp eyes. "Tell me what you know."

"They sent a text that said I could go to hell and that she could kiss her violin goodbye. I think they thought she was with us." Evan pulled out of her grasp. "Shit. Damn it. If they hurt her, I swear I'll kill them."

Adrenaline and worry surged through Bella's veins. She heard Caden talking to Joe; then he went to the front of the boat and pulled Jamie aside. A minute later Jamie was hulking over Evan and there was a flurry of pulling in fishing lines and worried voices.

"What the hell is going on?" Jamie demanded. His face was red, the veins in his neck plumped, snaking over tight muscles.

"I...I don't know. I swear I didn't know anything, Jamie. I swear it. I would never hurt Vera." Tears streamed down Evan's cheeks.

Bella had never seen Jamie as angry as he was now, pacing the deck with fisted hands. The boat roared to life and sped toward shore. The others gathered together, trying to figure out what was going on. Words of worry and confusion darted from their conversations. Caden dragged Evan to the opposite end of the boat with his back to Bella and the others. He paced a few steps, stopped and said something to Evan, then paced again. Evan shriveled beneath Caden's anger. Bella couldn't think past hoping that whatever was going on, Vera was okay.

# Chapter Twenty

CADEN DRAGGED EVAN off the boat and drove like a bat out of hell toward Seaside. Anger, worry, and guilt swelled in his chest.

"What the hell were you thinking, Evan? You should have said something to me the minute you got that text." He didn't mean to yell, but he had no chance in hell of quelling his anger. "Jamie trusted you. I trusted you. Damn it, Evan."

"I'm sorry. I texted them and told them not to go near her. You can check my phone. I thought they were just dicking around with me." Evan pressed his body against the passenger door. "Dad, I swear, I would never do anything to hurt her."

"How did they know about her violin?"

"They asked me to meet them one day when I was with Jamie, and I said no. That night we were joking around, and I said something about her playing the violin. I didn't think anything of it, Dad. I was just talking. I never thought they'd do anything."

Caden shook his head. "If anything happened to Vera..." What? There were no words to express how he felt. This was as much his fault as it was Evan's. He'd been so wrapped up in Bella that he hadn't spent enough time with Evan. He'd noticed all sorts of clues, but he hadn't spent enough time investigating them. What the hell had he been thinking?

"I want to know who is involved with this, Evan. Even if it includes you. And I want to know every last detail that you know." *Holy fuck. It had better not include you.* As he sped into Seaside and the police cars came into view, another reality slap slammed into his chest. If it came down to it, could he turn in his own son?

"Do not get out of this truck, and you'd better pray she's okay." Caden cut the engine and went into Vera's cottage. The smell of freshly baked cookies shot another piercing pain through him. A quick scan of the surroundings told him there hadn't been a struggle. Nothing was overturned. The officer, who he knew from the station, filled him in, and he headed back out to the truck as the others arrived.

Jamie grabbed his arm. "How is she?"

"She's okay, but they took her to the urgent care to get checked out."

Pain etched Jamie's face.

Caden quickly added. "It was precautionary. She was frightened, but no one touched her. Jamie, I'm sor—"

Jamie was already climbing into his car.

Kurt and the others were talking to another officer. Bella ran to Caden.

"What happened? Is she okay?" Fear riddled her words and filled her eyes.

He spoke fast as he hurried back toward the truck. "She was frightened. They took her to the urgent care center. I'm taking Evan there now."

Bella kept pace with him. "I'll go with you."

Caden stopped walking. He fisted his hands, fighting the urge to take her in his arms and tell her Vera would be okay and that he'd deal with Evan. He struggled against the ache burning a hole in his gut because this whole mess was his fault, and when he finally forced himself to speak, his serious, controlled voice surprised him.

"I think I'd better handle this alone. I'm sorry." He climbed into the truck and sped out of the community, feeling as though his world was shattering around him.

BELLA RAN INTO the urgent care center with Amy and Jenna on her heels. Leanna, Kurt, and Tony had stayed at the cottages so as not to overwhelm the urgent care center. The policeman at the cottages had told them that the kids broke in, and when they saw Vera was home, they took off, but the intrusion had shaken Vera up very badly. She hoped and prayed that Vera was okay.

They found Evan standing against the far wall of the waiting room with his back to the door. Caden was nowhere in sight. Bella went to Evan.

"What's happening?"

Evan turned with a shrug. His face was pale, his eyes sorrowful. "They won't tell me anything. Dad's in with Jamie. Bella, I swear, I didn't know they were serious when they texted."

"Okay. I believe you." She turned and nearly toppled over Amy and Jenna. "Jesus. Let me go see if I can get any information." She left them with Evan and went to the registration desk, where she was able to speak to Bones.

"Hi, Bella."

"Hi. Sorry to bother you, but our friend Vera Reed came in and I wanted to see how she was doing."

Bones's eyes softened. "Oh." He stepped closer and lowered his voice. "She's with a police officer and her grandson. I can't let you back unless she gives us the okay."

"I don't need to go back. I just want to know if she's okay."

He nodded and held up a finger; then he disappeared down the hall. When he returned a few minutes later, Bella was relieved to see him smiling.

"She's okay, and she's talking up a storm. They're just monitoring her. I'm sure she'll be released soon."

"Oh, thank God. Can I bother you to just ask Caden Grant, the officer who's with her, if he wants me to take his son back to my place? I hate to leave him here." She pointed to the waiting area, where Jenna and the others were hovering around Evan.

"Sure. Hold on." He left again, and returned quicker this time. "He said to leave Evan here and he'd take care of him."

*He said to leave? Leave?* Caden's response took her by surprise. She thanked Bones, even though she was tortured inside, and drew in a few deep breaths before returning to the others.

"Well?" Jenna asked.

"They said she's okay and she'll be released soon." She touched Evan's shoulder. "Are you okay?"

He shrugged.

"Your dad should be out soon. Do you want me to stay with you until he comes out?"

"No. I'm okay."

Bella didn't hesitate before wrapping her arms around him. She was surprised when he returned the embrace.

"Call me if you need me, okay?"

He nodded. "Bella, I swear, I really didn't know about any of this. I told Dad everything I knew."

"That's good, Evan. I'm just glad she's okay."

They went back to Seaside and joined Leanna, Kurt, and Tony on Leanna's deck. Pepper pawed at Bella to be petted, and Bella crouched to love him up as she filled them in. They sat in silence afterward, digesting the terrible turn of events.

"Man, Bella. Was Evan into some deep shit, or was he just hanging out with the wrong kids?" Tony asked. "I never would have expected this."

"No one did. I think—I hope—he was just hanging out with the wrong kids. Last night he told Caden that he wasn't going to hang out with them anymore, and from what he said on the boat, they got pissed because of it." She rubbed the back of her neck. "Who does this sort of thing? They could have given Vera a heart attack."

"What did Caden say?" Jenna tucked her hair behind her ear. "Can you imagine? He's not just a parent, but a cop."

"I don't know. He said he wanted to handle it alone. I guess he'll call when things settle down." The way he'd looked when he'd told her he had to handle it alone made her stomach sink. Then again, this wasn't like everyday bad behavior. This was a hundred times worse.

They turned at the sound of Jamie's car pulling into his driveway. Amy's eyes filled with tears. Tony put his arm around her as they descended the stairs to the deck. Jenna grabbed Bella's hand.

"Thank God she's back," Jenna whispered as they went to greet him.

Jamie opened Vera's car door and reached for her hand.

"Goodness gracious. What a welcoming committee." Vera smiled and patted her hair. "I must be a mess."

"You're perfect, Gram." Jamie walked with one hand on her lower back, the other firmly holding her arm.

"How do you feel, Vera?" Bella asked.

"Oh, Bella dear. I'm okay. I was just a little rattled, that's all. I don't think those boys expected me to be home, and I think I startled them as much as they startled me." She shook her head as they entered her cottage. "The police thought they were after my violin, because when I came out of the bedroom, one of them had it in his hands, but he dropped it before he ran back out the door."

"I'm so sorry—"

Vera interrupted her with a gentle touch on her arm. "Bella, I know you're worried about Evan, and believe me, if I thought this was Evan's doing, I would say so. As I told Caden—bless his heart, he is as devastated by this as poor Jamie is—I don't think Evan orchestrated this. He was too remorseful. Call it a gut feeling." She lowered herself onto the couch, and Jamie fluffed a pillow and slid it beside her. "Thank you, dear."

Bella wanted to know how the whole awful situation had come about in the first place and how Evan was holding up, but Caden could fill her in later.

"I'm sorry, Vera. This is my fault, too. I brought Evan here and introduced him to Jamie." She lifted her eyes to Jamie's and ached at the disappointment in his dark eyes. "Jamie, I'm so sorry."

"You couldn't have known, Bella," Jamie said flatly. "I think we'd better let Gram rest."

Outside the cottage, Kurt breathed a sigh of relief. "Thank God she's okay. What a nightmare."

Bella had a sinking feeling in her stomach. She needed to find out the complete story, not only for her own peace of mind, but for everyone else's, as well.

She wanted to call Caden and see how he was holding up. She knew he was devastated, but she also knew that he needed time to deal with Evan.

"We're going to stay at the house tonight," Kurt said as he pulled Leanna close. "Will you call if anything comes up?"

"Of course," Bella said.

Leanna hugged her. "Hang in there, Bella. I know you're worried about Caden and Evan, but you heard Vera. She doesn't think he was involved. And he did speak up when he thought something was going on. Call me if you need me."

"I will, thanks."

Tony draped an arm over Bella's shoulder. "Come on. Let's all go to my deck and commiserate."

"I'm going to get some munchies. I'm starved." Jenna hurried back to her cottage.

"I'll get iced tea." Amy ran onto her deck and disappeared into her cottage.

Bella leaned against Tony as they walked back to his deck. "Tony, how will we get past this? No one will ever look at Evan the same again."

Tony tightened his grip around her shoulder. "Bell, I think I remember hearing a story about three girls who snuck out one night, broke into a certain family's cottage, and drank all the beer in their fridge."

Bella had buried that memory long ago.

"And the way I heard it, those girls lied about being involved and admitted it only after a certain skinny little blonde puked her guts up." He stopped walking and shifted his eyes to Amy, heading down the gravel road toward them.

"Do you have a point, or are you just into reminding me that I was once a delinquent, too?"

"First of all, my chunky-dunking, firework-exploding, toilet-carrying friend, you are still a little bit of a delinquent. My point is, did everyone treat those teenagers any differently afterward, or were there a few days of disappointed looks and meaningful discussions to help the girls understand why they shouldn't have done it?" He arched a brow and kissed the top of her head. "It's gonna be okay, Bell. We all love you, and I don't think anyone here will assume the worst about Evan unless you tell us that this was all his doing."

"What are we talking about?" Amy carried a pitcher of iced tea. She'd thrown a sundress on over her bathing suit and she was juggling plastic wineglasses.

Tony took the pitcher and glasses from her arms. "I was just telling Bella to breathe."

"That sounds like good advice."

Jenna joined them on Tony's deck a few minutes later with a bowl of pretzels and a container of hummus. "Terrible situations make me hungry." She lowered herself into a chair, then patted Bella's leg. "Any word from Caden?"

"Darn it. My phone's in the car." Bella rose.

Tony patted her on the shoulder. "I'll get it."

Amy stared after him with a dreamy look in her eyes.

"Hey, puppy eyes." Jenna tossed her a pretzel.

"Sorry. Habit." Amy shoved the pretzel into her mouth.

"You guys, tell me what you're thinking right this very second." Bella prepared for worries about Vera followed by, *It sucks to be you. I can't believe Evan lied to everyone. How can we ever trust him again?*

"I'm so relieved that Vera is okay, and I wish Jamie hadn't looked at you the way he did," Amy said. "Oh, and Tony's got a nice ass."

"You noticed that look, huh?" Bella asked.

"I noticed that look, too. I'm glad Vera's okay, and I wish *you* didn't look so worried." Jenna popped a pretzel into her mouth. "Oh, and I agree about Tony's ass."

"Ugh." Bella buried her face in her hands. "That look sucked, but I don't blame him." She reached for a pretzel. "So, you're telling me that neither of you is sitting here thinking about how Evan effed up? Or wondering if he was behind the whole thing, if he *sent* them to Vera's?"

Jenna and Amy exchanged a concerned look.

Amy touched Bella's hand. "Bell, he said he wasn't involved, and he turned them in. Have a little faith."

*Faith.* There's that word again. "I've been thinking about fate, and I do have faith in Evan. I believe him, but I'm worried that everyone else might not be as forgiving. And what if he *was* behind it? How will I ever face Jamie and Vera again? And Caden? I know he blames himself. I saw it in his eyes."

"In a case such as this, Bella dear..." Tony dropped her cell phone in her lap. "Do as my mama always said. *Wait until the coffee brews to determine if it stinks.*" He settled into a seat beside Amy with a loud sigh.

"Come again?" Bella said as she scrolled through her phone.

"Wait until you talk to Caden to worry about what's next. Don't stress over things that aren't clear." He grabbed a handful of pretzels and handed a few to Amy.

"He hasn't called." Bella sighed.

"It might be hours. He's got a lot to deal with right now, and he's probably grilling Evan so he can have those kids arrested. The police said they were gone when they got here." Amy topped off her glass with iced tea. "I'm glad I'm not in that house tonight."

"Funny, I'd give anything to be right there by his

side. No matter how hard it gets."

# Chapter Twenty-One

CHIEF BASSET'S OFFICE was silent, save for the sounds of Evan's rapid breathing and the blood rushing through Caden's ears. Evan sat board straight, with his shoulders pulled back and his hair pushed out of his eyes. He was putting on a brave face, but Caden noticed the slight twitch in the left side of his mouth and his fingers fidgeting with the seam of his shorts. The whole situation sucked. He and Evan hashed and rehashed what had gone down at Vera's, and Evan told him that two of the other boys were behind the recent rash of break-ins. Caden still couldn't shake the feeling that if he hadn't let himself get so involved with Bella, he would have been more attuned to what Evan was going through and more attentive to the changes in his behavior. Hell, he might have been able to avoid the situation altogether, but he knew better than anyone that there was no going backward. He knew what he had to do, and that started with teaching Evan a hard lesson about responsibility, which was why they were at the police station.

"It's all there on my cell phone." Evan pointed to

his phone, which he'd placed in the center of the chief's desk. "It was Mike and David who broke into all those places—the campground, the cars at the beach and at that auto shop—and it was them at Vera's too. I swear I haven't deleted messages or anything. You can even look at the records." The strain in Evan's voice nearly did Caden in. "You can do that, right, Dad?"

"Evan, are there any other kids involved besides the two that you've told us about?" Chief Basset consulted his notes. "Mike Elkton and David Farrell?"

"What about Bobby?" Caden asked.

"No. I told you. Bobby didn't do anything. It was Mike and David who broke into those other places, and I only know David did it because Bobby told me so. That's why I stopped hanging out with them." Evan's eyes pleaded with Caden to believe him, even though he'd already pled his case back at the house. "I thought they were kidding when they said they'd *fingered* a car at Nauset, but then I started putting two and two together, and I asked Bobby about it and he told me a day later that they weren't kidding. They're the ones who were breaking into places."

"But not Bobby Falls?" Chief asked again.

"No. I swear it. You can ask him. He stopped hanging out with them when I did." Evan wrung his hands together and looked from Caden to the chief. "I would never do something like that. Bobby told me that they thought that since my dad was a cop they'd be safe. Like, if my dad found out, there was no way he'd turn them in if I was involved. That was the night I got pissed. Remember, Dad? When Bella was there for dinner? Me and Bobby were chatting online when he said they told him that. I confronted them last night, and I guess that breaking into Vera's place was payback or something."

"Evan, we're going to bring these kids in, and we'll

ask them for their side of the story." The chief leaned across the desk. "You realize that we have to listen to all sides."

"Yes, sir. And I know they might try to say that I was involved. But that's why I'm giving you my phone, and Dad said you could get the records from our online chats. That will also prove that I wasn't involved." He shot a worried look to Caden, and his voice escalated. "They can't fake that, can they? You can search IP addresses to see what messages came from our house, can't you?"

Caden placed a hand on Evan's forearm. He held on tight and hoped that Evan would take comfort in his touch.

"Evan, they can do all those things," Caden assured him. "What Chief Basset wants to know is if there is anything you want to admit to so that he hears it from you first. Remember my rule. Please, of all times, this is the time to honor it."

Evan nodded. "I know." He drew in a breath, and Caden felt him shaking beneath his touch. "We went to Payton's Campground one afternoon, and I didn't do anything, but Mike and David left me and Bobby for about twenty minutes, and when they came back, they told us to get the heck out of there." His tone was apologetic, and his hooded eyes were dreadfully sorry. "That was the time Bella said she saw me and I said she didn't. I'm sorry, Dad."

The day just got even shittier.

Evan brought his attention to the chief once again. "Bobby told me later that night that they told him they'd broken into a trailer and stolen some stuff, but he didn't know what. I should have said something, but I was afraid to. I'm sorry, Dad. I'm sorry, Chief Basset. If I had said something, maybe they wouldn't have had the chance to break in to Vera's cottage. And

I take responsibility for that." Evan sat back and covered his face with his hands. "I'm so sorry." He drew in another deep breath. "Dad, when we're done here, I want you to take me to Vera's. I need to talk to her and Jamie."

"I don't know, Evan. This isn't a little thing. Vera could have had a heart attack. They could have hurt her in some other way. She's stressed. She feels violated and unsafe in her own cottage. Jamie's livid. His grandmother, the woman who raised him, was put in danger. Do you understand that?" He didn't give him a chance to answer. "I'm not sure they'll be receptive to talking to you just yet. They might need a few days to get past this." Or a few weeks, or years. He had no frigging idea if Jamie and Vera would ever get past it. Hell, he needed time to digest it.

"Please? I know all that, Dad. That's why I need to talk to them," Evan begged.

"I think that's a good idea, Caden." Chief Basset held a steady gaze on Caden. "You'll be there to buffer the situation. Unless you worry they'll retaliate in some way, I think it's important to give Evan a chance to make amends."

"Yes, sir." Caden realized that he hadn't said no just because of his concerns of how Jamie and Vera might react, but also because he wasn't ready to face Bella just yet.

"What will happen to David and Mike?" Evan asked.

Caden found it interesting that Evan wasn't asking about what would happen to him. He must have truly come clean, which was honorable, even if he should have come to him sooner.

"Well, son, that'll depend on how the investigation goes, and if Mrs. Reed presses charges. And, of course, if those other thefts are confirmed. If you don't mind,

I'd like a word with your father alone. You can wait right outside the door by Ms. Palken's desk." Chief Basset nodded a dismissal to Evan.

"Yes, sir." Evan left the office, and Caden's eyes tracked him through the glass until he disappeared in the direction of Kristie's desk.

Chief Basset leaned back in his chair. "That's a pisser, huh?"

"That's one way to put it."

"You okay?" Chief Basset asked.

"Yeah. Fine. Just, you know...When it's your kid, all sorts of shit goes through your head." *Like if we never moved, this wouldn't have happened.*

"Yes, I do know. Like, what if he had been involved? What if he'd been the one to break in?"

Caden rose to his feet. "Yeah."

"Don't be too hard on him, Caden. He did the right thing."

"I know. Thanks, Chief."

On the way out of the station, Evan apologized again.

"I know you're sorry, Ev. You did the right thing by telling us. I just wish you would have come to me sooner, but in the end, you did the right thing, and I'm proud of you for that."

Evan had been strong throughout the last few grueling hours. He hadn't shed a tear since they left the boat, and he hadn't lost his cool. Now, at his father's words, his eyes dampened again.

"I didn't mean to mess up so badly, Dad, but I swear to you that I didn't have anything to do with any of the break-ins. I just wanted friends to hang out with, and then, when I realized what they were into, I didn't really believe it at first—then I did..."

Caden pulled Evan into his arms. His thin frame shook within Caden's stable embrace.

"I'm sorry, Dad. I'm so sorry."

Caden cupped the back of his son's head and held him close. He'd held him through scraped knees, broken fingers, and hurt feelings. He'd held him through tears shed over an absentee mother, and George's death, which had sent them both crumpling to their knees. But this, holding Evan after watching him do what most adults wouldn't have the courage to do—snitch on kids he'd have to face on a daily basis in the fall—this was powerful. Petrifying. This was why he needed to be there for Evan every damn minute he could.

On the way out of the parking lot, Evan asked to see Vera again.

"Evan, she's had a terribly hard day. It's seven o'clock. I think it might be better to wait until tomorrow."

Evan pressed his palms to his thighs. "Please, Dad? I want to talk to them."

"As I said, they may not be very receptive."

"I know. That's okay. You've always taught me to say I'm sorry, and I don't want to wait to say it." Evan's eyes were hooded, tired, but his voice was determined.

Caden knew that Evan would stay up half the night thinking about it if he didn't take him to see Vera now. He also knew that the longer he waited to talk to Bella, the more difficult it would be.

"Okay."

The sun was beginning to set when they pulled into Seaside. Evan's eyes jumped over each cottage on the way around the gravel drive.

"No one's outside," he said.

"It's been a tough day." Caden looked at Bella's cottage and caught sight of a shadow through the window. His chest ached with the memory of being

280

with her last night.

He parked by Vera's cottage and told Evan to wait in the car so he could ask Jamie if it was okay for Evan to come in. He knew this wasn't going to be easy for any of them, but Jamie had looked like Caden had felt earlier in the day when they were at the urgent care center—ready to tear someone's head off. He couldn't protect Evan from what he went through with those kids, but he could, and would, protect him from whatever else he was able to. Jamie had a right to be angry, but Caden hoped he'd be able to control his anger where Evan was concerned, at least until he heard him out.

Jamie answered the door with surprise in his eyes. "Caden."

"Hi, Jamie. How's Vera?"

"She's okay. Would you like to see her?" He stepped to the side, and Caden saw Vera sitting on the couch, reading.

"Actually, Evan's in the car, and he'd like to talk to both of you."

Jamie furrowed his brow.

"Jamie, I tried to dissuade him, but he really wants to make amends. We're just coming back from the police station. He didn't have anything to do with any of this, and he feels horrible."

"Jamie Joseph, you let that boy come in and say his piece," Vera said from behind Jamie. "Hello, Caden. How are you, dear?" Vera peered around her grandson.

"We've seen better days. I'm truly sorry, Vera."

"Yes, dear. You told me that at least a dozen times today, and I do appreciate it. You know I think I scared those boys as much as they scared me. They left as quickly as they came when they realized I was here. I think they expected the place to be empty. Please bring Evan inside. I'd like to speak to him."

"Thank you, Vera." Out of respect, Caden also deferred to Jamie. "Jamie?"

"Of course. Bring him in." Jamie sat down on the couch.

Caden went to the car and leaned over Evan's open window.

"They'll see you, but, Evan, don't expect this to be easy. No matter what they say to you, I expect you to remain respectful. Got it?"

"Yes. I know." Evan stepped from the car. "I know this is my fault, Dad. I can handle it. I owe them an apology." Evan followed him inside the cottage. He brushed his hair out of his eyes and stood before Vera, who had settled back onto the couch again.

Caden's chest constricted as he watched the boy he'd raised stand up and act like a man.

"Sit down, Evan. Please," Vera said.

Evan sat in a rocking chair beside the couch. He drew in a deep breath before turning his attention to Caden.

"Dad, can you please give us a minute?"

Caden was taken by surprise. "Are you sure?"

"Yes. Please?"

The confidence in Evan's voice was another surprise. He had no idea what his son might say, but he left him to make amends and hoped for the best. He'd handled himself well with the chief, and Caden had a feeling he'd do just fine with Vera and Jamie, too. He walked out of the cottage and over to the grassy area behind Bella's cottage. He couldn't stay away. He heard dishes clanking inside, and as he neared her deck, Bella glanced out the window and their eyes met. Caden's chest constricted as she came outside.

"Hi. How's Evan?" She hooked her finger in the waist of his shorts.

"He's okay. He's with Jamie and Vera." Jesus, he loved her. He loved her generous heart, her thoughtfulness, the way she claimed him with one small finger in his waistband. She went up on her toes, and he met her halfway for a tender kiss. He took her hand in his and brought it to his lips. "Bella..." He heard the devastation in his own voice.

Her smile faded. "Caden? What is it?"

*Don't do it. Don't say a word.*

"Caden. You're worrying me." She searched his eyes.

"Bella, I think I need to take some time and focus on Evan." *Stop. Fucking stop before you screw this up.* He hadn't realized he had come to this resolution so definitively until the words left his lips.

"Of course. I assumed that's why you hadn't called." She sighed. "You scared me. You looked so..." She searched his eyes. "Oh God. Caden?"

"Babe." He reached for her hand, and she pulled it away. "Look at what's happened, Bella. Vera could have been hurt. Evan could have gotten into real trouble. If I were more focused on him, this might never have happened."

"Wh-what are you saying?" Her lower lip trembled.

"Bella, you know what I'm saying. I need to focus on Evan and make sure he gets straightened out." The pain in her eyes sliced through every fiber of his being.

"I don't understand." She lowered her voice, and a tear slid down her cheek.

He wiped the tear with the pad of his thumb and gritted his teeth against the sadness that snaked around his heart and squeezed so tight he could barely breathe. "I'm sorry, Bella," he whispered. "I'm so sorry, but I'm obviously not very good at being a father and a boyfriend. I've failed Evan. I think we need to take a break."

"I don't need a break, Caden. *You* need a break. I want to be there for you and for Evan." She crossed her arms and turned away. "I thought you were all about commitment."

"I am. I always said that Evan was my top priority. I never hid that from you." He touched her shoulder, and she pulled gently from his reach. "I'm sorry, Bella, but I think Evan needs me around right now."

She turned to face him again with damp eyes. "So this is what you do? The going gets tough and you...*end* things?" Her shoulders rounded forward.

"That's not a fair statement. The going gets tough and I...Hell, Bella, I think I'm doing the right thing for Evan. We're adults; he's a kid. He needs guidance and attention. I didn't say I wanted to *end* things. I said *take a break.*" He didn't even know what he meant. He wanted to be with her every second of every day. But he needed to be there for Evan and make sure he got back on the right path without feeling cast aside, and how the hell could he do that if his heart was drawing him out the door?

"I *want* you, Bella. I just—" He'd kept his eyes off of Evan for too long, and look what almost happened. He needed to remain strong. For Evan.

"Please don't say any more." She turned away again, and when she spoke, it was with the same compassionate tone that had reeled him in when he'd first gotten to know her.

"I understand, Caden. I really do. But please, just go. It's too hard."

He stood behind her, desperately wanting to wrap his arms around her and press his cheek to hers. He wanted to tell her everything would be okay, but how could he, when he first needed to make sure his son was okay?

He lifted his hands to touch her shoulders—to comfort himself as much as to comfort her—then he lowered them to his sides without ever touching her, feeling impotent and sad.

So fucking sad.

## Chapter Twenty-Two

BELLA HAD BEEN lying on her bed staring up at the ceiling for hours, vacillating between thinking that Caden was doing the admirable and right thing and thinking about how the right thing felt like hell. Then guilt swallowed her whole for the latter thought. She'd pretended to be asleep when Jenna and Amy came over and peered into the bedroom. She'd ignored Jamie when he called through the bedroom window, and she'd ignored Pepper's barking when she heard Leanna returning to her cottage and calling across the road to Amy, explaining that she'd forgotten something.

She tried to doze off. A laughable thought. She had a meeting with the school board in a few hours, and she wanted to be rested, but she couldn't have slept if her life depended on it. She didn't want to think or feel. She wanted to pretend today never happened.

*Damn it.*

She didn't want to be this person, either. A woman who pined over a man who was only doing what was right for his child. A woman who pined over a man at all. She'd had a plan this summer, damn it. Her decisions were supposed to be made based on what she wanted, separate from any man or relationship.

*What the eff?*

*Why did I cave?*

*When did that happen, exactly?*

She caught sight of the bookmark Caden had given her and she groaned aloud. How was she supposed to just push aside her feelings for Caden—and Evan?

*Eff this.*

She tore off her clothes and wrapped herself in a towel, stomped to the kitchen and grabbed a bottle of Middle Sister wine, slipped her feet into a pair of flip-flops, and left her cottage.

*A break! An effing break.*

It was well after midnight and the lights in all the cottages were off. She went to Jenna's bedroom window, put her mouth up to the screen and shielded it with her hands.

"Jenna," she whispered loudly. "Jenna, get your ass up."

She heard Jenna grumble in her sleep. "Jenna Ward, I need you."

"Bella?"

Bella heard feet shuffling across the hardwood floor. Jenna's face pressed against the screen.

"Are you okay?" Jenna asked in a sleepy voice.

"No. Chunky-dunking. Now." She left no room for negotiation. "Hurry."

Jenna's face disappeared into the darkness. "We came by earlier," Jenna said as she shuffled around the room. "You were zonked."

"I was wallowing," Bella said through the screen.

Jenna's front door creaked open. She tiptoed across the grass in her towel and matching flip-flops. Her hair was pulled up on top of her head and secured with a plastic clip.

"Are you still upset over Vera and Evan?" Jenna looped her arms into Bella's and wiggled her toes. "Like my nail polish? Amy's are red. Mine are blue. We'll paint yours tomorrow. You got stuck with white."

"Nope. I'm not getting stuck with anything I don't want."

They walked across the quad and between Tony and Leanna's cottage, then crossed the gravel road to Amy's cottage.

"It's just nail polish. What were you wallowing over?" Jenna asked as they went around Amy's cottage to her bedroom window. "Jamie said Evan apologized and explained everything to them. Apparently, he shed a few tears, too. Poor kid. Being a teenager is so hard."

"Ames," Bella called through the screen. "Amy! Get your skinny ass up."

"What?" Amy pressed her nose to the screen and shielded her eyes, peering down at them. "Chunky-dunking? Oh goody! Hold on!"

They made their way down the gravel road, taking swigs of wine and passing the bottle from one to the next.

"Bella wasn't sleeping when we went over; she was wallowing," Jenna explained as she fumbled with the lock on the pool gate. The heavy metal chain clanked against the metal pole.

"Shh. Do you want to wake Theresa?" Bella grabbed the chain and held it still while Jenna inserted the key into the lock. "I'm wallowing because Caden said he needed an effing break."

Amy and Jenna gasped in unison.

"Tell me about it." Bella closed the gate behind them. "We'll talk after we're in the water. I need to clear my head." She and Amy walked to the far end of the pool by the stairs while Jenna dropped her towel on a table by the gate and hurried from one end of the pool to the other, nude, with her mammoth, bright white breasts swaying from side to side.

"Jenna!" Bella whispered. "Jesus, woman."

"Why does she always leave her towel up there?" Amy asked.

"God only knows. It's probably an OCD thing." Bella watched Jenna tiptoe onto the first step and lift her feet in quick succession, sucking in air between her teeth.

"Chilly. Chilly. Chilly chipples." Jenna laughed.

Bella set the bottle of wine on the table and draped her towel over a chair, then walked down the steps, passing Jenna, and went shoulder deep into the cool water. "God, I needed this. Just get under, Jen. I swear your boobs are like headlights. Get in before you wake Theresa and we all get in trouble."

"Okay, okay." Jenna spoke in a harsh whisper, as was their practice when they chunky-dunked. She went down one more step; then she went back up to the top step again with her fingers daintily spread out to her sides. "Cold. Cold. Cold."

Amy put her towel on the chair and crossed her arms over her small breasts. "Come on, Jenna. We'll go in together." She took Jenna's hand and they both sucked in air as they descended the steps and finally sank up to their chins in the water.

"Brr." Amy crossed her arms over her chest. "I don't remember it being this cold."

"It always is," Jenna said.

"It's not that cold, wussy girls." Bella dove under the water and swam like a dolphin to the far end of the pool. Jenna and Amy sidestroked across the pool.

"Bella, spill the beans. What the heck happened? I thought you and Caden were fine. More than fine."

Amy held on to the side of the pool and reached for Jenna's hand, then pulled her over. They were in the deep end, and in the dark, the water beneath them looked pitch-black.

Bella kicked her feet to stay afloat and to stay warm. Her body was so cold her limbs were shaking, though she'd never admit it after giving them a hard time.

"He said he needed to focus on Evan. That if he had been, this mess wouldn't have happened." Bella swallowed past the lump that lodged in her throat. "And I told him that I didn't want a break, that I'd be there for him and Evan no matter what."

"Of course you would." Amy's teeth chattered.

"Does he blame you somehow?" Jenna asked.

"No." Bella huffed a breath. "I guess Mr. Commitment doesn't keep commitments to women." She dove under the water to keep from crying and swam the length of the pool to the shallow end.

Jenna and Amy moved along the edge of the pool, hanging on to the concrete edge all the way to the four-feet-deep area, where Jenna could stand.

"That doesn't make any sense. He's all about commitment," Jenna said.

"Don't kill me, Bell," Amy began, "but this does kind of mean he's really committed, at least to Evan."

"I know that. But it sucks, right? I just don't understand why he needs a break from us to do it."

"Yes, but *break*? Or *break up*?" Now Jenna's teeth chattered, too.

"Break."

"Then you're not really broken up." Amy swam closer to Bella. "He'll be back. Just watch."

"Then does that make me pathetic if I want him to come back? Desperately?" Bella held her breath, fearing a *Yes.*

"No," Jenna said. "It means you love him."

"I do, but you know what? Maybe Leanna was right about fate." Bella cleared her throat to gain control of her emotions as she tried to spin the situation to her liking. "Maybe this happened so I can make my decision about where I live without the influence of our relationship." And in that second, she made a decision.

"Yes, I'm sure that's what it is," Amy said.

Bella wished she had as much faith in that scenario as she claimed.

A light clicked on in Theresa's house.

"Shh," they said in unison.

"Bella, come over to the edge." Jenna grabbed her arm and dragged her into the darkest corner of the pool. "Shh."

They clung to one another in the cold, dark corner of the pool until the light went back out.

"We'd better get out," Amy whispered.

They scrambled out of the pool, and Jenna's white ass wiggled all the way up to the far end of the pool, while Bella and Amy were wrapped in towels and ready to go in seconds.

Bella snagged the wine and headed for the gate. "Jen, if a car drove in, they'd see you in all your glory, running from one end of the deck to the other."

"Hush up," Jenna said as she wrapped her towel around her and reached for the gate. "I always leave my stuff there."

A flashlight shone in on them. Theresa stood at the entrance with a stern look in her eyes. She wore a pair of men's pajamas beneath a maroon robe, tied around her middle, and on her feet were indoor-outdoor slippers.

"Are you effing kidding me?" Bella mumbled as she slid the bottle of wine beneath her towel.

"Ladies." Theresa stared at Bella.

"Hey, Theresa." Bella feigned a smile. "We were just...closing the umbrellas. We thought it was supposed to be windy tonight." Water dripped from the ends of her hair onto her shoulder. She reached up and touched the drip. "And my shower pressure is just awful tonight, so I used the shower."

"Yeah. We all did." Jenna took a step behind Bella.

"Is that right?" Theresa pulled the gate open, allowing them to pass through. She shined the flashlight on Jenna's wet footprints, which led from one end of the pool to the other. "Because I'd hate to think you were breaking the rules and swimming. That's dangerous in the dark, and we can't have such risks being taken in the community."

"Oh no. Of course not." Amy swatted the air.

"Good." Theresa closed and locked the gate. "Because I know how enticing it can be to swim after dark."

Jenna sidled up to Theresa and whispered, "Do *you* want to go skinny-dipping?"

"Jenna!" Bella pulled her away from Theresa. "She's kidding." She dragged Jenna up the hill toward Bella's cottage, feeling the heat of Theresa's stare following them up the road.

"I think she knows we were swimming," Amy whispered. She clung to Bella's towel.

"Gee, ya think?" Bella glared at Jenna.

"And the toilet, too. Of course she knows it was us." Jenna's eyes widened.

Amy gasped. "Maybe she likes this whole game as much as we do."

"Or maybe she's plotting her sweet revenge," Bella suggested.

This was exactly what Bella needed. A distraction. Or many. She was either going to collapse into a pit of sorrow or sidetrack herself with her girlfriends. She tightened her grip on Jenna's arm and reached for Amy's hand. If only they could remain glued to her side until the pain subsided.

Or she died.

Whichever came first.

## Chapter Twenty-Three

THE NEXT FEW days were a blur of merely making it from one minute to the next, each moving slower than the last. Caden did everything he could to try to ignore the emptiness that threatened to suck him under at any moment. He went for morning runs after staying up at night, fighting the urge to call Bella to try to win her back. Every time he drove by Seaside, it took all of his willpower not to pull into the development, bang on her door, and forget trying to give Evan his full attention. Each day after his shift, he spent time with Evan, and while he tried to enjoy their time together and he knew he was doing the right thing for his son, without Bella, he felt like a piece of him was missing.

"Dad. Dad!"

Evan's frustrated voice pulled Caden from his thoughts. Evan stood on the front porch with one hand on the doorknob. His eyes were clear, and although his tone was frustrated, the old familiar ease that had once surrounded Evan with every breath had returned almost completely, confirming to Caden that he'd done the right thing. At least where Evan was concerned.

"Are you ready to leave? Should I lock the door?" Evan asked.

Today was Friday, and they were going to Boston for the day. "Sure, buddy. I'm ready." Except he was anything but ready. He'd invited Bella on the trip, and he'd been looking forward to showing her around his old stomping grounds and introducing her to his friends and to his parents.

"I can't wait to get there," Evan said as he climbed into the car. He no longer had his phone, since it was turned in to the police as evidence. He was chattier without it, and while Caden usually enjoyed their talks, he was too sidetracked to hold much of a conversation. He tried to push aside his thoughts of Bella, but their sharp edges refused to be ignored.

"Me too, buddy."

"I told Vera I would come by Sunday and clean up around her garden. Is that okay?"

"Sure."

"I'll bike over." Evan turned on his iPod and pressed an earbud into his ear.

Caden touched his arm, and when Evan pulled out the earbud, he said, "I'm proud of you, Ev. No one forced you to apologize or offer to help Vera. That says a lot about the person you are." He was thankful that both Jamie and Vera had accepted Evan's apology. Evan had told them everything, just as he'd told Caden and Chief Basset. Vera was very gracious with him, and although Caden still felt the hint of a fissure between Jamie and Evan, Jamie had said he had forgiven Evan, and Caden could tell that he was working on letting it go. He knew it had to be difficult. Hell, it was difficult for Caden at first, too, and Caden was his father. But love heals, and he knew their friendship would, too.

Evan shrugged. "I guess."

"And I think telling TGG about what happened was the smart thing to do. It's a small enough town that people will hear about what went down, and this way it's not a skeleton in your closet." They'd just come from TGG, where Evan was accepted as an apprentice for five hours each week, even after his confession. It was a start, and it was something that Evan was excited about and proud of.

"I know, Dad. I get it." He pushed the earbuds back in and looked out the window, leaving Caden to indulge in his painful thoughts until he felt as if he were drowning.

Two hours later, they pulled up in front of Caden's parents' house. The one-story rambler was nestled between two similar homes on a quiet residential street. He climbed from the car, remembering the night he'd brought Evan home for the first time. He remembered his mother's hand covering her mouth, her eyes filled with tears, as she reached for the sleeping baby. Now, as he walked up the front stoop with Evan beside him, he remembered how difficult it had been to hand him over—even to his own mother. In those few short hours between Caty placing Evan in his hands and Caden arriving at his parents' home, Evan had already become his world.

"Leave your skateboard on the porch," Caden said out of habit before they walked inside.

In a few short years, Evan would be off to college, and before he and Bella broke up, Caden had allowed himself to think of a future with her. He'd imagined lazy weekend mornings in bed and evening walks holding hands. He'd pictured them visiting Evan in college the way his parents had visited him, and one day, being the grandparents waiting on the stoop for Evan and—he hoped—his wife to hand them their first grandchild. And now sadness burrowed deep inside him.

"Hey there, bucko." Caden's father, Steven, was a burly man with thick arms and a belly that could use a little less of Caden's mother's home cooking. Steven embraced Evan and smiled over his shoulder at Caden. Caden had called his father Wednesday and filled him in on everything that had happened.

"Hi, Grandpa." Evan pulled out of his grandfather's arms, but before he could escape to follow the aroma of fresh-baked bread toward the kitchen, Steven ruffled his hair. Evan reached up to do the same to him and laughed when his grandfather playfully swatted his hand.

"Go say hi to Grandma." His father held Caden's gaze for a beat before embracing him.

Caden closed his eyes and reveled in the comfort of his father's arms. He'd always been Caden's rock, his sounding board.

"He's giving you a run for your money, isn't he?" Steven searched his son's eyes and furrowed his brow. "How are you holding up?"

"I'm good, Pop," he lied.

Steven slung an arm around his shoulder and guided him toward the kitchen. "I'm not sure I'm buying that, but come say hello to your mother."

What his father really meant was, *Let's see if your mother believes you.* Caden felt as transparent as Saran Wrap.

They found his mother pulling a hot loaf of bread from the oven. She smiled as they entered the cozy kitchen. Amber Grant was tall and thin, with auburn hair and hazel eyes that could stop a clock. Baking was a weekly ritual, and because of that, the house always smelled warm and inviting.

"Caden. You didn't tell me that Evan grew an inch." She set the pan on the top of the stove and took off her oven mitts. Her hazel eyes roved over Caden's face before she patted his cheek. "You okay, honey?"

"Fine, Ma. It's good to see you." Caden embraced her. "Did Ev grow? I guess since I see him all the time, I didn't notice." *Par for the course these days, but I'm working on that.*

"Oh, honey." She swatted the air. "There was one summer when you grew five inches and your father didn't notice until I mentioned it. I think it's a man thing. You men have busy minds or something."

*Or something.*

"Dad, Austin wants to meet me by the school. Do you mind if I skateboard over?" Evan asked. "I think we're gonna hang out with everyone for the day, but I can be back by dinner."

"Don't you want to spend some time with Grandma and Grandpa?" Caden asked.

"Let him go, honey. We'll catch up over dinner. Besides, I'm sure his friends are excited to see him." His mother sliced a piece of bread and wrapped it in a napkin. "Here, Ev. Take this so you're not hungry."

"Thanks, Grandma. Okay, Dad?"

"Sure." For a fleeting second, worry passed through Caden. He knew these boys, and he trusted Evan. Caden took his phone from his pocket and handed it to Evan. "Just call here if you need me. Be back by six, and behave."

Evan rolled his eyes. "I know."

Caden's mother sliced the bread and brought it to the table.

"Sit down, honey. Would you like some tea?" she asked.

"Sure." He wasn't the least bit hungry.

His father scrubbed his face with his hand and leaned back in his chair with a loud sigh. "So, parenthood is getting dicey." Steven had spent thirty years running the construction division of Eastern Pipeline, a company that ran underground piping for commercial buildings. He worked hours outside in the freezing cold and sweltering heat, and when Caden was growing up, he had no patience for laziness, procrastination, or disrespectful behavior. *Laziness has no place in a father's world, and one day you'll be a father, so get off your butt and get working*—on his homework, in the yard; what he was doing didn't matter. It was the message that mattered, and not only had Caden heard it loud and clear, he'd lived by it.

"You could say dicey. I might use a different word."

"Caden, is there anything else that's happened since the break-in? Has Evan admitted to being involved in any of it?" His mother nibbled on a piece of bread, her thin brows knitted together.

"No. He came clean, and there haven't been any new developments. He's about a hundred times calmer since all this came out, and without his phone, he's out of the loop from all that stuff. He also blocked the kids who were involved from his online activities." *Thank God.*

"What do you hear about the other kids?" Steven asked.

"They admitted to what they did. All of it, and surprisingly, they didn't try to implicate Evan. But they did admit that they thought if he helped them, I'd look the other way to protect him from getting in trouble with the law."

His father crossed his thick arms over his chest and looked down his nose at Caden.

"Pop, I took Evan straight to the station once I heard everything he had to say. I wouldn't have looked the other way."

His father nodded. "Good, because kids don't learn

a damn thing if they're not held accountable for their actions. But then again, I hope you didn't come down on him too hard with this, because he did snitch, and that takes balls."

"Steven," Caden's mother snapped.

"Sorry. That takes...Aw hell, Amber, that's the only thing that fits." His father covered his mother's hand with his and squeezed.

She shook her head and slid him a loving look that Caden had seen pass between them a million times. As much as it warmed him to see how much they loved each other, it made his heart ache for Bella.

They passed the afternoon with small talk. His parents brought him up to date on friends around Boston, and when his mother hadn't asked him why he was wearing a broken heart on his sleeve, he felt like he'd dodged a bullet. He knew she'd seen right through his feigned smiles and off-the-cuff answers.

His father liked to be busy, and after they'd exhausted easy conversation, he helped his father mow and edge the yard. Neither Caden nor his father needed much conversation. After that, they ran errands, another favorite pastime of his father. They went to the hardware store, the pharmacy, and finally, the grocery store to pick up a few last-minute items for dinner.

They were heading back to the house when his father pulled over at the ballpark where Caden had played as a kid. He left the car running and sighed. A combination so familiar, it sent a cold rush of air through his chest. When Caden was young and his father wanted to talk with him about something serious, he'd pull up at the ballpark and begin with a sigh.

"What's up, Pop?" He wasn't a kid any longer, and the longer the day stretched on, the wider the miles felt between him and Bella, making him feel agitated on top of feeling so fucking sad that he wanted to punch a hole in something.

"Son, obviously whatever's gotten under your skin isn't just Evan, because if it was, you never would have let him ride off to see his friends. You want to talk about it?" His father slid his warm brown eyes Caden's way. Looking at his father's face was like looking in the reflection of a time machine. They had the same angular nose, the same thin brows and cleft chin, and he knew that in twenty years, Evan would be thinking the same thing about him.

"Not really." His father couldn't fix his relationship with Bella. Nothing could, because he'd done the right thing for Evan, no matter how difficult it was for him.

"Fair enough. How about you give me a glimpse into what's going on anyway, or I'll have to deal with your mother hounding me until the next time you drag your ass out here. You look about as distraught as you did when you lost George. I know you're going through a lot with the move, a new station, and Evan, but..." He rubbed his chin.

"It's nothing I can't handle." Caden clenched his jaw against the acidic taste of the lie.

"Okay, play it your way." He put the car in reverse. "You mother thinks this has to do with a woman, and, son, if she's right, then good luck to you."

Caden wanted to tell his father all about Bella, that he loved her and that he'd made a mistake by saying he needed a break, but saying the words would only make it harder to digest.

"I have a feeling I'm shit out of luck, Pop."

His father huffed out a low laugh. "So, this *is* about a woman. Well, then, let me clue *you* in on something. I dated a few women before I married your mother, but when I met her. *Pow!*" He flicked his fingers forward, as if he were casting a spell out into the world. "Our eyes met and I could think of nothing but her every minute of every day afterward. Still can't." He shook his head and a smile spread across his face. "That's how you know it's real love, son. There's no ifs ands or buts. There's only life with her or hell without her."

*Hell. That sums it up perfectly.*

His father had never led him astray, and as they drove up to the house, Caden decided to open up to him.

"Well, Pop. I've got Evan. I have more to think about than just how I feel about her."

"Caden." His father paused as he pulled into the driveway and cut the engine. He turned to face Caden with a serious look in his eyes. "You've done a great job of raising Evan for all these years. Everyone who knows you recognizes how much you've given up for him, and despite this crap of hanging with the wrong kids, he's a damn good kid. That's because of you, Caden. All because of you. But, son, you must know that a man who never puts his own needs first can't be the best parent all the time."

Caden sat up a little taller, defending the fine job he'd done of raising Evan, despite his recent trouble. "I think I am a better parent for putting his needs first."

"You probably are a better father than you might have been if you hadn't done that, but, son, any way you cut it, a happy man is *always* a better father than an unhappy man. And for the first time in years, you're carrying around a banner with a frigging frown on it. Christ, Caden. You seem like you've lost George all over again, and I guess in a sense, if this woman is that important to you, then maybe you have." His father reached across the seat and settled his hand on Caden's shoulder. "Think about it. That's all I'm saying, son. If I can sense the unhappiness, so can he." He pointed to Evan riding his skateboard toward the car.

He'd been doing nothing *but* thinking about it since Tuesday night.

# Chapter Twenty-Four

BELLA UNLOCKED THE front door of her Connecticut home and stood in the doorway. Tears threatened, as they'd done since Caden said he needed a break. She tried to convince herself that this was all fated to be. *What if fate wants me to be in Connecticut? Shut up!* She had to believe that fate wanted her to follow her plan. Or maybe that fate sucked ass and she just had to make sure in her own goddamn mind where she belonged. She had a plan. She might have gotten waylaid, but she was back on track now, and she intended to stay that way. *Lead with my mind, not my heart.*

Two more companies that had been referred to her had signed up for the work-study program, meeting her twelve-company goal for the program. She'd met with the Barnstable County school board and had miraculously been able to hold her emotions at bay long enough to get an offer for full-time employment. When she'd gone to the Cape for the summer, getting that job offer was her top priority, and she was proud to have accomplished that goal.

It had been a tough decision to leave the Cape and return to Connecticut, even for just a day or two, but she had to walk into the school again and see if she still felt the desire to leave the place she'd called home for the last five years. Even before meeting Caden, she'd been excited about starting over in her favorite place on earth. But with her emotions all over the map, she had to be one hundred percent certain that she was either accepting her old job in Connecticut or the new job in Cape Cod for the right reasons—and those right reasons had to be her own. That's why, despite pleas from Amy and Jenna not to go, she took off that morning and drove almost four hours back to Connecticut. She couldn't shake the feeling that she'd forgotten something back at the Cape. The feeling had grown heavier with each mile she drove. By the time she arrived home, she realized that the something she'd left at the Cape was Caden and Evan. The distance between them felt terminal.

The house smelled and felt different. Empty. Still. *Lonely.* She'd lived in the house for four years, and it had never felt lonely before. She closed the door behind her and set her keys and purse on the table in the small foyer. She'd bought the Cape Cod–style home as a foreclosure and had been pleasantly surprised that there weren't any major underlying issues. She'd painted the interior top to bottom, which had taken weeks, but she'd enjoyed making the house her own. She'd even patched two holes in the drywall, but she'd had to hire a plumber to fix two broken pipes in the basement and replace a bathroom sink.

She meandered through the cozy kitchen, the dining room she'd never used, and the living room where she watched *Justified* and *Grey's Anatomy*. She wondered what it would have been like to watch those shows with Caden and Evan, and a shiver ran down her spine despite the warm summer day. As she ascended the stairs, she rubbed her arms to chase away the goose bumps. There were two small bedrooms upstairs: the master bedroom and a guest bedroom. Her bedroom was similar to the bedroom at her cottage, with a pink comforter and lacy throw pillows, white sheer curtains with pleated blinds, and a charcoal-gray shag area rug over hardwood floors. She ran her finger over the top of the dresser and picked up a framed photo of her, Jenna, Amy, Leanna, Tony, and Jamie from a few summers ago. As she stared at the photo, she couldn't help but envision Caden and Evan in the mix. She set it back down and walked to the window. Her neighbor, Jeannie Mace, and her thirteen-year-old son were playing catch in their backyard. Her mind traveled to Caden and Evan. Her throat thickened. She drew in a jagged breath and turned away. She wanted to bury her face in her fluffy pillows until the pain of missing them subsided. The urge was so tempting that it sprouted wings and hovered around her, taunting her. *Go ahead. Lay your head down and give up on your plans, your future. Wouldn't it feel good to disappear into your broken heart?*

Yeah, that was the problem. It would feel too damn good—for a few minutes. And then it would suck again. Big-time.

Bella wasn't the kind of person to fall apart.

Then again, she'd never been in love before.

And she was damn sure that what she felt for Caden was love.

She eyed the bed. *You know you want to flop onto your belly and have a good cry,* the urge said as it zoomed around her head.

"Eff you," she said to the empty room.

Bella ran down the stairs, snagged her keys and

purse, and sped out of the driveway toward the school.

Her sandals clip-clopped along the linoleum floors as she hurried down the hall toward her classroom, breathing in the unique smell of high school. A different scent filled the halls during the school year than it did during the summer months. During the school year, the halls smelled of perfume, testosterone, and teenage lust, with a hint of the other scent most teenagers gave off—adolescent angst. Images of Evan flashed in Bella's mind. She remembered the first moment she'd seen him, the evening of the beach bonfire, walking so close to Caden they could have banged shoulders and looking at his father with a mix of adoration and intrigue. She smiled at the memory of Evan and Jamie deep in conversation the night of the barbeque in the quad and the way his eyes lit up when Jamie invited him to stop by and learn about programming. Sadness pressed in on her as she recalled the way Evan had stormed out the back door of Caden's house the night she joined them for dinner and the petrified look in his eyes when they were on the boat.

God, she missed him. Was he holding up okay? Was he feeling less stressed or clamoring to move back to Boston?

She was with teens all day nine months out of the year. How had Evan torn off a piece of her heart so quickly?

She entered her classroom and drew in another deep breath. Her phone vibrated, and she pulled it from her pocket, hoping it was Caden. *Jenna*. This was the third time she'd called in as many hours. Bella shoved her phone back into her pocket. She couldn't talk to Jenna yet. She couldn't talk to anyone yet. She wasn't sure she was capable of talking without losing her voice to sobs.

She looked around the classroom. *I loved teaching here*. She loved her fellow teachers, and she even loved the way her windows faced the courtyard. During many stressful afternoons, she'd lost herself for a few blessed minutes gazing into the courtyard. Yes, she loved this place.

*Loved*. That was the operative word.

She could spend the next several years teaching the same classes and probably be content. But one thing she realized over the past few weeks of creating the work-study program was that she was missing out on the very things that excited her. Challenge. Diversity. Creativity. *Content* was no longer enough.

Each determined step she took down the hallway and toward the administrative offices solidified her decision. She was sticking to her effing plan, damn it. These were *her* decisions.

After meeting with Kelsey and firmly turning down the job offer, she went home and began packing. She couldn't keep her mind from wandering to Caden and Evan. Had they gone to Boston, and if so, had it made them both feel better? Did it bring back the sadness of losing George? If so, was Caden still sad when he returned, or was he strong and self-possessed as usual? Oh, how she wanted to call and ask him all those things, but if she called, she'd never make it through the day, and she had things to get done before she allowed herself to hear his voice again. She had to be strong. She was always strong.

Except she wasn't always strong, and Caden understood that.

He loved that about her.

She forced herself to focus on packing. She reached up to the top shelf of her closet and brought down a shoebox. Her lips curved up into a half smile. She lifted the top of the box and her smile faltered; her hands began to shake. Tears welled in her eyes.

*OhGodohGodohGod.* She reached into the box she hadn't opened in years and ran her fingers over the pink fuzzy handcuffs. A single tear slipped down her cheeks as she picked them up and clutched them to her chest. The sadness she'd been fighting so hard to repress and ignore coiled in her belly, hot and venomous.

*Caden. Oh God. Caden. I love you.*

She sucked in a breath as the sadness seared through her body, stealing her strength and her rationale. She collapsed to her knees, rocking forward and back and wailing like an abandoned child. The handcuffs were a joke. They were silly. *Stupid. Asinine.* But damn it to hell, they brought the whisper of Caden's breath against her cheek, his voice in her ear: *Tonight I just want to be close. No games, no props, no diversions. I just want to love you.*

*I just want to love you.*

The memory tore her insides to shreds. Racked by unyielding sobs, she rolled onto her side on the bedroom floor, where she lay until the sun dipped from the sky. Then she rolled onto her back and caught sight of her fluffy pink comforter, lacy pillows, and sheer, frilly curtains.

"What the hell am I doing?" She stared up at the ceiling and swiped at her tears. "Get up," she commanded.

*No, thanks. I'll just stay here. Me and the urge to wallow in sadness. Constant companions. Maybe strength is overrated.*

"The hell with wallowing. Wallowing sucks." She reached under the bed to retrieve her cell phone from where it landed when she shoved the damn silent thing away from her, but it was too far away. She stretched her arm under the bed, inching her fingers along the floor. Her fingertips brushed the edge of the phone. She pushed her shoulder as far under the bed as it would fit, cursing the low-style frame she'd fallen in love with. She could feel the edge. One more push and—*damn it!* She'd pushed it farther away.

"Now is not the time to mess with me, you little electronic shit." She swung her foot under the bed and sent the phone spinning across the floor. On hands and knees, she retrieved the electronic nemesis, pushed to her feet, and flew down the stairs and out the front door.

She came out of the convenience store ten minutes later with an armful of chocolate. Chocolate didn't make stupid decisions. Chocolate didn't ask questions. Chocolate was the perfect companion.

If only Caden were there to share it with her.

# Chapter Twenty-Five

SUNDAY MORNING CADEN went for a long run on the beach to keep from calling or texting Bella. Gray clouds hovered ominously over the bay, and they felt like a direct reflection of his heart. It was getting more difficult to be apart from Bella, rather than easier. Wasn't time supposed to heal all wounds? He felt as if his heart had been torn open, the very core of his soul exposed. The wound was so raw that he feared it might never heal. When he ran to the point where he usually turned back, he slowed to a walk. He missed Bella so much. Would it be treacherous if he called? Just once? Just to hear her voice?

He ripped the Velcro band from his arm and withdrew his cell phone. Just a quick call. He could ask her if he left his tool belt at her cottage. Yes, that might work. She might buy that. He pressed her speed-dial number and closed his eyes, trying to calm his racing heart.

"Caden?"

Her sleepy voice filled him with sadness. "Yeah, hi. Sorry to call so early."

He heard her repositioning herself and pictured her at the cottage, cuddled up beneath her pink comforter. Oh, how he wanted to be there with her.

"It's okay. Is Evan okay?" she asked.

His throat thickened. Of course her mind went to Evan. Caden was so trapped in his own longing to hear her voice that he'd lost track of the fact that she didn't have any updates on how Evan was getting along.

"He's fine. Good, actually. Helping Vera out at her cottage, and he starts with TGG next week."

"Oh. Good. I'm glad to hear that."

He looked out over the bay and paced. "I miss you, babe." His voice was so soft that he hoped she heard him. She didn't respond, and he thought he must not have spoken after all. "I just...Can I come by and see you?"

"I'm not in Wellfleet."

He stopped pacing. "You're..."

"Back in Connecticut."

He forced himself not to ask why, or if she'd taken the job there.

"What time is it?" she asked.

"I don't know. Seven thirty maybe. I'll let you go. I just wanted to hear your voice."

By the time Caden circled back toward home, the sun streaked through like glimmering lights of goddamn hope. Hope that he didn't have much of anymore. She was in Connecticut. *Connecticut.* Was she there for good? Was that her way of finalizing their *break*? He could kick himself for not asking if she'd taken the job there, but he'd been struck mute by the fact that she was no longer a few miles away.

He arrived home drenched in sweat, which felt right for his frame of mind lately. He ripped off his shirt as he went inside and snagged a towel from a kitchen drawer to wipe the perspiration from his body.

"Hey, Dad." Evan sat in the living room poring over one of the computer books Caden had bought on his first date with Bella.

He remembered that evening as if it were yesterday. Oh, how he wished he could turn back time and go back to that night and skip over Tuesday altogether.

"Hi, Ev. What are you doing up?" He'd practically had to beg Evan to watch a movie instead of playing PC games last night. When he'd decided to be more focused on his son, he hadn't taken into account that Evan might not be as excited about the prospect of the two of them spending more time together as he was.

"I told you I was helping Vera today, remember? This book is awesome. Did you buy it for me?" He flipped through a few pages.

"Right. I remember." He wiped his face with the towel. "I bought that book so I could read up on what you were interested in. You can read it. It's like a foreign language to me." He didn't care about the damn book. He cared about Bella, and damn it, now she was gone. How was he going to make it through eight hours of work?

"Thanks." Evan's hair was still wet from his shower, and Caden was glad to see he'd put on clean and unwrinkled clothes.

He forced himself to focus on Evan. "I'm working until five. Want to cook burgers on the grill tonight?"

Evan shrugged. "Bobby wanted to hang out."

Caden's stomach clenched. "Evan, I'm not sure that's a good idea."

"Bobby doesn't hang out with those guys anymore. I swear it. You can ask him, and he didn't ever do anything bad."

"I don't know, Ev." Bobby had been cleared of any

wrongdoing, just as Evan had, but Caden was nervous about Evan spending time with any kids until he knew them and their parents personally. Maybe it was time to change that.

"I'll tell you what. Call Bobby and tell him that after my shift I'll come by to meet his parents; then you and Bobby can spend the evening here."

Evan closed the book he was reading and sighed. "I've been spending all my time here since this whole thing went down. Don't you trust me to do *anything*?"

"Yes, I trust you." Caden sat beside him on the couch and leaned his elbows on his knees.

"No, you don't. If you're not working, you're here with me. Except when you run, but then I'm usually sleeping." Evan rose to his feet. "You never even go out with Bella anymore."

"This isn't about me, Evan. You want to spend time with Bobby? Then I need to meet his parents." Caden was not bending on that rule ever again.

"I don't care about that. Fine. Whatever." Evan shoved his hands into his pockets. "But why do we have to sit around here all night? It's boring, Dad. It's summer. We want to go hang out, and there's a movie playing on the back of the town hall building in Wellfleet tonight. We were going to ride our bikes over and watch."

Caden ran his hand down his face. He was glad Evan was getting back into life, and he'd done the right thing, so there was no reason not to trust him.

"Fine. I'll meet his parents after work. You have your new phone?"

Evan pulled it out of his pocket. "Thanks, Dad. Why don't you go out with Bella tonight?"

*Because we broke up.* "How about you worry about your own social life, and I'll worry about mine?"

Evan looked at the floor, then back at his father

with a pinched look on his face. "You broke up, didn't you?"

"We're...taking a break." He was done with this fucking break. Why the hell had he thought it was a good idea in the first place?

"Why?" Evan's face contorted. His cheeks heated. "Why'd you break up? Was it because of me?"

"No, it wasn't because of you, and I said a *break*, not that we broke up for good." How could Bella not have known that? How could she have left? How could he have been so stupid in the first place to think he needed this break? Bella understood Evan, maybe even better than Caden did at times.

Evan paced. "God, Dad. I really like her. Why'd you break up if it wasn't because of me?"

"It's complicated, Evan." He rose to his feet and started down the hall toward his bedroom.

"*Complicated*. That's your standard answer," Evan said as he passed him. "Well, that sucks, Dad. You finally get a life, and somehow you manage to do it with a woman I really, really like spending time with, and then I fuck it up for you."

Caden closed his eyes for a beat to try to gain control of his mounting anger, but days of frustration came tumbling forward, and he stalked back down the hall to Evan. "First of all, don't say *fuck*. Second of all, I've always had a life, and—"

"You have not ever had a life. You've had work and me, and that's it. I've never seen you with a woman until Bella, and I liked her, Dad, and whether you want to hear it or not, I liked you even more when she was around. You were happier." Evan fisted his hands.

Caden realized that Evan was as upset over this breakup as he was. They were both on the same damn page.

His voice softened as he tried to rein in his anger.

He'd thought he was making things better, but he'd only made things worse for both of them. "Did it ever occur to you that you and work *are* my life?"

"I don't care." Evan stepped into his room and slammed the door.

Damn it to hell. Would things ever go back to normal?

Caden went into his bedroom and sat on the bed. He always did the right thing. *Always*. Damn it. He'd hurt Bella, Evan, and himself, all because he thought he was doing the right thing. His father was goddamn right. He couldn't be the best father if he wasn't whole. It was time he took his life into his own hands and did what *he* wanted for his own heart. What he needed to be whole.

He loved Evan and he loved Bella. There was no reason he needed to be exclusive with his love—he had enough to give to both of them.

He paced the bedroom. *If I hadn't done a good job of raising Evan, he would have been in the thick of the trouble—not the one who turned them in.*

He looked at the bed, and his chest constricted. He'd had dreams of loving Bella in that bed, waking to her in his arms, making plans for the day with her *and* Evan. He pulled out his cell phone, then scrolled to the picture of him and Bella in the Wellfleet fire tower.

"I miss you, babe. I miss you so fucking much it's killing me."

He had to show Bella that he was fully committed to her, and there was only one way to do that.

## Chapter Twenty-Six

CADEN'S PHONE CALL had breathed new life into Bella. She'd gotten up right after the call and started packing. She'd already packed most of her don't-ever-throw-out stuff. The items that she would never need again but couldn't bear to part with—prom dresses, love notes from boys in elementary school, letters from her Seaside friends. She couldn't help but try on some of the prom dresses and was surprised that she could still fit into a few of them. As she moved around now in one of the light pink frocks and caught a glimpse of herself in the mirror, she didn't look anything like the Bella everyone knew and loved, but she felt more like herself than she had in years. She was a woman and she was ready to take charge of her life and fucking roar.

She was startled when her phone rang, and she scrambled to find it among her boxes. Jenna's name and picture flashed on her screen.

"Don't kill me for leaving," Bella said before Jenna could say a word. She heard Jenna say, "She answered. She answered!" Then she heard the telltale empty box sound of the call being put on speakerphone.

"God, woman. We would have gone with you. Leanna and Amy are here with me. Are you okay? Please tell me you're okay. I tried to call you yesterday and you didn't answer your phone." Jenna's voice was full of worry. "I was ready to drive to Connecticut, but Amy wouldn't let me. She said you needed to sort this out without us. Is that true?"

She heard the hurt in Jenna's last words. "Yes, it was true. I'm so sorry, Jenna, and thank you, Amy."

"I've got your back, Bells," Amy said.

"Oh," Jenna said quietly. "But we love you."

"I know that. I love you guys, too. I just...I couldn't deal with it, Jenna. I needed to clear my head, and if you guys were with me, you'd let me cry for as long as I needed to. You'd make me feel better and you'd help me figure it all out."

"No shit, Sherlock. That's what girlfriends are for," Jenna said.

*Sarcasm*. Bella smiled. "This was something that I needed to figure out on my own. I knew you'd understand."

"I do, but next time can you just answer your fucking phone and tell me? I cleaned my cottage for three hours, and you know it wasn't dirty to begin with. I even had Amy mess up my shoes so I could reorganize them."

Bella laughed. "She's a good friend to do that for you."

"Yeah, she is," Jenna said.

"Bella, it's Leanna. How are you holding up? Are you okay, or do you want us to come there and be with you?"

"I'm good, Leanna. Caden called, and we talked."

"And?" Jenna asked.

"And it made me feel better. I know he needed

that time with Evan. I finally made a decision. I turned down the job here and signed the papers to sell my house."

"Bella. You're doing it after all?" Jenna asked.

"I am. You know, Tony was right. I am the epitome of strength and confidence. But Caden knows me even better than I know myself. He saw right through my public persona."

"Fate," Leanna said. "I knew you two were meant to be together."

"So, what about your plan?" Amy asked.

"You mean my *modified* plan? I don't *need* a man to be whole, and I don't *need* a man as a reason to make my decisions. I can *want* a man without *needing* him." Bella knew she'd made the right decision, and she heard little happy noises that weren't laughs or squeals, but were the types of sounds that came straight from that happy place rooted deep inside her friends. She imagined them holding hands, smiling for her, with her, and waiting with bated breath for the rest of her decision.

"And?" Jenna finally asked.

"And I want Caden."

THE NEARER BELLA got to Caden's house, the faster her heart raced. This was it. Her now or never moment. This was *her* life, and she was going to tell him exactly what she thought of his needing a break. She drove down Route 6 and turned down the side road toward his house. She was breathing so hard she had to pull over for a minute just to take a few deep breaths.

*Okay. Okay. Okay. I can do this.*

She tugged at the hem of her dress, then pulled at the flimsy ribbons holding up her top. With one last loud exhalation, she drove back onto the road and turned onto his street. His driveway was empty.

*Shit.*

She hadn't even considered that he might not be home. She blamed her error on the sugar rush from eating all the chocolate she possibly could. He could be anywhere—fishing with Evan, or at a beach, at work. *Damn it.* This was supposed to be easy. Knock on his door, say her two cents, and either—*Oh. My. God.* Caden's truck pulled into the driveway behind her.

She couldn't breathe.

She watched in her side-view mirror as he stepped from the truck in his uniform, looking exactly like he had the first night they'd met. When his eyes caught hers in the rearview mirror, she felt her heart swell. Only this time the sadness in his eyes mirrored how she felt, but she couldn't let that dissuade her from where she was heading.

His powerful legs carried him one sure step at a time toward her car. Her breathing became shallow, and when he reached for the door handle, she no longer felt like she was a woman who needed to roar.

She just felt like a woman, and that was enough.

CADEN COULDN'T BELIEVE his eyes. Bella was right there, stepping out of her car wearing—*good Lord.* What the hell was she wearing? Some pink polyester number that hugged her breasts and hips and appeared to be held on by two thin ribbons that tied around her neck. There was a pink satin bow at her waist, and the fabric stopped above her knees in the front and hung to her heels in the back.

"Stop looking at me like that." She crossed her arms, and her shoulders rounded forward. She drew them back and lifted her chin.

"I'm...Bella..." *Jesus, say something.* "I'm sorry."

"So am I." Her eyes narrowed.

*Shit.*

"I'm going to tell you something," she said with a serious tone. "And I'm only going to say it once."

Caden touched her arm.

"I can't think if you touch me."

That made him smile, which brought a narrowing of her eyes. He stared at his hand before peeling his fingers from her skin.

"I'm sorry. But you're here. Even if you're annoyed with me, I'm happy you're here." How could he not smile? He'd missed her so much, and here she was, wearing some ridiculous outfit, angry and fucking adorable. The sound of her voice was like a new heart to a dying man.

"God, I missed your voice," he admitted.

"You." She poked his chest. "Hurt." *Poke.* "Me." *Poke.*

He grabbed her finger and pressed her palm to his chest. She tried to pull away, but he held on tight.

"Damn it, Caden." Her voice trembled. "You hurt me. A lot."

"I'm sorry." He took a step closer and she peered up at him, then lowered her eyes to her hand, trapped beneath his. "I hurt me, too."

At that, she lifted her beautiful eyes to his, and he could see her struggling to sound angry when he knew she felt as compelled to fall into his arms as he did to wrap them around her and hold her close.

"You waited too many days before you called me," she said just above a whisper.

He shook his head. "I didn't know if I should call."

Her eyes narrowed again. "You should have."

"I couldn't be more sorry." He wanted to pull her into his arms and kiss her, hold her, make both their pains go away, but before he could move, she spoke.

"Damn it, Caden. You're standing there all

323

handsome and apologetic, and...hot in that stupid sexy uniform, with that look in your eyes like you love me more than life itself, and..."

"I do," he said.

"You..."

"I do love you more than life itself."

She clenched her jaw and looked away, and when she turned back, her voice was determined once again. "Oh. Wait. I have...I love you, too, but damn it, I need to finish."

He smiled. "Sorry."

"It's okay." She bit her lower lip and furrowed her brow, as if she was trying to remember what she was saying. "You let me be strong, but you also make me weak." She shook her head. "But you don't really *make* me weak. You love me in ways that make me feel safe enough to forget I'm strong, and that scares the daylights out of me—even though I love that feeling. I've never had that feeling before, but you, Caden Grant..." She fisted her hands in that silly pink getup, and a second later she poked his chest again. "You." *Poke.* "Are." *Poke.*

He grabbed her hand again and held it tight.

She drew her brows together. "You are the man that I want to be with. I like how you make me feel, and damn it, Caden. I'm embracing it. See?" She swatted the skirt of her ridiculous dress. "I like how you take care of me. It makes me want to take care of you and Evan. But I won't be jerked around. I won't be treated like I'm expendable. You either take me or leave me, but there is no in between."

He tightened his grip on her hand. "I don't have a lot of experience with being in love or taking breaks." His heart squeezed as her words took root, and he softened his tone. "Or realizing I was the biggest fool on earth."

"You..." She hooked her finger into the waistband of his pants. "What?"

"I was an idiot. I blamed Evan's hooking up with the wrong friends on my not giving him enough attention because I was so wrapped up in us that I couldn't see straight."

"You made a commitment to Evan, and I respect that." She stared at his chest. He lifted her chin with his finger.

"I made a commitment to you, too, Bella. To us. I thought I needed to focus solely on Evan, but, babe, I was wrong. *We* need to focus on Evan. Together. I can't be a good father when I'm spending my emotional energy missing you. I can't sleep. I can't eat. I can't do a damn thing because I love you, Bella, and without you, seeing straight isn't even an option." He paused to let his words sink in. "I made an impulsive suggestion because Evan is..."

"*Everything*, as he should be," she said softly. "I overreacted. I was selfish and I'm sorry."

"No. You're wrong about Evan being everything. Evan was everything until I met you. He is my son, and I love him. But the space he fills in my heart is the space that only a child can fill." He cupped her cheeks and took a step closer, so they were thigh to thigh, as they should be. "You're my soul mate. My lover. My friend. The woman I want to spend my life with, and maybe one day, if you want to, you'll be the mother of *our* child. That side of my heart that Evan fills has room for more, but the other side of my heart? Your side? It only has room for you."

Her eyes dampened. "Caden."

"Let me finish, please." He touched his forehead to hers. She sighed, and when he pressed his hands to her cheeks and lifted her face so he could look deeply into her eyes, a warm tear slid over his thumb.

"I love you, Bella. I love your strength, your loud laugh, the way you think of Evan even when you should be thinking about your work. I love the way you love your friends and your hidden adoration of all things pink. I will always love you, Bella, and I want you in our lives."

He sealed his lips to hers, and all those empty spots that had appeared over the last few days filled with Bella.

With *them*.

When they drew apart, he reached into his pocket and pulled out a piece of paper the size and thickness of a business card. "I wanted to give you something to show you that I'm serious about my commitment to you."

He put the paper in her palm and folded her fingers over it; then he pressed a soft kiss to the back of her hand. Caden kissed her forehead.

"Before you open it, please tell me what you're wearing."

Bella looked down at her dress and her cheeks flushed. "It's a prom dress. I bought it to wear to my high school prom, but that was before I realized that girly girls got taken advantage of."

"So you didn't wear it?" He loved her so much his heart ached.

She shook her head. "I wore a black dress. But when I saw it in my closet, I remembered how you saw right through me and how you loved that side of me. And how you said to embrace it." She lifted one shoulder in a shrug.

He kissed her again, and she melted against him.

"Maybe we should go shopping for something from this decade," he teased.

"Maybe shopping can wait," she said against his lips.

The sound of tires on gravel drew their lips apart.

"Bella!" Evan dropped his bike and wrapped his arms around the two of them. "You're here. Jenna said you were in Connecticut, and I thought..." He hugged her again. "I thought you decided to take that job."

"I missed you, too, Evan." She ran her eyes between Evan and Caden. "How could I take a job that was so far from my favorite two men?"

He shot a look at Caden. "You're back together?"

Caden nodded, and Evan did a fist pump. "Thank God. Please take him out of here, Bella. He's been moping around and driving me crazy."

"Oh, I think I can handle that," she said with mischief in her eyes.

"Um." Evan ran his eyes down Bella's dress. "You might want to change your clothes first. I'm pretty sure that went out of style in the fifties."

"Nineties," Bella corrected him.

"Whatever." Evan headed for the front door.

*Whatever*, said with a smile. Music to Caden's ears.

Evan stopped halfway to the door and returned to Bella's side with a serious look in his eyes. "Bella, I'm sorry for lying to you about being at the campground that day. I was afraid I'd get in trouble, and...well, I won't lie again."

Confusion flashed in her eyes. Caden realized he hadn't even had a chance to tell her everything that Evan had told him yet.

"That's okay, Evan. I'm glad you did the right thing in the end."

"Cool. Thanks." He headed inside.

"Thank you," Caden said to Bella. "I have a lot to tell you, but I'm proud of him for apologizing. I never asked him to."

"He's an amazing kid, Caden."

Bella unfurled her hand and read the note on the

card. She fisted her hands in Caden's shirt. "A get-out-of-jail-free card? Did you steal this from a Monopoly game?"

"No, but I copied the idea from the game, sort of." God, he loved her.

"Don't you *ever* compromise your beliefs for me. I love you for your convictions."

He kissed her softly. "Oh, sorry. That was meant for me. In case you decide to use your fuzzy handcuffs and forget to respect our safe word." He arched a brow and she laughed.

"Turn it over," he whispered.

She looked down at the card.

"Read the other side." He held his breath as she flipped over the flimsy card. He felt her heart beat harder against his chest. She looked from the card to him, then back again.

"Is...?" Her eyes welled with tears again. "Is this a joke?" She read the words again.

*Marry me.*

"I've never been more serious in my life. I love you, Bella. I knew it the moment you fell into my arms that first night. I want to be your YMCA guy. The guy who does or doesn't fix your deck, depending on your mood. I want to wake up with you in my arms and I never, ever, want another frigging break from you. Will you marry me, Bella?"

"But...Evan?" Her lower lip trembled.

"I'm not asking you to marry Evan, but if you're worried that he will be upset, he won't. He was ready to clobber me for messing things up with you. I have only one stipulation."

Her eyes widened.

"I don't ever want to be not-a-husband with you. I want the real deal. You in a white dress, me in a monkey suit. I want you to have the wedding you secretly dreamed of."

Tears streamed down her cheeks. "How do you know I've dreamed of anything like that?"

He touched her dress. "Anyone who kept a dress like this, dreams of a real wedding. Please don't make me wait any longer for an answer."

"Yes, Caden. I want to be your real wife, and never, ever be your not-a-wife."

*The End*

Please enjoy a preview of the next
*Love in Bloom* novel

# seaside
## Hearts

### Seaside Summers, Book Two

### Love in Bloom Series

### Melissa Foster

NEW YORK TIMES BESTSELLING AUTHOR

# MELISSA FOSTER

## seaside
## *Hearts*

*Love in Bloom: Seaside Summers*
Contemporary Romance

# Chapter One

THERE SHOULD BE a rule about drooling over construction workers, but Jenna Ward was damn glad there wasn't. She sat on the porch of the Bookstore Restaurant, soaking up the deliciousness of the three bronzed males clad in nothing more than jeans and glistening muscles that flexed and bulged like an offering to the gods as they forced thick, sticky tar into submission. Their jeans hung low on strong hips, gripping their powerful thighs like second skins and ending in scuffed and tarred work boots. What red-blooded woman didn't get worked up over a gorgeous shirtless man in work boots?

God help her, because she needed this distraction to take away her desire for Peter Lacroux, which went hand in hand with summers on the Cape and consumed her in the nine months they were apart. She zeroed in on one particularly handsome blond construction worker. His hair was nearly white, his jaw square and manly. She wanted to march right out to the middle of the road that split the earth between the restaurant and the beach and be manhandled into submission. Right there on the tar. Wrestled and groped until all thoughts of Pete evaporated.

"Wipe the drool from your chin, *chica*." Amy Maples handed Jenna a margarita and, pointedly, a fresh napkin, as she settled into the chair across from her. "Good Lord, woman. What's up with you this summer? I swear you're in heat. I can practically smell your pheromones from over here."

Jenna gulped her drink and righted her red bikini top, which was trying its damnedest to relieve itself of her enormous breasts. Even her bikini top was ready for a man. A *real* man. A man who craved her as much as she craved him.

Jenna reluctantly turned away from Testosterone Road and faced her best friends. The women she had spent her summers with here in Wellfleet, Massachusetts, for as long as she could remember and the women she hoped would help her through her most important summer *ever*.

Okay, she'd self-defined it as such, and it was probably a poor excuse for *most important*, but that's how it felt. Huge. Momentous. Gargantuan. *Great*. Now she was thinking about other huge things...

"You've been here for a week, and you still haven't told us why you're all claws and hormones. Want to clue us in, or are we supposed to guess?" Bella Abbascia was a brazen blonde—and she, like Leanna Bray, the disorganized brunette of their bestie clan— had already found her true love. A feat Jenna only dreamed of. Ached for might be more accurate, and Bella was right; it was time to come clean.

Jenna downed the last of her drink and slapped her palms on the table.

"I don't care what it takes; this is *my* summer. I'm done pussyfooting around. I want a man. A *real* man." She slid her eyes to the construction workers again.

*Yum!* She tried to convince herself to feel something more for the construction worker, but the only person her mind found yummy was Pete—and it didn't seem to want to make room for others.

She wasn't above faking it to pull herself through the charade. Maybe if she tried hard enough, she could talk herself into believing it.

"So, you're going after Pete?" Leanna sipped her margarita and arched a brow. "How is that any different than every single one of the last five summers?"

"Oh no. Peter Lacroux can kiss my big, sexy ass."

"Jenna!" Amy Maples's eyes widened. The sweetest of the group, she was perfectly petite, with kindness that sailed from her blue eyes like a summer breeze.

"You do have a mighty fine ass, Jen," Bella said. "But you've had a wicked crush on that man forever. If you're going to focus your attention on someone—" Bella bit her lower lip and shook her head as one of the construction workers wiped sweat from his brow, pecs in full, drool-inciting view. Bella raked her eyes down his sculpted abs. "Um...Okay, yeah. They're pretty damn hot. But why throw Pete away?"

Jenna had been over this in her mind a hundred times. She locked her eyes on her glass and exhaled. "Because I'm not going to spend another summer chasing a man who doesn't want me. And this is a tough summer for me. I have to break up with my mother, and that's enough heartache for a few short weeks."

"Break up with your mom? Can a person do that?" Amy glanced around the table.

"I gather she's not taking your dad getting remarried well?" Leanna asked. "I had such high hopes when she didn't fall apart during the divorce."

Jenna rolled her eyes. "So did I. You'd think that two years after her divorce, she'd be able to sort of compartmentalize it all, but, girls, you have no idea." Jenna shook her head and held up her glass, indicating to the bartender that she needed another drink. She could have gotten up and retrieved the drink herself, but Jenna wanted the diversion of the sexy waiter who would deliver it to their table. She'd take as many diversions as she could get to keep from thinking of Pete.

"She's gone...hmm...how do I say this respectfully? She's not gone cougar, but she's definitely acting different. She's dressing way too young for a fifty-seven-year-old woman, and I swear she thinks she's my new best friend. She wants to talk about guys and sex, and what's worse is that she suddenly wants to go dancing and to bars. I love my mom, but I don't need to go to bars with her, and talking about sex with her? *Please.*"

"I was wondering what was going on when she texted you a hundred times last night." Bella pulled her hair back and secured it with an elastic band. "She's going through a hard time, Jenna. Give her a break. She was married for thirty-four years. That's a long time. I'm not even married to Caden yet, and if we broke up and he married a younger chick, I'd be devastated." Bella and Caden met last year when Bella had been busy rearranging her own life. She'd started a work-study program for the local school district, fallen in love with Caden Grant, a cop on the Cape, and now she was as close as a mother to his almost sixteen-year-old son, Evan. The Cape was a narrow stretch of land between the bay and the ocean. Bella and Caden lived on the bay side in a house that Caden had owned when they'd met, and they would be staying at Bella's Seaside cottage on and off this summer.

"I get it, okay? I just...God, it's just so hard to see her struggling with her looks, and honestly, you know I adore her, but she's sort of making a fool of herself. It's been two years since the divorce. She just needs to get over it and move on. I do feel bad because I had to take a firm stand and tell her that I wasn't going to come home until *after* the summer."

"Why do you feel bad? That's what you do every summer." Amy eyed one of the construction workers, a water bottle held above his mouth, a stream of wetness disappearing down his throat. "Holy hotness." She fanned herself with her napkin.

Jenna watched the guy wipe his mouth with his heavily muscled forearm. "Yeah, but she wanted me to come home to *hang out* with her a few times." The sexy waiter brought Jenna her drink.

"Thank you, doll." She watched his fine ass as he walked away.

"Doll?" Amy giggled.

"See?" Jenna bonked her forehead on the table. "That's *her* word. Doll? Who says that? You have to help me. She'll ruin me, and I swear if I spend one more summer lusting after Pete, then I'll be empty on all accounts. My mother will hate me, my hoo-ha will be lonely, and I'll use words like *doll*. Jesus, do us all a favor and shoot me now."

"Yeah, well, about that whole Pete thing?" Leanna nodded toward the crosswalk, where Pete Lacroux was crossing the road carrying the cutest damn puppy.

*Holy mother of God, he is fine. I want to be that puppy.* Those construction workers couldn't hold a candle to Pete, and Jenna's body was proof as her pulse quickened and her mouth went dry. His shoulders were twice as broad as those of the boys on the pavement, his waist was trim and—*holy hell*—he shifted the pup to the side, giving Jenna a clear view of the pronounced muscles that blazed a path south from his abs and disappeared into his snug jeans. Those damn muscles turned her mind to mush. Yup. She'd gone as dumb as a doorknob.

"Breathe, Jenna," Amy whispered. "You are so not over him."

Jenna couldn't tear her eyes from him. Years of lust and anticipation brewed deep in her belly. *Just one more summer? One more try?*

*No. No. I can't do this anymore.* "The man's one big tease. I'm moving on." She forced herself to tear her eyes away from him and guzzle her drink.

And then it happened.

She felt his presence behind her before he ever said a word. Jenna, the woman who could talk to anyone, anytime, had spent years fumbling for words and making atrocious attempts at flirting with the six-foot-two, dark-haired, mysterious specimen that was Peter Lacroux, but despite catching a few heated glances from him, she remained in the friend zone.

Regardless of how her body reacted to him, she didn't need to beg for a man she could barely talk to, or follow after him like that adorable puppy snuggled against his powerful chest.

She was totally, utterly, done with him.

*Maybe.*

PETE EYED THE women from the Seaside cottage community, or the Seaside girls, as he'd come to refer to them, on his way across the street. They hadn't spotted him watching them as they ogled the young construction workers from the patio of the Bookstore Restaurant. Pete had done the community and pool maintenance for the cottages at Seaside for about six years. He was a boat restorer by trade, but when he'd begun working at Seaside, his career hadn't yet taken off. By the time word got around that he was an exceptional craftsman, he was too loyal of a man to stop doing the maintenance work. Besides, the girls were fun, and he'd become friends with the guys in the community, Tony Black, a professional surfer and motivational speaker, and Jamie Reed, who'd developed OneClick, a search engine second only to Google. And then there was Jenna Ward, the buxom brunette with the killer ass, a cackle of a laugh, and the most intense, alluring blue eyes he'd ever seen.

*Fucking Jenna.*

He watched her eyes shift to him as he neared the restaurant. Other than his craftsman skills, reading women was Pete's next best finely honed ability—or so he thought. He could tell when a woman was into him, or when she was toying with the idea of being into him, but Jenna Ward? Jenna confused the hell out of him. She was confident and funny, smart, and too fucking cute for her own good when she was around her friends. Just watching Jenna sent fire through his veins, but when it came to Pete, Jenna lost all that gumption, and she turned into a...Hell, he didn't know what happened to her. She grew quiet and tentative when she was near him. Pete liked confident women. *A lily to look at and a tigress in the bedroom.* His mouth quirked up at the thought. He wasn't a Neanderthal. He respected women, but he also knew what he liked. He wanted to devour and be devoured—and with Jenna, who swallowed her confidence around him, he feared his sexual appetite would scare her off. Besides, with his alcoholic father to care for, he didn't have time for a relationship.

Jenna turned away as he stepped behind her. Her hair was longer this summer, framing her face in rich chocolate waves that fell past her shoulders. Pete preferred long hair. There was nothing like the feeling of burying his hands in a woman's hair and giving it a gentle tug when she was just about to come apart beneath him.

He held Joey, the female golden retriever he'd rescued a few weeks earlier, in one arm, placed his other hand on the back of Jenna's chair, and inhaled deeply. Jenna smelled like no other woman he'd ever known, a tantalizing combination of sweet and spicy. Her scent, and the view of her cleavage from above, pushed all of his sexual buttons, despite her tentative nature around him. But he had no endgame with Jenna Ward. No matter how much he wanted to explore the white-hot attraction he felt toward her, he respected Jenna and treasured her friendship too much to take her for a test ride.

"Hello, ladies."

"Aww. Can I hold her?" Amy jumped to her feet and took the puppy from his hands. Joey covered her face with kisses.

"She's a little shy," Pete teased. He'd found the pup in a duffel bag by a dumpster behind Mac's Seafood, down at the Wellfleet Pier. The poor thing was hungry and scared, but other than that, she wasn't too bad off. The first night Pete had her, the pup had slept curled up against Pete's chest, and they'd been constant companions ever since.

"Yeah, real shy. How's she doing?" Leanna asked.

"She's great. She sticks to me like glue." He shrugged. "I was just coming over to get her a bowl of fresh water, maybe a hamburger."

"Hamburger?" Leanna wrinkled her thinly manicured brow. "How about puppy food?"

"Puppies love burgers." Chicks were so weird with their rules about proper foods. He glanced down at

Jenna, whose eyes were locked on the table. She usually went ape shit over puppies, and he wondered what was up with her cool demeanor.

"Want to join us for a drink?" Bella slid a slanty-eyed look in Jenna's direction.

He felt Jenna bristle at the offer. He should probably walk away and give her some breathing room. She obviously wasn't herself today. He was just about to leave when Amy grabbed his arm and pulled him down to the chair beside Jenna. *Great.* Now Jenna had a death stare locked on Amy. Pete was beginning to take her standoffishness personally.

"Sit for a while. I want to play with Joey anyway." When Amy met Jenna's heated stare, she rolled her eyes and kissed Joey's head.

"How's the boat coming along?" Leanna Bray was a quirky woman, too. Her cottage had always been a mess before she met her fiancé, Kurt Remington. Every time Pete had gone by to fix a broken cabinet or a faucet, she'd had laundry piles everywhere, and sticky goo from her jam making seemed to cover every surface, including herself. Almost all of her clothing had conspicuous stains in various shades of red, purple, and orange. Kurt was as neat and organized as Jenna. He'd taken over the laundry and didn't seem to mind picking up after Leanna. In any case, her place was much more organized these days.

"She's coming along." Pete had been refinishing a custom-built 1966 thirty-four-foot gaff-rigged wooden schooner for the past two summers. Working with his hands was not only his passion, but it was also cathartic. He'd spent the last two years pouring the guilt over his father's drinking into refitting the boat.

"What will you do with it when you're done?" Amy Maples looked like the girl next door, with her sandy blond hair and big green eyes, and acted like a mother hen, always worrying about her friends.

Pete shrugged. "Oh, I don't know. Maybe I'll sail someplace far, far away." He'd never leave his father, or the Cape, but there were days...

That brought Jenna's eyes to him. Jesus, she had the most gorgeous eyes. They weren't sea blue or sky blue or even midnight blue. They were more of a cerulean frost, and at the moment, pointedly icy. *What the hell did I do?* He racked his brain, going over the last two weeks, but he hadn't seen Jenna for more than a minute or two. He couldn't imagine what he'd done to warrant her attitude.

Jenna raised her eyebrows in Amy's direction. "Time for *me* to go away." She rose to her feet, bringing her red-string-bikini-clad body into full view. The tiny triangles barely covered her nipples and the bottom rode high on her hips, exposing every luscious curve.

Pete shot a look around the patio—every male eye was locked on Jenna. Jenna wasn't even five feet tall, but she had a better body than any long-legged model. *How the hell can a woman have a body like that and not be one hundred percent confident at all times?* He stifled the urge to stand between her and the ogling men.

"Where are you going?" Bella's eyes bounced between Pete and Jenna.

"I'm going to do what I came here to do. There's a construction guy with my name on him over there." Jenna lifted her chin toward the sky, and her pigeon-toed feet carried her fine ass off the patio, across the grass, and directly toward one of the young construction workers.

"What's she doing?" Pete narrowed his eyes as Jenna approached a ripped construction worker. He expected Jenna to put her hands behind her back and sway from side to side like she did when she spoke to him—reminiscent of an excited girl rather than a sensual woman—adorable and confusing as hell.

"Oh. My. God." Bella rose to her feet, her eyes wide.

"Nothing, Pete. She's...Oh God." Amy put Joey in Pete's lap. "Take her. I um...Darn it." Amy reached for Bella's hand as they gawked, mesmerized by Jenna's bold move.

Her shoulders were drawn back, her beautiful breasts on display—proudly on display! *What the hell?* She put one hand on her hip, and holy hell, Pete didn't need to see her face to feel the slow drag of her eyes down that bastard's body in a way similar to how she usually looked at *him* when she thought he wasn't looking. But then she'd go all nervous when he'd approach.

*What the fuck?*

"Holy shit. She's going for it." Bella sat back down, as Jenna put her finger in the waistband of the guy's jeans and shrugged. "She's something this summer, isn't she?"

Jealousy clutched Pete's gut.

"Yes, and this summer's rock fixation? What's up with pitch-black rocks? She's never collected them before." Amy's voice trailed off as she watched Jenna in action.

Pete made a mental note of the rocks Jenna was collecting this summer. He'd spent five years taking mental notes about Jenna. Every summer she collected different types of rocks—egg shaped, all white, gray, and oval. There was never any rhyme or reason that Pete could see for her rock selection, but she knew what she liked, and the ones she liked ended up all over her cottage and deck.

Jenna's eyes were fixated on the guy. *That* was the

Jenna Pete had hoped would talk to *him*, and now...Now he was getting pretty damn pissed off.

"Those aren't local guys; they're contractors," he warned. "They probably have women in every town around here. Want me to intervene?" Jenna wasn't his to protect. They'd never even gone out on a single date, but somewhere in his mind, despite his confusion, she *was* his. Summers to Pete meant six to eight weeks of seeing Jenna, and over the last two years, while his father buried his troubles in alcohol, seeing Jenna meant even more to him. But until this very second, he never realized how much he wanted her, or how much she meant to him. Joey turned her tongue on Pete's chin. Frustrated, Pete lifted his face out of reach.

Leanna shook her head. "God. Look at her go."

*Look at her go? You think this is okay?*

"Pete, have you heard something bad about them? Should we worry?" Amy's voice was laden with concern. "Bella, maybe we should..."

Pete watched Jenna take her phone from her pocket and type something. A second later the blond guy took his phone from his back pocket and nodded.

"She gave him her number. I can't believe it," Leanna said.

"She wasn't shitting us," Bella said. "Damn, our girl's getting her groove on." She settled back in her seat and petted Joey. "Oh, Pete...*tsk, tsk, tsk.*"

"What's that supposed to mean?" He clenched his teeth so tight he thought they might crack.

"Nothing." Leanna smacked Bella's arm.

Bella set her eyes on him. "A woman like Jenna only comes around once in a lifetime."

He was just beginning to realize how true those words were.

"Bella, don't," Amy warned.

Bella shrugged. "Just sayin'."

He didn't know what to make of the woman who was a wallflower around him and a sex kitten around a random dipshit in the street. Jenna sashayed back toward the table with a grin on her face. That was Pete's cue to get the hell out of there before he was stuck listening to Jenna going on and on about that dipshit. He rose to his feet with Joey in his arms.

"Wait. Don't leave," Amy pleaded. "You didn't get Joey her water."

"I've got to get going." With Joey in his arms, he headed off the patio. Jenna brushed past him without so much as a word, and it pissed him off even more. He couldn't escape fast enough.

"Guess who's going to the Beachcomber tonight? Oh my God. He's even hotter up close." Jenna's voice echoed in his mind as he crossed the street to get Joey a bowl of water from Mac's.

*Holy Christ. Like I needed to hear that shit.*

(End of Sneak Peek)
To continue reading, be sure to pick up the next
LOVE IN BLOOM release:

SEASIDE HEARTS, *Seaside Summers*
Love in Bloom series

Please enjoy the first chapter of the first
*Love in Bloom* novel

# Sisters in Love

## Snow Sisters, Book One

## Love in Bloom Series

### Melissa Foster

"A beautiful story about love and self-growth and
finding that balance to happiness. Powerfully written
and riveting from beginning to end."
—*National bestselling author Jane Porter*

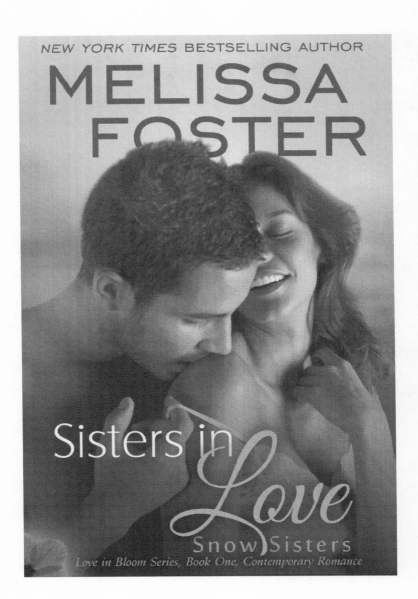

NEW YORK TIMES BESTSELLING AUTHOR

# MELISSA FOSTER

## Sisters in *Love*

Snow Sisters

*Love in Bloom Series, Book One, Contemporary Romance*

# Chapter One

THE LINE IN the café went all the way to the door. Danica Snow wished she hadn't taken her sister Kaylie's phone call before getting her morning coffee. Living in an overcrowded tourist town could be a major inconvenience, but Danica loved that she could walk from her condo to her office, see a movie, have dinner, or even stop at a bookstore without ever sitting in a car. Every minute counted when you lived in Allure, Colorado, host to an odd mix of hippie and yuppie tourists in equal numbers. The ski slopes brought them in the winter, while art shows drew them in the summer. There was never a break. Every suit and Rasta child in town was standing right in front of her, waiting for their coffee or latte, and the guy ahead of her had shoulders so wide she couldn't easily see around him. Danica tapped the toe of her efficient and comfortable Nine West heels, growing more impatient by the second.

What on earth was taking so long? In seven minutes they'd served only one person. The tables were pushed so close to the people standing in line that she couldn't step to the side to see. She was gridlocked. Danica leaned to the right and peered around the massive shoulder ahead of her just as the owner of that shoulder turned to look out the door. *Whack!* He elbowed her right in the nose, knocking Danica's head back.

Her hand flew to her bloody nose. "Ow! Geez!" She ducked in pain, covering her face and talking through her hands. "I think you broke my nose." Each word sent pain across her nose and below her eyes.

"I'm so sorry. Let me get you a napkin," a deep, worried voice said.

Two patrons rushed over and shoved napkins in her direction.

"Are you okay?" an older woman asked.

Tears sprang from the corners of Danica's closed eyes. *Damn it.* Her entire day would now run late and she probably looked like a red-nosed, crying idiot. "This hurts so bad. Weren't you looking where—" Danica flipped her unruly, brown hair from her face and opened her eyes. Her venom-filled glare locked on the man who had elbowed her—the most beautiful specimen of a human being she had ever seen. *Oh shit.* "I'm...What...?" *Come on, girl. Get it together. He's probably an egomaniac.*

"I'm so sorry." His voice was rich and smooth, laden with concern.

A thin blonde grabbed his arm and shoved a napkin into his hand. "Give this to her," she said, blinking her eyelashes in a come-hither way.

The man held the woman's hand a beat too long. "Thanks," he said. His eyes trailed down the blonde's blouse.

*Really? I'm bleeding over here.*

He turned toward Danica and handed her the napkin. His eyes were green and yellow, like field grass. His eyebrows drew together in a serious gaze, and Danica thought that maybe she'd been too quick to judge—until he stole a glance at the blonde as she walked out of the café.

*Asshole.* She felt the heat of anger spread up her chest and neck, along her cheeks, to the ridge of her high cheekbones. She snagged the napkin from his hand and wiped her throbbing nose. "It's okay. I'm fine," she lied. She could smell the minty freshness of his breath, and she wondered what it might taste like. Danica was not one to swoon—that was Kaylie's job. *Get a grip.*

"Can I at least buy you a coffee?" He ran his hand through his thick, dark hair.

*Yes!* "No, thank you. It's okay." She had been a therapist long enough to know what kind of guy eyes another girl while she was tending to a bloody nose that he had caused. Danica fumbled for her purse, which she'd dropped when she was hit. She lowered her eyes to avoid looking into his. "I'm fine, really. Just look behind you next time." Not for the first time, Danica wished she had Kaylie's flirting skills and her ability to look past his wandering eyes. She would have had him buying her coffee, a Danish, and breakfast the next morning.

Danica was so confused, she wasn't even sure what she wanted. She chanced another glance up at him. He was looking at her features so intently that she felt as though he were drinking her in, memorizing her. His eyes trailed slowly from hers, lowered to her nose, to her lips, and then settled on the beauty mark that she'd been self-conscious of her entire life. She felt like a Cindy Crawford wannabe. Danica pursed her lips. "Are you done?" she asked.

He blinked with the innocence of a young boy, clueless to her annoyance, which was in stark contrast to his confident, manly presence. He stood almost a foot taller than Danica's impressive five foot seven stature. His chest muscles bulged beneath his way-too-small shirt, dark curls poking through the neckline. *He probably bought it that way on purpose.* She glanced down and tried not to notice his muscular thighs straining against his stonewashed denim jeans. Danica swallowed hard. All the air suddenly left her lungs. He was touching her shoulder, squinting, evaluating her face.

"I'm sorry. I was just making sure it didn't look broken, which it doesn't. I'm sure it's painful."

She couldn't think past the heat of his hand, the breadth of it engulfing her shoulder. "It's okay," she managed, hating herself for being lost in his touch when he was clearly someone who ate women for breakfast. She checked her watch. She had three minutes to get her coffee and get back to her office before her next client showed up. *Belinda. She'd love this guy.*

The line progressed, and Adonis waved as he left the café. Danica reached into her purse to pay for her French vanilla coffee and found herself taking a last glance at him as he passed the front window.

The young barista pushed Danica's money away. "No need, hon. Blake paid for yours." She smiled, lifting her eyebrows.

"He did?" *Blake.*

"Yeah, he's really sweet." The barista leaned over the cash register. "Even if he is a player."

*Aha! I knew it.* Danica thrust her shoulders back, feeling smart for resisting temptation.

(End of Sneak Peek)
Check online retailers for the Snow Sisters series
SISTERS IN LOVE, SNOW SISTERS, Book One
*Love in Bloom Series*

# Full LOVE IN BLOOM SERIES order

Love in Bloom books may be read as stand-alones. For more enjoyment, read them in series order. Characters from each series carry forward to the next.

## SNOW SISTERS

Sisters in Love (Book 1)
Sisters in Bloom (Book 2)
Sisters in White (Book 3)

## THE BRADENS

Lovers at Heart (Book 4)
Destined for Love (Book 5)
Friendship on Fire (Book 6)
Sea of Love (Book 7)
Bursting with Love (Book 8)
Hearts at Play (Book 9)

## THE REMINGTONS

Game of Love (Book 10)
Stroke of Love (Book 11)
Flames of Love (Book 12)
Slope of Love (Book 13)
Read, Write, Love (Book 14)

## THE BRADENS (coming soon)

Taken by Love (Book 15)
Fated for Love (Book 16)
Romancing my Love (Book 17)
Flirting with Love (Book 18)
Dreaming of Love (Book 19)
Crashing into Love (Book 20)

# SEASIDE SUMMERS (coming soon)

Seaside Dreams
Seaside Hearts
Seaside Sunsets
Seaside Secrets

# THE RYDERS (coming soon)

Duke Ryder
Blue Ryder
Trish Ryder
Jake Ryder
Gage Ryder

## Watermelon Jam

3-pound seedless watermelon*
2 1.75-ounce packages of powdered pectin
8 cups white cane sugar
2 tablespoons lemon juice

Before starting the jam, boil the jars and lids in large saucepan so when you fill them they won't break from the heat of the jam. Scoop out three pounds of seedless watermelon and place in blender. Finely chop the watermelon so that there are still small chunks. Place the watermelon in a 8-quart saucepan and bring to a boil; then add the pectin slowly. Keep stirring so that nothing sticks to the bottom. Bring it back to a boil and add the sugar very slowly so that you don't drop the temperature of the mix too fast. Bring back to a boil for 1 minute and then fill your (already hot) jars. After filling the jars, turn them upside down for 5 minutes and then back upright. This will seal the jars. This recipe will fill 10 eight-ounce mason jars.

*It might take a large watermelon to get three pounds of fruit, so look for the largest one you can find.

AVAILABLE at www.AlsBackwoodsBerrie.com, Amazon, and other retailers.

# Acknowledgments

I have been spending summers on Cape Cod since I was a toddler, and Wellfleet, Massachusetts, is truly my favorite place on earth. When I was writing *Read, Write, Love* and I met the Seaside gang, it was the perfect time to bring my favorite place to life. Much of the inspiration for this series comes from good times I've shared with friends at the Cape, whose names I will keep secret for fear of embarrassing my chunky-dunking crew. However, Seaside is a fictional community. If you scour the Cape and happen to come across a community called Seaside, please understand that it was not the basis of this series.

Our sinfully sexy police officer, Caden Grant, was named to honor a reader's son. Kim Shaw Clark contacted me and touched my heart with the story of her handsome warrior, Caden. I hope I have done him justice. Thank you for reaching out, Kim, and for giving me a high bar to strive for. I'd like to thank Stacy Eaton, one of my best friends and colleagues, for answering all of my cop-related questions—and for laughing when I changed the outcome. I have taken fictional liberties in my story. Any and all errors are my own.

Many thanks to my editorial team: Kristen Weber, Penina Lopez, Jenna Bagnini, Juliette Hill, Marlene Engel, and Lynn Mullan. Thank you, Natasha Brown and Clare Ayala, for your endless patience and expertise.

And a special thanks goes to Al Chisholm of Al's Backwoods Berries, my partner in the creation of Luscious Leanna's Sweet Treats and the best damn jam maker around. If you're ever in Wellfleet during the summer, you can find Al and Luscious Leanna's Sweet Treats at the flea market, or visit his website noted on the recipe page in this book. Luscious Leanna's Sweet Treats are also available on Amazon.

Last but never least, thank you to my supportive husband and family, who make my writing possible.

Melissa Foster is a *New York Times* and *USA Today* bestselling and award-winning author. Her books have been recommended by *USA Today's* book blog, *Hagerstown* magazine, *The Patriot*, and several other print venues. She is the founder of the World Literary Café, and when she's not writing, Melissa helps authors navigate the publishing industry through her author training programs on Fostering Success. Melissa also hosts Aspiring Authors contests for children and has painted and donated several murals to the Hospital for Sick Children in Washington, DC.

Visit Melissa on her website or chat with her on social media. Melissa enjoys discussing her books with book clubs and reader groups and welcomes an invitation to your event.

Melissa's books are available through most online retailers in paperback and digital formats.

Made in the USA
San Bernardino, CA
22 August 2014